LIES OF THE GODDESS

LIES of the GODDESS

LILA SAMSON

Weaver's Light Books

Cover Art and Design: Lila Samson

Formatting and Illustrations: Lila Samson

Map of Zekhar: Lila Samson

First Edition Printing, 2025

ISBN: 979-8-9906103-6-1 (Hardcover Dust Jacket)

ISBN: 979-8-9906103-7-8 (Hardcover Laminate)

ISBN: 979-8-9906103-5-4 (Paperback)

ISBN: 979-8-9906103-8-5 (eBook)

LCCN: 2025911539

Weaver's Light Books is an imprint of Lila Samson.

For my mom, Lisa, who stuck with me through all my multiple crises over the years and celebrated each time I reached the other side.

Pronunciation Guide

Aarua - *Ah-roo-ah*

Abrahten - *Ah-brah-tehn*

Aleksander - *Ah-lek-sahn-der*

Alesathne - *Ah-less-ath-nay*

Aoife – *Ee-fah*

Asghar - *Ass-gar*

Bozkei - *Bo-z-kay*

Brevindun - *Breh-vin-dunn*

Bunc - *Bunk*

Caliphus - *Cal-ih-fuss*

Calvantia – *Cal-vahn-tee-uh*

Caoimhe - *Keev-ah*

Carissa - *Car-ih-sah*

Chione - *Key-own-eyy*

Clauden - *Clod-en*

Czeslawa - *Chess-wah-vah*

Demir - *Deh-meer*

D'orde - *De-ord*

Dzera - *Dzh-ehr-ah*

Elmere - *El-meer*

Elspeth - *El-spe-th*

Ethingar - *Eth-in-gaar*

Farnich - *Far-neech*

Fazhia - *Fah-z-ee-ah*

Femi - *Feh-mee*

Genoise – *Gen-oh-eez*

Halkin - *Hal-kin*

Homunculi - *Ho-mun-cu-lie*

Iscah - *Iss-cah*

Janek - *Yahn-ekh*

Kasajb - *Kahs-ay-eeb*

Kallendrine - *Cal-en-drine*

Kutsalyot - *Koot-sahl-ee-oht*

Lauklin - *Lawk-lynn*

Lenore - *Leh-nor*

Levana - *Leh-vah-nah*

Mekartlim - *Meh-kart-leem*

Nounet - *Noo-neht*

Ölmesuz - *Ool-mesh-ooz*

Orzei - *Or-zay*

Posheica – *Posh-ih-cah*

Pozhontec - *Pah-zh-on-tek*

Rodzjiek - *Ro-dzh-yek*

Rodzjiekim - *Ro-dzh-yek-eem*

Toprazi - *Tohp-rah-zee*

Tulathne - *Too-lath-nay*

Varek - *Var-ehk*

Wythane - *Why-thay-n*

Zekhar – *Zeh-khar*

Zekharyan – *Zeh-khar-ee-an*

Zure - *Zoo-rey*

The Country of
The Untamed
The Pozhontec Mountains
The Great Temple of Tulathne
Castle Brevindun
Kallendrine Estate
Aarua Manor

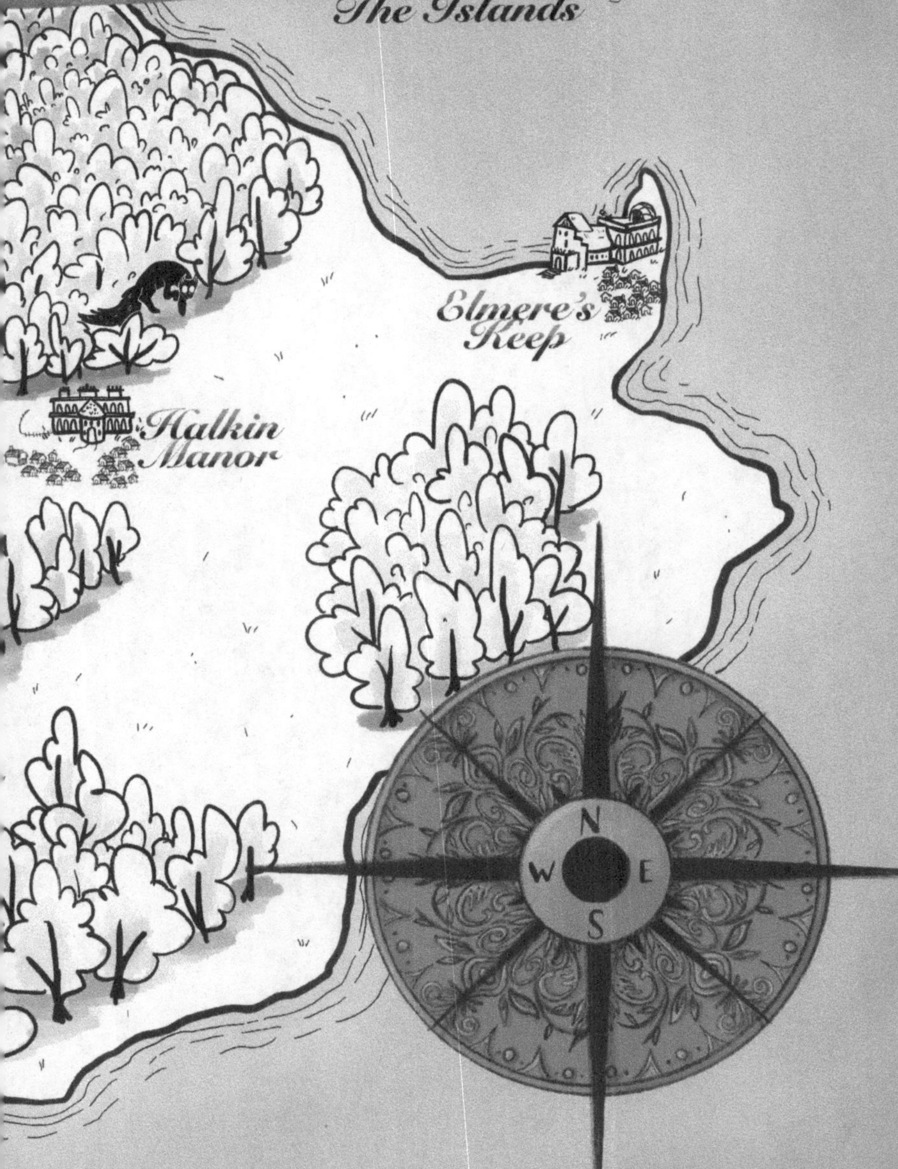

ZEKHAR
The Islands
Elmere's Keep
Halkin Manor
N
W
E
S

PART ONE

"It will never be as it once was."
- Line 12
The Prophecy of Alesathne
Seeress Aithne

PROLOGUE

THE NIGHT SKY ABOVE THE small cottage was clear. There were no clouds to cover the stars—regardless of the fact there were no stars on this night, anyway. Only the full moon shone down onto the small village, on the sleeping and wakeful alike, silent as she watched a young woman stumble into her home on the outskirts of the community.

So many matters of this world had become tiresome to her, but as she rose, great and glowing behind the mountain, the moon couldn't help but be fixated on the scene unfolding.

The young mother pressed her hands against her back as another wave of pain rolled through her. Clattering steps issued along the boards of the porch until she reached the door, already sweating from not only the heat of the day but the strain of the child now attempting to kick its way out of her. Inside, she filled a pot of water and placed it on a dying hearth. Her counters were full of herbs and talismans—different medicines she'd used all throughout her time while her baby grew.

There was no room aside from the floor for her to set out a bowl, a blanket, or even a place to lay the child once it was here.

No midwife would be coming. The child had sullied the mother, unwed as she was. No one in town was going to care should either of them live or die.

Sore knees pressed into folded blankets. Through layers of skirts, the woman felt for the position of her baby. She knew nothing about what to do. She was a healer, a setter of bones and remover of curses; there was nothing she knew about midwifery aside from when she'd watched her sister give birth years ago.

Her sister. How did she fare? It had been so long since—

A scream ripped from her throat, pain coursing through her pelvis, her back, her legs. Folded arms rested on a bench, her forehead pressing in to the embroidered fabric of her sleeves and the wood beyond. She counted the seconds.

One.

Two.

Three.

Four.

On to a minute when another round passed, strong and sustained. Blood flowed down her legs onto the blanket.

Her grandmother had woven it. Her mother had been swaddled in it. How fitting then, that the family that abandoned her would now be instrumental in cradling her new baby.

Provided she made it that long.

Everything was on fire. The mother counted her breaths, the minutes,, the jolts of pain, slick with sweat and still wearing her layers of clothes after a day in the marketplace. Glancing up, through the window, she saw the moon.

"I can't do this," she whispered, breathing fast and uneven. "Levana, I can't do this."

For a moment the pain faded, perhaps the goddess had heard her—then it was blinding.

Curling up on hands and knees, she screamed as a contraction tore through her. Knobby joints and wiggling fingers sent nothing but pain through her cervix.

She pushed, squatting best she could, hands slick with sweat and blood cradling a small head already full of hair.

Moaned prayers echoed through the small house. Blessings to every god she could remember in her muddled state, to the trees, to the ancestors—if they were even still with her.

Aside from her pain, the only sound was the wind softly whistling through the window that never fully closed, and the cracking of wood in the hearth.

One final push and the child slid free, screaming.

Resting her hips on her heels, pain still pulsing through her though not nearly as awful as it had been moments before, she wrestled the squirming newborn from her skirts.

Tears flooded down her cheeks—no longer caused by pain or fear, but instead rapt awe at the beauty of the child in her arms. Red as the dye used in Rodzjiek embroidery, her daughter shook with cries, tiny hands clenched in fists, toes the size of a lentil balled up, only to stretch out and ball up again.

The mother fell back against the bench, holding her girl to her chest.

In the sky outside, the moon paled. She was overjoyed at the safe delivery, yes. But something was wrong. Something would happen to the child, and her mother would be powerless to stop it.

She'd seen it often enough, though centuries always stood between the girls destined to bring a curse to the land—whether they wanted to or not.

Gentle fingers danced over the small nose bridge, between the eyes fluttering.

She was strong, this new addition to the continent, but would she be strong *enough*?

Still, the two clung to one another.

Little body and face now clear of fluids, cord cut, the mother wrapped her newborn in a swath of soft, worn linen. The dark hair on the little one's head stuck up in odd directions, and she squinted at her mother through puffy eyes, rich irises glowing in the firelight.

Shaking fingers smoothed out the creases on her wrinkly face. For the first time in years, the mother breathed a prayer of thanks. Thanks for a safe delivery. Thanks for her strength.

Thanks for the child, and please, any god who is listening, give her a good, long life.

Let no one hurt her.

The mother's eyes drifted to the moon and the space past her, where she caught a faded glimmer of a single constellation.

The only one bright enough to be visible on a full moon. *Please,* she whispered—to the stars, the moon, and the spirits within them—*please let Czeslawa be given a good fate.*

Chapter

ONE

LIGHTNING FLASHED THROUGH THE OPEN curtains, and it was just enough light for Aleksander to find his armor. It rung out as it struck against itself, and he winced. The walls were brick and sturdy, his door was closed, and the wee hours of night had just begun to settle. Nobody would be able to hear, he knew that. Still, with the storm outside waging a war against the drying grass and falling leaves, it was entirely possible no one was able to sleep.

He threw a passing glance to the tapestry in the corner of his room, on which the goddess stood silent and still as ever.

"Sorry," he whispered. Lightning lit up the white gown in the artwork, as well as the veil covering her face. He flattened his lips against one another. She'd felt distant ever since he returned, but that did nothing to quell the surge of guilt he felt when he would leave the room without a prayer to Her.

There was once a time where he woke up early to spend an extra ten minutes conversing with his goddess-mother.

Or, more accurately, an extra ten minutes talking *at* her. He never heard a reply, no matter how much he asked. Even that time in the Great Temple, just a handful of months ago.

That feeling was so foreign and distant, he'd convinced

himself he'd imagined it.

He held Aoife, the antique arming sword belonging to every incarnation of Alesathne before him, in his gloved fist. He calculated each move, careful not to let any of the straps or embellishments on the sheath make noise as he pushed open his door and crept down the hall.

Torches flickered in sconces on the walls, the warm light contrasting sharply with the harsh snap of the lightning. Each bolt made him jump.

Months had passed since he'd had lightning coursing through him as he attempted to sever the forearm of a traitor. He had gotten over Lord Terrell's betrayal of the crown and of Tulathne easily; well, as easily as one could expect. He had hardly known the man, and had certainly not known him enough justify the way his fingers shook when he woke suddenly in the night, dark blood painting his dreams, the tearing sound of—

He couldn't look at the courtiers the same way. Not after that. They swarmed him and the others now more than ever, asking for more stories, more speculation over the growing situation. Never mind they'd all walked away from that journey and fight changed. Never mind they'd walked away fewer in number.

Aleksander tried not to think about Iscah. In the first few weeks after, she was almost all he thought about. But lately, his dreams of her corpse had become less common. As the war council assembled plans to gather military intelligence and support took shape, he hardly slept anymore.

There were always too many thoughts rattling around in his head. Too many things to prepare himself for.

Sleep was for the safe, the idle. The walls of Castle Brevindun were thick, sturdy, and for the last few months, guards were placed at every gate. Still, any notion of peace that came Aleksander's way could never find reason to stay.

As he passed a window, lightning struck a tree out in the courtyard. He stumbled, dropping the sword to the stone. The loud crash was muffled by the snapping of wood as a branch broke free and fell into the bushes. Through the rain, smoke spiraled up from the shattered trunk. A hard, thick swallow worked its way down his throat and he picked up Aoife, continuing down the steps.

By the armory, the torches had burned down to mere embers. Oil-soaked wraps were blackened, hanging like shredded flags. Still, he managed to pick his way down the hall until he found the door that led out to the training ring.

It opened with a creak, and was instantly illuminated with a bright flash.

His heart jumped into his throat.

Maybe it's not a good idea to train in a thunderstorm.

But as the light faded, Aleksander let the door close behind him, and strapped Aoife to his waist.

He couldn't list all the nights he'd spent out here. When dreams became too much, or when he couldn't sleep at all, the Sword of Ages resigned to put on his armor and weasel his way out to the dusty ring, tracing step after step in the dirt until his entire body was so heavy he collapsed onto his bed and not even the darkest of nightmares could disturb him. Now, with the dirt beneath him turning to mud, his boots stuck in the pits where he'd retraced form after form, fighting imaginary homunculi and sorcerers, any thoughts of sleep were far from his mind.

The rain slid down his back, cold and thick and already carrying the decaying sweetness one finds mostly in leaf litter during the later months of the year. Trees had already started to turn, most of them dropping their leaves. And among those still cloaked with dying foliage, only a few still held to their rich golds and reds. Harvest festivals lit up the town on certain nights. On others, he could see through the windows in the Great Temple as the priestesses made their prepared offerings for the world's descent into winter.

From the very top of the castle Aleksander often convinced himself he could see all the way to Duke Elmere's Keep on the coast far coast. The trees were so bare, he'd catch a glimpse of a glittering...*something*. With stories of Elspeth's upbringing there floating around his mind, he couldn't help but allow himself to mistake the flash of armor or even a wayward wagon as the sun glinting off the rounded dome of the observatory.

He swung Aoife down, water slicking off the steel in a satisfying arc towards a dummy. Lightning struck somewhere in the distance, and he raised Aoife again, shifting his feet and throwing himself to the side. His boot stuck in the mud and he slammed hard against the ground, pain shooting up his left shoulder.

Thank Tulathne Varek didn't see that, he thought, pushing himself back to his feet and using his wet glove to try and brush as much mud from his pauldron as he could. A hiss escaped his tight teeth—a response to the protests from his hip.

His Ölmesuz trainer had been away from the capital city of Brewith for the last few weeks. With growing fear among the people and unrest in certain cities and towns, one of the primary topics of discussion was how to quell their fears. Mother Saoirse was right—those following the crown and trusting the royal family were sure in their steps. But those who weren't were already beginning to consider the alternatives. Varek had been sent to gather information and tend to alliances. His absence was expected, normal. But that didn't stop King Clauden from opening every meeting with, "In regards to Varek, nothing has been heard yet—but we expect news soon."

As Aleksander raised Aoife into the sky, another bolt shot

through the clouds. He stumbled once more, catching himself as the lightning struck a flagpole nearby.

"Should you be out here?"

He spun, eyes wide, heart racing—not just from the close strike. Through sheets of rain, he found the door open. A small flickering light hovered just at the edge of the overhang. The figure carrying it was obscured, but he could make out the long, heavy nightgown they wore, and the long curls flowing against it.

The tip of his sword fell to the mud, and he squinted. "Carissa?"

"Try again."

Her voice was low, commanding. Though, he noted, not devoid of the closest cousin of tenderness she could summon.

"Lenore?" Water dripped off his furrowing brow. He squinted, but the rain gathered on his lashes, painting the scene before him in warped watercolors.

"Come inside, child," she said, pushing the door wider.

Pushing through confusion, he shook his head. "No, thank you, I wish to train."

The small candle she bore floated back and dissolved into the darkness of the hallway. Lenore stepped forward into the torrent, wrapping her heavy shawl around her. It was woven with the colors of the family's crest—maroon, favored by Carissa, made up the backdrop of it. Thin lines of pale blue and green crossed through it and over one another, accented with gold embroidered vines along the edges. It was instantly soaked through.

She did not bother to hitch up her hem as she approached, her fine silk slippers sticking in the mud as she walked forward.

Aleksander had grown. He had not noticed it until he stood inches away from the woman, but when she looked up at him ever so slightly, he swallowed. The pair usually kept their distance. It maintained their hierarchy.

He never felt as though she was smaller than him, but... here he was.

Looking down.

"It's cold," she said, her tone measured, "it's late, and there is a storm. Come inside. Whatever musings you need to work through, do it over a cup of tea or hot milk."

A crack sounded overhead and both looked up.

"Don't stay out here where you face being struck."

When he looked back, the queen's eyes—as pale green as her daughter's—were fixed on his face. Carissa looked like her almost only in that aspect. But that was always something he appreciated. The queen wasn't as kind or warm as her husband, nor as nurturing as her daughter. Yet she offered a strange, stern comfort when Aleksander needed it.

He nodded. "Alright."

Lenore's mouth fixed in a straight line, one hand darting out from beneath her shawl to take his wrist and lead him back. Her touch was light. It wasn't that she didn't trust Aleksander; no, that wasn't it. With each glance she cast behind them, to the sky—with the swift shift from his wrist to his pauldron, guiding him in, he blinked at her.

The queen was genuinely worried.

She set the candle on a shelf and pushed Aleksander onto a bench, busying herself with undoing his armor. Deft fingers flitted around from hinge to strap, debating what to take off first. The queen's mouth fit into a tight line, her eyes narrowing as she surveyed the task she'd set for herself.

It took more effort than he'd expected not to smile at the kind gesture. "Usually I start with—"

"I can do it," the queen snapped, her hands stilling in the air. A slow exhale preceded her movement. Eventually, she undid a strap at his shoulder. "Tell me, my boy, what were you thinking?" With a powerful tug, she tore his pauldron off. The force pulled him aside and caused him to steady himself against the seat beneath him. "Going out in a storm, in all metal?"

Aleksander sat for a minute. He didn't know, to be entirely honest. He wasn't tired this evening, and it had become habit to get his mind or his body working instead of laying in bed, tossing and turning. "Couldn't sleep," he said with a shrug.

The queen scoffed. "We have teas for that."

She loosened the wrist-strap on his glove. Gripping the forefinger and pinkie, she gave it a tug, nearly stumbling back with the effort as the glove remained on. Blinking twice, she readjusted her grip. Another tug, and off came the glove, followed by the other. The pair dropped atop a pile with the other pieces of armor she'd extracted, muddied and dripping water in a puddle on the stone floor. After a moment, she cleared her throat. "I know you're... overwhelmed, Aleksander."

He lifted his head. "Am I?"

Her hands stilled their work, his gorget floating above his collar bone. "Aren't you?"

There was nothing that particularly weighed on him, he figured. Never mind he hardly felt comfortable in his skin anymore. Every sound made him jump. When he closed his eyes, he saw the light draining from Iscah's, the blood seeping from Terrell's throat. He would circle around the thought that none of this was over yet, that he still served a purpose and was needed in a battle. They didn't know when or where it would happen, how many men they'd be against...how many undead.

Slipping free of his thoughts, Aleksander's pulse thrummed through his fingers.

It was hard to breathe.

"I'm fine," he said.

Lenore huffed again. She shook her head lightly, long

curls slapping Aleksander's arm and spraying even more water over the floor. "Of course you are." She took off his breastplate without another word, followed by the faulds that fell over his hips, and the cuisse over his thighs. He was left seated in his nightclothes—a plain tunic and linen pants—and soaking wet. Folding her arms over her chest, she nodded sternly towards the door. "Go get tea. And go to bed."

Aleksander pushed himself up. After sitting for so long, listening to the soft crumbling crackle of the candle wick and the ringing of his armor, sleep had indeed began to settle in his limbs. He groaned with the effort of standing, and a small smile flitted over Lenore's lips.

"Or *just* go to bed," she said.

He blinked at her. Part of him wanted to fight, just for the sake of it. But the other part of him noticed how her eyes were lit with a tired, worried light.

He raised a hand, gently brushing her arm. "I will."

A deep breath leaked slowly from her nose. Her entire frame softened, and she raised an arm from her torso and gripped his bicep. "You're doing all you can," she said softly. "And you're doing well, Aleksander. Don't second guess that. Ever."

For the millionth time since the solstice, Aleksander wanted to cry.

He hated that.

He hated feeling his throat close and his eyes burn when there was nothing to cry about. And even when there was. It had become too much for him, this constant emotion.

So, the boy simply nodded, swallowed hard, and leaned forward, his chin resting on the queen's shoulder. Without thinking, he hugged her.

She stiffened as his arms encircled her. After a moment, he felt her fine hands pat his back and give a gentle squeeze before finding purchase on his chest and pushing them apart.

"Well," she cleared her throat. "I do hope you sleep well. Don't forget your armor."

"You too, my queen."

With the plate held tightly to his chest, rattling and clanking all the while, he offered a nod to Lenore who stood stock still in her place. She returned it without a word. During the walk back to his room, he couldn't help but smile.

He hadn't heard her speak his real name in years.

Chapter
TWO

$\mathcal{I}$ HEARD A RUMOR MY mother found you last night. Outside. During the storm."

Aleksander tore his eyes away from the oak he had watched split the night before. It was still billowing black smoke, though thankfully a lot less than it had hours earlier. As the gardeners waded through the faded greenery, Carissa stepped forward, hitching the hem of her gown over the fallen branches and waves of dirt. It was thick, velvet and fleece patched together to create a striking gown of deep red and purple that accentuated the life that had returned to her face. Her eyes met his, and she smiled.

"I'm hoping she did not. Only a handful of years ago, you'll remember, I was sneaking out to go to the Temple. It would be unfair of me to receive punishment and you not."

He couldn't help but smile back, memories of Clauden's lecture and Janek's worried expression seeming deeply funny in hindsight. "She did," he admitted.

"Ah, then I'll have to have a word with my mother. It seems she's gone soft-hearted," she chuckled. The skirt fell from her fingers, hem landing on the path with a puff; her attention turned thoughtfully to the tree before them. "Be thankful it was the tree, then, and not you." Out of the corner of her eye, she found him again; her grin widened. "We can't have our savior dying prematurely and unremarkably, now can we?"

Distaste churned in his stomach, but Aleksander laughed. The homunculi attacks had waned, as it seemed no others had yet discovered the mastery over flesh that Terrell had. Still, unrest was rampant. The events of last week were still fresh in Aleksander's mind—a small temple to Tulathne, a few miles south of Elmere's Keep, had been defaced overnight with praises for the Scourge and curses for him and his Mother. The paint was red, and the initial assumption had been that it was made from blood. The townspeople cleaned it up overnight, a small group of priestesses and Rodzjiekim.

The news was spread calmly, and it reached the castle days after the incident.

But the images conjured up—white columns stained with blood-red paint, threatening and menacing and evil—couldn't leave his mind.

Any mention of any town always came with an undercurrent of worry that the words following would tell of a disaster.

He'd often considered that he would rather not risk his life at all. If it must end in the coming war, he wished it to end quietly. "You just want to have more opportunities to frustrate me," he said, bumping her shoulder with his.

The collision jostled her to the side and she laughed wildly. It made Aleksander's heart lurch with relief. He couldn't remember the last time she'd laughed so heartily.

Carissa had returned from their time in the Untamed in a daze. At meals or meetings, she'd sit close to her husband, his hand tightly locked in hers, eyes downcast and empty. It was two months ago that she spoke up during a meeting instead of just whispering what she wanted to say to her husband, and it was a month since she had first delivered an honest smile. Not the ones she painted on at court events, or to the priestesses.

And this smile she held now, this was the most earnest of all.

One could hardly tell she was a husk just mere months ago.

Her eyes sparkled as they searched the tree's branches, cheeks pink and round. The appearance she held now was a contrast from the lean, regal woman who had stood with him on the terrace after the solstice, looking out over this same garden and this same tree, and an even greater contrast from who she had become on their travels, leeched of her strength and vivacity by her desperation and misuse of magic. "You're practically family," she chuckled, folding her arms across her chest. "That's just my duty."

"Not your only duty, though." It was only a half hour ago Aleksander had left the meeting room and the conversations therein. The war council, comprised of the royal family, Priestess Caoimhe, and Demir, had discussed their newest orders. And they were, for once, something he looked forward to. He grinned at his sister. "Are you excited to go?"

She pressed her lips together thoughtfully. "I am. Lord Asghar has some of the most skilled mages and Crafters within his fief. I'm looking forward to see what I can learn from them."

A raven had arrived from the south, and it was all they'd talked about that morning. The system of ravens was Varek's idea—an old communication tactic during wars, though Aleksander couldn't help but see the great fault in it should the enemy manage to shoot down a raven and retrieve the letter. Despite concerns, however, the king had been enthusiastically in favor of the idea. Over the last few months, the old Ölmesuz had been in and out of Brewith on his way to other cities and their lords, setting up this system.

The letter received had been from Lord Asghar, one of the few Ölmesuz who held such a title. His land was to the south, just a gulf away from the Ölmesuz homeland. Happily for the war effort, there had been rumors of unrest and the spread of Blight groups—"Blights" being what Lenore had taken to calling the followers of the Scourge—nearby his lands. When the letter spoke of the many skilled mages and Crafters in his patronage and how he wished to extend their knowledge to the dear princess, King Clauden had practically thrown himself out of his chair at the chance. They weren't to be spies, not officially, but anyone who heard Clauden's announcement knew that he was hoping they would gather intelligence regardless.

Aleksander was set to accompany his royal sister to the estate and remain there during her training, along with Elspeth. It was their duties to see if anything particularly interesting happened, or if any intriguing whispers made it to their ears.

Demir had nearly bitten a hole in his cheek with how hard he fought to keep himself calm. Queen Lenore had not been so presumptuous as to break the news of his staying at Castle Brevindun kindly. She held firm in her command of Demir staying to advise Janek in training new recruits. Though she'd mainly relegated him to desk work—being in charge of overseeing all raven communications to and from Castle Brevindun.

Aleksander had argued that Demir was a skilled warrior and deserved more. Even Caoimhe, who had only encountered him in their weekly meetings, had tried to change the Queen's mind. Their attempts were futile.

When the meeting had adjourned and Demir finally left the table, his forearms were like old ropes on a fishing ship—knotted and on the verge of snapping.

"I feel bad for Demir," Carissa said, wringing her hands. Aleksander looked at her abruptly—had she somehow heard his thoughts?

She continued, "He's put so much work into this and was willing to give up so much to follow us—" with a quick glance, she amended, "follow you, I mean. And only to be relegated to desk work..."

"He said he didn't mind it," Aleksander reminded her. But his mind turned back to the immense frustration and anger pouring off the Mekartlim's frame.

"And you don't mind being the Sword, and I don't mind my visions," she muttered.

"I've been meaning to ask about that." He turned to face her fully. "How have your visions been? Any new ones? Anything necessary to relay?"

The princess's answering sigh was slow and heavy. "They're

visions, what can I say. They utter messages I stay up all night trying to decode, only to find myself tired and frustrated and at a loss. None of them have been nearly as consuming as those from a few months ago, however. I'm thankful for that." Her eyes flickered with a strange memory as they roved the landscape, her expression shifting between amusement and confusion. "The newest one was interesting. I was standing on top of the mountains, looking over Zekhar as she burned. From my chest came this most magnificent golden light—like a string, leading me somewhere, but I didn't follow it. It wove around my hands and feet and stomach, then went out over the land. In my looking after it, I saw in the flames a wreath of daffodils. Then everything was put out by the most magnificent rainstorm."

Aleksander studied her. Somehow, a peaceful look had fallen over her features—it was almost as though she hadn't mentioned having yet another vision of her country burning.

"What do you think that means?"

Those green-gold eyes flitted back to the tree. "I'm not sure. But I don't feel grief over it, so I'll take that as a good sign."

Following her gaze, Aleksander watched as the tree was expertly sawed into pieces by the gardeners. "Why aren't they trying to save it? It didn't seem too damaged..." he shrugged. "I mean, it lost a limb, but that's nothing. It can grow another."

"It was only a matter of time before it fell," Carissa remarked. "Safer for them to tear it down than for it to fall over and crush someone. Besides, I'd heard one of them remark how the strike allowed them to see the rot that had been hidden away these past few years." Her hands settled on her hips. The curls at her cheeks twisted in the wind—gone was the updo she used to favor so heavily; instead, her curls fell long against her back in a thick braid ornamented with a maroon and gold ribbon. It seemed much more in line with her mother's style.

The style of a queen.

Aleksander pursed his lips. "Still, it's sad. I loved that tree."

◇ ✳ ◇

ALEKSANDER LAZILY PASSED a glance over the tapestries on the walls—some depicting tales from Zekharyan folklore, others depicting old rulers, like the First King of Zekhar, Ogaden W'tihyan, and, of course, Tulathne.

Aside from tapestries, old sets of armor and large floor vases overflowing with flowers made the simple, thin hallway into somewhat of a gallery. And a ways down, a few tapestries and vases away from the end of the hall, sat a hunched figure on a bench. Behind him, the expansive wings shifted awkwardly so as to not brush the wall. In his hands hung a small object on a string.

"Everything okay, Demir?" Aleksander stopped a few feet away, movements becoming wary.

Those pale, gold eyes found him instantly. The man smiled. "Of course, my lord Champion. I'm alright." With one swift move, the chain swung up, gathered into one of the man's large hands, and disappeared into the pocket of his doublet.

"Are you sure?" Aleksander's eyebrows pinched together on his forehead. "You seem... well, you seemed upset at the meeting and now you're alone in a hallway and you don't look comfortable."

Demir's smile slipped. It held to his face, still creased his cheeks and crinkled his eyes, but the sparkle within faded and did not return. "I am sure."

It certainly didn't sound like he was sure.

Guilt sunk into Aleksander's gut. "I'm sorry you aren't coming with us." It was a sad excuse for an apology when there were still so many more things to be said.

But Demir waved it off with brevity, standing and flexing his wings, wincing when his left caught and didn't open all the way. "I have a job to do here. I promised to serve you and the crown, to prepare for the war and protect our collective people—you'll be doing that in the south, and I'll be doing that in Brewith. Am I frustrated? Yes. But is anything I'm frustrated about something that is within my control? No."

"Still... I'm sorry." Sorry Demir wasn't coming with. Sorry for his wing. Sorry for Iscah.

Sorry for pulling him into this.

His stomach twisted. There was so much that Demir could have avoided if it weren't for him. How could he—

"Stop all your apologizing. You've done it too much and you don't need to," the Mekartlim said. His voice was low. It rumbled through Aleksander, and he knew the man had understood his words—and everything he'd left unsaid. "I left my family to find a purpose. To protect them. And if this is how I can do it, then this is how I do it."

He slung an arm around Aleksander, sauntering towards the door at the end of the hall that led to the grand staircase and the main foyer of the castle.

"How can you stay so happy," Aleksander asked. The question slipped out, but he didn't try to take it back. Instead he let it hang there.

A long silence stretched.

Aleksander focused on how the brown leather of his shoes was so warm in comparison to the stone in this part of the castle.

"I don't think I stay happy," Demir finally said. "I just try to find a way through every day. A bright spot. And I trust that when all this is over, the whole world will be a bright spot." The arm around Aleksander tightened, jostling him.

Whether it was the intended affect or not, Aleksander laughed.

Demir smiled again, chuckling with him. "There's a lot on your plate right now, I know that. But I've also woken up to see fresh tracks in the training ring, or cups of tea scattered in the garden. If you have time to train and drink tea, you have time to find a bright spot."

"Aleksander!"

Both turned, spotting Elspeth bounding through the door on the far end of the grand hall they'd walked into. Her dark auburn hair was pulled into a braid around the top of her head, her fangs catching the light in her wide, wild grin.

Warmth bloomed in Aleksander's chest; he raised a hand to wave back at her.

"Ah," Demir murmured through his grin. "I daresay there's a bright spot right now."

Chapter

THREE

YOU'RE GETTING SLOW, ALEKSANDER," SHE panted. Elspeth's sword wavered in her hands, footing unsure as she levied another strike towards him.

He side stepped the cut with ease. A flourish from Aoife deflected the following blow. "Oh, I'm getting slow?" Aleksander smirked, finding his footing again. "Look at yourself, El. Varek would be beyond disappointed."

"Varek's not here."

"And thank the goddess for that." He twirled Aoife in the air, taunting his opponent.

Her thick brows drew down over her eyes, forming a little crease from her nose to her forehead.

Aleksander smiled at that. The intensity in her gaze, the playful chaos swirling in her eyes.

She raised her sword once more to a ready position, feet shifting in the mud. "It's not easy with all this slop around my feet."

"You fought fine in the Untamed."

At this, Elspeth's countenance faltered—the sword in her grip wavered, and her eyes softened. Rapid blinks cleared the memories. Her brow fell back over her eyes, heavier than before. "Yeah, well, I wasn't myself in the Untamed." With a deep breath she charged forward, swinging at Aleksander. A series of clashes, and they stumbled away from each other, chests heaving. "Besides, I'm used to training here in dry dirt. This mud is different."

Even as she was talking, Aleksander watched her movements. After a moment, she shifted her arm ever so slightly in the wrong direction; he dove, she missed the parry, and his sword bounced off her armor.

"Gods!" she shouted, stumbling backwards and falling into the mud with a *plop*. "Why can't I just keep my footing in this *stupid* ring!" Her sword arm raised, and with a hearty scream, she whipped the blade off to the side. It didn't go far—the grip caught on a footprint and stayed there.

Aleksander jumped at the display. Despite the racing of his heart, he knew she would never throw her sword at him, in anger or otherwise. Metal-on-metal rang out through the open air as he knelt before her.

Her large, red-brown eyes gazed up at him, a mix of shock and frustration clouding the sparkling hints of gold. After a moment, she sucked her teeth, head dropping forward. Within moments her shoulders bounced with laughs.

Aleksander joined in, offering chuckles of recognition. His gloved hand came down heavy on her shoulder. "Are you alright?"

"Yeah," she muttered, shaking her head. Her face lifted ever so slightly, just enough for Aleksander to catch the light smile she wore. "Yeah, I'm alright."

With each inhale, crisp autumn air flooded his lungs. It was invigorating; the sharp chill imbued every inch of him with a new sense of life, joy, and strength. When he offered Elspeth his hand, he had a moment where he considered using it to his advantage and flipping her or pinning her, continuing the fight in the most childish way possible. But as the air cleared his eyes and his head, he pulled her to her feet and into an awkward, armored hug.

Her glove came down heavy against his back as she patted

him. The two stood nearly head-to-head now, and as they parted, her eyes flicked over his face and up to his disheveled hair. "Did you sleep at all?" she asked.

"I did." His hair caught on the coarse, cracked leather fingers of his glove. He managed to work the stuck strands free and meet Elspeth's raised eyebrow with a quick, "I did! What, do you think I'm lying?"

"I'm *thinking*," Elspeth said, slowly stepping back to retrieve her sword from the mud, "that your armor has dry mud on it and I *know* it's been cleaned since the last time it had rained. If you'll remember, I had lost a bet and cleaned that suit myself." She flicked the blade in his direction. "And I take my punishments seriously."

It was true, he did sleep. Muddy armor or not, after his conversation with Lenore, he had retreated to his room and tucked himself into bed and drifted off without any dreams. He'd woken early, readied himself, and attended the meeting before joining her out here.

Heaving a sigh, Aleksander trudged over to the table. The water in the jug was refreshing and crisp, the constant cold air acting better than the shade had in the summer. He poured himself a cup and leaned back against it as Elspeth sheathed her blade and slogged her own heavy boots through the muck to join him.

"I slept, but I *did* come out here first."

She shook her head, not saying anything. After having a variation of that same exchange over and over, Aleksander was glad she didn't push it further with chiding to take care of himself. He already got enough of that from Carissa.

A loud sigh punctuated the *clack* of the wood cup on the table. "Well, have you heard when we leave yet?"

"Tomorrow morning."

He couldn't help but mimic her giddiness when he met her gaze, crinkled by the great grin splitting her cheeks. "I'm excited," she giggled.

"It's going to be a new experience, that's for sure."

Aleksander raised his cup to his lips and took a sip. "I've never been to any estates in Southern Zekhar. Usually the dignitaries down there come up to visit us."

Elspeth filled her cup and drained it again in record time. A single stream of water dripped down her chin and she did nothing to brush it away—the girl was much too occupied by her inquiries about the manor they'd be staying in. "Do you think his estate is by the ocean? I've missed the ocean ever since coming here. Can't get good shrimp in the capital, it's just too far away from the sea for anything to retain its flavor." Her nose wrinkled with a memory. "It's all slightly rank when it gets here."

This was something he always appreciated about Elspeth. No matter what their situation was, or the conversation, she always managed to bring in something trivial that took his attention. When they'd sit in the garden at the tail end of summer, sweating through their finery and spending every spare second batting away a mosquito or a fly, she's always bring his attention to the shape of the clouds or the dessert that was served at the dinner the previous night. On the occasions she spoke of her upbringing, she had the ability to latch on to one tiny aspect of a memory and ramble about it for hours; the way her attending maid would always attempt to convince her to file her teeth down was what stuck out in Aleksander's mind the most.

When Elspeth had first told him, he didn't know how to react. The way she passed over it was so simple, so careless. He had asked her to explain what she meant by that, and when his friend obliged by telling stories of other Rodzjiekim who had been forced to take a metal file to their canines, his stomach soured. She didn't explain further, but he remembered when he'd chipped a tooth as a child, and the pain that had come from having the tender inner flesh exposed.

When he'd asked if it was painful, she'd nodded. "Oh, very. I'm glad I managed to keep mine."

And somehow, after that topic and others like it, both would manage to laugh. For the time they were together, no matter how sad or exciting or plain strange the topic, stress melted from his shoulders, and he enjoyed the conversation.

So, with a chuckle, he shrugged and tapped her shoulder with his cup. "We'll just have to see."

He took a drink. A moment passed, and he cleared his throat. "Do you think it'll be safe? For us to leave Brewith?"

Neither Aleksander nor Elspeth had left the confines of Brewith in the last few months—hardly even the castle, though it seemed Elspeth got out more than he did. She'd frequently return with tales of the modiste in town, or people and conversations she'd happened upon in the market.

Elspeth scoffed. "Of course. The king wouldn't send us if it wasn't safe. And they'll have Demir and Janek staying here to help with the war effort."

"War effort" was what they were calling it, though it was nothing like any war Aleksander had studied. Their opponent had not made themselves clear. There were no battle strategies, no intense training sessions, no encampments in different parts of the country. Just hearsay finding its way to them. Less and less bodies, more and more vague threats. Less destruction, but a constant thrum of unease beneath everything and within everyone.

It wasn't a war effort. Not yet. It was a country holding its breath, knowing the attempts at maintaining normalcy despite more armed patrols and more nervous whispers would eventually all stop in favor of the bloodshed that comes with a real war.

A wave fell free and brushed her cheek; she cocked her head to the side, staring out into the grey-filtered light painting over the training ring in smooth brushstrokes. "Let's think of this as a vacation. It's more for her highness's benefit than ours, anyway."

The notion of having a time of rest was appealing—Aleksander couldn't deny it. But as the door cracked open and a maid shouted that dinner was served soon, they parted to doff their armor and pack for a few days of travel before joining the meal and slipping off to bed. And all the while, Aleksander was rejoined by something he'd not felt for a few weeks.

At the base of his skull, right at the start of his neck, a cold, swirling presence awoke.

He let that Presence stay—even acknowledged it, greeted it. The last time it had appeared was so long ago he couldn't remember the exact moment. In the days, even the months after the Untamed, it was as though it had fallen asleep, exhausted by all they'd endured.

As much as he tried not to think about it, tried not to give in to the sensations and extra awareness it gave him, somehow, it felt good to have it back.

It stayed through dinner, where he chatted with Carissa and Janek about silly things like the premonitions she had before they were married *about* their impending nuptials. He tried not to think about the Presence too much. Tried not to speculate what it could be, why it was back, despite how calm he felt about it. Yet the questions wouldn't stop cycling through his mind. Was it just a manifestation of his own anxiety around what was happening? Or did something within him awaken when the Scourge's magic did?

Was it trying to warn him?

What if something was happening, something he could stop, and he ignored it?

Each smile over the course of the meal felt more and more false as the night wore on. The cold was nearly tangible—he feared the hairs on his neck would stand up, or goosebumps would ripple down his arms.

"Aleksander?"

He lifted his gaze from the chalice in his hand, filled with clean, sweet water, and found Elspeth looking at him with wide, concerned eyes. "Did you hear me?"

With a swallow, he shook his head. "No, sorry. What did you say?"

She smiled.

Both his heart and the Presence stuttered in their pace.

"I was just talking to Janek about Liadain. I was wondering what you've heard, seeing as you're supposedly the reincarnation of her husband."

Despite the strange topic, Aleksander smiled. "I've heard a bit."

"Like what?"

Stories flooded back from his days with the priestesses and he told Elspeth as much as he could remember about the Grey Lady, Liadain, wife of Alesathne, beloved of Zekhar. He told her about her diplomacy with the people, the skill she possessed with magic and how she used it to help her husband throughout their time together. She was beloved by the early Zekharyans, until the Scourge appeared and took her from them.

Aleksander's food began to cool on his plate, his fork and knife laid on the table cloth as he kept speaking. "Some say that's why Alesathne fought the Scourge in the first place. Not because it was his duty, but because he needed to avenge his wife as well as his mother."

Elspeth's eyes glowed as he spoke, devouring every word as her own food sat untouched. "How did they meet?"

"I don't know, actually. That was never covered in class."

His friend sniffed out a laugh, finally picking up her fork to prod at her dinner. Before taking a bite, she lifted her gaze to his once more. "If they were so bound, why isn't she reincarnated, too?"

At this, uneasiness took over Aleksander. The Presence felt heavy with grief. He shrugged. "Maybe she is. Maybe she's just not searched for as intently as...as the Scourge and I are."

A mirror of the grief he felt washed over her face before Demir interjected with a story from his people, about the Prince of the Orzei. As he talked and the mood lightened, the cold touch of the Presence slipped more in to a warm caress. Each time he met Elspeth's eyes, exchanged a joke, passed her food or drink, it dipped to his chest, further and further until that strange consciousness felt fully settled in his body for the first time ever.

The Presence seemed to be soothed by her—or, as the warmth in his chest grew, maybe it was just Aleksander himself.

Chapter

FOUR

GOLDEN SUNLIGHT, THAT KIND IN the early morning that somehow seems so much purer than that of sunset or midday, painted the interior of the great hall. Wavy, water-like ripples glinted off the ornate, ceremonial armor worn by the two guards standing at either side of the open double doors.

Aleksander nodded to them as he adjusted the bag on his shoulder. They hadn't been there before. There were guards on patrol in the castle, there always were, but to have them so prominent was new. To have them dressed in their best was even more unusual.

"There you are!" Janek shouted, striding through the wide doors. His hair was combed neatly to make the waves in his dark tresses seem somewhat uniform. That, paired with the clean, expensive doublet he wore both gave Aleksander comfort about the knights in ceremonial wear as well as a new sense of confusion and apprehension.

What on earth was going on that everyone was so fancily dressed for?

Before he could ask, his friend swept him into a hug. "How are you feeling?"

"I'm alright," Aleksander confided, "wish I could stay and help out here more, but it will be nice to see more of Zekhar."

"Oh, right!" Janek leaned back, his hand still on Aleksander's shoulder. "You've not been to the south!"

He shook his head.

"You're going to love it." His arm slipped around Aleksander's shoulders, walking him out to the front of the castle. "It's a lot like Brewith, but with some stunning Ölmesuz architecture."

"And you're choosing to miss all that?"

Janek pursed his lips. "I'm not *choosing* to, I'm needed here. There's work Demir and I are going to be doing, and I'm honored to do it."

At this, Aleksander perked up. "You mean training new soldiers?"

His friend squeezed his shoulders, a grin cracking up the side of his face. "Partially."

Passing through the front doors, the guards both offered them sideways glances.

"What's with the armor?" Aleksander whispered, not fully meaning to. Janek chuckled and nodded back to the soldiers before leaning towards his young friend's ear.

"Goddess knows, it was an order given by Clauden."

Speaking his name seemed all that was needed for the king to step into view at the base of the stairs, near the waiting carriage. Carissa was on his arm, with a bright, excited grin. Her braid curled into the hood of her cloak—a thick, soft wool lined with grey fox pelts. A shiver traveled down his back at the sight.

"What do I have to do to get a cloak like that?" he hollered, leaning on his sword, Janek's arm still around his shoulders.

The man swallowed a gruff laugh.

"Be a royal seeress!" Carissa shouted back. As the smile stretched between Aleksander's lips widened even more, she stuck her tongue out at him.

Janek jolted with a laugh, his cheeks growing pink at the sound held behind closed lips. He stared at his wife with a content, satisfied expression. "Oh, I love her," he breathed.

As overjoyed as Aleksander was that his sister was finally

back to herself—dare he say, even better than her old self—Janek was finally becoming himself again, too.

Carissa's state upon their return had weighed on Janek most of all. While Aleksander felt guilty about his failure to keep her safe, to keep her happy, Janek spiraled into guilt over not being there.

One night after Carissa had spent most of the day alone in the study, only to trip back to her room and fall asleep before the sun set, Aleksander had stumbled up on his friend in the kitchen. A pot of milk and spices bubbled on the hearth, and when he asked if Janek was okay, he answered that he was. Of course, he said that with a tight mask of fake-peace warping his features. The two had sat on small wooden stools, mugs of milk tea steaming in their hands, and talked. There was a lot Janek had discussed with Aleksander in those few hours, but the phrase that haunted him for days after was short and simple.

Janek had taken a deep drink, swallowed slowly, and muttered, "She's my sun, Aleksander. She's burned out, and I have no way to light her up again."

That did not stop him from being there for her in everything. In her nightmares, in her dark visions, in her potent bouts of all-consuming grief and guilt Aleksander experienced as well. Janek stayed by her in all things. Goddess help any guard who suggested he try to get sleep instead of staying up reading to her, picking flowers in dark starlight, or doing anything he thought had the slightest chance of bringing his wife back to her body.

Somehow, something he did worked.

"We should get going," Elspeth bounded down the steps after him, a similar cloak to Carissa's slung over her shoulders, though it was much shorter. It fell just about her mid-thigh, from beneath which Aleksander could see the pants she favored and her well-worn boots.

"You got a cape too?"

She blinked at him. "Did you not? It was a gift at the last harvest festival."

He scoffed. Of course it was. The festival where he spent

almost his whole time chatting with courtiers and taking the daughters of lords out on the dance floor for every song except his favorites was just the kind of place where he would have entirely missed getting the favor of the event.

"The sun is rising," Caoimhe said from her place over by the brazer. At her feet sat baskets of coals from the temple, and in her hand was a small jar of oil. She uncorked it and poured the liquid in a swirl around the brazer. "We'd best get moving, you'll be traveling all day."

"I'll let you lot get on with everything," Janek said, sweeping Carissa into a hug and peppering kisses along her cheeks and over her nose as she broke into giggles. Her thin hand raised and captured his chin, giving him a proper kiss before stepping back and adjusting her cloak.

"Love you," she murmured, patting his cheek.

"I love you too," he said, darting forward to kiss her nose one last time. He turned to Elspeth, placing a hand over his heart and bowing fully at the waist—a gesture she returned. Finally, Janek made his way back to Aleksander, pulling him once more into a crushing hug.

"Look after my wife, Aleksander," he whispered. "I don't blame you for what happened. But it cannot happen again."

Aleksander tightened his grip on his friend, raising his mouth to Janek's ear. "Of course," he said, "I promise."

This was the second time he made that promise to Janek and even though the man said he didn't blame Aleksander, the boy was still aware that the fault laid squarely on his shoulders. This time, though, it would be different. This time, he would not make that mistake.

It was not just Aleksander protecting Janek's wife, or the Sword of Ages guarding the Eyes of Time—he was protecting his sister. He'd known that on the last journey as well, but he hadn't known what that would fully entail.

And they all suffered from it.

He glanced around quickly. "Demir isn't coming?"

"No," Janek answered, his features tight, "he said he had

other work to do this morning. He does send his love and wishes for safe travels, though."

Aleksander nodded despite the sinking in his gut. The man had seemed fine at dinner, but he'd also been around him long enough to know that the Mekartlim was the best among them at not pushing his problems out onto others. Even when others offered him support with nothing wanted in return.

Janek retreated with King Clauden up the steps to the palace. The large doors swung shut with a heavy, echoing sound, and Aleksander turned to Carissa. She was still smiling.

"We haven't gotten to have a day out together much, have we?" the princess remarked, cocking her head to the side. Her hands rested on her hips, revealing that same gown she wore the day before. It hung looser around her, and Aleksander wasn't shocked she had neglected to tie the ribbons tighter. They'd be sitting for hours—tight clothes never fared well during long travels.

"You've got your training, I've got mine," he said, nodding towards Elspeth, "and as much as I'm your guard and brother and I will always enjoy accompanying you, El gets infinitely more enjoyment from your escapades into town."

The two exchanged giddy, bright-eyed grins.

"It's true," Elspeth planted her hands on her hips, "we don't get nearly as swamped by fans as we do with you, so we can focus more on the important things. I've seen more bards in the past month than I have in my whole life in the Keep."

His chest warmed at that. "I'm glad, El."

The girls turned away and that warmth turned to a dull ache. It felt childish. He was always the person who accompanied Carissa to town. And yes, they did get overrun with people searching for pardons, blessings, healing...but strangely, he missed it.

In the past few months, Aleksander hardly had time to think about them. His people. How were they? All his training, all his anxiety, it had been focused on the threat of the Scourge. His duty was to protect the common folk, but...

His stomach sank further, the slight sting of betrayal laced with a deeper vein of guilt.

He really hadn't given much though to them. The people he was doing all this for.

Had they been getting the help he usually gave? Was the city okay?

The dull ring of coals into the brazier beside the steps drew his attention away from the downward spiral he had started on. The apprehension which caused his stunted sleep the night prior returned. His fears were unreasonable, he knew that. Still, he couldn't help but worry that this would go terribly wrong, or the castle would be attacked without him here to defend it, or something would happen to Carissa or Elspeth or anyone else down there, and the tragedy would be on his head.

He swallowed hard.

Now, as if those thoughts weren't enough, he added the people to his list of reasons to stay.

But the whole country was his, wasn't it? All the people in Zekhar were his, not just those in Brewith, even if they were the ones he felt he truly knew.

He held to this notion as he approached the brazier; as he greeted Caoimhe formally and raised his hands; as the flame burst to life and they began reciting prayers for a safe journey, thanking the goddess for all She'd given them so far.

This journey wouldn't be one that ended in his abandonment of his people. Had he failed to dedicate himself to them earlier, he stared into the flames, resolve settling in his soul.

With the final words of the prayer, he twitched; that sentient chill, that Presence, raced down his spine.

It never liked it when he prayed.

Chapter

FIVE

𝓔LSPETH DREW THE CURTAINS SHUT. The thin, delicate glass beyond shook with each crash of thunder, each sheet of rain. The sound was enough to make everyone nervous. With the heavy fabric now between them and the storm, Carissa nodded, appreciative, to Elspeth. "Thank you for that."

She gave the princess a hesitant smile. "Of course."

A safe journey.

Aleksander almost scoffed at the thought. That was what they'd prayed for. And here they were, huddled in the carriage while their driver was pelted with rain, the horses frustrated whinnies carrying through the sounds of the storm. It didn't shock him. Lately, every prayer he'd made seemed to be answered with a direct counter to what he'd asked for.

Maybe it would have been safer if Aleksander hadn't led the last prayer. Maybe that one action cursed their whole trip.

Another rumble, and he pulled back the curtain just enough to see the world beyond. For mid-afternoon, Aleksander was met with a world washed with the thin ink of an early night. He couldn't pick out trees, much less the line where the road ended and the countryside began.

"Maybe we should stop," he offered, dropping the fabric.

"Where *would* we stop?" Carissa's fingers found her pendant of the goddess, twirling it around where it hung from her neck. "We passed the last town an hour ago. It would be foolish to turn around now."

"At least the rain would be at our backs?" Elspeth offered. She shifted uneasily in her seat.

The light in the carriage was dim. With no candles and no sunlight, now with the curtains drawn, Aleksander could barely make out the woman seated across from him. And as for Elspeth, his only assurance that she was still beside him was the occasional brush of her leg against his, or the sharp inhale at a crack of lightning.

The carriage jolted to a stop. Within moments, the door swung open, and a spray of rainwater fell across Aleksander's face.

"Your highness. My lord," Bunc was soaked to the skin, his teeth chattering, his cloak hanging off him as though it were wet paper and not oiled leather. "I must insist we pull off and wait out the rain. I have knowledge of a cave nearby, large enough to fit the horses. Though, the carriage will need to stay outside." The man was shouting, yet Aleksander could barely make out what he was saying. "Do I have your permission to take us there, my lady?"

Carissa nodded. "Do what is needed, Bunc. If you think we should wait out the storm, then we shall wait out the storm."

After the door closed it was hardly enough time for Aleksander to settle back in his seat before the cart burst forward. Each rock, pothole, and puddle sent Aleksander's hands scrambling for purchase on the wall, the roof, the door—anywhere that would give him a semblance of security. At last he wrapped his fingers around part of the adorning fringe meant to cover the rod on which the curtains hung. It shifted under his weight as he was bounced, heart racing, eyes wide.

He found Carissa in a flash of lightning, gripping tightly to her seat.

A hand enclosed on his bicep, strong and unrelenting; in another flash, he was able to make out Elspeth, gripping the curtain rod on the other side with one hand, the other firmly latched onto him. He shifted and gripped her knee in return. Curling his fingers into her leg, past fabric and muscle, he felt the frantic, fluttering heartbeat they all shared.

A sudden jolt sent them leaping out of their seats.

A gasp from Carissa in the air, a grunt from Elspeth as she slammed down.

She cursed, a mix of fear and frustration coating her tongue.

"We'll be there soon," Aleksander said, though his voice wavered. "Bunc said it wasn't far."

Before he could finish speaking, the carriage rumbled to a stop. Without the okay from Bunc, Aleksander threw open the door and jumped out. Rain pounded down on him. Each swath that came tried to weigh him into the earth.

If he awoke tomorrow covered in bruises, he wouldn't be surprised.

A flash of lightning illuminated the mouth of a cave. Bunc had already pulled the horses inside. Through the chaos of the storm, the mares nervous whickers just barely reached Aleksander's ears. The man looked back at the flash and straightened when he saw Aleksander.

"Here, my lord." In a surprisingly spry move, he launched into the driver's seat and lowered down a lantern—the only one still lit, and even it was struggling to flicker. The driver nodded to Aleksander. "I'll get the ladies in, you go put things to rights inside. Start a fire if you can."

Aleksander held the lantern out in front of him. Its dim oil-fueled glow danced over the walls as he stepped inside, and the roar of the storm rose to a deafening howl. Each sheet of rain reverberated off the curved walls, the stones, the cracks and crevices. A bolt of lightning flashed overhead—the resulting crack of thunder was enough to make Aleksander wedge his head between a shoulder and his free hand.

His blood chilled.

There was... something. In the darkness. He saw something, he was sure of it. Up near the back, where the stones littering the floor became larger and harder to navigate.

Another streak of lightning and... *there.*

He held the lantern out in front of him, taking each step as slow as he could. It looked like a person, the figure he'd seen. And there hadn't been homunculi lately—only a few strange sightings here and there, and they couldn't do much.

Clauden's voice from the war council two weeks ago echoed in his mind. About how there was a sorcerer trying to figure out how Terrell did what he did. The abominations this man made were even more bloodthirsty, and much less humanoid in appearance, with extra limbs and eyes and rows of teeth. Either he had found an easier way past the Flow's toll, or he had ripped the power from it, and the worse state of the abominations was seen as punishment by the magical force.

That sorcerer had been killed, the king had said. Varek had been sent to the town he was operating in, east of Kallendrine's land. The man was dispatched, and as many homunculi as were nearby were destroyed as well.

No one could escape the Ölmesuz, and he had no reason to lie about failing a mission.

But still, he had come back with scrapes and a new depth to the haunting in his eyes.

"How is it?" Elspeth called from the entrance.

Sick warmth flooded Aleksander's stomach. "Shh!" he hissed. "There's something in here."

"What?"

Aleksander turned, chest rising and falling at too fast a rate. In the entrance stood Elspeth and a cloaked Carissa, backlit by rain and lightning. He held a finger to his lips, then pointed over his shoulder.

Immediately, Elspeth drew her sword. No sound came from her steps, careful as they were; by the time she joined Aleksander, she aimed a hand loosely at the lantern and slowly swept her fingers up.

The flame rose, brightening the cave just enough for Aleksander to make out the figures huddled on the ground along the wall.

Bile rose in his throat. "Oh, goddess help us," he whispered. The lantern met the ground with a dull metallic clank. His shadow climbed the walls, dancing with the boulders and stalactites and warped images from the sheets of rain through which lightning filtered. Aoife slid from her scabbard, hovering in the air before Aleksander's face, reflecting the odd array of light.

"Are they..." Elspeth's voice was thin.

"For their sakes I hope so." Each breath was forced deeper than it should have been. The air he took in was moist, cold, and smelled of stale cave air and mildew from decaying leaves. Nothing rotting, not yet.

Or perhaps he had just gotten used to the smell.

Finally, Aleksander knelt down before the figures—the people. He reached a trembling hand forward, gently brushing back a thick, dark lock of hair that obscured the face of the person most easily accessible.

His stomach roiled at the sight he uncovered.

Their jaw was almost entirely gone, eyes pale and dull, staring into nothing. Blood caked what was left of their throat and clothes. Aleksander couldn't help but notice the pendant clutched in the person's hand—the same kind that Carissa wore around her neck.

Their face was in a later state of decay. His eyes didn't stay long on the beetles picking at their open flesh.

Swallowing his nausea, he managed two words. "They're dead."

Elspeth knelt beside him silently, her hands out and hovering over the corpses, nostrils flaring. There were five in total, ranging in age from adult to child. Much to his pain, the first he had found was the least mutilated.

"We need to burn them," she said after a moment. Her voice was low enough that Aleksander could hardly hear, especially over the echoing storm.

"El, we can't, look outside." He didn't move as he spoke. His eyes were locked on the group. They were human. He could tell by their clothes, by the lack of fangs in the gaping holes torn into their cheeks and jaws. "You and I both know exactly what did this. We need to burn them when we can."

"Clauden said that man was killed. More homunculi shouldn't be possible."

"It doesn't mean all his creations were killed, does it? And what about all the other things we've been hearing, El? You don't think he was the *only* person trying to recreate what Terrell did, do you?" The Presence snaked around Aleksander's spine, just as terrified. Every inch of him was set on edge, heart pounding, lungs aching to release a scream, stomach rolling. Images of the solstice, of that traitor's cottage... Homunculi didn't care for the whole person. As much as they hungered, they never craved a full meal, it seemed. It was just destruction and death and any bit of blood and chaos they could scavenge to satiate their ravenous, rotting bellies.

Whether more were possible or these were the victims of stragglers not yet caught, Aleksander did not want to find out.

Burning them was the only thing that seemed to work to make a body unviable as a homunculi. The village they'd passed through—Teallach—was proof enough of that.

Lightning crashed outside and Bunc's soothing calls to the horses bounced off the walls along with it. Elspeth sat back, staring at the corpses.

"You okay?" he said quietly.

She shook her head. "No. Of course not."

"We have to wait, El." He patted her shoulder. "Come rest, there's nothing we can do."

She swallowed hard, and when it became clear she wasn't going to move, he stood, ankles cracking, and made his way over to the rest of the group.

Carissa sat on a folded blanket she'd managed to get out of the carriage and into the cave without completely soaking. He passed her a smile before sitting on a rock before the small bundle of sticks Bunc was trying to work into a fire.

"What's over there that has Elspeth so captivated?" Carissa said, throwing a glance over her shoulder. "Weirdly-shaped stalagmites?"

Aleksander followed her gaze back to where his friend sat. They'd spent time together over the last months, he and Elspeth. Between shared training sessions and separate duties, they'd find moments to sit in the garden or on the parapets, watching the stars or the clouds or the bees. He'd seen the distance that had now engulfed her face only a handful of times in the past. Only when she talked about the homunculi.

They got under her skin the way nothing else did.

"I watched when they got Iscah," she had told him, her hands buried in her skirt on a late summer afternoon. She hardly wore dresses—usually she favored pants tailored tight against her legs, with any ribbon up the side she felt was reminiscent of Rodzjiek embroidery—but that day she'd worn a dress. It crumpled in her fists as she continued, "It was going for her face. I think it wanted to... eat her. Like I saw the others do at the solstice. Got a slash across her throat just as she ran it through."

They only talked about the events of the first journey twice. This was the second, and the last.

The same haunted look that had fallen over her features then was etched into them now. Looking back at her from where he sat, all that was visible was her hair and the back of her hunched form. She'd drawn her knees up under her chin and hugged them. After a moment, a single finger released its grip and gestured towards the lantern. The light in the lamp diminished, and as it did, Aleksander sighed."Remember Clauden telling us about Varek's most recent mission?" he started slowly. His sister nodded, and he continued. "I don't think he got all the homunculi. There are...people back there."

His sister's face paled, cheeks and eyes hollowing. "And... they're..."

He nodded.

She swallowed hard, nodding once, then twice, then repeatedly as her gaze drifted back to the fire. Trembling hands drew her cloak around her. Aleksander knew the jittery movements of her fingers weren't brought on by the cold.

"It's been a while since we've seen homunculi aftermath," he whispered. "She's... it's hard for her to move past it. After what happened."

The princess's nodding continued even as she sank back against a small boulder, knees drawing up in a mimic of Elspeth's pose. "I understand," was all she said.

Chapter

SIX

RAIN DRIPPED STEADILY ON TO the roof of the carriage. Gone was the deafening roar of the rain and the crashes of thunder. The storm had left sometime after Aleksander's watch ended, and as he awoke now, he found Elspeth, again, kneeling by the bodies.

Her crown was undone and fell in a single braid down her back. As he rose, her head cocked in his direction. "Do you think they died quickly?"

By the way they were holding one another, anyone who found them would know they hadn't. But Aleksander sighed, his boots scuffing along dry stone as he approached her. "I hope so." His knee hit the ground and she turned, burying her face in his shoulder. Wet eyelashes flicked against his neck.

"I keep forgetting," she breathed.

"It's okay." He rubbed circles into the space between her shoulder blades. "It's not your fault."

Aleksander didn't know what possessed him to say that. What wasn't her fault? The bodies? The homunculi? Not knowing? Regardless, he tucked his head against hers. It was true. It wasn't her fault.

She stayed silent for a long moment before whispering, "I wish this never happened. I wish the prophecies had never existed."

He sighed deeply. "Me too." A shock ran through him at his own words. They...weren't a lie. As much as he thought they should be. As much as they *really* should be. Elspeth nuzzled closer and he sat back, pulling her in. A fresh, soft breeze echoed through the cavern, bringing with it the scents of rain and fading plants. They inhaled deeply with a synchronized breath. "I don't understand why everyone was so excited when I was born," he said, "if the birth of the Sword means...things like this."

"They're selfish," she muttered. An awkward shrug bounced off his arm. "The courtiers are excited their savior is back. Most are too excited about that to really care what it means for the rest of us." A deep sigh echoed and her shoulders relaxed in his embrace. "We should burn them."

"Yeah," Aleksander nodded, his chin against her hair, "They deserve peace."

Once they stood and brushed dust from their pants and hands, they worked together to move the dead past the sleeping bodies of their comrades and into the pink morning light. Elspeth arranged them in funeral poses; chins up, hands folded over their chests. Two adults, one around their age, and two younger.

As he took his position at the head of what was to become the burial pyre, Elspeth split off into the nearby bushes, dragging out a limp, crumbling form.

Aleksander jolted back. "What is that?"

The rotten flesh and exposed bones were enough to tell him what it was, but Elspeth still answered him. "I think it's what killed them." Unceremoniously, she tossed its rickety limbs over the rest of its body, and Aleksander could see not only where the magic had been struggling to hold it together, but where it seemed a good sized dagger had sliced into its ribs.

"Did they kill it?"

"That's my guess. Found it when I was pacing last night after the storm let up." With a pointed stare and a snarl, the body burst into flames. "It doesn't deserve the reverence they do," she said, making her way back over to the family. She found her place beside Aleksander. Gone from her features was the rage she'd felt at the monster. Now, all that remained was the dull, empty, endless pain that never seemed to leave any of them.

Aleksander averted his eyes from them as Elspeth raised her hands. Palms open down and towards them, her fingers trembled. Without a thought, he steadied her with a hand on her lower back. A deep breath rose her shoulders, and she curled her fingers ever so slightly, twisting her palms slowly to the sky. He swore he could see the fire racing beneath her rich skin, bright and wild and terrible; but not once did it leap out.

A glow started within the bones of the dead. He watched out of the corner of his eye as Elspeth deepened the inferno, causing flames to crack free and engulf the whole of them. Once a blaze steadily burned, her hands dropped to her side.

Embers crackled behind burning irises. He studied her, entirely transfixed on the scene before them. Beneath the awe washing over her features, grief thrashed. Beside it, anger. Tears caught the light on her lash line and unease tightened Aleksander's chest.

Everything on her face was so raw, and yet vacant. It felt wrong to stare at her, so he simply stood behind her and held her, arms around hers. His chin rested on her shoulder. "You did good."

Not well.

Good.

For a moment, she stood there, unresponsive, staring at the flames. Aleksander debated letting go—it was strange, standing here and hugging her when she did not reciprocate. Loosening his grip, he began to pull away. Two firm hands wrapped around his wrists drawing them back across her chest, holding him there. Warmth collected where their skin met, a contrast to the cold, damp morning.

She didn't let go for a long time.

◊ ✳ ◊

ALEKSANDER TOOK CARISSA'S hand as she stepped into the carriage, maneuvering her muddied skirts around the benches as she took her seat. The curtains were drawn now, and despite the awful night of sleep on hard stone—and the events of the early morning—Aleksander found himself relaxing in to the padded seats with ease. It cradled him in a way it never had before. Or maybe this was just the first time he noticed it.

"Would you read more?" Elspeth asked, leaning forward and wedging her hands beneath her thighs.

"Read more of what?"

Across the way, Carissa gently placed a hand on her stomach as she leaned forward, retaining a regal stature as she dug through a small pocket at the edge of her seat. When she sat up again, she held a small book between her fingers.

The worn, pale green of the linen cover lit up a memory in Aleksander's mind. "Is that Varek's book?"

He had never gotten a good look at the small novel the man had carried around all those weeks together, but the faded foil printed on the cover in the imitation of a branch with budding leaves had caught in the firelight often enough for Aleksander to recognize it all these months later. "Why do you have Varek's book?"

"He lent it to me," Carissa said with a shrug. "He said he'd read it often enough and thought I might like it, so I've been reading it on our trips to town. I'm hoping to finish it by the time we see him next so I can return it." She leafed through the book, head bowed, until she came upon a small, dried leaf pressed between the pages. She took it and passed it to Elspeth, who tucked it behind her ear.

For a moment, Aleksander saw images of her in the field beside the castle, running with Carissa, both wearing flower crowns as the girls often did in Brewith during the warmer months. Carissa and he had spent time galavanting about there as children. Had Elspeth ever experienced such simple freedom?

She didn't speak in detail about her upbringing, but the walls of the Keep seemed much more stern than those of the castle. Especially for the low-borns.

"Is it any good?"

"It's interesting," Elspeth said. "It's about this boy who is attending a school for mages, only his family can't afford the school even though his father was once a lord. The school and the other nobles there don't know about his father's fall from grace, so he's trying to find ways to stay in attendance as well as hopefully regain his family's lost wealth, and maybe even elevate himself one day to the palace."

Aleksander rolled his eyes, but leaned back anyway. "Sounds boring."

Elspeth's eyes went wide. "Oh, no. He's a horrible person and the drama is so tragic. It really pulls you in. Just listen."

"*Chapter twenty four*," Carissa began. Her eyes flicked up to Aleksander's. "Janus has been put in public service due to a mishap at school, and he's just found his way into a tavern where an Ölmesuz girl he knew from school is performing on stage like a minstrel. She has ties to the palace but because she was born lowly and raised in Ölmesuz culture, he doesn't know whether he sees her as a friend or as an animal." Her legs shifted one over the other, leaned forward, then sat up and adjusted her neck.

"It's an older book so some of the language is expected," Elspeth admonished, "but the author still makes it clear that Janus is in the wrong for his views towards the Ölmesuz, and especially Kinneret. I personally think she's one of the best characters in the story."

"Are you going to let me read?"

The carriage fell silent. Carissa's eyes returned to the print.

"*Little as she was, Kinneret threw herself between the men.*" Her eyes dashed up to Aleksander's. "Janus and his sworn enemy, Brutus, have both stumbled upon Kinneret's performance—oh, you'll figure it out."

Elspeth patted Aleksander's shoulder and shifted, readying for the story.

"*Her iron-dark hair hung in curls over her shoulders, the*

glint in her eye cold as steel. She had never looked at Janus that way before. "Curious," he thought, "she seems as if she truly thinks I may be in the wrong here, instead of her fellow creatures." The notion of running her through with his blade before turning on Brutus was a potent poison, but he swallowed it down and lowered his sword."

Aleksander crinkled his nose at the language. There was once a time people truly thought like this, calling Ölmesuz, Rodzjiek, and Mekartlim 'creatures' instead of people. Never mind the arcane and scientific advancements the Ölmesuz contributed throughout history, nor the music and medicine of the Rodzjiekim. That's to say nothing of the textiles and food brought by the Mekartlim. Yet he couldn't help but be drawn into the story. Every word from Janus's mouth and mind made Aleksander's blood boil, and there was more than one time when his eyes flicked over to Elspeth and found her unconsciously baring her fangs, small licks of flame sparking from her eyes and curling around her lashes.

Kinneret was an easy favorite, as Elspeth said. She was strong, and smart, and clearly knew that Janus was trying to use her, even if Janus himself didn't; still, Aleksander found himself drawn to Tiber, Janus's best friend. Something about his blind hope, his desire to use his station for good, even amongst the cruel noble offspring plotting their own rises to power... it sat well in Aleksander's chest.

He had never been so enthralled in a story before. Most books he'd read were about the history of Zekhar, folklore, or religious texts. Somehow it never occurred to him that stories of pure fiction could exist, much less be so intriguing.

Night fell, and Carissa was still reading thanks to a small flame summoned at the tip of Elspeth's fingers. At one point the carriage paused for Bunc to inform them it was only another hour or so until they reached Hadiqin, the town home to Lord Asghar and Aarua Manor.

They thanked him and agreed to continue moving as quickly as they could. The moment the door was closed, they turned back to one another, losing time to the story once more.

It was deep into the evening when Carissa flipped to the last page. Elspeth's cheeks were wet with tears, and even Aleksander was blinking back the urge to cry.

Carissa sniffed deeply, opening her eyes as wide as she could to see past the tears. *"'Nothing would change for him—Kinneret's songs would echo through mead halls and forests, but she no longer would. If he plugged his ears, he could endure life in the city. But as he kissed Eleanora's hand, blinking into her bright blue eyes, a smile formed on his villainous face.*

'He could make sure he never heard those echoes again. After all, he'd silenced Lord Brunn, and Brutus, and Tiber. He could. The country would be his, the songs played would be his favorites, the names given to children the names he deigned fair. It may come to pass, he noted, that time would not be kind to his rule. But as Eleanora smiled back at him, he was thankful he was right in one aspect—'"

Elspeth nearly growled.

"'—the blood in his veins was more than water. It was power. And no one would wield it like he would.'"

The book snapped shut. It echoed through the carriage, eventually fading into the rumbling of the wheels and the clopping of hooves on cobblestones. Even as the carriage slowed to a stop everything was silent. Only when Bunc's feet hit the stone did Aleksander dare to move, to speak. "So, he won? He got to get away with killing everyone and just... became king?"

A squeak sounded from beside him as Elspeth ground her teeth. "I'm... devastated. But also that was stunning. But awful."

"I need to ask Varek if there are more after this," Carissa's voice was far off, her fingers trailing lazily over the laurel on the cover—that is what it was, Aleksander had learned. "That can't be all."

The door opened with a creak. An exhausted Bunc stood before a grand staircase up to a manor haloed in moonlight. Carissa tucked the book under her arm and took his hand.

"Villains don't win," Elspeth shook her head.

"They do, though," Aleksander said. "They do win. In real life. That's why fighting them is so important, because they don't deserve to win."

"But who fought Janus?" Elspeth took Bunc's hand, muttering her thanks. Her eyes roved the manor's facade, seeing it but not at all taking it in. "Brutus, Tiber, Kinneret—they tried and lost."

A strange jolt of rage flew through Aleksander's jaw. "Tiber didn't deserve what happened to him. None of them did."

"That's why I want to know if there's more," Carissa said. The bags under her eyes were visible in the low light—while not dark, they were puffy. "If a villain wins, that means there must be a hero that will take them on later. I don't understand why the author wrote this if she doesn't plan on having Janus overthrown."

"Perhaps I'll lend you the rest of them once you get some of your training completed, your highness."

At the sound of the deep, rumbling voice, Aleksander jumped and, for some reason, had to fight the odd urge to race up to the Ölmesuz sauntering down the steps and greet him with a hug.

Elspeth, on the other hand, gave in to that urge instantly.

"Varek!" she shouted, shooting from Aleksander's side like a crossbow bolt. Varek stumbled back, his foot catching on a step as the comparatively small Rodzjiek girl rocked him off balance. "I didn't know you'd be here!"

"Just so happens, my old friend's manor was closer to my last assignment than Brevindun." He shrugged, patting Elspeth's back as they parted. "The king mentioned some of my favorite nuisances would be coming by this evening, and Lord Asghar was more than happy to accommodate me." His eyes, ringed with dark bags and deepening wrinkles, found Aleksander. "I figured now would be as good a time as any for the god-child and his friend to show me what they've perfected while I've been away." His hand slowly moved to the blade on his hip.

Blood ran cold in Aleksander's body. He was tired, distracted, and admittedly not much improved since Varek's last match with him. But before he could say or do anything to rebut, Varek smirked, his hand falling limp.

"Well, maybe I'll give you a chance to rest up. A fair fight isn't as fun as a heavily favored one, but it works all the same."

Nothing offered more relief than the moment a footman appeared and took his trunk, guiding Aleksander through the darkened hallways to his new room.

Chapter

SEVEN

N O BED HAD CRADLED HIM the way this one had. After a night on the floor of that cave and a full day traveling the rest of the bumpy, horrible way to Aarua Manor, the plush mattress had picked away all the stress and pain in his body. He could have stayed there all day if he had been allowed.

His senses had not yet gotten used to his new surroundings. With each glance about the ceiling, he grew more and more entranced, catching small details in the stone, in the fabric draped over him, a rich, thick, glowing red in the early light. Birdsong, still bright despite the chill leeching through his open windows, had awoken him. It did not cease, and the high ceilings allowed for their music to soar and dance around him.

He lifted a hand into the shaft of sunlight streaming just above his headboard, marveling at the way the light turned the edges of his fingers pink. Between his digits, dust swirled. With a light smile, he swished his fingers, a gentle mimicry of how he'd seen Elspeth dance with smoke.

The room was not opulent, not like the bedrooms in Brevindun. But goddess-on-high, it was comforting beyond belief.

A door squeaked slightly and he froze, turning his face just enough to see a wavy auburn curtain and one piercing eye peek through the door.

"Aleksander!" she hissed, giddiness already leeching into her voice.

His hand fell to his stomach and he rolled over with a groan. The blankets welcomed him. He wanted to stay here all day, and goddess help anyone who dared try to—

He jolted to the side, splaying his arms out as the mattress beneath him buckled and shook. One sturdy, dark arm landed before his torso, trapping him on the bed. He gazed up into that tangle of red hair, only to find his friend leaning over him, radiating warmth. A feral smile split her face.

"I smelled really good food on the way here. You should get up and come eat with me."

Despite the energy lacing every muscle of her, he relaxed back into the pillows. "Couldn't you just bring it to me?"

Her eyes flashed, a mix of annoyance and amusement. "I'm not a servant, you'll remember."

A lazy smile turned the corners of his mouth as he studied the way the sunlight made her hair catch fire. A safe blaze, though that concept never fully fit her.

She blinked, gaze flashing over his face. With a raised eyebrow, she continued, "I can just as well go down first and make sure everyone else eats, and you're left with nothing. If that's what you'd prefer."

"Fine," he relented. "Bring me my dressing gown, please."

"Why?" Elspeth screwed up her face. "Not like I haven't seen you change out of your armor before, it's basically the same thing."

Except it wasn't. The fabric of the night clothes Asghar's estate provided was soft, luxurious, and very finely woven. It was nothing like the thicker cotton underclothes they fit beneath their gambesons and plate. He set his jaw, face burning. "Elspeth."

She mimicked his expression. "Aleksander."

"Please."

Her lips twitched in a smirk. "Alright, if it makes you feel better I won't look."

Fighting his way out of his blankets, he landed a shove on Elspeth's side, sending her toppling onto the other half of the enormous mattress. A wave of lavender floated after her, puffing up with a gentle burst of dust and linen when she landed on the heavy blanket. That smirk still stayed pressed into her cheeks, even as she closed her eyes and stretched indulgently over the bed.

"They're so comfortable here," she murmured.

"I thought we were going to get breakfast together," Aleksander chided, racing across the room to wrap himself in the fine dressing gown that had been hung outside the wardrobe for him by whatever unseen servant had been assigned to him. His movements were fast and clumsy, but by the time Elspeth huffed out a breath and rolled off the bed, he was presentable. "Yes," she said, "but I've never been on a bed this luxurious before. Let me live, Aleksander."

"Neither have I," he retorted, tying the cord around his waist tightly as she adjusted her own robe. "But I'd like to eat if you're forcing me out of bed."

The dressing gown she wore was much more suited to her than the others he'd seen her in—gone were the wintery blues and purple-reds favored so heavily by the royal family. Ash-green fabric draped loosely off her shoulders, drooping down to where a matching sash tied it around her midsection. Like his own robe, it shimmered with every movement.

Noticing his attention, she crossed her arms. "What?"

"Nothing," he said. And it was nothing. It was nothing, the way her whole self seemed more alive than she'd been before. It was nothing, the giddiness she so freely expressed.

It certainly was nothing, that feeling that swelled more and more in his chest when she would look at him.

She pursed her lips. "Alright. Well, I don't doubt Varek is eager to get us training again today, so let's go fill our bellies first."

The notion of getting out of bed only to be thrust into an

arena and forced to be knocked down by Varek over and over again was not a pleasant one. Aleksander gritted his teeth. "Oh, is he?"

Elspeth shrugged, raking her fingers through her hair. "We knew this was part of the deal. Carissa works on her magic, we work on our swordsmanship, and now with Varek here, it's only going to be more important."

"I know, I know," he muttered. The boy dragged a hand down his face. Just because he knew this was going to happen didn't mean he wasn't still upset by it. It was different than training at home, or in the middle of the night. Those instances, when he chose to train, he had control. He could lose himself in his drills. He even found joy in it, now and then. But when Varek was there, everything was agony. Each step, each swing, each barked correction from the old man...

"Come on."

Aleksander looked down at the words, finding Elspeth's fingers weaving through his. She gave a gentle tug, her smile softer and encouraging.

"Neither of us are doing it alone today."

With a heavy sigh, Aleksander stepped forward, allowing her to lead him towards the door, through it, and down the hall. All the while, her hand stayed in his, warm and sure, coursing with energy.

If he focused, Aleksander could swear he felt her fire racing along her bones, jumping out to meet his touch.

His hands suddenly became very clammy.

At the bottom of the steps, Aleksander pulled his hand free and cracked his knuckles. It did not bother him when Elspeth shot a frown his way. But he did immediately speak to shift her attention. "Any idea what Varek has in store?"

At this, she grinned, bouncing in her steps. "Not a clue, but I think it's safe to say there's going to be a lot of sweating, cursing, and bruises."

The Presence balked at that, but nonetheless, Aleksander chuckled, a joyless—though not humorless—sound. "*Wonderful.*"

On the terrace the constant crash of waves from the sea and the salty air, faintly warm with the relentless talons of summer, mixed with the breakfast spread in a scent that made Aleksander's mouth water. Unlike Brevindun, there were no guards by the terrace doors. There was no table where everyone sat to scarf down a platter of eggs, sausage, and whatever fruits or vegetables were available. Instead, Elspeth strode towards a single table piled high with eggs prepared various ways, pastries, fruits, yogurts, and flatbreads. On the far end there were dishes stacked, stained with the remainders of breakfasts already devoured. It wobbled with every movement Aleksander took in gathering his food.

One dish he'd never seen before caught his eye—eggs surrounded by tomatoes and onions. It smelled heavenly, and when he scooped a forkful of it into his mouth, his intuition was proven right. Rich spices exploded on his tongue, and after filling his plate a second time, he watched Elspeth glance towards the door before digging a spare spoon into the platter and shoving it straight into her mouth.

Most of the dishes had already been picked clean.

"How late did I sleep?" With careful precision, Aleksander took the last lemon scone and placed it on the corner of his full plate.

"Late," Elspeth said. She shoved half an egg, topped with spices and parsley, into her mouth. "It's easily midmorning."

A pang of guilt shot through him, but then the pair walked to the edge of the terrace and the wind took that feeling away.

It was stunning.

Aleksander had never been this far south before, and while most of the foliage and animals were all the same, the geography was different. Elmere's Keep sat atop a cliff, in the colder waters of the northern sea. Its waves simply *looked* icy, even at the end of summer. Here, the water was warmer. It sounded deeper, softer, as if he could laze about in the currents without freezing to death. Thin forests—nothing like the ancient Untamed—littered the southern half of Zekhar and their borders stopped near the town, leaving space for a rocky shoreline to meet grassy fields. But behind Asghar's estate, gardens stretched from the level below the breakfast terrace all the way to the sea. It didn't matter that the plants and trees were all falling dormant for the coming winter—the spectacular shades of red, orange, and gold were a beauty in themselves.

His plate clinked against the stone railing of the upper terrace. A cold breeze blew his hair back from his face, his ears, and he remembered that, though they were further south than Brewith, it was still autumn.

"You should have grabbed a cloak at the festival," she chided, sing-song as she speared a slice of late-season strawberry. "You Zekharyans don't have heat in your bones like we do." A playful smirk twisted her lips before she turned her gaze back to the sea, chewing thoughtfully.

Even as she turned away, he watched her. Loose and long, her hair twisted in the wind, catching on her shoulders to create a magnificent cowl. Everything about her shone. As one strand fluttered around her nose and she scrunched it up in response, something stirred within Aleksander's chest.

"You seem to be having a good time," he said. Every word was measured, soft. "I'm glad."

She turned to him, eyes glowing. "You know, so far I am." After a moment, her fangs cracked through in a smile. "I don't know if you're aware of this, my lord Champion, but I don't travel much."

That smile. How could one not return such a pure expression? As he smiled back, however, a pressure built within his throat. It nearly sent goosebumps down his arms. It wasn't a feeling he was familiar with—it wasn't a scream, nor a cry aching to be released.

No, he wasn't sure what that pressure was caused by at all.

He swallowed hard, turning out back to the sea and shoveling four too many forkfuls into his mouth.

Beside him, Elspeth snorted a quiet laugh and resumed eating her own breakfast.

"You must be the Lord Champion," a deep voice behind him rumbled. The man owning it stood tall, even towering over Varek. He approached with long strides. A wide grin, bright as the sun itself, greeted them. "A pleasure to meet you one on one, Lord Wythane."

Chapter

EIGHT

ORD ASGHAR WAS NOT A man easily forgotten. Though it was uncommon for him to attend matters of court and even most of the festivals hosted by the royal family, when he did appear, his statuesque form and smooth, powerful gait made him stand out in every room and in everyone's memories.

Beside him, Elspeth's eyes widened, a rosy blush blooming in her cheeks.

Aleksander had to fight not to roll his eyes.

Another thing not easily forgotten was his affect on almost all women. And a good amount of men.

"Lord Asghar," Aleksander pressed his hand to his heart, offering a bow. "Thank you for allowing us to accompany Princess Carissa here while she pursues her studies."

The chains and hoops adorning the lord's ears swung when he bowed in return, fingertips loosely touching his forehead, as was the Ölmesuz custom. "Of course." Sun glinted off his deep bronze skin as though he were entirely molded from the metal, not just reminiscent of it. His high cheekbones shone brightly, contrasting with the pale gold of his hair, falling like a river down his back and shoulders. Small sections throughout were braided and adorned with beads. "I would be remiss to not bring Varek's favorite student and the princess's protector into my demesne when I am already hosting the other half of your party." Sparkling amethyst eyes turned to Elspeth. "And you must be Lady D'orde."

He took her hand, his own bedecked with various rings and bracelets. Even with Asghar bowing at the waist, Elspeth's hand was level with her head as he raised it to his lips and brushed a kiss over her knuckles. "Lovely to meet you. Varek has told me much."

"Oh?" She blinked rapidly, clearing her throat. "I mean, of course, why wouldn't he? We're not special, certainly not me. We're just his students. And you're his friend. It makes sense that he'd talk about me—us."

This time, Aleksander did roll his eyes, but only in an attempt to fend off the churning in his stomach.

The lord stood, not responding save for an amused, if slightly uncomfortable, smile. His gaze shifted away from them and out to the sea beyond. "I will never understand why my ancestors chose to travel north and settle here, but I'll forever be glad they did. If you are here into the snow season, you should return to this terrace." His eyes flashed. "The sea is wild and magnificent. There is truly nothing like it, not even on the northernmost coasts of Ölmess."

Aleksander turned back, casting an eye out at the already churning waves. He couldn't imagine the rolls crashing onto the stone being any larger; and once his mind did allow him to visualize it, the image terrified him.

"Have you seen much of the estate yet? Your carriage came in late and I was told you went directly to your chambers."

They both shook their head, and Asghar practically jumped in excitement.

"Ah!" Asghar exclaimed, clapping his hands. "Please, my Lord Champion, Lady D'orde, come with me."

With a sweeping gesture that caught the wide sleeve of his ornate robe in the breeze, Aleksander left his now-empty plate on the stone wall and followed the man inside.

Through tall, open hallways they meandered. The ceilings

were vaulted, often decorated with flourishes of vines and geometric patterns. A few murals crawled down the walls, depicting stories from various folklores—Ölmesuz, Zekharyan, and even some Rodzjiek. Asghar was good at pointing out various stories immortalized in the murals, especially ones Aleksander and Elspeth were likely to be familiar with. The man glowed with pride when Elspeth gasped and raced up to a wall, excitedly exclaiming that this was a Rodzjiek tale she knew well, one of the only ones she grew up with in the Keep. A sweeping gesture here or there down various halls was accompanied by the explanation of the wings, where the armory was, the kitchen, the training halls, the other rooms for in-house Crafters and mages, and so on. His smile stretched wider than it had been prior, and he pushed open a large set of dark wood doors. Within, stretching and winding farther than Aleksander could see, were rows and rows of books, scrolls, and other written volumes.

The estate's library.

Aleksander immediately understood why Carissa wanted to study here. In fact, he couldn't help the frustration that he was not a mage, and as such likely had little use for this room.

"Are you coming by to use my library?" A voice crooned as soon as Aleksander crossed the threshold. "Or are you just stopping for a tour?"

He could not see the speaker, no matter how hard he tried. Shuffling sounded from among the tall bookcases that snaked through the room and lined the walls, stretching nearly to the vaulted, painted ceiling. The wood on them glistened as though they were freshly oiled. A hand-lettered sign at the end of each denoted which books were where—reference, history, medical, arcane, and so forth.

"Just a tour at the moment, Chione," Asghar responded, his gaze wandering the room.

Aleksander could not stop his own attention from dancing about the room either; metal lanterns with cut out shapes dangled from the ceiling, flickering with firelight inside. The colored glass in them sent scattered arrays around the library.

It was magnificently grand.

"I suppose I'm not surprised, the mages have already gathered most of their books this morning," she continued. Finally, a figure emerged from the stacks, a tower of books leaning against her chest. She met the small group with a slow, gentle smile. "Ah. My Lord Champion. Forgive me for not bowing, my hands are full." Her gown swept the floor, long and pale blue, with a shimmering silver caplet that draped all the way down to her elbows. It complemented her steel skin and hair perfectly, drawing attention to the two large, sapphire eyes that routinely flicked from her path, to the books in her embrace, to Aleksander's own eyes.

He waved it off quickly. The notion that he was a guest and not a member of the royal family had settled in his chest as he followed Asghar down the hall during the early part of the tour—formalities felt strange now.

"I feel like I should be bowing to you," he said, awkwardly.

She laughed as she reached the desk at the front, placing her hands upon it on either side of her stack of books to steady herself. "No, please," she turned, leaning back against the desk. "That is not necessary."

With a long sweep of her arm, she bent at the waist. Her straight hair shimmered over her shoulders, nearly whispering with the same metallic voice one hears from thin necklaces when placed together, or chainmail. "It is an honor to have you visit our archives, my Lord Champion." She stood, hand above her heart. "I am Chione, daughter of Akila and Darius, head librarian of Aarua Manor."

Aleksander found himself placing a hand on his heart as well. "Aleksander Wythane, son of Tulathne, Sword of Ages. And this is Elspeth, daughter of..." He trailed off awkwardly, realizing that he did not know the names of any of Elspeth's parents—by birth or otherwise.

Noticing the gap, Elspeth's jaw twitched. Her lips flattened for a split second before she inclined her head towards the librarian. "Daughter of the Untamed. Sworn Hand of the Sword of Ages."

Sapphire eyes shifted to the girl beside him, and her smile widened ever so slightly. "A pleasure to meet you, my lady."

"Has the princess come for her studies yet?" Asghar asked.

"Yes, she arrived shortly after breakfast this morning. She was taken to the chapel so that she might offer prayers to her goddess before being handed off to Mage Theresas."

"You have a chapel?" Aleksander's heart raced.

Growing up, he always felt more connected to Tulathne when he *needed* to be. On travels, where temples and oratories were few and far between. During holidays. During birthdays. Any time when he was consumed with something else. Perhaps this would be a good place to connect with Her, a place so like the palace yet so unlike anything he'd encountered before. An embarrassing sense of desperation overtook him, paired with a sudden, forceful feeling that he *was* Tulathne's son, and he had to start acting like it. He wrung his hands together even as he asked, "Can we see it?"

Chione's eyes flitted towards Asghar, the brightness in them faltering. "Yes," she said after a minute. "But, my lord, please be aware that as we have mostly Ölmesuz and Zekharyans living and working at this estate, the chapel has been made to be a place of worship for both followers of Tulathne and those who venerate the Kutsalyot and the Mother."

Again, Aleksander waved his hand, dismissing the thought from the air. "That's no problem. I want to see it." Truthfully, that made him all the more intrigued. Not only could he get closer to his mother, but he could finally learn more about this faith he's seen displayed so infrequently yet so earnestly.

"As you wish," Chione said. A smile appeared on her face, but her eyes did not crinkle in that earnest way. "Follow me."

The chapel, it turned out, was only a few paces down from the library. Already, Aleksander could smell the rich incense burning from within. Though it was not part of Tulathne worship, the smell gave him a sense of comfort.

It all fell away like a cloak the moment he turned in the

doorway, taking in the room.

The chapel was beautiful. That was not the issue. There was a section for Tulathne off to the left, with pews lined up and equipped with plush velvet kneelers. They got her colors right, the statue of her was clean and well-designed. The rest of the chapel was simple wooden pews, row after row, facing towards the front of the room. Lit by candles and lamps, the statues seemed almost alive. It was there, as his eyes alighted on the figure in the center, that panic began to turn his stomach, to lock his lungs in a vice.

He immediately knew which member of the Kutsalyot was the most venerated. He could tell by the downturn of her nose, the thick lashes they captured so perfectly in stone, the way her bangs separated ever so slightly in the middle of her forehead before blending into the tendrils that always framed her face.

Never had he seen her so serene—except maybe when she had her head in Demir's lap all those months ago, asleep under a starry late-summer sky.

Chapter
NINE

*I*SCAH.

Aleksander froze to the spot. A scream built up in his throat, tightening with each breath. It felt like he'd seen a ghost. But that grief, that visceral, angry, broken grief, clawed up his throat. A strange choking sound was all he made through tight-clenched lips. It was as raw as the moment he'd watched her fingers go limp, entwined with Demir's.

A sharp gasp sounded next to him and without looking, he caught Elspeth's hand in his own.

Her grip answered his in a desperate vice.

Neither of the Ölmesuz accompanying them spoke, and after a brief glance, Aleksander discovered neither had entered the chapel. They stood right outside, hands folded, silent. The lord's face was calm, empty save for the regret in his eyes. Beside him, Chione's eyes were wide with worry. Apology.

Pity.

His heart ached. He turned back to the visage before him.

Footfall sounded against stone, slow and hesitant, and he realized he was walking forward. Elspeth's grip stayed in his, and soon she walked with him.

The statue was tall. It seemed to be on a slightly larger-than-lifelike scale. At her feet, covered by the draping, traditional clothes she was depicted in, were candles, notes, flowers, small treats wrapped in parchment.

Petitions, he figured. Prayers. Condolences.

Veneration.

There were more scattered around the feet of the other Kutsalyot in the space.

The Honored Dead.

The Honored Ancestors.

Of which now Iscah was a part.

Every inch of the statue had been carefully brushed with paint. Someone who knew her well must have overseen the process, because everything was a perfect match to her real coloring. Layers of purple made the carved eyes glisten their proper deep amethyst. A subtle blush graced her ashen cheeks.

He wanted to touch her. To reach out and gently brush his fingers along the back of her hand, still gripping a sword lowered to touch the ground. To somehow climb high enough and look into those eyes carved to stare into the high distance.

From the corner of his eye, he saw Elspeth's hand raise, sliding up along Iscah's wrist.

A voice shouted in his mind to stop her. Art is not to be touched, especially this kind of art—but he turned to his friend's face and in response to the pain strangled there, to the twisted expression warping her features and bringing water to her eyes...

In answer to that, the voice fell silent.

She tried to hold that hand, the one gripping the sword. Her fingers wrapped around the cumbersome stone before her, and Aleksander gave the hand he still held a squeeze.

The burning in his eyes worsened, and the statue before him blurred as tears began to fall.

An awful collection of feelings consumed him. Grief tore at his chest, guilt at his throat, and his whole body seemed to slowly crush beneath the weight of immense sorrow and longing. She was a friend. A friend he didn't talk much with, but she was there. She'd smiled at him. She'd helped Carissa and laughed and fought beside them. This stone visage was honoring her, he knew that. It gave her the peace, the respect she deserved—the respect Aleksander immediately knew he did not give her enough of. Yet he couldn't help but stare at it, unblinking

She should be here, breathing. Not like this.

"We didn't know how to tell you," Chione's silken voice floated through the chapel. Aleksander hardly heard it. His pulse throbbed in his ears as his mind repeated over and over the unfairness of the situation.

Anger was the foremost feeling within him. And he let himself be angry.

His lips pulled back to bare teeth. "So you let me just wander in here and find her?" Oh, how he *hated* the emotion that cracked his voice. It was deeper than usual, rumbling and scraping along stones of sorrow that lined his throat.

Elspeth's hand tightened around his.

No other words came.

"If it's any comfort," Chione continued, "we believe she is now in a safe place, where she may live for the eternity she was... kept from...on earth. And we believe she will watch over those she loved in her life here. Death is not the end for us it's merely... a transition."

A transition. Did that mean anything to Aleksander? He supposed not, as his heart ache grew worse and the tension running down his arms threatened to snap his bones. She was gone. It was his fault, he knew that now. He had known the moment it happened.

She wouldn't have been there if not for him.

But nothing he said now could shift that.

Iscah stared off into the distance of the chapel and whatever lay beyond, and no matter how hard he tried to push down his feelings, they erupted in his chest, violent and unbidden.

It should have been him.

"She still looks beautiful." It was all his tongue would let him say, for it was the only positive thing he was thinking.

Clearing his throat, he tore his eyes away from the sculpture. It was everything he could do to not fall to the ground, wailing and screaming like a child—though that was all he wanted to do. Tired, watery eyes scanned the chapel. The other Kutsalyot there were designed similarly. Their poses varied, their dress similar—all the draping, fine fabrics of their people. And there, in the corner, pale and in a pose he'd seen hundreds of times, stood Tulathne.

Any excitement or drive he had once had to find his place at that kneeler before Her and connect with his goddess was gone.

As he blinked, a hand appeared before him. He flinched, so did the fingers. When he met Elspeth's gaze, she pressed her lips together hard and continued reaching forward, wiping her thumb along the bottom side of his lashes. Rough was her touch, pulling at his skin to rid it of the tears there, but he'd be a fool not to see the kindness pooling behind her eyes, red with tears and doused embers. Her bottom lip quivered, sticking out no matter how tightly she held them together.

Once she was done, she rubbed her fingers on the collar of his shirt. Their eyes met. She opened her mouth to say something, but quickly closed it again.

He had no strength to respond with anything but, "We should go find Varek. No use wasting time we could be training."

◊✳◊

ALEKSANDER'S ARMOR WAS heavy. It weighed down on him in a way it never had before. Sure, the autumn sun offered no help to relieve him of that oppressive weight, but it wasn't a great contributor to his strain either.

The arena wasn't small. When he trudged his way in, squinting into the light, dust stretched out on either side of him nearly twice as much as it did back at Castle Brevindun. Aside from seats along the wall where fighters might take pauses from their training, there were stands. What kind of events would be held here, Aleksander did not know, but it was clear they often required a large audience.

In the center stood Varek, clad in his usual dark linen shirt and dark purple pants. The need for him to be armored during their training left long ago. A few weeks after they'd come back from the Untamed, he pit Aleksander and Elspeth against each other with the intention of seeing who was stronger. When the match raged for nearly an hour, both of them panting and drenched in sweat, he'd finally stepped in and called it off.

Now, someone had to forfeit or take the other down before they'd be let go for the day.

Aleksander swallowed hard, watching Elspeth wheel her arm around. Her sword flashed in her grip as she stretched out her joints.

He wasn't in the headspace to give her a fair fight today, and part of him felt bad for that. She was a good soldier—she deserved fair fights.

Through warm ups, where orders were barked by the gruff old Ölmesuz from his new perch on the side of the wall, Aleksander's mind wandered. Through the chapel, around the statue of Iscah. They'd made it so fast. And with so much care. Each fold of her garment, each wave of her hair...it was as though she'd posed for a portrait. But she was in the ground, deep in the Untamed, near the Pozhontecs. And there she would stay.

Aoife curved down, blocking the imagined hit Varek shouted out.

His mind continued its journey out the front doors of Aarua Manor, down the road, still just as rainy as it was when they traveled here.

A flash of steel—the blade curved up.

He blinked away the violent image of the people in the cave.

You're getting distracted, stop it.

But that flickering shadow on the wall, missing a jaw...

He swung his sword out to the side, a fraction of a second too late. He couldn't see Varek, but he felt the frustration radiating off the man.

The next command he heeded perfectly, and then he was back in Brevindun.

Janek. At the thought, his chest ached. Why did he always

have to leave people? Not all of them, but enough to feel bad. And Janek—he'd accepted, both times, that he couldn't accompany his wife. If only the king and queen didn't care for image that much. Perhaps Aleksander could have stayed to help Demir with his duties and Janek could have accompanied his wife for once.

Demir. His wing. Guilt stabbed at Aleksander's chest—

Aoife swung up to block again, then out to execute an invisible parry.

—but it wasn't his fault. Demir had done all he could. The rain had bogged him down.

What was he doing now?

I should consider writing him a letter—

A boot slammed into the back of Aleksander's knee and he tumbled forward. "Pay attention," Varek growled. On the sand beside him, Aleksander saw the towering shadow. He could almost make out the snarl on the man's face. "Your enemies won't take kindly to daydreamers."

Aleksander had no strength to form a witty retort. He merely stood, shook out sand from beneath his kneecups and greaves, and lifted Aoife into the air once more.

Before he could start back on his routine, however, a sword met his. Vibration rang through his arms, startling him from his spiraling thoughts. He parried it—loosely, poorly.

Another strike came in and he reached for Varek's sword hand, catching his wrist and forcing it away.

Aleksander's heart raced. "What are you doing?"

Varek grabbed Aleksander's wrist, the two in a stand off for a mere moment. Then, the larger man shoved. The boy's feet came out from under him and he splayed on his back in the dirt. Pain bounced around his spine, his arms, his head. A cloud of dust swirled above him.Through it, strode Varek. He crouched beside Aleksander, brown-gold eyes roving his face. As far as Aleksander could tell, there was no anger in them—only curiosity.

"What was that for?" Aleksander croaked.

Varek raised an eyebrow. "You're the one who got distracted. You should tell me."

He grit his teeth and sat up, struggling all the while. "I don't need to tell you anything."

Besides, there was too much to tell. In that short time they were running drills, Aleksander had unearthed too many questions. He blinked, studying the man, shoving his thoughts away for later.

Those tiger-eye irises roved his face, peering through squinted, wrinkled eyes.

Was Varek aware of the statue? Of what she had become to their shared people?

Aleksander chewed the inside of his cheek. "Why are you down here, again, Varek?"

The old Ölmesuz rolled his eyes and held out a hand. With a pull, Aleksander was on his feet. "I believe I told you."

"You were out to set up communications and then you got sent here to dispatch that one sorcerer, right?"

"You said it just like the king did," Varek snorted.

"That can't be all, can it? I mean...you killed that guy a week ago. And it wan't even down here, it was further east."

Something flashed through the man's eyes...uncertainty, perhaps? He blinked it away before Aleksander could figure out what, exactly, it was. The feeling it left was a sinking pit in his stomach.

Aleksander swallowed.

After a moment, Varek spoke. "You're right, Elias Armstrong was taken out days ago. I came here on request of Lord Asghar. He wanted me to investigate the unrest occurring in his lands."

Elspeth's armor clanked as she approached. "It's happening here too? We haven't heard anything about it."

"That's partially why you were sent here," Varek said over his shoulder, "whether you were told or not. To protect Carissa. If we all end up going in to town, you're to be extra eyes and ears."

Elspeth came into view, sheathing her sword. Auburn wisps stuck to her forehead with sweat; she made a futile attempt to wipe them free with her stiff glove. "I'm always ready for a day in the shops, but that can't be what you need us for. Unless you just need some time off? We could all go for a day out, Varek, it may help your mood."

Varek's lips pressed into a thin line. "We'll go when we need to, and there's a strong chance it won't be for something as simple as shopping. For now, we need to work." A few pats on Aleksander's back knocked sand free. "Elspeth, Aleksander, I'd like to see a duel."

This brought a grin to Aleksander's face. "I've beat her the last three times."

"He's exaggerating." Elspeth's eyes were half lidded with a mix of humor and annoyance. "Last time it was muddy and I tripped."

"And what about the time before that?"

Her cheeks burst into a furious blush.

Aleksander couldn't help but laugh. Her eyes widened, fixing on him with such childish rage. An angry pout set to her lips. There was nothing intimidating about the expression. He'd seen her furious before, he'd seen her feral—this was simply hilarious.

His own ears and cheeks began to burn, his shoulders bouncing with stifled giggles

"You want a duel, Varek?" She flourished her sword. "You'll get a duel."

Elspeth sunk into her stance, her eyes not leaving Aleksander's. He smiled, stepping into ready, leveling his sword in a challenge. "It's not muddy this time, I expect you to stay on your feet."

She sucked her teeth, scowling at him.

"Fight till one of you yields or falls," Varek said, his usual declaration before a duel. "Go."

The Rodzjiek girl threw herself at him, shouting as she swung her sword precisely. Aleksander blocked, and the force she hit Aoife with sent him staggering back. A nervous laugh exploded from his chest as he regained his footing.

It only egged her on.

Blow after blow, Aleksander parried, reaching to get his own strikes in here and there. Sand shifted beneath with each step. It was more difficult to navigate than their usual packed dirt training ring, but stars of difference from that night in the mud.

"Watch your shoulder, Aleksander!" Varek shouted from the side.

Aleksander tucked it in moments before Elspeth swung, narrowly missing his pauldron.

"Elspeth, back foot!"

"I know what I'm doing!" Her fangs flashed, snarling.

A shock of cold ran through Aleksander's veins. That deep, gravely voice was one he'd only heard a few times prior—the most prominent in his memory was a scene by Terrell's cottage, where she was surrounded by homunculi and flame.

As much as Elspeth did not scare him, he would be an idiot not to recognize that she was capable of immense catastrophe if a whim compelled her.

She swung her sword down.

Or if she allowed her vision to tunnel towards one goal.

He raised Aoife to block—the impact shuddered through him, and she kept pressing forth. Before he slid her sword free, he caught the glow in her eyes just as it burst into flame.

Metal slid against metal and he backpedaled away from her. "El." Aoife brushed the dirt. He did not want her out in front— did not want his weapon to stand between them. Not as her eyelashes flickered with flame.

Her shoulders heaved with deep, frenzied breaths. The armor covering the back of her hand began to glow red, then gold, warping around her leather glove and melting to drip into puddles that sizzled on the sand. The leather itself darkened, smoke hissing out through the seams.

"Elspeth!" Varek shouted.

Her lips dropped over her teeth, erasing her snarl. Those burning eyes flicked over to him. "Yes?"

"Control yourself, or I'll have to stop the fight."

Thick brows knit together in confusion. "What?"

"Your hands," Aleksander croaked. "You're... El, look at yourself."

Looking down, her eyes widened at the sight of her burning gloves still wrapped around the hilt of her sword. The weapon clattered to the sand, aggressive stance broken as she stumbled back, desperately trying to pull off the leather mitts.

"Easy, easy," Varek barked, striding towards her. He reached to help, but she pulled back.

"No! I..." Frantic breaths sent the smoke whirling. One glove flew off, smoldering on the sand. "I can do it myself." She hissed, pulling back from the melted metal as it scalded her fingers.

Varek took another step closer—Aleksander followed suit.

"I said no!" She was shaking now, sweat pouring down her face. The second glove slid free and she looked at her hands. Beneath her skin wove veins of lava, flickering and glowing through the swollen, red flesh of her palms. Panic flooded her face, her eyes locking on Aleksander.

"Are you okay?"

She blinked once, then shook her head. "I...I think I need a break."

Aleksander nodded, and to his surprise, Varek remained silent. The towering figure beside him dropped his hands to his sides and nodded once. It was enough—Elspeth took off for the gates, undoing her armor as she went.

The door slammed shut.

Aleksander raised Aoife, turning to Varek. Before he could speak, the man raised his hand. "I think that's enough for today." A strong hand patted Aleksander's back. "Go rest. I expect to see you early tomorrow morning."

Chapter

TEN

$\mathcal{D}$ AWN CREPT OVER THE TOP of the trees, and Aleksander was in a training ring painted pink. Varek drilled him until he was pouring sweat, panting and begging for a break.

"Are you a child, your holiness?" he sneered. "Or did your goddess-mother just birth a weakling?"

Aleksander gritted his teeth and hit the man harder.

They missed breakfast, training through until noon, when the sun floated at the perfect angle above them to blind Aleksander each time he lifted his sword. Lunch was brief—they removed their armor, devoured healthy plates of beans, flatbread, and spiced chicken, then returned to the ring.

By dinner, Aleksander had been talking and interacting with only Varek. Aches ran up and down his muscles, and before he could ask where Elspeth was or if she'd be joining for the meal, Carissa strode in to the great dining hall, decorated with one grand table laden with food and just enough places for Aleksander, Elspeth, Asghar, Varek, and, of course, Carissa

In the two days they'd been here, he hadn't seen her since they'd gotten off the carriage. He jumped up to greet her, wincing at the stiffness in his neck and shoulders. Once all the pleasantries were exchanged and he'd given an update on how training with Varek was going—

"Exactly how you think."

—the pair sat down and began to spoon heaps of cucumber, pepper, tomato, and dill salad on to their plates. It didn't take long for Varek to join, as well as Lord Asghar.

A fifth cushion remained empty on the terrace, and even as Carissa talked, Aleksander found himself glancing towards the door.

Where is she?

"Long story short," Carissa said, waving her fork, "I've been going about healing all wrong."

"I didn't even know you were working on healing," Aleksander said, stuffing a slice of roasted pepper into his mouth. "Aren't you focusing more on transmutation and such?"

"Yes, transmutation and scrying and so forth are what I'm supposed to be working on, but healing is the foundation to working with the Flow. Well, basic healing, at least. Especially on plants. It's the base for transmutation, and when it comes to scrying I need the familiarity that healing gives me with the Flow to actually do it properly. Mage Theresas says my original teacher at Brevindun showed me the most complicated way, and that's why it's been so hard for me to engage otherwise." She set her fork down, adjusting in her seat.

To some end, Aleksander was grateful for the months at Brevindun when they were both heavily absorbed in their respective studies and worlds—it prepared him for seeing Carissa at a breakfast, then not seeing her for a few days, and then catching up over dinner. But sitting across from her and listening to her chatter on about things that he would never be able to do wrapped him in a blanket of nostalgia.

Her hands stretched forward as she talked, showing the different gestures she'd use to transfer energy and shift the Flow to remove an illness or instill new life, he suddenly found himself sitting across from her in the garden, surrounded by lilacs and lilies, an open bottle of pomegranate juice between them.

So many evenings had been passed in just that way when they were young. When she could make mistakes in her magic and laugh it off, learning more the next day. When he would train for a handful of hours and spend the rest of his time in the Great Temple or wandering the castle grounds. When things were simple. Before they'd become burdened with...all this.

He smiled as she finished her explanation. The blush in her cheeks made her look younger than ever, and with the slight weight she'd been steadily putting on, her face was glowing.

"You seem to be doing well with Theresas."

Her grin widened. "I am. Honestly, I think most of my problems back in Brevindun were simply that the Flow works differently with different people. The mages that taught me were mostly men, and their tactics tended to be blunt and produce immediate results, regardless of the quality of that result. Working with the priestesses and seeresses, everything was slower, more intuitive. That's how Theresas works. Slow, deliberate, intuitive..." she pinched a portion of a raspberry free between the nails on her thumb and index finger, "The Flow is living, though not exactly in the same way we are. We need to form a relationship with it." Popping the fruit in her mouth, she smiled. "I'm beyond grateful for Tulathne granting me the chance to study here."

Aleksander did not like how his stomach twinged at the mention of the goddess. The Presence seemed to be frustrated by it, too. He felt the sentience peering over his shoulder, frowning.

"Lord Asghar was very kind to extend the invitation," he said, sipping his lemonade. A wash of mint followed the bite of the lemon—he had to stop himself from chugging the whole glass and immediately asking for more.

Carissa nodded at the man, seated at the far end of the table. "*Of course.*" She raised her glass to the lord lounging at the end of the table. "Thank you, my lord, for your gracious hospitality and your generosity in sharing the wisdom of your mages and Crafters with me."

The lord smiled, his cheeks full of fragrant rice and beef. "It is my pleasure, your highness."

She set her glass down and turned back to her food, slicing

off another piece of roasted pepper and scooping some of the filling into the boat she'd made. "Enough about me, though, how's training going for you? More than you've said earlier, please, I'd like to hear details as I used to."

He shrugged. "Training is training. We run drills on blocking, parrying, strikes. I train with weights. I train with my armor. Sometimes we duel. It's going as well as it can."

"No, it's not," Varek said around a mouthful of beef. "Elspeth hasn't shown up in a full day, and you clearly lapsed in your training when I left."

"He practiced every day, Varek." Carissa's eyes narrowed. "I saw him sneaking out many a night to practice alone, in fact."

Aleksander's cheeks burned. So he wasn't quiet about that after all.

"Well, he didn't practice the right things." A sip of lemonade broke the conversation. The engraved red glass clacked on the table, and Varek continued. "I'm sure his holiness ran through his forms time and time again, but when it comes down to it, all he drilled into himself was a sloppy wrist, tight shoulders, and..."

Aleksander stopped chewing when Varek's eyes met his.

The man sniffed, turning back down to his food. "But it's nothing we can't fix."

Silence fell over the meal. Waves crashed in the distance, harmonizing strangely with the clattering of silverware on ceramic.

In the peace of the evening, Aleksander's mind turned to one place only: Demir and Janek. Lately, their evening meals at Brevindun had been lively thanks to the joviality both men held to. Dinners at Brevindun, he figured, must now be just as boring as the ones here. Full of occasional chatter and long silences.

Somehow he couldn't imagine Lenore engaging in any witty banter with the Mekartlim Aleksander had come to love so dearly.

Demir would know how to talk to Elspeth. Demir got Carissa to relax more than once, something few people could boast.

"How would I go about writing a letter to Demir?"

Aleksander said.

Varek raised an eyebrow, but kept eating.

"Juss-ah," Asghar held up his fork as he finished chewing. "Just a normal letter? We have ravens that go between here and the castle in the capital, so if you'd like, you can send messages through them when the need arises."

Shoveling more rice into his mouth, Aleksander responded with a nod and a smile.

At the corner, between Asghar and Carissa, Aleksander stared at the empty seat. His chest ached. It wasn't that he missed her—they'd had to go a few days without seeing one another at Brevindun. He'd only met her a handful of months ago. It *wasn't* that he missed her. It was simply that he couldn't bear staying so separate from her after the chaos that had endured yesterday.

A whole afternoon had passed with nothing from Elspeth. Aleksander had gone back to his room after training and cleaned himself up. Servants were already preparing a bath for him, and one clarified that it was only at the behest of Lady D'orde, as she had also requested a bath after training. Most of the afternoon he'd spent in those warm waters. Dinner was brought to his room with an apology from Lord Asghar—there was another dinner meeting that took precedence. And finally, he slunk back into his bed, where the faint scent of lavender and rosemary lingered where she'd stretched on it hours earlier.

He'd contemplated walking the few steps down the hall to her room. Knocking on her door. Asking if she was alright.

But he didn't.

They were friends, but she'd been so...

Angry wasn't the right word, he figured. He didn't know what the right word was. The only one that seemed to fit was scared, but then that would make him a bad friend for not visiting her, so he didn't choose that one either.

"Aleksander?"

His head bobbed up, scanning the table for who called his name. "What?"

Carissa leaned forward. "Theresas and I are working on a spell, and I'll need a few components. We're going to try a new method of scrying. Do you want to accompany me to town tomorrow?"

He straightened, smiling. "Yes! Just yesterday, I was talking to Varek about that, so—"

Varek twitched his head. "If you go into town, take precautions." he lifted his gaze, passing it between them through narrowed eyes, "On second thought, maybe I should come with. A couple of...pampered Zekharyan royals wandering Hadiqin? You wouldn't last a moment alone."

At this, Asghar's fist pounded the table in time with a hearty laugh.

Varek chuckled along, a smirk gracing his lips as he lifted his glass to them once more.

"What's that supposed to mean?" Carissa's brows sunk low over her eyes, drawing deep caverns between them.

"Only that, with no offense meant to your gracious highness," Asghar managed through guffaws, "our ways are different than yours, and while Hadiqin still belongs to your beautiful country, the town is still deeply Ölmesuz. You would do well to have an interpreter with you, or at least someone of the culture." He patted Varek's shoulder with a large hand, shaking the man a few times and prompting a hearty laugh. "This one may be a poor example, but he's still one of us."

"Come on," Varek said, shoving his friend's arm away. "You and I both know I'm more Ölmesuz than you ever will be."

"In age only," Asghar laughed again. "Did you know this man had taken almost four hundred lives by the time I was ninety-two?"

Varek's broad smile faltered, waning to a hesitant grin. He turned back to the table, shuffling his food around his plate with the tip of his fork. "Yes, well... I didn't have your mother there to smack me upside the head and tell me not to."

Asghar's own smile faltered, and he sipped his drink.

Aleksander half considered excusing himself simply to get

away from the uncomfortable mood shift. As he made it halfway to standing, Carissa beat him to the punch.

Rising to her full height with a speed that startled Aleksander so he had to brace himself on the low table to keep his balance, she brushed her hands on her skirt before resting one, daintily, on her belly. "I am entirely full, so I will take this chance to retire." A shallow bow towards Lord Asghar, "Thank you once more for a decadent meal. I've never had stuffed peppers before, they were delightful."

The lord nodded his thanks. "Please, either of you, take a plate to Lady Elspeth." He pushed himself off his divan and leaned forward to fix a plate—before anyone could stop him, it was piled high with a large stuffed pepper, oranges, fresh cucumbers, and a spread of garlic, oil, and chickpeas. Aleksander patted his mouth with his napkin and stood, taking it from the lord's outstretched hand.

"I will. I've been meaning to check on her anyway." His heart pounded at the words, but now he had a reason to see her.

She did need to eat.

Dishes and utensils still ringing out against one another faded as he made his way into the hall. In the evening, the lamps were dim flickers, casting warped shadows on the walls. He wasn't shocked he'd not noticed the intricacies of the building the night they'd first arrived—it seemed like a different building entirely in the dark. Through doors with open windows, a cool breath of air flooded the hall. It sent a chill along his scalp, ruffling his hair. The waning thickness of sea air in the summer still floated on it, however faded.

Aleksander passed his door, continuing down the dim corridor towards the other three doors. First in the hall was Carissa's. Then Aleksander's. It would make sense the next was Elspeth's, though he was not entirely sure.

Shifting the wobbly plate into his left hand, he knocked.

"Elspeth?"

Silence came from within.

Did he choose the wrong door?

He knocked again. Still, nothing. Aleksander's heart sank. He *must* have been wrong; Elspeth's room was further down the hall, then, or maybe not even in this hallway all together. No, he should stop speculating and go ask someone. A servant? The housekeeper? But how would he find them? He turned his back to the door and peered one way down the hall, then the other.

Behind him, the door creaked.

"Aleksander?"

The speed with which he spun to face the timid voice was almost enough to send the roasted pepper toppling off the plate.

From the crack in the door, stringy auburn hair fell over a half-lidded eye. At the sight, his throat grew thick.

"El," he managed. "I brought you dinner."

She eyed the plate, not opening the door any more than it already was.

"It's stuffed peppers and oranges and some cucumbers and hummus," he swallowed hard. "I figured...well, I don't know if you've been eating today."

Her eyes darted back up to him. They were puffy, red.

She didn't look well.

"Can I come in?"

Elspeth pressed her lips together. "I don't know if that's a good idea."

"What? What do you mean it's not a good idea?" Aleksander pressed his hand to the door, pushing—Elspeth's own hands flew to counter the movement. Aleksander's jaw tensed in frustration. "Elspeth, come on. It's me."

His words seemed to give her pause. Her eyes roved his face, as if trying to determine whether he was right or not.

Whether he was really Aleksander.

After a minute, she peeked her head out and glanced down the hall, then stepped back and beckoned Aleksander in.

His heart sank as he took in the state of her room. "El..."

"I've been trying to control it," she said, walking in front of him, keeping her eyes downcast. "I think I'm getting better."

The hands that took the plate from his were swollen. Dark

streaks of splitting lightning crossed over the inflamed knuckles.
Burns.

Chapter

ELEVEN

E CAUGHT ONE WRIST AND lifted her hand to his face. "Elspeth, what—"

She pulled away quickly, steadying her plate and taking a few steps back from him. "I told you, I've been trying to control it." The fork split the skin of the pepper. Elspeth devoured it like a starving animal.

"El, you need a healer."

"I'm doing just fine," she snapped, rice spitting across the floor. "They're fading anyway."

As she ate, Aleksander glanced about the room. Before the open window, blowing in a sharp, cold breeze through burned, tattered curtains, sat a washtub. It was similar to what he had used. The water was darkened by soot. Most of her valuables had been stacked in a corner. Some had finger and hand prints burned into them, including the fine fur cloak she'd worn on the journey here. The only thing seemingly unharmed was her bed, unmade and tousled as it was. That, and the parchment scroll curled on her bedside table.

The parchment was cool in his fingers. Entirely unburnt. Raising it towards his chest to open it, Aleksander noticed it didn't even smell like smoke.

"That's not for you," she said, a hand snaking around his

shoulder and snatching it away. "Don't worry about it."

He squinted at her in the dim light. "What is it?"

"Nothing." The parchment crumpled as she shoved it into the drawer of that same table. It rocked with the force of her slamming the drawer shut. "I visited the library late last night. Chione thought this might help."

"Did it?"

Elspeth chewed a big chunk of pepper and shook her head.

A heavy breath escaped Aleksander's chest. He sat down on the bed and Elspeth followed suit. The frame creaked slightly as she settled. The plate was all but empty by now; orange juice dripped down her chin as she stuck the flesh between her teeth and pulled the skin free. Her hair was bedraggled in the worst way—full of knots, stringy with water and oil, near matted in some areas. It was thick with the smell of smoke. Aleksander lifted a hand, gently brushing back a strand.

She leaned into the touch, closing her eyes. Aleksander fought to push down tears that appeared with great confusion and no warning. His fingers snaked into her hair, around the back of her skull. Slowly, he scratched her scalp.

A shuddering breath, tinged with the sour of oncoming tears, shook her shoulders.

"El," he whispered, "are you okay?"

Her eyes fluttered half open, dropping down to her plate. She selected another slice of orange. "No."

Aleksander's lips flattened. "Can I brush your hair out?"

It wasn't just that it looked awful—though it did. And it wasn't that Aleksander, after a life in the palace, had developed a strange complex around hair care—though he actually had. It was more that, in this moment, as he took in the shuddering frame of his friend, everything seemed wrong and he couldn't figure out why. And if he couldn't figure out why, he couldn't fix it. So he could, at the very least, brush her hair.

She blinked at him before placing the plate on the floor and turning her back to him. "Oil's on the windowsill."

Before he could even fully register his movement, he was up

and had gathered the oil and a comb before plopping back down on the bed. The force of his drop on to the mattress made Elspeth bounce.

His gut twinged when she didn't even chuckle.

Still, his fingers began to section her hair into locks the width of his palm, like he'd done for Carissa on days they'd stayed up too long, or after late nights at the temple, studying every word of every prophecy ever.

No wonder he couldn't remember any of them. As his fingers massaged oil into Elspeth's scalp and began to work it down to the ends, his mind went blank. How much time passed, he didn't know, but he had gotten the third section, his concentration was broken.

Elspeth's shoulders shook with quiet sobs.

He didn't say anything. Just let her cry as he combed the oil through her hair, slowly working out knots until what was once a clump lay smoothly against her back, those elegant waves once again catching candlelight.

"I didn't mean to," she whispered. Aleksander had heard her say it time and time again over the last few months. As if she was trying to convince him.

"I know," he muttered. "It's okay."

A shaking breath sent tremors down her arms. "But what if I end up being dangerous?"

Aleksander snorted. "We've been over this. You're going to be fine."

"But—"

"Elspeth. Stop." The flickering of the flame in the single oil lamp beside her bed danced with the gentle scrapes of the bone comb on her hair. "I still mean what I said in the garden. And the library. And any other time I've told you this. You're dangerous, yes, but you're not *a* danger. Not to us, not to me."

A deep sigh slumped her shoulders. "I know, I never mean to be. I just... I worry."

"Don't." Aleksander shifted to another lock of hair, sweeping the finished section over her shoulder. She winced as the comb tugged on the first knot. "Sorry."

"It's okay."

It took a few more tugs until that knot was able to be worked out. "How did you get the burns?" Aleksander asked.

"Fire in my veins," was all she said.

A few more knots, then, "Why do you still have the bath tub?"

She sighed. "It gets hot, under my skin. After a while. The wind keeps the water cold."

They fell into silence. Aleksander combing her hair, Elspeth breathing, crying, calming herself, and crying again.

How many hours passed, Aleksander knew not. Though sometime late in the night, when the moon's light angled just so through her window that it cast a long, pale blue shadow over the bed and blended with the lamp to create a beautiful watercolor over her hair, his fingers ran through her dark copper tresses, marveling at the way it bounced free and glistened with oil and renewed health.

"That's better," he muttered. Mainly to himself, but when Elspeth nodded, he was glad she'd heard.

"Thank you." One fine hand, looking as though it would eventually blister, tentatively reached up wove through her hair. She swept it all the way to the ends where it drifted free—not nearly as airy as when it was freshly washed, but still much better than when he had found her. The bed frame squeaked as she turned to face him.

Her eyes were drooped with exhaustion, her cheeks stained with tears. Still, she found his gaze. She held it. "I... appreciate you, Aleksander. You're a good person. You're a good friend."

He smiled. His thumb brushed the tracks of tears away best he could. Beneath his touch, her skin was flushed and warm. "You seem tired."

Eyelashes fluttered. "I am tired."

"Are you going to come to training tomorrow?"

Her gaze flickered, drifting down to her hands folded against her legs, then back up to him. "Do you want me back at training?"

"I do." And he did. "You're missing out. Besides, you're a buffer for Varek's criticisms. He doesn't want to be *as* mean as he can be if you're there."

This made her laugh. It was a light sound, not one that had much intense joy in it, but it made Aleksander's heart flutter. Oh, how he wanted to bottle the sound and store it within her, so she'd never lose that laugh again. "As if my presence makes any difference."

Aleksander hadn't been lying. It did. When Elspeth was in the ring, Varek was more cooperative, more explanatory—with Aleksander, it was demands and, when a demand was not met, punishment.

"It does," he said softly. "You do."

There was that glow again. Caliphus contained in a skull. It made the fluttering in Aleksander's chest grow wilder, flapping around his stomach and hastening his breathing. He wanted to stare into those eyes forever. Hold her flushed cheeks in his hands, never to part. The soft smile on her face did nothing to calm him or distract him from that strange notion he had. She slowly raised a tired, quivering finger and delicately brushed a mussed lock of hair from his eyes. "Well, thank you for thinking that."

Though her hands were not on fire anymore, the place where her finger brushed his forehead felt as though she'd left a trail of coals.

His head and chest were thoroughly muddled, the only response able to leave his lips a simple, "Yeah."

A smile twitched her mouth.

"I'm not lying," he continued. "I can't. I don't. You know that."

Her brows scrunched together. "Oh, do I?"

"Well, you should."

Outside crickets chirped. Elspeth's mouth stretched open in a deep yawn, baring her fangs and seeming momentarily more animalistic than human—well, as humanlike as Rodzjiekim were.

When her mouth closed again, however, she slumped forward. Her head rested against Aleksander's chest; a reminder that she was, indeed, just a girl. His hand smoothed her hair again, doing his best to steady the shaking in his hand, caused simply by the pounding in his chest. She couldn't hear his heart hammering away, could she?

"You should sleep."

"Hmm."

He shifted her off of him and onto her bed, wrestling the mound of tangled sheets and blankets free that he might drape them around her. They were as soft as the ones in his room, if a bit smokier.

She nuzzled into them all the same.

He leaned down, chin on her mattress, cheek to her pillow. His forehead pressed against hers. "You know I'm here for you, right?"

She nodded, bumping their noses together. "Yeah."

"You ever need anything, and I mean *anything*, ever again, you—"

"I'll find you, Aleksander." Her eyelashes fluttered open for a mere moment. "I promise."

It was those eyes he focused on as he fell asleep. Not the fact that he didn't pray to Tulathne. Not the statue of Iscah down the hall. Not Demir or Janek, not the ache in his muscles or the fact that he knew he would have to endure it all over again come morning. Just her.

His hands still smelled like rosemary.

Chapter

TWELVE

ALEKSANDER STUMBLED BACK, TRYING HIS best to wipe water from his eyes. It slipped beneath the collar of his doublet, beneath his armor, heating instantly in the warmth radiating from his chest. He frowned at the blurry image of the Ölmesuz weighing another water bladder in his hand.

"Come *on* Varek!" he whined.

The man's eyebrow arched up, and he took another, wheeling one at his head and another at his feet. Aleksander danced to the side, ducking as he moved.

"Good!" Came the shout from beside Varek, where Elspeth was already drenched in the water bladders she failed to dodge.

But his feet twisted beneath him, and in moments, Aleksander was flat on his back again, sand sticking to every ounce of moisture on his skin and armor.

It had started with them both standing still, one at a time, all the while dodging the white water-filled intestines and attempting to slice the blackened ones. A sure-fire way to learn Ölmesuz agility, Varek said.

Elspeth went first, and despite her sure steps and unwavering gaze, every inch of her was rigid. Her spine was straight and tense, her arms stiff as she attempted to swing her sword. Gone were the fluid movements everyone had become familiar with.

And Aleksander? He'd been even worse. Constant duels and drills had reminded him of his stature, where to keep his center of balance. But when your body had to contort to avoid more than one attack at a time...

"Disappointing," Varek droned, "I wish I could say I'm shocked."

His head fell back into the sand. Above him, thin clouds passed through a pale blue sky.

"But," came Varek's amendment, "you were not horrible enough that we can't make this work." Aleksander lifted his head in time to watch Varek toss his chin towards the side of the ring. A small archway separated the fighting grounds from the bullpen, and to the side of the bullpen was a fountain in the wall. Water flowed into a basin, glistening and cool and gorgeous. "Get a drink."

Elspeth dropped her sword belt into the dirt, already undoing her armor and letting it fall in a trail in the sand behind her.

Aleksander quickly followed suit.

His gloves came off, then his vambraces, his pauldrons, his rebraces and gorget—he slipped his chest plate off over his head and fell to his knees, dunking his face in the fountain. The water was cool, flooding over his face and into his nose. Coughs sputtered from his mouth as he came up, then dunked his face again and drank even deeper than the first time.

It was autumn, the sun was not nearly as hot as it had been in past training exercises, but sweat coated him as if it were the middle of summer, and the cool fountain brought a much needed rush to his head. By the time he sat back on his heels, breathing slowly, his face and hair dripping with water, Elspeth was already at the arch, collecting her armor and strapping it back on.

"You're doing fine," Varek said.

Aleksander held his breath. The rushing of the water nearly drowned the sounds of their voices—especially with Varek speaking so softly.

"Fine doesn't feel like enough," Elspeth responded. Her armor clanked as she adjusted it. It bounced off the tile wall in front of Aleksander—with the fountain, it almost sounded like wind chimes.

"You're a good fighter," Varek spoke again. "I know you can do this, though. I mean, look at what you're doing already."

Aleksander's brow furrowed. Varek had never spoke to him like that. Never been so... encouraging. He leaned forward, letting his forehead rest on the decorative tile edge of the pool.

"Yeah, but that's making it harder."

"So your fire is hard to control. Guess what, you're still controlling it. You and I both know it's only a matter of time before you master it." A pause. "I'm proud of you, you know. For coming back today. And for telling me what happened."

Silence stretched between them. The rattle of armor became quieter, more specific, as Elspeth finished tightening the leather straps and shrugging herself into the suit. "Thanks, Varek."

The man grunted, and eventually, steps receded into the ring. When Aleksander raised his head, it was not Elspeth leaning on the archway anymore, but Varek, his arms crossed, banded-gold irises trained on him. "Done with your bath, your holiness?"

Aleksander's heart soured. "I care about her too, you know." The words were a lot harsher than he'd intended, his tone much more clipped.

Varek's eyes softened, almost imperceptibly. "I know you think do." Before Aleksander could open his mouth and offer a venomous retort, there it was in the man's face—the softness he'd heard moments before, entirely open and earnest. "I know you *do*."

Aleksander's mouth closed.

He stood there, surveying the boy leaning against the fountain. Aleksander couldn't help but feel there was something he was missing, something incredibly important that, somehow, he had failed to take notice of. Beyond that, Varek's gaze was almost...pitying.

"I do," he said. The words were soft. "I do."

"I know," Varek repeated. "She's just...there's..." a deep sigh broke his words, the vulnerability retreating behind a wall of practiced stoicism. "Get your armor on," he said with a nod, "we're not done yet today."

◊ ✷ ◊

IT WAS TOO quiet. After waking early to train, the hustle and bustle of meal times and bathing and the flurry of servants preparing his bed for him, he was sore, full, and weary. Sound had been bombarding him all day, and now, his ears rang in the stillness. The single candle flickering on his desk, by the latched window, seemed to echo through the room.

He swore he heard mice in the walls.

Hours passed. The candle burned down, leaving him in the dark, and yet it was *too* dark. No light came through the window —the moon had been full the night before, it's light should not yet be so dull. Yet it was.

He sat up, running a hand through his hair. Back home, at the castle, he would have donned his armor, gathered Aoife to him, and gone down to train. Here, though...

Within the walls of Aarua, overwork felt like a sin. Maybe it was the candles, the mosaics. Maybe they were enchanted thanks to all the mages wandering the halls. Or maybe it was simply the fact that Brevindun was his home, and here he was simply a guest.

And guests do not wander or snoop.

The floor was cold on his feet. Wind whistled in through the crack in his window, bringing with it the smell of decaying leaves and rotting flowers. A warm scent, despite the chill it came in on. From the moment he'd arrived, the weather began to swiftly turn towards winter. He flung his robe over his back and slipped his arms in, tying a knot at his waist, and stepped into the hall, barefoot. Aleksander had no plan as to where he was going—he simply needed to move.

The lamps in the hallways were beyond dim. Every corridor had one or two flickering; not nearly enough to properly illuminate a path for an unfamiliar visitor. Yet he felt his way, fingertips lightly grazing the wall as he went, feeling as the space around him shifted from painted stone to a rare tapestry to detailed, carved columns. Eventually, voices found his ears.

"You're sure you've not heard anything else?"

Asghar.

"I wouldn't be telling you this if I had, Femi."

Aleksander skidded to a stop. *Varek.*

A deep sigh echoed from the lord, followed by what Aleksander could only assume was an Ölmesuz curse. "We're losing ground."

"We're not losing anything. There are still supporters in the city. And outside it. I talked to them, they still stand with us."

The heart enclosed within Aleksander's ribcage began to race. Dropping into a crouch, he inched along the wall until he felt it give way—beyond was a terrace. It wasn't one Aleksander had ever visited before. This one was smaller than the one they ate on daily, with an ornate fence and railing going around the entire outside edge of it, from wall to wall. There were no stairs— the only way in and the only way out was the door he now crouched beside. On a low table, flanked by divans, a single, dim lantern flickered beside an unused tea set.

The lord stood by the balcony railing. His ears drooped, his hair piled atop his head in a frazzled bun; a few braids still hung down, bedecked with their beads, curling at the ends. But Asghar's whole countenance had been shed. His back hunched as he looked out over the city below, glistening faintly with lamps along the streets and out from windows. Everything about him was heavy. "Varek, this is useless."

A figure beside him shifted—Aleksander watched as the man tugged down his mask. It was the same one he'd worn when they'd found Lord Terrell's cottage, though the rest of his outfit was not one Aleksander had seen ever before. There was nothing familiar in those clothes. This new dark, leather doublet was cut close, his black pants made from loose linen tucked and into calf-high boots. The whole outfit was worn, but still in good condition. A high collar brushed under his beard, laced from hem to throat—straps went under his arms and across his back, each holding what looked to be a small dagger. His boots were the same black leather as the rest of his outfit. Every step was so silent, Aleksander wasn't entirely sure the man was moving. Perhaps his eyes were playing tricks on him, unaware of how to translate Varek's silent movement any other way. He leaned on the balcony, facing the door. His empty gaze landed on the lantern and the tea set, and Aleksander's heart leapt into his throat.

Varek had always been menacing. There was something about him that made the hair on the back of Aleksander's neck stand up, even from that first meeting. There was always that knowledge that he had been an assassin, a mercenary.

But in this outfit, in this setting...it was suddenly very real.

Aleksander swallowed. Varek's ear twitched, and he stopped breathing until the man spoke again.

"We still have the loyalty of the *h'met'res*, and a good number of trades people. I've heard word that our contact in Duke Elmere's court is making progress with the young Lady, and just this morning a crow arrived from Fazhia. She and the Duchess Kallendrine are entirely on board."

At this, Asghar looked at Varek, wide-eyed. "Fazhia is siding with us? The heretic?"

"The convert," Varek corrected, his low voice edged with a threat. "She may love the Zekharyan goddess, but never forget she was born one of us. Never forget she still *is*. That's enough to keep anyone's head on their shoulders. Even some Zekharyans are siding with us. Not everyone trusts what's been popularized by the priestesses." He shrugged, his gaze wandering to the top of the door, inspecting the dying ivy that swayed in the evening breeze. "If we can work Aleksander enough, I daresay we may actually have hope."

"He would never betray his goddess. Or his family. Don't forget, the boy is as royal as they come," Asghar spat.

"He wasn't, not always." Varek blew out a breath. His fingers tapped the railing. "His family were farmers by the Pozhontecs. If he was anything but Zekharyan, he'd already be on our side."

A strong wind blew through, ruffling pair's hair.

The assassin shrugged. "He's getting closer with Elspeth. Perhaps we can use that, the charm of a girl born and raised in the caste he should have been in. Or Carissa—seeing as they're family."

"Not the princess," the lord straightened, hand out. Disgust etched his face. "I may have had hope for her once. But not anymore, not after what I've seen today. No, if she has any inkling about our...our *treachery,* as you like to say...our heads will be on spikes."

Through the pounding in his ears at the word "treachery," Varek's laugh echoed into the night. His stomach dropped.

"Zekharyans don't do that anymore," he laughed.

Asghar didn't appear too convinced. "Either way," he said glumly, "our guts will be spilled."

Wind swept through. Aleksander felt sick in the passing silence.

"Better us than the others. They've suffered enough." Varek's voice broke. He huffed, curling his lip back in a snarl directed at no one. "I will not stand by any longer, Femi. I have devoted too many years to this."

I have to go. Aleksander stumbled to his feet, his back cracking as he straightened.

Both men on the terrace snapped to face the door. Varek drew a blade from where it had been tucked at his chest.

Tulathne, mother, if you're still honoring any *of my prayers,* Aleksander tried desperately to slow his breathing, taking measured steps backwards, *grant me the speed of an Orzei.*

Varek took a step forward. "Someone's been eavesdropping," he growled.

Aleksander sucked in a deep breath.

And ran.

THIRTEEN

Each step sent shocks up his legs. The slap of his feet on the floor echoed, but he didn't care; the wind moving past his ears, muffling nearly all sound, was enough to encourage him to just keep going. Keep running. *Don't look behind you, that'll slow you down.* His breath came in desperate pants until his chest burned, eyes watered. Every inhale was agony—he'd been working with Janek to build up his stamina, hopefully overcoming whatever weakness Tulathne had seen fit to curse him with, but they hadn't done much, and it still didn't seem to be enough.

It was hard to hear over his own breath and footfalls, but he swore there was a shift of fabric behind him.

A hard swallow choked down his dry throat.

His head began to pound, his throat burned—until he ran smack into a body and tumbled to the floor.

"Oh, gods!" Came the muffled shout.

Finding the blurry, darkened figure beneath him, Aleksander shut his mouth to stifle a dry cough as he scrambled away from them.

"My Lord Champion, are you alright?"

"Aleksander?"

Two people? He looked around, forcing his breathing to slow

—in through the nose, out through the mouth. It caught, and he coughed.

"He's having an episode—Theresas, get a stick of clean ginseng root. Go!"

His hands and knees pressed into the cold floor. *Focus on that*, he told himself. *Focus on the cold, and breathe slowly*. Yet his throat caught, time and time again. Gentle hands cupped his face, tilting his eyes up—in the dim, watery lamplight, he made out two pale green eyes, wide and nervous.

"Theresas is going to get your medicine, you'll be okay, just stop coughing, please." The panic in Carissa's voice was audible. It made his heart race, which made him breathe faster—relief came instantly when something cold and damp brushed his lips. The ginseng crunched immediately between his molars, letting that potent, fragrant oil flood into his nostrils and down his throat. He sucked on it like it was a well in a desert. With each swallow, the tightness in his throat lessened, as did the seizing in his chest.

Finally sitting back against the wall, his eyes closed, he took a deep breath. It made him cough, but he slowly took another, and another, until his breathing steadied enough.

Opening his eyes, he found two women seated before him in the dimly lit hallway. One, his sister, concern etched in her soft face. There was an air of franticness about her—her nightgown was rumpled, her dressing gown untied, her hair unbraided, curls everywhere. The other, crouched beside the princess, was a woman he'd never met before.

She had dark skin, like Mother Saoirse, with milk white eyes that stared blankly ahead yet somehow seemed fixed on him. Her face was slight, kind, and she, too, seemed relatively frazzled. Wrapped around the top of her head was a blue silk scarf, and from the line where the silk was pulled tightly against her forehead, small spirals of curl broke free. The bags beneath her eyes were visible, but not enough to be worrying. "My young Champion, are you alright?"

"You must be Mage Theresas," he said around the root still

caught between his teeth.

The woman nodded. "Yes. I apologize if I stepped in your way, I thought the hallway was clear—"

"No," he coughed and sucked down more of the oil from the ginseng. "No, it's my fault—I was..." Aleksander trailed off. What was he doing? He was running from Varek and Asghar after he overhead them talking about treason.

A glance down the hallways in each direction confirmed that, had Aleksander been followed, his pursuer had given up. At least for now.

Opening his mouth to speak, he was seized with another coughing fit. Carissa's hand gripped his shoulder tightly until it stopped, the root all but flattened between his clenched teeth.

He should tell her. He should spill everything he just heard on that terrace... But something stopped him. Whether it was the strange trust he still felt towards Varek, or a fear that the man was still hiding out around a corner, ready to strike should he need to, the words died before they even reached his tongue.

Now was not the time.

Lifting his head once more, he gave it a slow shake. "I can't see in these hallways, I was trying to get back to my room."

"You're on the wrong side of the building for that," Theresas chuckled, feeling for her staff on the ground before pushing herself to her feet. "This is the mages wing. Nothing but our rooms and research stations over here."

For the first time since clearing his vision, Aleksander's eyes settled on Carissa. "What are you doing here? It's late, you should be sleeping."

She pressed her lips together firmly. "And I will. I just needed to check on something with Theresas first."

Aleksander took her arm, both of them standing. "Are you alright?"

Her eyes darted to the mage beside her before nodding. "Yes, everything is fine. We've just...hit a block of sorts. I'm anxious to find a way around it."

"Her highness is impatient, young Champion," Theresas

said. "She's skilled, but cannot accept when the goddess forces her to pause her studies."

"Because there is no time to pause." A sharpness crept into Carissa's tone. She eyed the woman beside her. "I have a duty to uphold and a crown to bear in a matter of months, this is not the time for me to be slowed down."

At this, Theresas laughed. She threw her head back, shoulders shaking, pale eyes squinting shut with her smile. "You royals will never cease to be the funniest creatures I have worked with. And I've worked with a *lot* of odd creatures." One hand slithered around the princess's elbow, tugging gently. "Now, please escort me back to my room, so that we can each get some much needed rest this evening."

A smile turned Carissa's lip, following an exasperated sigh. "Of course, Mage Theresas." That smile fell away when she met Aleksander's gaze once more. "You get some sleep too."

He nodded and watched until their silhouettes melded with the darkness of the hallway.

Now, he was sure he was alone. There were no sounds echoing through the small corridor aside from his feet shifting, his own breathing, and the occasional crack of his teeth further loosening the fibers of the root between them.

He couldn't go back to sleep. Not now. There was too much on his mind.

The gentle smell of incense had been hanging in the air, but he hadn't noticed it until he was finally able to take a deep breath —*of course*. This is the wing for the mages, that means the chapel and library should be...

Aleksander kept his hand on the wall as he walked, carefully noting shifts from paint to bare stone, from pillar to wall. Eventually, his fingers grazed over the closed wood of a door, and—upon finding the handle—a metal bar. With a tug, it creaked open.

Again, Aleksander's heart sank.

There Iscah stood, lit by votives and surrounded by candles. Revered in every way she should never have needed to be revered in.

Her name should be chanted through streets, written into epics—not murmured in prayer, in funeral songs.

The Presence snaked down his back. It felt...sad. *Very* sad.

Its grief almost hurt to carry.

It took every ounce of resolve left in Aleksander's tired, oxygen-deprived body not to slump before the statue of his friend and instead slump before the statue of his mother.

Supposed mother.

He shrugged off the discomfort, leaning into the kneeler. It was hard to pray lately. Ever since the knowledge about others seeing him as a fake, seeing the royal family as tyrants he was no more than a victim of...his stomach churned.

They were wrong, of course. He knew that.

But when the name Alesathne crossed tongues in reference to him, whatever pride he used to feel would be washed out by a wave of discomfort. Nausea would force anger up his throat, and some small voice, deep in the recesses of his mind crawled forward to whisper, "*That's not you.*"

His knees hurt. The kneeler here was not ornate, nor was it incredibly plush. The Ölmesuz, he gathered, likely didn't worship on their knees like Zekharyans did. The only pews with those velvet bars were the ones over in the corner, before Tulathne's shrine.

Somehow, the way that the goddess was treated like a guest didn't frustrate or disturb him as he knew it ought to. To the people here, to Lord Asghar himself, She was.

Her veiled face peered down, hands out as to give or receive something.

It was quiet. Peaceful. The priestesses would have killed for such a secluded, intimate moment with the goddess, that he was certain of.

He took a deep breath and closed his eyes.

No words came to him. No requests for peace or guidance. Opening his eyes, he leaned on the bar before him, hands folded, forehead resting on the smooth, oiled wood.

I should feel something, *shouldn't I?*

The Presence fluttered with grief and frustration. Instead of ignoring it or only acknowledging it, Aleksander took a moment to breathe. To lean in. It felt simultaneously as though it was an extension of him, and something entirely separate, tacked to his soul with strings.

His eyes took in the shadows cast on his knees by the lamp light flickering through the bars of the railing before him. And after a moment, he closed them again.

Tulathne, still frozen before him, seemed to materialize in his mind. But here She was... much less cold. She had that warmth he missed, the kind he'd been used to feeling. Or at least, the kind he *thought* he'd been feeling.

"Hello, mother," he muttered. In his mind, Tulathne turned towards him. There, in whatever void he'd created, the pair just... stared at one another. Aleksander swallowed. "Sorry I've been away."

Anger ran from the Presence, down his spine, and flooded his body.

He opened his eyes, and the sensation stayed. He didn't dare look up at the statue—even in the real world, where he was sure She was no more than stone, he felt Her eyes on him through that carved marble veil. And from behind hovered that Presence. Nearly tangible. His heart pounded, though it felt far from dangerous. More than anything, it felt...annoyed.

Slow apologies languidly slid off his tongue. "I'm sorry I haven't been keeping up my prayers," "Sorry I've been doubting You," and so forth. There was no thought behind them. Just the things he knew he needed to say to Her.

It was strange asking for absolution after so long. The last time he remembered praying—truly kneeling and focusing and praying—was in the first week after coming home. Desperate to regain normalcy, he'd spent all night in front of that tapestry in his room, begging for Iscah to come back, for the goddess to make things right.

Nothing ever changed.

His prayers now were tasteless. Empty. Stuck to his teeth like dried taffy, devoid of any nuance or feeling.

He stopped, his mouth open, tongue poised—there was no need for this.

His eyes drifted up now, once more. "I'm scared. And things are... clearly not as safe as I'd been expecting," he muttered, "and all I ask from you is guidance. Proof that I'm on the right path."

Comfort slid down his spine. There was no emotion with it, that tangible sensation kin to a hand stroking his back. But he could feel fine fingers traveling from nape to right between his shoulder blades, where they pressed momentarily.

Suddenly, Aleksander was very aware of the statue a few feet to his right, her carved eyes staring off into the distance, one hand floating just beneath her chin, wrapped in a golden chain with the Crafter's seal dangling, the other still gripping her sword.

He almost couldn't bear to look. The expectation of those bright eyes being trained on him was too vibrant, he felt Iscah's attention thrum through his body as clearly as his own pulse.

A sharp swallow scraped down his throat, and he turned.

Her eyes still gazed into the distance. She hadn't moved.

He still did not exhale.

Aleksander surveyed every inch of the carved visage, his heart leaping with each candle's flickering shadow, each illusion of movement. But there was none, not really. She was stone, after all. Painted stone. Devoid of breath.

Finally, he breathed.

He chewed the skin of his bottom lip, leaning towards the image of his lost friend ever so slightly.

"I am sorry, Iscah. I really am."

The silence that echoed after left a hollow void in the center of his chest.

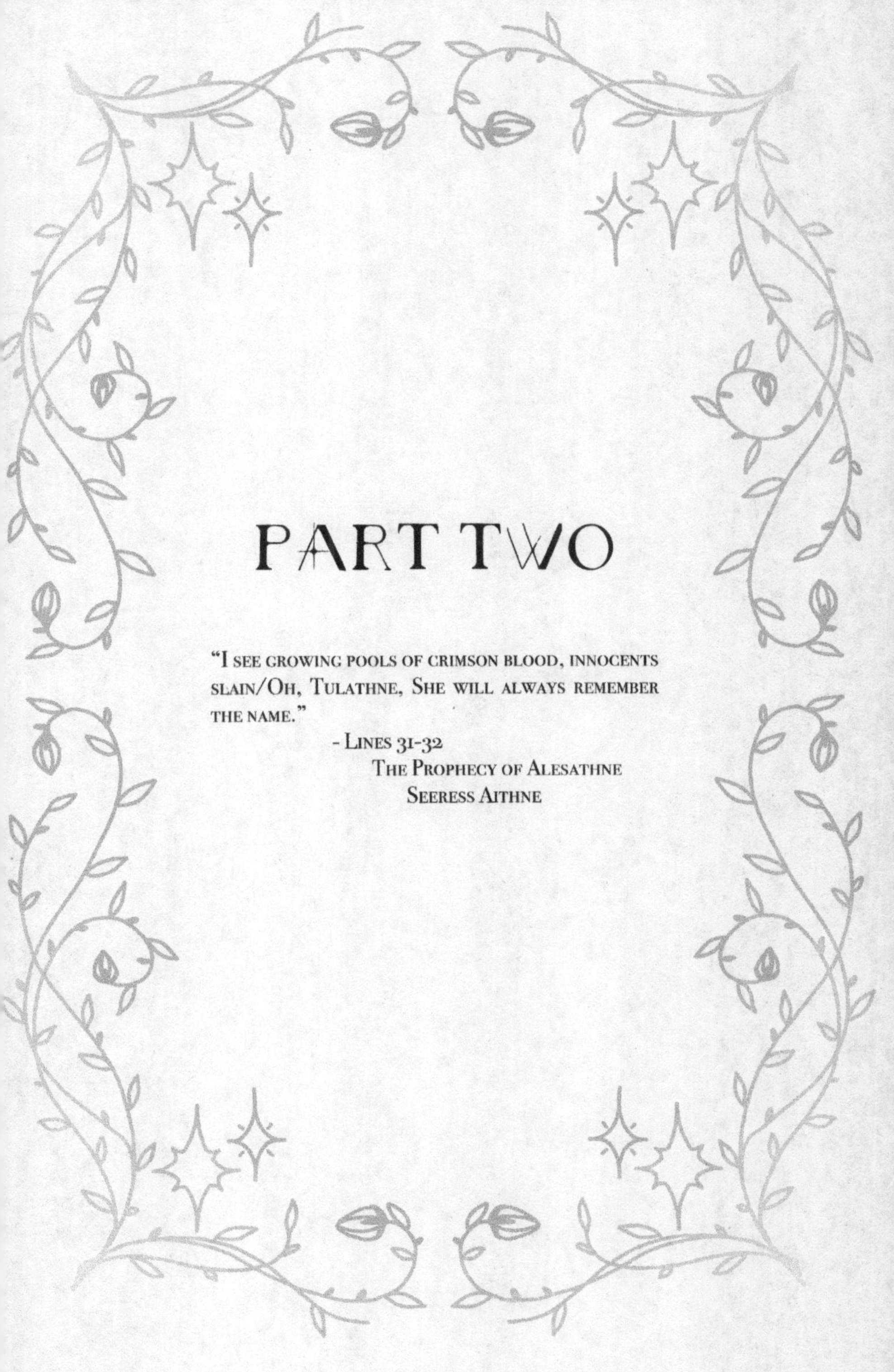

PART TWO

"I SEE GROWING POOLS OF CRIMSON BLOOD, INNOCENTS SLAIN/OH, TULATHNE, SHE WILL ALWAYS REMEMBER THE NAME."

- LINES 31-32
THE PROPHECY OF ALESATHNE
SEERESS AITHNE

Chapter

FOURTEEN

"ID YOU END UP SLEEPING at all last night?" Aleksander asked the woman beside him as he slid Aoife off his belt and handed the bundle of metal and leather to the footman at the back of the carriage. Deep within his chest, something twinged at the feeling of that ornate scabbard sliding from his fingertips.

"Oh, did you have trouble sleeping?" Elspeth chirped, strapping down the empty trunk in the back of the carriage. Carissa planned to fill it with spell components.

Carissa eyed the two of them. "I slept fine, thank you. Did you?"

Elspeth pressed her lips together, turning back to the cart and pretending to tighten the strap again. "Why wouldn't I?"

Aleksander watched as she tugged on it a few more times then brushed two fingers along her hairline to part airy waves that had escaped her crown braid. With a swift turn, she planted her hands on her hips. The new vest she wore parted open, revealing the ruff of her thick woolen blouse. Intricate embroidery depicting birds and flowers ran along the hem of the rich red doublet.

Her gaze landed on him. "What about you? Did you sleep well?"

"Fine," he said. "I slept fine." With each word, he refused to meet his sister's eyes. It was not a lie, he had slept. He'd slept fine enough to wake the next morning and have enough energy to pull himself out of bed. He'd slept fine enough that he did not ache from the day prior. He just had not fallen asleep until late. The chapel housed his exhaustion, grief, and fear for long enough, and eventually he'd pulled himself to his feet and wandered back to his room. In the hallway, he met Varek. It was too dark to see what the man had been wearing at the time, but he'd felt the leather beneath his hand when he'd pushed himself around the Ölmesuz.

"And where are you coming from?" The rumble had stopped him in his tracks.

"The chapel."

No use lying.

Silence followed, then footsteps, and finally Varek had patted his shoulder. "Make sure you get sleep. Grief and religion are not things to fortify a body."

The touch was nearly enough to make Aleksander crumple. He prayed Varek wouldn't hear the pounding of his heart, see the wide panic in his eyes.

"I'll see you in the ring tomorrow?"

Aleksander had said yes then, only to walk towards the armory and training ring the next morning for Elspeth to stop him on her way back, reminding him that they were going to town with Carissa.

Shaking off the memory, Aleksander met his sister's eyes. "Actually, I didn't sleep well."

The victory was short lived, her smirk fading quickly. "Well, there you have it."

Into the carriage she went. It rocked under her weight, and once she was seated, Elspeth swung in. Dirt and stone crunched beneath its wheels.

Aleksander's foot just landed on the step when the sound of boots down stone steps caught his attention.

Varek bounded towards them.

Seeing the man in daylight turned Aleksander's stomach. He was acting so...normal. Well, as normal as he could. Breakfast had been full of quips and slights which were brushed off with laughter, and now, as he swung into the carriage behind Aleksander, taking his place next to Carissa with an uncharacteristically gracious nod...

Aleksander's eyes stayed on him, unblinking.

He could not let him out of his sight.

Varek's eyes locked to his, and the dread that sunk in Aleksander's gut almost made him break the stare. But it held. He held. Varek raised an eyebrow, his eyes flicking over Aleksander's face, his hands clenched together in his lap, the feet firmly planted on the floor, and back up.

Ever so slightly, a smirk flashed across his face, and the old man raised his chin.

Carissa raised a hand, rapping the roof. "Drive on!"

The carriage lurched forward, jostling apart whatever terrifying challenge Aleksander had accidentally issued to the man. Suddenly, the scenery was much more interesting, and he soon found himself lost in the detail on each and every building. They held to the usual Zekharyan bases, of wood and stucco and stone, but windows were latticed, open to the breeze. Patios were covered in painted tiles, swept clean to display the bold blues and reds and yellows, as well as the designs painstakingly painted on each of them. Arches were not solid stone but instead were bent wood, or sometimes they too were tiled like the patios they covered.

People milled about in heavy clothes, or light garments with more than five layers. There were Ölmesuz and Zekharyans walking alongside one another, trading, buying, sharing a drink. The crowds parted without more than a glance to the carriage.

When it stilled, one woman eyed the fancy coach, only to turn and shout to her friend, the scarf over her head flapping in the autumn wind. "This is the first stop," Carissa said, swallowing hard. She adjusted the satchel slung over her shoulder. Nervous fingers worked on the clasp with no intended outcome.

The door swung open to a bustle of noise. Aleksander stepped out into a swell of people that shifted around him effortlessly, as if they were not even patrons trying to move, but trees that sprouted and must simply be avoided. Carissa took his outstretched hand and stepped carefully down the bouncing stairs of the carriage.

"Is everything okay?" Aleksander asked, a whisper against her hair as she passed.

The princess pulled back, studying his face. "Of course. Why wouldn't I be?"

Metal and wood creaked as Elspeth exited the carriage, and finally Varek, but nothing took the Sword's eyes off of his sister and that tight smile she'd plastered across her face.

Still, he nodded.

"What is this place?" Elspeth asked, peering up at the painted sign swinging in the breeze. "I can't read whatever language that is."

Aleksander squinted, clearing the glow of the sun off the gilded letters just enough to make them out. The writing looped and curled, accented with dots and what looked like it could almost be small stars.

"Our language," Varek said.

Unease slithered down his spine, but when he looked at the man behind him, those stone eyes he feared would be trained on him were instead studying the calligraphy. "It says *Inaya's Apothecary*. Not a very catchy name, someone should speak with Inaya."

"And who exactly would you suggest speak to me, boy?"

Aleksander squinted against the sun, focusing on the woman leaning in the doorway. Her ears drooped with heavy, large earrings of gold and jewels. Wrinkles creased her golden skin, more than Varek's. Her cheeks rounded into a smile. "Visitors from Lord Asghar's residency, no doubt."

She stepped out, one aged, knobby hand pressing her loose gown against her abdomen as she bowed. Thick, copper curls fell from her shoulders, nearly brushing the ground. "I am honored to be of service to those studying with the mages."

When she came back up, her eyes alighted momentarily on everyone. A passing smile to the guards on the carriage, curiosity at Elspeth, and intrigue as she flitted between Carissa and Aleksander. Her eyes caught Varek's, then immediately returned to Carissa's. "My lady, you are the princess, are you not?"

Concern sunk in Aleksander's gut. The look at Varek had been too fast, too...knowing.

Could she be...

No. There was no way. Not every Ölmesuz was a spy, secretly in league with Varek and the lord who was betraying them.

He was just paranoid.

A blush of embarrassment at his own rashness flooded his cheeks, and he hoped Inaya mistook it for a chill.

"I am," Carissa answered. Her voice wavered momentarily; she cleared her throat before continuing. "I'm studying with the Mage Theresas. She's requested I gather certain ingredients in town. And seeing as my Champion and the Lady D'orde have never been south before, it was an excellent excuse for me to get what I need while also allowing them to explore."

Citrine eyes passed over Aleksander and Elspeth. "The Champion, and the Rodzjiek girl who fought alongside our Kutsaly." The old woman pressed a hand to her chest. "It is an honor."

Elspeth smiled. The expression was tense, it tugged at her face in all the wrong places, and all Aleksander wanted was to smooth it out. "Lovely to meet you, Madam Inaya."

A smile, broader than the one she'd offered earlier, squinted her eyes. "Please, come in."

Chapter

FIFTEEN

ᐯAREK HARDLY HAD TO DUCK through the door, and once inside he straightened fully, still far from the arched ceiling. The ghost of a smile dusted his face.

"Nice to be the average height, for once?" Elspeth asked, jabbing the old man in the side.

A low chuckle answered her.

Ahead of them, Carissa followed Inaya as she wove around stacks and tables, listing all the ingredients she was looking for. The names floated to Aleksander's ears in a muddle—it didn't take long for him to split off and wander the shop, eyes drifting along the vaulted ceiling strung with dried plants and lanterns. Along each wall were shelves interspersed with glass display cases, each stacked to the brim with various herbs, bones, teeth, tufts of fur, and so on. Some housed stones, others liquids. One entire case was filled, floor to top shelf, with olive oil in varying sizes of bottles.

If Carissa didn't find what she needed here, Aleksander would have been shocked.

"Aleksander," Elspeth hissed, bending sharply to stick her nose next to a selection of knives with carved antler handles. "Look at these."

A quick glance at the price made him wince—150 gold pieces.

"What would you use it for?"

She shrugged. "Anything, I suppose. I don't even know if I want it, it's just beautiful." Still bent, she shifted over to the jars of stones next, each labeled with its name. Aleksander scanned them, finding one of red jasper.

"Here," he said, holding the bottle up. "This is your stone."

The chips shimmered in the shaft of light he caught, and soon Elspeth's face was next to his, eyes wide, savoring the way the color shifted.

"Why mine?" Gentle fingers took the bottle from him to study it closer.

"Oh..." he shook his head, eyelashes fluttering. It was suddenly too difficult to make eye contact. "Your eyes look like red jasper."

In the corner of his vision, her face lit up. That smile broke out across her face and she clutched the jar of jasper to her chest, empty hand roving the bottles. "Okay, here." She lifted one. "This is yours."

A small jar of light blue chips, shifting in hue like the mountains in the winter and streaked with thin veins of brownish-gold, hovered in front of his face.

Aquamarine.

Blush crept up his neck, but he took the bottle, muttering his thanks. "Do my eyes have that brown in them?"

She crept closer, eyes wide, peering into his. "Yes. Just around the middle, though." Falling back, her hand and eyes went back to roving the bottles. "We have to find ones for Carissa and Varek now."

Aleksander scoffed. "Like Varek would care."

Elspeth bucked back, frustration clouding her face. "You don't know that."

With a heavy sigh, Aleksander picked up a jar of Tiger's Eye. "This. This is his eyes."

His friend blinked at the jar in his hand, taking it slowly, inspecting it to see for herself. "Yeah," she finally said. "That's it."

After a few more minutes of looking, Elspeth settled on a bottle of Prehnite for Carissa. With Aleksander holding whichever ones she could not, minutes passed as she weighed whether or not to purchase any of them.

Eventually, they all got placed back on the shelf. "I just don't know what I'd do with them," she said, peering through the glass of the cabinet next door. "I'd love to use them somehow but I'm not a mage, and I'm not good enough at sewing to...oh gods."

A hand latched around Aleksander's forearm, pulling him closer.

"What?"

"Look." A thin finger pointed at the second shelf from the top—particularly, the set of twelve vials suspended in a carved wooden case. Each one had a stopper on the top, cork. Inside sat a thick, coagulated sludge, mostly black with strange grayish-red chunks here and there.

"Why is she collecting homunculi remains?"

The question left his lips no louder than a whisper.

"I don't know," Elspeth responded. Her fingers brushed the glass. "I can't...I can't tell how old they are. I never remember how quickly their remains deteriorate." A glance at Aleksander, then back at the case. Her irises flickered in the reflection. "Should we ask Carissa how old they are?"

"Best not interrupt her highness."

Aleksander jumped at the sudden, conspiratorial whisper uttered between him and Elspeth's heads. Varek grinned at the reaction. "She's busy with Inaya, and who knows. Maybe one of the components she was sent to get *is* homunculi remains."

Elspeth tore her gaze away to study the old man's eyes. "But aren't they too volatile?"

Varek straightened himself, bones shifting and cracking back into place as he did so. "Suppose they must have figured out a way to make them less-volatile. You can ask her yourself."

Aleksander glanced at the apothecary bending over her desk, stacking vials and stones and other things wrapped in linen he couldn't quite make out. Carissa leaned with her, arms wrapped around her abdomen. Her head tilted at just the right angle to bounce lamplight off her curls and gave her a fading halo.

"No," Aleksander turned his attention back to the case. "It's not my business."

"If you have a question," Inaya's voice rose, traveling easily across the shop, "then you can ask it. Anything in here is your business if you wish it to be."

He did not wish it. In fact, in this instance, Aleksander would have very much preferred to turn around and leave, never thinking of the apothecary or her shop or the things in it ever again.

It seemed though, that Elspeth did wish it. "We were just wondering why you have so many homunculi samples," she said. "They deteriorate quickly, don't they?"

At that, Carissa straightened, her face paling. "Homunculi?"

Inaya waved her hand. "They do, that's why they're in there. I've had them for the last few months. Most mages are too worried about using them. Can't blame them, I suppose. The magic they were born of is not safe magic." At that, she chuckled, turning back to the contents laid out before her. "Not that any magic is truly safe, but you know what I mean." Glass chimed against itself as she organized the box before her. "There, that should be all."

Carissa lifted her head, a nervous smile breaking to earnest for just a moment. "How much do I owe you?"

Inaya waved her hand. "I'll send the bill to Theresas. She buys enough from me, I know how to get it to her."

Carissa reached out to grab the box, only for Inaya to slide it away. "You," she looked pointedly at Varek, "Carry this for her."

"What?"

"I'm perfectly capable of carrying it myself."

The apothecary met the princess's indignant expression with one of stern warning. Each word was laced with a nearly lethal tone. "You will let this young man carry it for you."

Elspeth scoffed, and Inaya's glare turned on her. The girl's face wiped clean of any expression that was not embarassment.

"I'm sorry, madam Inaya, it's...I just..." She appraised Varek, gesturing with a limp hand that quickly situated behind her back.

A soldier's resting pose.

"He's not young," she said.

Inaya squinted at Varek. "You're younger than me. That makes you young. Carry this."

Varek's jaw flexed, and Aleksander swore he saw a hint of a smile appear on the woman's face. She pushed the box further across the counter, her long fingers tapping along the top impatiently. "Come on."

In two strides Varek stood beside the counter and took the box, holding it to his chest. "Anything else, ma'am?"

Inaya's smile grew. "Oh, I do so love it when the younger generation still proves to have manners. Yes, as a matter of fact, I have a small parcel I've been meaning to deliver to our lord." A drawer clattered open and in a moment, she held out a small paper wrapped package. "Could you see he gets it?"

Varek leaned forward, trapping the flat object between his long forefinger and the box.

"There's a good boy. Now run along. I'm sure you have many other errands today."

Carissa left the shop first, trailed by Varek, and behind him, stifling giggles best they could, were Aleksander and Elspeth.

"Do you think you could carry my shopping too, young man?" Elspeth quipped.

"Watch it kid," Varek growled. "I could still kill you if I wanted."

"Hey," Aleksander barked, smile splintering across his face. "Who are you calling kid, 'young man?'"

Satisfaction bubbled in Aleksander's chest the moment a tinge of red became visible in Varek's cheeks.

a free with the was used to respect at once. Often...
...ans from young women, Prayers and blessings and...
...A Kordai Woman—one of the Few born pure in this...
...served her eyes when they met his...
...not make eye that was...

Chapter

SIXTEEN

THEY WERE ONLY FORTY-SEVEN steps from the carriage, if they took big strides. Aleksander counted as Carissa led them further down the street, weaving through swells of pedestrians and stepping over puddles left from the last fall rainstorm.

After Inaya's, she'd been tasked to stop at a shop run by a local Crafter. An old friend of Theresas, the mage had apparently contacted the Crafter a few nights ago to request a special conduit for Carissa. It was unlikely the Ölmesuz artisan had finished it yet, but Carissa would likely have to attune anyway. The princess and the mage had both agreed it would be best for her to stop by and check. Carissa slipped inside the small shop, close to jostling trinkets and Creations off the shelves on either side of the thin aisle, and after a moment of attempting to follow her, the three warriors decided it would be best to wait outside the door.

Any time someone stared too long at Aleksander's outfit or the finely brushed golden waves of his hair, he wished he had not taken Aoife off before getting in the carriage.

Had people always stared this much?

Had he always reached to grip the hilt of his sword in response?

In Brewith he was used to respectful nods. Giggles and screams from young women. Prayers and blessings and...

A Rodzjiek woman—one of the few he'd seen in Hadiqin—narrowed her eyes when they met his.

...not whatever that was.

The young lord cleared his throat and looked away.

Across the street, a local vendor was selling small statues of the Kutsalyot. Some of the classics, images Aleksander had come to be familiar with like the kneeling form of Lady Nounet and the strong, sword-bearing stance of Lord Abrahten. And of course, brand new carvings of Lady Iscah.

He watched as a young girl with dark skin and long, straight-steel hair picked up one. The figurine turned over in her slight hands, and she smiled, chattering with the artist.

Only a few words were able to be understood at such a distance. "Good for protection" was the full statement that he made out.

Wind rustled the canvas cover of the booth, picking up the girls hair and making it float and twist in a new dance. She brushed it over her ear and nodded to the shopkeeper, digging in the satchel at her waist and taking out a handful of coins.

"Varek?"

The man's name tripped off his tongue, so silent he hardly noticed he said it.

"Yes?"

"What do the Saints stand for?"

Beside him, the man shifted.

Aleksander's eyes didn't leave the girl at the booth.

"Well, it depends. Nounet watches over musicians and storytellers. In her time here, she fought for Ölmesuz to be allowed a place in those jobs. She herself wrote many pieces about liberation. Abrahten, he was a soldier who fought in the wars of Ölmess. He's seen as a champion for the Mother, much like how you're a champion for Tulathne. They all have their different domains, mostly inspired by their lives and what they stood for."

"So Kutsalyot are only people who've done commendable things?"

"The public ones, yes. Each family has their own Honored Dead, their own Saints."

The artist wrapped Iscah in sheets of pink, purple, and white paper before stuffing it in a small bag and handing it to the girl, who only made it a few steps before undoing all that wrapping and peering at the little Kutsaly in her bag.

A smile crossed her face.

Aleksander's throat tightened. "What about Iscah?"

In the corner of his eye, Elspeth pushed off the pillar she was leaning on. His eyes flicked to her for a moment, and he followed her wide gaze to the same stand he had been watching.

Varek exhaled a heavy breath. "She's for...those who need strength. She's new, so people use her for a lot of different things, pray a lot of different prayers. But I've seen mostly women gravitate towards her."

The girl looked around, catching Aleksander's gaze. A look of unease passed through her features before she offered a smile.

Aleksander tried to reciprocate. He knew the expression didn't reach his eyes.

"People who pray to Iscah see her as a...beacon, of sorts. For the lost and weary. And the scared."

He patted his pants pockets, feeling for the coin purse he knew he had on him. But as he met the gaze of another small Iscah, perched above a selection of other Kutsalyot, his hands dropped.

No matter how much he needed her guidance, he had to admit it would be a little strange for him to carry around an icon of his deceased friend.

It was too hot. His body was too stiff. Aleksander stretched his shoulders back, loosing a tight breath that had been trapped in his lungs for goddess knew how long. "I need to go for a walk."

Elspeth regarded him with concern. "I don't think that's smart, you don't know the area."

"I will be just fine." Despite the clawing discomfort in his chest, he was able to shoot Elspeth a smile.

After a moment, she gave one in return. It was forced, and Aleksander knew it.

As he walked into the flow of people, Varek's stare still burned like a brand on the back of his head. Even as he was swallowed into a crowd, somewhere between the saint's booth and the next one carrying purses and satchels, eyes were on him from every angle. People in the street brushed against him, and the sting of their touch burned up his arms, his back, his legs.

His throat closed.

An opening appeared and he ran, stumbling to a stop on a bench, breathing heavily.

"Are you alright?"

Aleksander jumped at the voice, soft and delicate. Looking up, two dark, obsidian eyes met his, creased with concern.

Over the young Ölmesuz's shoulders was slung a bag, and from the open clasp, Aleksander saw the icon he had just watched her purchase peeking at him, face perfect and bright.

"I'm..." he met the girls gaze again. "I'm alright."

The smile she gave reminded him of the one Elspeth had worn moments earlier. "Okay," she said. "Are you sure?"

A breeze swept through, and Aleksander inhaled deeply, scanning the image before him. "I am." Again, he caught a glimpse of Iscah. "Can I ask you a question?"

Her drooping, dark ears twitched as she nodded.

A shaking finger wagged in the direction of her bag. "What do you see in her?"

His words came out wrong—he knew it the moment a flicker of rage passed over her face, those dark irises darting around his form. He could practically hear her thoughts:

You're a Zekharyan, you don't deserve to know.

How dare you disrespect my religion?

But before she opened her mouth, her eyes met his again, and she softened. "A lot of reasons, but...things are worrying me. And I get too deep in my fear sometimes. Lady Iscah didn't, from the stories I've heard. She was a Crafter, not a soldier, but she fought. She was brave."

Tears clogged Aleksander's throat. He nodded. Desperate, rapid blinks kept them from spilling.

The girl's face contorted, her attention lingering on the glistening at his lash line. After a moment, she parted her lips in a gasp and extended a hand. "Ishan," she said.

He grasped her hand gently. Her fingers were cold in his. "Aleksander. And you're right, she was."

Before either of them could even think of anything else to say, shouts echoed down the street. Aleksander bolted to his feet, offering a bow to Ishan before turning and running, Varek's booming tone echoing off the buildings around them.

"Take. A step. Back."

Carissa hadn't made it two feet outside the door to the Crafter's shop before two men began berating her. Guilt seized his gut, only for a glimpse of Elspeth through the din to quell it.

He did not leave his sister alone. He left her with the person he trusted the most.

Instinctively, pushing through the crowd that had gathered, he reached for Aoife. His heart jolted with the realization that she was not there, but as Varek loomed over the young Ölmesuz and Rodzjiek men who were still cursing Carissa, that fear abated.

"—to what your family has done, and revoke your claim on this land!" The young Ölmesuz man, eyes like emeralds, hurled his words at Carissa, who did not flinch.

"That's *enough*," Varek snapped.

Under his gaze, the young man shrank—though only for a moment.

For now, he would trust Varek.

For his sister's safety.

"Oh, grandpa wants to fight, does he?"

"Didn't your grandpa teach you to respect your elders?"

Varek's retort earned a wad of spit on his boot. His large hand clapped around the teen's bicep, shoving him back.

"Guess not."

"I hope you get lost in the Untamed and are ripped apart by the Dzera, you vile lump of murderous flesh!" The Rodzjiek boy spat at Carissa's feet, only for Elspeth to step in the way, fangs bared. He glared at her. "You're a disgrace to your people."

Pain streaked across Elspeth's features, but the other young man just sneered. Regardless, the girl squared her shoulders, embers flickering in her eyes.

"What's going on here?"

Aleksander forced his way in behind Elspeth as the crowd began to part. Walking through it was an older man, Zekharyan, though clothed in an array of Rodzjiek and Ölmesuz fashions.

"Kieran," a man from the side said, pointing at the tense scene. "Her royal highness has paid us a visit today, and these boys decided it would be a good time to cause a scene."

The man—Kieran, apparently—raised an eyebrow. He was big, with a stature that insinuated he spent most of his time building. The faint dusting of wood shavings in his hair was mostly dispelled with a breeze, but he still stuck a calculating, gruff stare to the young men. "Go."

The Rodzjiek boy opened his mouth, but Kieran repeated himself. "I *said*, go."

Casting one last glance at Varek, whose expression would have incinerated him on the spot if he were able, the pair slunk off through the crowd.

Kieran turned an eye on Carissa, bowing at the waist. "I'm sorry, my lady. Kids these days, they don't see nuance. There's a lot of trouble going around. Both of them have family they lost, either years ago"—a glance to Varek—"or recently." Pain crossed his features, momentarily, when they turned to Aleksander.

No sound of movement came from behind him, but from the towering man's relaxed shift in expression, he assumed his sister gave some sort of thanks and acknowledgement.

"I beg your forgiveness for their sakes," he continued. "Not all in Hadiqin hate you."

"But enough do?"

The sharp tone whizzed past Aleksander's ear in a perfectly

aimed arrow.

When it struck, Kieran's face faltered. "Not enough, your highness. Never *enough*, not here."

That sour, anxious worm in Aleksander's stomach writhed more, and he lifted his chin, stepping further in hopes of fully blocking the man's view. "Thank you for your apology and your assistance with the situation. We'd hate to keep you from your day, as much as I'm sure you'd hate to keep us from ours."

A discerning eye scanned Aleksander's face, painting swaths of amusement, realization, and a dash of frustration around the older man's strong features. Finally, he nodded, taking a step back. "Of course, your *holiness*. Of course."

Varek waved the crowd away with the large man, and after a single deep breath, Carissa stepped around her brother, shoulders tight. "Well, we've still a list of things to accomplish here today."

Her shoes clicked a deliberate pace on the stones, dress swishing beside her.

"Varek," Aleksander whispered, stepping to follow her.

The old man looked down at him, then off in the direction of the melting crowd. "I know. It's alright."

"But they—"

"It's alright." To Aleksander's shock, embers of concern burned in those banded eyes when they met his. "I'll take care of it, don't worry."

He nodded before taking his place beside Elspeth to escort his sister. With Varek only a few paces behind, he tried to stop himself from looking back.

Oh, how Aleksander wished he could trust him.

SEVENTEEN

Silence flooded Aleksander's ears as the swirling sounds of his dream gave way to the world around him. The contrast was sharp, and he blinked awake with discomfort. Gone was Demir's laugh, the rustle of trees, and the warmth that had danced over his skin like fingertips on polished stone.

How he missed his friend.

He still hadn't written him a letter.

The draping fabrics above him were painted in a dull, watery hue, shifting with the rivulets of water pattering down on the other side of his window. Tapping rain mixed with the distant crashing of waves on the terraces, and it was almost enough to drag Aleksander back in to the soft cradle of sleep.

Lightning snapped. He bolted upright.

It was daylight. Yes, his room was dark, and yes, the sky beyond those panes of glass were a roiling mottle of greys and dark blues, but the glow within those clouds was not solely lightning. Somewhere behind it was the sun.

Sweeping his feet around that he might sit up taller on the soft down mattress, a tired mind surveyed its body.

He felt...rested. That was, as much as it felt wrong, the best word for it. A heaviness laced his limbs, and he was still partially tangled in the blankets he'd tossed and turned in for most of the night. Thinking back, he wasn't sure when he'd fallen asleep. But he had slept, and it had helped.

As much as that notion frustrated him.

Surveying the room, Aleksander found the clock swaying in the corner to read well into the morning. Even nearing noon. Breakfast was likely already cleared, and a midday buffet would soon be laid out on the terrace instead.

He dragged a hand down his face, mind slogging along with thoughts of what the day entailed, and what he'd missed—until they stopped completely.

Fear shot through him.

No one woke me up.

Not Elspeth, not a servant, not Varek himself.

Aleksander's heart began to pound.

What if Varek and Asghar's plan—whatever it is—happened? And everyone's dead but me?

Within the next breath, he scoffed to himself. The man could do it, that wasn't out of the question—but assuming he'd throw whatever coup into place already, when the discussion on the terrace seemed to favor more planning?

Beyond that, who was to say Varek truly was going to kill everyone? Squeezing his eyes shut, Aleksander shook his head. He'd made that up. No where in the conversation he'd overheard had either of the older men mentioned that. They'd mentioned going against the crown. They'd mentioned being viewed as traitors. But none of that came with threats towards Aleksander or his family.

He needed to calm down.

Varek was a lot of things. Scary, mean, and dangerous to name a few. But impulsive? Bloodthirsty?

Aleksander had to admit: neither of those were traits the old Ölmesuz posessed.

In a breath, the boy shucked off his blankets and traded their wrappings for the loose drape of his dressing gown. His feet tucked into soft, fur-lined slippers.

Outside his door, lamps glowed at intervals down the storm-darkened hall.

There was no plan in his mind as he set out. Only a vague sense of hunger in his stomach and disquiet in his chest that made the thought of sitting alone in his bed unbearable.

Through his wanderings down halls and wings he'd not frequented in the last few days, he couldn't help but be drawn to the images on the walls. He'd seen them before, some of them quite often, but he still found his eye latching on to them as he passed. What had initially been a simple painting of an unknown figure now had a story.

His steps slowed before one depicting a woman stepping down to the earth and walking among the early peoples of Toprazi. She was not Ölmesuz, but she met with a man who looked every bit to be one of the long-lived. The story progressed as the hallway did. Aleksander traced her courtship with the man, the man's friendship with her father, and the moment Time and his Daughter blessed the man with long life, that he might spend near-eternity with his beloved.

The pair were married. They had children. He watched as they multiplied and devoted themselves to the stars above and the study of the arcane.

One figure, a son, stood out. He was painted differently than the rest—with wide, bright, gold eyes. Everyone else had small lines to denote lashes, but his were detailed. Eerie. Everything began to crumble around him, and in the last image, Aleksander stared up at him.

The figure was impaled on swords, spears—any weapon available. Purple, shimmering veins traced his form, and even the gold of his eyes had been traded for the amethyst hue.

Aleksander swallowed hard.

"The first of the Lunatliyot."

Panic gripped him, sending the boy spinning and almost tripping on his own slippers before he flung a hand out to steady himself on the wall. Lightning flashed, mixing with the lamps in the hallway and illuminating Chione. She smiled, a hint of satisfaction and amusement playing in her eyes.

"You didn't scare me," he said. He hoped it was convincing.

"Oh, I'm glad, I would have hated to hear that I did." Her raised eyebrows told him it wasn't. Still, she refocused on the painting behind him. "It's an interesting painting, isn't it."

Aleksander allowed his own attention to redirect to the art. "Did it...actually happen?"

Chione shrugged, a musical "hm," floating from her closed lips. After a moment, her fingers raised, hovering a breath away from the stone. "History has a way of warping. Even for us, your holiness," she said his monicker with a light laugh. After a moment her hand dropped, and she took a step back. "We say his name was Isgaar. He was the second son of our Mother. He was the first to realize that, as one whose mother was never born and whose father was blessed to never die, he could speak with the Flow. Time and magic are so entwined, you see, and...for us, it's like breathing. But he was too ambitious. Saw too much, wanted too much." Chione's lips flattened against one another. "So his mother killed him. And magic became forbidden to wield by all Ölmesuz."

He blinked. It was so strange to hear Chione repeat such a story while simultaneously being so blasé about it. Her eyelashes half-covered her sparkling gaze. It was unnerving, the care with which she looked upon a painting full of utter destruction and pain. "But," he asked slowly, "even after that, people still tried to wield magic, right? I thought I remembered Varek saying something about that."

Chione shrugged. "People are people. They are greedy and power hungry, and even history cannot be enough to change it." She swallowed hard. A shadow passed over her immaculate face. "Especially when that history is forgotten or rewritten."

Aleksander stared back at the image. The man in the flames, holding his sword high—for an instant, he thought of Varek. The man would never give himself up to the Cursed Dead, but in that moment, with the words from the balcony floating back to him, he seemed like he'd be willing to do anything for his cause. Whatever that may be.

"Are you alright, my lord?"

He blinked, breaking away from the painting. "Chione, have you seen Varek?"

Her eyebrows raised. "You didn't hear? A raven arrived last night—he left before the dawn, and the storm."

A rock sunk in Aleksander's gut. "What did the raven say? Who sent it?"

She shrugged, smoothing back a strand of hair with a delicate sweep of her fingers. "I don't know the details. I just know it's outside Hadiqin, and he'll be gone for a few days. He left in a hurry, too. We were just sitting down to a late tea when it came in."

His head swirled. It could be the Blight... or it could be something from one of Varek's allies. Which was worse? The regrowth of a terrible darkness, or a new poison from within the court?

Within the court. Terrell had been within the court.

Aleksander's skin grew cold.

Maybe the court had always been poisoned.

"My lord Champion?"

The boy fought from his tunneling thoughts back into the present, finding the towering woman bent over, her face level with his. Concern pooled in her eyes, a single hand reaching forward and brushing his bangs away from his forehead.

"Are you alright? You're pale."

"I..." how could he answer? No, he's grappling with news of possible treachery. Yes, he's just... cold?

He *was* cold.

"I'm just a little cold, I suppose." Even to his own ears, his voice sounded distant.

An arm wrapped around his back, leading him away from the wall. "Come with me," she purred. "We'll set you up by a fire and I'll call for tea."

Aleksander's body went through the motions of walking down the hall, siting in a chair, wrapping a blanket around him, but his mind was full of what he needed to do. Of what he could do. He could tell Carissa. He *should* tell Carissa.

A touch brushed down his cheek. Chione said…something. Aleksander nodded, though he was unaware what he'd agreed to with such a gesture.

The sensation left, and Aleksander knew he was alone.

The court had to be safe. It had to be.

But Terrell.

Asghar. He and Varek had mentioned others that night, others with *Duke* and *Lord* before their names.

And now, Varek has left. To where? He didn't know. But he was gone and that meant—

No.

Aleksander's heartbeat ricocheted up into his shoulders, his jaw.

This is a good thing. If Varek is gone…I can get proof. I can find things to show Carissa. Maybe even Lenore and Clauden themselves.

A hard swallow worked down his throat.

I can stop this.

Heat pricked at his palms. His soul slammed back into his body, and his eyes focused on the rippling, brown surface of his tea.

His heart still pounding, rational thoughts began to soothe the panicked ones.

He did not care much for the man, that much was true. But he would be a liar to say he didn't care at all, or if he ignored the strange sense of loyalty he felt towards the Ölmesuz.

There was time to figure this out. He needed to learn more. The conversation he'd overheard was out of context.

Maybe, the thought crept in, *if I know the context, they wouldn't be traitors. Not really.*

Everyone in Zekhar was his to protect, and that included the two Ölmesuz. They deserved his respect. They deserved for him to hear out their point of view.

Even if it did end up being a blasphemous one.

A fire crackled to his right—they were in the library. In some far corner of it, barred from the rest of the room by towering shelves and flickering oil lamps alight on small, intricately tiled side tables. Chione sat across from him. Her hands were folded in her lap. She leaned forward. "What's going on, Aleksander? You seem... unwell."

Aleksander swallowed hard at the use of his name. No one in this place, save for the people he'd come here with, used it. It was always "my lord Champion," or some variation. The Presence shimmied to consciousness around his neck and shoulders, and Aleksander found himself lean into it. A deep sigh released from his chest. "I'm... just having a hard time, Chione."

She nodded. "I don't doubt it. You've been training nearly every day, Lord Asghar says you don't converse much at meals anymore; even the young lady D'orde says there's something strange about you ever since the two of you'd begun learning our fighting tactics."

"Elspeth's talked to you? Why?"

The librarian shrugged. "She had questions. I'm the keeper of answers. Why wouldn't she?"

That scroll, unsinged and free of smoke, came to mind. The speed with which Elspeth had snatched it away—the fact that she'd never brought it up again. "She said you gave her a scroll," Aleksander raised the cup to his mouth, slowly taking a sip. It was hot, but not bitter. He actually quite liked it. "Were those the answers you gave her?"

At this, Chione shifted. Her eyes darted around the small alcove she'd placed them in, landing on the fire and lingering a moment before returning to Aleksander. Now, the warmth held within them was clearly forced. "Yes," she said, "though I fear they weren't satisfactory enough."

"Do you have a copy?" Aleksander found himself saying. "I'd like to—"

"What questions do you seek answers for, my lord?" Chione cut him off, leaning forward even more. Her pale eyes narrowed. One ear twitched and the jewelry on it twinkled momentarily. "It's clear you have them."

Now that question was unexpectedly frustrating. There were so many things Aleksander wanted to know—trivial things he'd wondered since he was a child, about the sun and the moon and stars and so on. There were questions regarding the history of Alesathne and the Scourge, to see if anything was kept out of the archives in Brevindun that may truly help him in this instead of the basic, bland encouragement everyone had seemed set to offer him. Then, there were answers about Varek, about Asghar—even if he did get the courage to ask them, it was unlikely Chione would answer them even if she did know the truth.

"Have there ever been any other Rodzjiekim to wield fire the way El—" he caught himself, "Lady D'orde does?"

Why that was the question he chose to speak, he didn't know. But the Presence seemed pleased, so he let it hang in the air.

Chione didn't move. For a moment, Aleksander earnestly wondered if he'd imagined her being real, if she had somehow turned to stone or been a statue this whole time. Perhaps all this stress had gone to his head and he'd imagined the kind librarian and her gentle voice.

Then she blinked.

"It is very rare. But there have been others, yes. We don't keep records of Rodzjiek mages, not well at least."

"Was that what the scroll was about?"

The woman pursed her lips in thought. "Not intentionally. I had merely selected a cutting of poetry I had hoped would give her peace."

Peace. That word sank into his chest. Even though he'd found his friend worn and scared afterwards, he nodded. "Thank you."

"It did not do much, she's told me as much," the woman continued, "but of course. I do what I can."

Logs crackled in the silent void after her words. Aleksander did not know what to say next, nor did he know where to take this conversation. He took another sip of his tea.

"Do you know the prophecy of Alesathne and the Scourge?"

Aleksander blinked at the switch in topics. "Yes, of course."

"Could you recite it for me?"

He nearly laughed. The last time he'd read it was years ago, and the last time he'd recited it was even further in the past. "I don't think I'd do it justice."

A small smile turned the corners of Chione's mouth. "Try it, then."

She did not blink as she waited. After a stretch of silence that made Aleksander realize she really wanted him to try it, he cleared his throat. "It's something like, 'After Alesathne falls, he shall return. His father a man, his mother a woman, and only his soul shall know his true name. In regards to the cursed, who... who rose sword to...'" after a moment, he nodded. "Who rose sword to heaven and slandered the name of our Lady, our Keeper, they too shall be revived and remain fit for the reaper.'" As he finished the line, a smile lit his lips. "I do remember that part. It rhymes."

Chione nodded. "It's close enough. Keep going, if you can."

Aleksander scoured the depths of his mind. "I only remember the last lines were something like, 'the world grows dark, again people live in fear; the dark *shall* return, be ready.'"

"'It's face shall be different/ Alesathne, keep your head steady./ There will be many who rise to do harm,/ To slaughter daughters in towns and farms,/ Those uninvolved, who serve other gods, /Defend them—defend us!'" Chione's eyes drifted shut. "Those are the real last words. Though it seems no one remembers them."

"That can't be right," he muttered. He'd studied the prophecies for years, recited them over and over—he'd even recited one of them at his vow ceremony. He'd have remembered a line as dramatic as that.

"It is." Chione rose, disappearing into the stacks for a moment. "There was a time when your kind were new to this continent. My people and those born of its soil and skies worked to record the early years. Though..." the sound of leather and linen slipping against one another whispered through the dim room, "it's not always kept well." When she re-emerged, in her hand was a small, leather-bound tome. Its edges were frayed, worn in at the corners. She held it with complete reverence and desperation.

The chair creaked as she sat back down.

Her hand smoothed out the cover, wiping away an invisible layer of dust. "This is the record of the Seeress Aithne. I think you remember that name."

"I do."

She was the one who worked closely with the first Alesathne, the true Alesathne. In fact, a few historians speculated that she was Alesathne's true wife, not the lady Liadain, though all other accounts pointed toward something nearer to complete disregard for Aithne."

The notion was not new. Aleksander heard it many times in his classes—the Lady Liadain was the true love and wife of the sword, but So-and-So from five hundred years ago and Mr. Whoever from over two thousand years ago and whoever else throughout time thought her no more than a seductress bent on destroying him, so "we must always keep that in mind."

For some reason, that had always annoyed him. Their discounting of Liadain in favor of a seeress.

The leather creaked as she opened it. Worn pages, made intricate with borders and paintings and fancy calligraphy, crumpled as she flipped through them. Only when she found the page she was looking for did she turn the book and allow Aleksander to read it.

And there they were. Much less measured than the words he'd remembered, much more... desperate. They were recorded in a scrawl, the illuminating artwork did nothing to hide that fact. But there were the lines Chione had recited, the lines he had entirely forgotten.

His brow scrunched together. "I honestly don't remember this."

"I don't expect you to." Her voice was soft. No voice had ever been so wary. When he looked up, she was staring at the fire. "A lot of us believe that the translations of the original prophecy—

spoken in old Zekharyan, I'm sure you know—are incorrect. And some of the lines are omitted. Especially that one, since it is so held to by Ölmesuz and Rodzjiek individuals."

Something felt wrong. An itch began in the palms of Aleksander's hands, crawling up to his shoulders and his throat. He wanted to throw the book across the room and run. He wanted to never return to the library, or speak to Chione again.

His traitorous fingers clenched the leather tightly. He leaned forward. "What do you mean?"

Chione breathed slowly and deeply. "I mean," she drawled, "that the royal family does not like that verse, because we see it directly condemning their actions."

"What actions?"

Aleksander wasn't even sure he spoke, but Chione's face turned towards his. The expression etched there was too multi-faceted, too confusing to parse.

"We believe, aside from the fact that they stole you and are using the prophecy to manipulate the people of Zekhar...that they use it as an excuse to butcher us."

Chapter

EIGHTEEN

THE THOUGHT WAS REPULSIVE. No, worse than that—whatever worse than repulsive was. He shook his head, the book still firmly in his grasp. "No," he said, "no that's not right. How would they even do that?"

Chione bit her lip. Firelight flickered over her skin, her hair—she seemed to glow. "What do you know about the first Scourge?"

"I know they desecrated the Great Temple and attempted to curse Tulathne. I know they murdered Zekharyans and Alesathne was ordered by his mother to kill them and avenge Her."

"She." Chione leaned forward, a slender finger flipping through the pages until a specific one appeared—on it was the image of a woman, sword high, bleeding from her chest while her gown caught fire. "The first Scourge is not 'they'—the first Scourge was a 'she.'"

There was something familiar about her. The way her strange pale-brown hair streamed down her back, fluttering in the imagined wind, the way her eyes blazed with rage, even as she succumbed to her fate, even as her lips paled and her skin blistered.

"She wasn't Zekharyan, in fact, she was...like your friend,

Lady D'orde." Chione whispered. "So whenever there is a young girl found to be excessively skilled in magic—usually Rodzjiek or Ölmesuz, since the Mekartlim have no magic tradition—she is..." the woman pursed her lips, cutting off her own words. After a moment, she spoke with immense care. "I've seen and heard of more than there ever should be falling to Zekharyan steel because of the fear that, if she's allowed to grow up, she'd become the death of them."

Aleksander's throat felt thick. First, he discovered they don't believe he is who he was raised to be, and now, he learned they see this whole prophecy as a condemnation of their daughters. That all of this was nothing but a desperate lie.

His fingers trembled over the page.

"It's a difficult concept to hear, I know."

"No," he said, voice thin. "No, you don't know."

His mind began to swim again. They wouldn't do that. His family wouldn't *do* that, they wouldn't sanction the murders of innocent girls because of their fear for a prophecy. Their sages were too careful, their mages to smart.

No, this isn't right.

The dull snap of pages closing echoed off the stone. This was blasphemy, this was treason. Finally, he raised his eyes from the worn leather clutched in his fingers. "Why do you help us if you don't think anything we're doing is right? I think you tell on yourself," he pushed himself up, blanket falling to the floor. "I think the fact that all of you still help us and revere us is because you know, deep down, that this is right. That we are right, and that you are wrong."

She looked up at him. Her eyes shifted, glittering sapphire deepening to a cave-pool. Aleksander's heart stuttered—for a moment, he truly feared being swallowed by her gaze. "There's another option, my lord."

"And what is that, Chione?" His words were clipped, harsh.

He sounded like Varek.

Her lips wavered before she spoke, but when she did, there was no malice—only grief. "Perhaps we're scared of you."

◊ ✳ ◊

THE BOOK PRESSED into his stomach. He'd been loathe to take it, but Chione had insisted, and for some reason his hands seemed keen on betraying him and tucked it beneath his shirt without a second thought. His heart pounded every time he felt the leather brush his skin, the spine poke into one of his ribs. It was a thin, smaller volume—just enough to conceal under his clothes.

It made him want to vomit. Not from anything physical the book was doing, but simply the things it stood for. The things it insinuated. It was translated by a Rodzjiek woman whose name he couldn't pronounce, the art was by Zekharyan and Ölmesuz alike. Everyone working on it had agreed to its accuracy to some extent. And yet, it was a cursed object if ever he had encountered one before.

Part of him planned to burn it when he got back to his room, or run down through the terrace and into the rain, letting the paint and ink soak and bleed together so that the writing may be washed away before he braced himself against the sea wall and threw it into the raging waves. But when he pushed open the door and saw the candle on his bedside still burning, the rain pounding at his window, and Aoife resting on the cushion before it, he couldn't stop himself from pulling it out again and leafing through.

So many people believed this. Why?

One page caught on his thumb, and despite the panic building in his chest, he read it.

It was another quote from the Seeress Aithne, after her delivery of the initial prophecy. The one he, apparently, couldn't remember right.

> *Let us all find peace, please,*
> *In the manner which I have ascribed.*
> *They shall return—all of us do*
> *But in their lifetimes there shall be pain.*

It cannot be stopped, it cannot be lessened
Not unless you look in their eyes,
Utter their praise.
Yes, even hers, who's you so wrongly stain.
As I said before—a wrong for a wrong in service of a right.
You cannot pretend—

Aleksander closed it. The candle was smaller now, the flame would not be enough to catch onto the pages. And he didn't want to soak himself to the bone in a frozen late-autumn rain.

Aside from that, he couldn't ignore the small voice in his head whispering its intrigue over the book. This was full of lies, manipulations, treason against Tulathne herself, most likely...

He tucked it beneath his mattress.

There was no way he'd remember putting it there. Within days—maybe even hours, if he was lucky—it would be gone, at least in the way that mattered most to him. He didn't think about it as he shucked off his robe and slippers, he didn't mull over any of the words as he strapped Aoife over his worn training clothes, and he absolutely didn't stop at the doorway and glance back towards his bed.

His fingers itched.

There's a really good chance just having it there will give me bad dreams, he thought. But the door closed, and he started down the hall, content to find something else to occupy his time.

Each thud of his boots down the hall seemed so much louder than ever before. It managed to somehow drown out the pouring rain outside and the racing of his heartbeat in his ears. Aleksander just needed to train. That's all. Training cleared his head, it always did. Just him, the sword, and the imaginary opponent in front of him—the blurry image of the Scourge. Only it wasn't blurry anymore.

She wasn't blurry.

He threw his shoulder into the door out to the training ring. Rain battered down on his shoulders, his head, but he kept going.

Thank goodness I didn't bring the book with me, passed the thought, *it would absolutely be ruined.*

Guilt nauseated him. He should have brought the book, he should have ruined it. But he didn't, so he drew Aoife and began to swing.

The sand stuck to his boots differently than the mud in the castle's ring. It didn't tug at his feet as much, just formed strange clumps that made him stumble to and fro as he moved—still, he continued.

One, six, block seven, dodge left—

It was almost like she was here, that form from his dreams. The rain shattered everything past the reach of his sword into flickering, broken images. The shadows beyond certainly could house two glowing eyes.

Nine, parry four, duck—

Was this really worth his time?

Three, four, seven, eight—

No, it wasn't. It was stupid.

Seven, block eight, nine—

He shifted, spinning out of form; his hip met the sand with a grinding squish. Aoife's blade scraped along the particles. Aleksander's chest heaved.

It was stupid. It was.

He shouldn't be thinking about that. He should be thinking about his duty. About his training—

Aleksander's head hit the ground. Rain splattered his face, his splayed arms and legs; his doublet soaked through, putting a chill into his bones.

Everything in him felt heavy. Unbearably heavy.

He had a traitor to watch and a demon to kill. No matter if the demon was a girl. No matter if the traitor was close to him.

This wasn't what should be taking up his time.

Yet the curling, shuddering Presence seemed to want to latch onto the image of the woman in the book. There was something there he was missing, he was sure of it. But that was for later. Not now. And it shouldn't even *be* for later.

Aleksander sighed heavily.

He knew it would be.

With a grumble, he pushed himself up to his feet and scooped Aoife from the ground. Sand stuck in all the small filigree of her cross guard and pommel. He did his best to clear it with a short, cracked thumb nail—it didn't do much.

There was something so mortifying about dragging himself back into the manor, soaking wet, covered in sand, after training for no more than ten minutes.

Thank the goddess Varek wasn't here to witness it.

His boots no longer thudded—instead they squelched. With each step, rage built inside him. It was that awful, burning rage, the kind that made his fingers start to shake and his head feel like it was floating and about to explode all at once. He hated the squelch of his shoes, he hated the rain dripping down his back, he hated the sand sticking between his fingers, and most of all, he hated how he couldn't get that awful, blasphemous, liar of a book out of his head.

He didn't want to admit that it made him think.

He didn't want to admit that it reminded him he wasn't Alesathne; at least to these people.

His own mind reminded him enough already.

Fresh incense wafted by as he passed the chapel. Inside, furtive, panicked prayers mixed with the curling smoke. A glance out of the corner of his eye, and he stopped in his tracks.

"Carissa?"

The praying stopped. The figure, hunched over her hands before the statue of Tulathne, slowly lifted her head. "Aleksander?" Carissa turned.

Forget rage. It drained from his body the moment he saw her tear-stained cheeks, the red rimming her eyes and swelling her nose.

Goddess, she couldn't be doing it all again, could she?

He stepped inside, not minding his clothing or the state of them. "What's going on?"

She reached out a hand, beckoning him closer. He obliged.

The kneeler creaked under their combined weight, but Carissa just looped her arm through his and rested her head on his shoulder.

A forceful sniff broke the pattern of whimpers and gasps.

One sand-encrusted hand raised to push back a lock of curl from her sweaty forehead.

She was still whole, that was the main sign that this wasn't as awful as he'd first expected. Her cheeks were plump, her eyes unshadowed. There were no signs of the Flow draining her like it had before. She must have figured out a way to appease it—he hoped so, if she was working so closely with Mage Theresas.

Even though Carissa was whole, however, she still seemed... desperate. Broken.

"Carissa," he pulled his sister closer. "What's going on?"

The princess shook her head. "What if it will never be enough?"

"What do you mean?"

A tear plopped onto his sleeve. "What if all my studies are for nothing, what if I can't use magic anymore or have visions and what if I ascend the throne and do *nothing* to help my people?" She was shaking now. "What if all of this is useless?"

Aleksander prayed she couldn't hear how loud his heart was beating. "What did you see?"

She didn't answer.

"Carissa," damp fingers pressed to her cheekbone. He forced his sister to meet his gaze. "What. Did. You. See?"

Bloodshot eyes blinked once. Then twice. "I saw two paths," she whispered, "and in both...we are separated. Forever."

ALEKSANDER SHOOK HIS HEAD. SHE'D had visions like this before—visions that he'd betray them and side with the Scourge, visions that everyone on their council would die. Carissa's visions were the pride of the priestesses, but they often brought her nothing but pain.

He had yet to see any of the truly horrible ones happen, and he wasn't about to start believing them now.

"You don't know that."

"I do," she whimpered. "I watched the battle. It's that same field—it's always the *same* field. First, you were leading the charge, and I was behind you. It was just us two against a raging wall of fire. You saw the destruction wrought on our land and cried so hard your tears doused the flames. Left in its wake were...burned, mangled corpses. And you melted away with them. Then it was like...everything flew backwards. The fire leapt onto your shoulders and you didn't burn." Her breath caught. "But when it leapt to mine..." Again, she shook her head, lower lip quivering. "And I know it's right, I know that's the future I'm leaning towards. The second one."

Panic gripped him. "Stop," he snapped, "stop with this, you cannot just accept your visions."

"Why not?" Her lips hung half-open, swollen from crying and

exhausted from prayer. "It's all decided anyway, isn't it?"

"It's not." He slid off the kneeler, dragging the princess with him until they both sat, cross-legged and opposite from each other. Bridging the gap were their hands.

Aleksander held to her tighter than she held to him.

"The fact that you saw two outcomes means it was not decided. And even if you had seen only one... Carissa, do you remember the one about me siding with the Scourge?"

After a moment, Carissa nodded.

"Right, and will that happen?"

She breathed steadily, eyes fixed on their joined hands. Aleksander's heart tripped a beat—he realized he was hoping she would say no. He needed to hear it from her.

Carissa shook her head. "No, of course not."

"No, of course not," he echoed. Aleksander squeezed her hands. "So we will work together and find out a way to make sure we *both* walk off that battlefield. Okay?"

She met his eyes. "Okay." A shuddering sigh tugged her eyes shut. "I'm just... we're trying to learn how to reroute the Flow. Like the Rodzjiekim do. So it doesn't take a physical toll on a mage's body. My body, specifically."

Words echoed back to him—words said beneath fluttering leaves on a hot summer evening. "You can't be serious."

She blinked up at him. "What?"

"You're not actually trying that, are you?" Terror slithered down his spine. "Carissa, you said that's what Terrell did."

Any human who tried to conduct the Flow in a way outside what the mages had learned would go crazy. That fact had been established in his mind since he was a child. The Flow needs *something* in return for what it gives, and if it's not physical it's mental.

Terrell was proof of that. The other man—Elias—he was proof too.

But Carissa nodded. "It's my only hope right now, Aleksander. I need to be a... a battle-ready mage. Who knows when the Scourge will make their next move? I can't sit here unable to use magic because of—" her eyes slid to the side, her lips pressing shut. A frustrated huff blew out her nose. "I can't use magic if I don't figure this out, Aleksander."

"Why not?"

She chewed the inside of her cheek. "Because I can't take it anymore. My body is not... it's not safe to do. Not right now, I'm not strong enough."

Aleksander scoffed. "It was never safe. That didn't stop you."

"Yes, well, I can't afford to be selfish anymore. They...our *people* need a leader who takes care of herself, who is there for them." Her teeth sunk into her bottom lip. "I can't be there for them if I kill myself protecting them. Or even just in figuring out how to protect them." A hand numbly swiped at her eyes. Her shoulders sagged. "Aleksander, have you heard any of the reports since coming here?"

He shook his head. Nothing specific had gotten to him, though the ravens coming and going throughout the day and night were as obvious and constant as the sun itself. "I know Varek left because of something, but—"

"There was a man who went on a spree in a little hamlet to the east, nearer the southern woods—" she shook her head, "he killed *goddess knows* how many people, all Zekharyan. Someone who got away overheard him say it was to cleanse the world of Tulathne's scum."

While Carissa may not have gone into detail, Aleksander's mind did. Warped, twisted bodies painted themselves across his mind's eye—some were killed cleanly with a single stroke to the neck. Like Lord Terrell.

Like Iscah.

Others were ravaged, chests ripped open, throats torn, limbs half hacked off. Like the homunculi were wont to do.

Who would have the stomach to commit such horrors? The only people Aleksander could think of were the people he'd encountered—his team, who had mainly slaughtered homunculi; Terrell and the creatures themselves, who mauled and killed without remorse.

On some level, the perpetrator had to be just far enough from human to act with such brutality; not in the way that the Rodzjiekim, Mekartlim, and Ölmesuz were non-human. But fundamentally, deeply inhuman. It wasn't a problem of birth, of which people they belonged to—it was the utter rot present in their souls.

A rot Aleksander saw for the first time at the solstice, then the cottage, then in the mirror. But it never stayed long in his reflection—for that he was grateful. He felt as if he still had a chance.

"Clearly, he had to be Ölmesuz," Carissa continued. "No Zekharyan would commit such an act."

Aleksander gritted his teeth. That's why they sent Varek. An immortal for an immortal. A murderer to catch a murderer.

A traitor to catch a traitor, whether they knew it or not.

Was Varek currently hunting down one of his own men?

He blinked the thought away. As far as he knew, Varek truly did hate the Blight and those who sided with the Scourge. Untrustworthy as he may be, Aleksander couldn't imagine the man crossing *that* boundary for the simple sake of going against the crown.

Carissa had fallen silent, staring contemplatively at their entwined fingers. Her forefinger curled and uncurled against the palm of his hand. It took everything in him not to pull away—she knew it tickled him, but the vacancy in her eyes told him she wasn't aware of much right now.

Janek, he silently called out, *if only you were here.*

His voice would draw her out of this. Aleksander was sure. But yet again, Carissa needed her husband and only got her brother. He tried his best.

"Carissa," he kept his voice low and smooth as he could. It was not even vaguely similar to Janek's, but the tone was reminiscent. *Please be enough*, "I think you should go lay down. How about I walk you back to your room?"

She blinked, her shoulders rising and falling in a slow, deep breath.

"No. I'll walk myself."

Her skirts rustled as she stood. A heavy shroud of exhaustion fell over her shoulders and Aleksander had to stop himself from offering to help her. With her hands extended to the sides, eyes fluttering half-closed, and a slow exhale, she seemed to be steeling herself to do everything alone.

He stood too, watching, waiting.

Slowly, her hands drifted to her sides.

"I'm here if you need anything, you know."

She nodded, eyes still closed. "I know. Thank you." As they opened, she found his face, features softening. "Tulathne did not see fit to give my mother any other children, so I have no siblings," she muttered. A small smile appeared. "But She did see fit to bring you along. I'm glad I get a brother after all."

Aleksander's jaw quivered.

Ten, almost eleven years since he'd come to the palace. Five since he started calling Carissa his sister—they were raised like siblings, but no one made them feel like they were, except for King Clauden. Even then, sometimes it felt like the only people who saw them as family were each other.

Yet all that, and this was still the first time Carissa uttered that word.

Brother.

He swallowed hard. This was a remarkably stupid thing for him to cry over, but the tears threatened to spill all the same. Without a second thought, he pulled her into a crushing embrace —one she returned with equal desperation, equal love.

This time he didn't stop the tears from trailing down his cheeks.

"And I'm glad I get a sister."

Chapter

TWENTY

E SWORE HE COULD FEEL the book beneath his mattress as he slept. Each time he rolled over he felt the pages shifting, a spine or corner pressing into his ribs. Even when he moved to one side of the large bed, it felt as though there was a heavy slant to the surface.

Time had slowed to a stop throughout the night. Aleksander would roll over, stare out the window at the stars beyond, memorize the clouds he'd see, close his eyes, roll again, and try to sleep. When he'd inevitably sit up with a frustrated tug on his blanket, there would those clouds float, barely moved.

His fingers dug into the pillows so firmly he heard his nails squeaking against the soft cotton. Pain streaked up his fingers, his arms—combined with the tension in his shoulders, he fought against his impulse to hurl the pillow right at the stack of decorations and ink wells on his desk. Or maybe the window. It shouldn't break anything, but...oh, he *wanted* to break something.

It was not just the book's content at this point, but its existence, and the discomfort he'd wrought from it. It was the book's fault he wasn't sleeping. Not the fault of his own mind, too keenly aware of the small volume. Not his spiraling thoughts of fear—what this could mean for the country, for him.

It was the book's fault.

Its very existence was a sin.

Rage laced each breath, tight in his chest. Bunching up the pillow as best he could, he sucked in a deep breath and buried his face in it, letting out a long, violent scream. It tore into his chest, his throat. Heat pricked up all over his body, every drop of energy in his body channeling into his scream. Shoulders heaving, he lifted his head and fell back. Mercifully, his eyes closed.

"I'm just so... sick of this," he said. Not to anyone in particular. "Gods, just let me sleep." His eyes snapped open. "Goddess," he corrected. "Tulathne, let me sleep."

But his heart now raced. How dare he reference other gods? Tulathne was the only one that mattered—the only one anyone should really respect. It was blasphemous to suggest otherwise.

"I'm sorry, my Lady," he whispered. "Please, mother, let me sleep."

No voice came back through the silence of his room in an answer. Even the Presence stayed relaxed. But every part of him twitched with anxiety.

Stop, he told himself, *She's understanding. She knows I've been around people who don't believe in Her, who use words differently. She knows.*

Aleksander gathered the softest blanket draped across the bed in his hands, wrapping it around his head and body in a cocoon. Curling up against the headboard, he worked to slow his breathing.

"She knows. It's okay."

He sat there, staring out at the large windows and the starry evening beyond.

The room was suddenly quite cold.

◇✳◇

AN EVENING OF restless sleep sent buzzing vibrations up his arms, his legs, even into his face as he blinked into the early golden sunlight. Bound by the blanket, his body ached; he'd somehow managed to stay in his seated position all night.

While the sunlight offered relief from the uneasy night he'd endured, a stone sunk into his stomach moments after a wave of peace abated.

Night was over, but what followed was a day of uncertainty. Of no plans and no ways to occupy his mind. Sure, the library was always an option, but the moment the concept of visiting Chione and her tomes crossed Aleksander's mind, he remembered the one he'd hidden. The one that had kept him up all evening simply through its presence.

In a flash, he was across the bed, hand beneath the mattress. The leather cover slid free with ease. It caught the early light, showing truly how old and well-loved it was.

Before he could stop himself, he opened the pages, flipping through until something caught his eye.

Time is a friend, though we may not be worthy.
One must remember from where we have come,
The battle we've just finished,
The pains we've endured already.

You fear, you say, for our future?
Good, I hope you do.
I only slather salt into our wounds
That we might correctly identify where to suture,
For if correction is left aside,
We may all shrivel and die.
Not in body, no, never in body—
But in spirit.

"Fear for the future," he muttered, his eyes lingering over the following line. *Good, I hope you do.* Part of him wanted to flip to the page before, gain context, learn exactly why he should be fearing for the future—no, no. To learn why *she* said the people were fearing for the future. The stone in Aleksander's gut sunk further.

There was no need to fear a future that was already here.

A glance towards the window. It was no longer raining, and he had no candles to light the pages with. He supposed he could still sprint down to the sea and toss it in...

He stood and slid it back into its space beneath his mattress.

He'd deal with it later.

Doing his best to banish any thoughts of the content he'd consumed, he brushed his hair, splashed his face, and donned a simple doublet and pants. Training was indeed an option this morning, and it would have been a good way to pull himself from his mind...

But the doublet pulled at his shoulders in a way that made him want to rip it off and throw it into the sea—his armor wouldn't be better.

The soft shuffling of his boots down the hallway were the only thing he focused on while he made his way to the terrace. There, breakfast was just being set up. A servant caught his eye and nodded before placing a coffee pot beside the tiered display of fresh fruit.

"I'm the first, I assume?"

Again, the servant nodded. His ears bobbed as he did so, sparkling green eyes flitting up at him every now and then.

He leaned against the doorway. "I'll just wait," he said, the words strangled and awkward on his tongue. "Don't worry about me."

However, the servant clearly did. Each movement he made was preceded by a glance, a shy smile, and a quick nod. Before putting the cups out, before situating the bowl of yogurt between the meat and the fruit, before folding a napkin and placing it in the holder.

Aleksander pressed his lips together. He tried to focus on the sea out past the terrace, to give the man any amount of freedom, yet each time he'd glance over their eyes would meet and he'd have to return the servant's nod. Discomfort flooded his stomach. There was nothing he could say or do that would make the man more comfortable. He'd seen it at Brevindun often enough—leave the servants to their work and they'll do it well, but watch them and they'll be more nervous than a thief.

"I think I'll take a walk through the manor," he finally said, brushing his hands off on his pants.

Relief flooded the man's face, but his words were still desperately polite. "Only if you wish to, my lord. You're more than welcome to stay here as I set up."

Aleksander shook his head. Already, he'd stepped back into the hall. "I've just woken up. A walk will...do me good, I think."

The chilled salt air followed him on his way. He tried his best to firm his attention on the patterns in the tile flooring. They were beautiful—he hadn't noticed the intricacies before. Some were a lovely bright orange background with white and blue swirls, put together against others to create what one could see as waves or as flowers. As he got further, it shifted to white tiles with green and gold accents.

The colors immediately brought to mind the fields he used to play in as a child outside the castle. Overlooking the city, just a walk from the Great Temple, was a field the royal family occasionally let their horses out in. When they weren't there, however, Aleksander and Janek would run out with wooden swords or just themselves after their classes for the day. Sometimes the grass would be up to Aleksander's shoulders, waving green and gold in the setting sun, the bunches of seeds atop stalks bursting like fireworks. Once, he and Janek laid there, obscured by grass, watching the birds fly overhead to the mountains. That's how they knew summer was ending and winter was on its way—when the grass swallowed them and the birds left.

Then, the tiles stopped. Ending in a line of dark polished stone, Aleksander's eyes slid up the ornate wooden door before him. It wasn't rounded or stylized the way the doors for the chapel and library were, it was single, with rope-like carvings up the sides, and flowers within the borders.

There was no doubt—this was a wing he'd never been in.

"Oh," he muttered to himself. *How am I going to find my way back?*

Just as he began to turn, his eye caught on a small placard beside the door. It was gold, inscribed with the flourished letters he had seen on the shops in Hadiqin. Below it, however, was the alphabet he was familiar with.

Office of His Lordship

Femi Asghar

Immediately, a thought whispered in Aleksander's mind —"*go in.*" Whether the Presence had learned to speak, or his own thoughts had suddenly gotten loud, he wasn't sure.

All he knew was he shouldn't listen to it.

But maybe he could find paper here. Maybe he could write to Demir.

Yes. That's what he would do.

But I won't. I'll turn around and go back and find paper somewhere else.

The brass doorknob was cold in his hand and the hinges swung silently. With two steps, he threw himself inside, the door latching softly behind him.

Chapter

TWENTY ONE

ALEKSANDER'S HEART ALTERNATED BETWEEN RACING like he was being chased and failing to beat at all.

Before him expanded Asghar's private office. Bookshelves lined the walls, starting on each side of the door behind him and extending around to stop at each side of the massive glass doors leading to a remarkably small balcony. There seemed to be only one chair there, and a small mosaic-topped table with a teacup.

Was he here already? Will he be coming back for his tea?

"What am I doing?" Aleksander muttered. Yet he stepped carefully over the ornate rug, woven with a mix of geometric and floral patterns, all the way to the desk.

He knew what he was doing. The moment he began scanning the papers scattered on the glistening wood, echos from a few nights ago floated through his memory.

Letters brought in on ravens.

Fazhia.

Contacts.

Varek.

Anything related to the conversation he'd heard on the balcony. His fingers itched, hovering above the polished drawer handle. It opened smoothly—inside the first one was nothing but extra ink, pens, and paper. The second one held the manor's ledger. Aleksander scrambled to put it on the desk, planning to read it after checking all the drawers.

With each slide of wood on wood, Aleksander's eyes flicked up to the door. He had *never* done anything like this before—never had he snooped in private quarters, and especially had he never been looking for evidence to prove that the lord of this manor was complicit in treason.

A stack of letters, bound with a ribbon, was the next thing to land beside the ledger.

He was a good kid. A holy man. The son of a goddess, a *good* goddess. He had no business doing something like this.

A drawer caught. Aleksander bit his lip and carefully wiggled his fingers into the drawer, pushing down the item that seemed to be the culprit. It slid open—the corner of a book was bent. He put it on the desk anyway, not bothering to check the contents and see if it would actually be helpful.

He had *no* business here. He was being distrustful and unruly, his behavior was shameful—oh, if Lenore could see him now, he just *knew* she'd sit him down and have a long discussion about his duty and his station and how that means he should carry himself. He was the Sword of Ages, not a spy. And beyond that, it was highly disrespectful and downright rude to behave this way when he was a guest. When his host was a member of court, no less.

He flipped open the ledger. Just reading the first words made his stomach dip. They were exchanges at the beginning of the year, for fur and thread. Nothing important.

The boy concluded he may be the Sword of Ages, he may be a lord and thus above this...but he couldn't deny the thrill coursing through him.

It was strange, having such intense fear and excitement and guilt carried in his body all at the same time.

At the bottom of the page was a nondescript exchange for 200 silver pieces. Despite his upbringing, draped in jewels and fine fabrics from head to toe that cost more than that, the number made him stop.

But the thing that annoyed him most is it came out of

nowhere, and the note beside it was a scrawl he couldn't make out.

Leaning closer, he was finally able to make out the slightly darker lines within the smudge.

"P...pay... oh, payment. Okay, 'payment'...to..." he sounded them out carefully, eyes squinted. *Damn, this is hard to read.*

Muffled voices echoed down the hall, and Aleksander's blood ran cold. He hadn't seen if there were any connecting hallways while he wandered, nor what other doors were in the area. For all he knew these people could be going straight past the office he was currently trespassing in...or they could be heading straight for it.

A drawer squeaked as he yanked it open, shoving the last book in and slamming it shut before carrying on the the next and the next.

The voices grew louder, but the pounding of his blood in his ears took out nearly all the aspects of speech that alert the listener to the speaker's identity.

A string of curses he'd heard Clauden mutter over the years slipped from his lips. Everything seemed slightly too delicate, slightly to slippery—he couldn't grab anything fast enough, couldn't place it where it should go smoothly enough. What if a paper bent and Asghar noticed? What if he somehow left something that let them know it was him?

He shook his head, pausing just long enough to hear the voices echoing just on the other side of the door.

Papers rustled, wood slid, and just as the last door locked into place—the ledger secured firmly within it—and Aleksander slid around the table, the knob rotated.

He felt as though he might faint.

"Oh!" Lord Asghar blinked at him, his hand frozen on the handle, the other reached back in a gesture to invite someone in. "My lord Champion. To whatever do I owe the pleasure of having such an esteemed individual in my office at such an early hour?"

"Aleksander?"

If Aleksander's heart wasn't going to burst before, it certainly was about to now. Pricks of ice crawled up his cheeks, at the same time burning with panic.

Elspeth stepped around Asghar. Her hair fell down her back in a single braid, hands clutching a fur-lined cloak she'd donned, likely to keep the chill of late fall from piercing through the thin fabric of her nightgown.

The bags beneath her eyes were the same Aleksander had seen beneath his own this morning.

With every fiber of his being trying to steady his breathing, control his appearance, he allowed a smile to slip across his face. "Lord Asghar, Lady D'orde! I was...looking for paper!"

The door swung shut, keeping the trio inside. "Oh?" Lord Asghar adjusted one side of his robe, sweeping his hair in front of his shoulder. Each step towards his desk was measured.

Aleksander prayed Ölmesuz couldn't smell fear.

"Was there not any in your desk? I tried to ensure they were fully stocked with pens, ink pots, really anything—"

"No, sorry!" Gaze darting to Elspeth, Aleksander nodded to her. "I offered them to Lady D'orde, as I didn't have any use for them and, in fact, she used them all up. Brainstorming...um, battle plans and training exercises. And...other things."

Her dull eyes met his, wide and tired, laced with the red of a sleepless night and confusion. But she nodded. "Yes," her voice was raspy. "I used them as my journals as Chione and Varek suggested—as I work with my fire more."

She must have just woken up.

"Aleksander and I had planned to meet early this morning, which was why I uh...told him I wanted to speak with you. He must have figured he could...get more paper while waiting. Even though I'd told him to just wait at breakfast."

Despite the too-big circles her eyes had turned into, despite the too-high arches in her brows, she sounded convincing.

Asghar's fingers splayed across the desk.

Aleksander tried to maintain composure when the man gathered his sleeve in his hand and wiped away a smudge of oil on the polished wood

"It's alright. We've discussed what we needed to, haven't we?" Those amethyst eyes flicked between them. Amusement glinted more than the sunlight. "With Varek gone, I do suggest you have some fun. Though, do not entirely neglect your training. My old friend would have your heads if he found out I encouraged entire abandonment of your skills for the day."

"Yes, of course," in three steps, Aleksander was beside Elspeth, gripping her bicep in a vice. "We wouldn't dream of doing such a thing."

"Ow," Elspeth hissed.

Aleksander hauled her back a few steps. "Assuming everything is alright with you two and your meeting is concluded, we'll go now."

"Actually," Asghar held up a hand, "I've one more thing to give Elspeth, and a few more words to share." His lips curved into a grin. "If you'd be so kind as to wait in the hall, my young Champion."

"Of course." He leapt back from Elspeth, ripping the door open so hard a jolt of fear that it might fall off its hinges ran through him. "It's entirely my fault for invading your space in the first place. I just...I had figured it would be easy to find here, and the bookshelves were so stunning I got distracted."

"Surely it's nothing compared to the library. Chione told me you had spent some time there yesterday."

Aleksander nodded. With each word, he pulled the door closed more and more. "It was, and it was lovely—you two finish your meeting, I'm so sorry for interrupting!"

The latch clicked into the mortise and everything fell silent. A great weight descended on Aleksander's shoulders, sending an intense, buzzing ache down into his fingers. Slowly, agonizingly, a whine crept up to an irritating volume in his ears.

He was quite sure he was going to fall over.

Aleksander stumbled sideways until his hand met the wall and he slid down against it. Adrenaline—or the sudden lack of it —set each of his nerves alight in a similar way to how his skin prickled when there was too much electricity in the air before a storm. A shaking hand pressed to his heart in a needless attempt to keep the organ raging there from flying from his ribcage in a gruesome display.

That was close. Too close.

But he'd almost found something...maybe.

The Presence swirled to life, prodding at that part of his consciousness that was itching to get back in there and dig for more.

He had found something. What it was, Aleksander had no clue, but there was proof that something strange was going on. 200 silver was a large amount for anyone normal, but just small enough for a lord to do something discreet. And what about those letters he hadn't gotten a chance to leaf through? There had to be some sort of correspondence there. When he'd heard Varek and Asghar talking, he'd heard them reference their contacts. Contacts had to have a way to get *in* contact, yes?

All at once, his pulse stilled.

They'd mentioned Elspeth.

Not just that, they'd mentioned using Elspeth to work on *him*.

Cold dread settled in his bones.

They'd gotten to her, hadn't they? That's why she was in a meeting, she's been turned to their side, that's the only—

Shut up. Aleksander ran a hand down his face. *She wouldn't do that. This is Elspeth we're talking about. She's too smart for that.*

Head tilted forward between his knees, he heaved a deep sigh. All this was getting to his head. He'd started the day trying to focus on his job, why he was here. To train and get better and maybe, when Varek is away, have a day of fun. Or at least free will. And here he was, overthinking everything. Breaking in to a private office, going through someone else's property. Fearing that his best friend was committing treason and betraying not only the crown but him.

It was a good thing the Sword of Ages was never meant to be a spy. He made a rotten one.

He pursed his lips together. She was his best friend. Ever since they'd met, they'd been the only person to see the other clearly. Fully. Yes, Carissa saw him, but that was different. He'd always be a child to her.

When Elspeth looked at him, she saw a capable young man, a friend. At least, he hoped so.

Whenever he looked at her, he saw a girl he would give the world to—if it were not so large. Aleksander was sure no one could hold it with the care and excitement she could.

The latch clicked and he shot to his feet. Nervous hands tugged at his doublet.

"Thank you again, Lord Asghar." Elspeth smiled. It was a hesitant expression, small and contained and not at all the grin Aleksander loved.

It reminded him of all the measured kindness Carissa and Lenore offered to the courtiers.

He had certainly overreacted—a girl smiling like that was not a sign of conspiracy.

The lord bowed, his intricate braids jingling together as they fell over his shoulder. "A pleasure, my young Lady. I do hope I was able to give you answers, or at least point you in the right direction to where you may find some."

She nodded. "You did, yes." Her eyes flicked to the side, catching Aleksander's, before returning to meet Asghar's gaze. "I'll leave you to your morning. Aleksander and I should go eat something before we begin our expedition for the day."

"Of course. You children have fun. Should you choose to visit my town, do ask a footman for shop recommendations. Aryel knows all the good ones, in my opinion." He cast a glance between them, a wink at Aleksander, and stepped back. "I'm sure I'll see you both for breakfast tomorrow."

The two stood stock still as the door swung shut. The moment the latch clicked, Elspeth pushed a box into his stomach.

"What is this?" The package fumbled, and within, he heard a heavy glass roll.

His friend raised an eyebrow. Amusement ignited within her gaze. "It's the paper and ink you were so desperate for, *my lord*."

TWENTY TWO

ELSPETH KEPT HER GAZE TRAINED on him as they ate. Aleksander, on the other hand, kept his face to his plate, hardly saying a word as he nudged his spoon at the blueberries and strawberries nestled into a bed of sweet whipped cream. Still, he couldn't stay quiet around her. And with that strange moment in the office, he couldn't exactly expect El to leave it be.

"That's all?" she said, after a particularly long silence.

He nodded, shoving a scoop of cream and berry into his mouth. "Yeah. That's all."

The explanation he had given her consisted of the facts: he had time before breakfast, wanted to see if there was anything related to the Blights or other riffraff that was being kept from them—from him specifically. He didn't tell the Lord Asghar because he panicked and did not want to be known as a snoop.

It wasn't a lie. It was just...a very carefully selected truth.

Draining her glass of fresh orange juice, Elspeth leaned back on her hands. Wind tearing off the sea tugged at her braid. "Am I supposed to believe that? Because I don't."

He rolled his eyes, finally looking up at her. "Yes. Because that's what happened."

"The Aleksander I know would never stoop so low as to break into an office when he could simply ask. You're easily the most diplomatic among all of us." She bobbed her head to the side. "Besides Demir, at least."

"Well, maybe the Aleksander you know isn't all of...the Aleksander."

Elspeth's eyebrows raised, a smile playing on the corner of her lips.

When he didn't speak further, just fixed her with a frustrated stare, she sighed, a foggy breath puffing from her lips as she gazed out over the terrace. Another wind gusted through the carved balusters. Aleksander watched as it smoothed out the harsh lines that had begun to take up residence in his friend's face.

The past few times he'd seen Elspeth, this morning included, there was a heavy air of stress and exhaustion over her. Their conversations were laced with fear and reassurance, cryptic statements, and uncertainty. Here, though, the areas around her eyes finally relaxed. Her thick eyelashes fluttered against the wind, blinking away the dryness it brought. A few strands of hair flew free from her braid. They caught on the furs, flicking at the ends.

Elspeth's lips parted slightly with another exhale and Aleksander's cheeks warmed.

"I'm glad you seem... calmer," he said.

Sparkling gold-red eyes flicked over to him, and he could swear they flickered brighter the moment they met his.

She shrugged, gazing back out at the sea. "I may have grown up in the Keep, but nature is in my blood." A smile passed over her lips for a moment, the brightness lingering in her eyes. "We Rodzjiekim are born from the Untamed, you know."

Another burst of cold air blew across the terrace. Aleksander's napkin flew from his lap, which he barely caught, throwing his body sideways to reach it. When he turned back, he couldn't stop a smile from cracking open his face.

Elspeth leaned into the wind, eyes closed, chest slowly rising with a measured inhale. "Hi," she whispered.

As if in answer, the wind blew stronger.

Her hair caught on it, twirling around before her face, brushing her cheeks. Her nose scrunched, fangs forming two silly bumps on her bottom lip with her smile stretched so strangely.

When her eyes opened, she turned to him, ready to speak. Whatever words she had planned died on her tongue. After a moment, her fangs peeked from her lips in an answering smile. "What?"

Aleksander's eyebrows scrunched. "What?"

"Why are you smiling like that, what's so funny?"

He shook his head, but the smile did not dissipate. "No reason."

"Sure," she said. Tiny bits of rock crunched between her feet and the stonework of the terrace flooring as she stood. Her laugh echoed, warm and deep and shining. Strong fingers caught her fur cloak and regained it from the wind that dared attempt to steal it.

"Do you really have a journal?" He wasn't sure why the question came, but it did.

She smirked, staring down at him. "Yes, I do. I feel like most people do. Don't you?"

"No. What would I write in it?"

"I don't know, secrets? Things you're going through and thinking about. It's a nice way to work through your thoughts, get out emotions, anger, whatever and not have to face any judgement from others." Breathing in another gust of autumn sea air, her shoulders dropped. "I'm figuring it out, by the way."

Aleksander's eyebrows rose. "Really?"

She nodded. Slowly, she began to pace as she spoke. "I've been using the training ring at night. Like you did back in Brevindun. It helps, I see why you did it. The silence, the darkness...it helps a lot with focus." Still gripping her cloak, her fingers flexed, fidgeted. "Still gets really hot, though." Her feet stilled, lips pressed together for a moment, a flash of pain crossing her momentarily-serene features. Then, she lifted her chin, spun slight to face Aleksander again, and smiled. "So, what are we doing today? Despite Asghar's encouragement with training I do think we should waste the day having fun."

Aleksander blinked at her. "You actually want to? I was just —"

"Of course! Lord Asghar said the town had some lovely shops, and honestly I think we need to get out for a little. Judging by the bags under your eyes, neither of us are sleeping well."

Raising a hand, he brushed the soft skin beneath his eyes. "Do I look awful?"

Elspeth didn't respond. Instead, she looked down at the still-burned cloak wrapped around her nightgown and gave it a swish. "I think a new gown might be a needed addition to my wardrobe."

"I feel like I hardly see you in dresses," he said.

"Just because you don't see me in them doesn't mean I don't want them. I'm just very picky about the ones I *do* want." Her eyes danced through the sky as she spoke. "Or maybe we could go find some food we've never tried before, or get some jewelry. Oh!" She found Aleksander once more, crouching before the plates and cups they'd set up for their breakfast. "We could even go on foot, pass through the woods." Her grin widened, feral. "Maybe the Dzera comes this far south, we could say hi."

His heart was pounding too much to go cold from fear. A nervous laugh pushed him to his feet. "No, I'm more than content to never run into it again."

"Understandable." The girl stood, adjusting her furs to raise her arms over her head, twisting her spine this way. "Regardless, I haven't had a day to do what I want in...months. We should take advantage of it."

"In months?"

"Since I met you." Her smile softened.

Something pinched in Aleksander's chest—whether it was guilt or something else, he couldn't place. There was something in that simple statement that did make him feel guilty. What freedoms had he taken from her, without even knowing it?

Before those thoughts could take hold any further, she extended a hand. "Well? What do you think?"

That small voice in his mind reminded him of the book, the treachery he had yet to garner proof of, the training he had to continue. But for the first time in days, he pushed it aside with ease. Her burns were merely discolored patches of skin, warm and soft against his palm.

"To be honest..."

Elspeth's grin faltered, her grip tightening.

"I don't think I've ever just had a normal day in a town. It's always been accompanying Carissa or for ceremonies." And it was true. When he was a child he had more freedom, but once he was ten, once he took his vow, everything changed. Not only did the idea of exploring a new town sound fun, but doing it with Elspeth? There was no doubt in his mind that his friend would show him things he'd never considered before. "Let's do it."

◊ ✳ ◊

"Why do I have to wear this and you get a whole new outfit?" Aleksander tugged at the collar of his new doublet. Well, new was not the correct word—it was new to him, but upon their agreement to sneak into the town and explore, Elspeth got the idea to go in disguises. She'd chosen a Rodzjiek skirt he'd never seen her in—long and dark, with embroidered flowers around the hem—and a red velvet vest, finished with her furs. Over her shoulder draped that single, glimmering braid.

Aleksander had told her she was beautiful, a compliment she'd laughed at, but had spun in her skirt and given a dramatic curtsey regardless. It was the truth—not that Elspeth was not beautiful otherwise, but something about the colors of her outfit made her shine.

His, on the other hand...

"It's a very nice doublet, leave it alone!"

The back of his hand stung after a quick swat. "Ow!" Shooting her a glare, he picked his way around a pot hole. "Be honest, El, is there any reason to wear these? We've already been in the city, a good few people have already seen us."

Elspeth hitched up her skirt, stepping over a rather large rock in the road. "Yes, but when we were here last we were in uniform. And with Varek and the princess. *That's* what people will remember, not us. Trust me. I've been on the other side often enough to know that when shiny armor and jewels are in the mix, that's mostly what people notice." She tossed a nod to a passing horse and rider. "Besides, we don't want people to think you're from the capital, or that either of us are anyone important." With a huff, she crunched a leaf beneath her foot. "Your accent will do that enough already."

"My accent?" Aleksander didn't know whether to feel offended or confused. "What accent? What does the way I speak have to do with anything?"

They slid to the side to allow a cart to pass. The driver nodded at them, Elspeth nodded back—Aleksander had to stop himself from bowing.

Stepping back out into the road, Elspeth shrugged. "You must have noticed most of us don't sound like you." She shot him a glance from over her shoulder. "Even *I* don't sound like you."

"I just thought that's because you're Rodzjiekim." The words sounded stupid coming out. They *felt* stupid coming out.

A comment that Aleksander feared would make Elspeth defensive was brushed off with a quick shrug. "Yeah, but I was raised in the Keep. I speak like all the low-born there." He could hear a smile appear as she said, "With an added lisp on a few letters, because I'm Rodzjiekim. You, however," she lifted her chin, mimicking his diction, "Every word you speak has been expertly chosen, and even when you're relaxing, it's still refined."

He had never thought much about the way he talked—he just knew there was a specific manner around those in court. But as they got further and further into the town, as the buildings became more noticeable and closer together, as the foot traffic became more congested, he started to understand what Elspeth was saying.

It wasn't just the words they used, but *how* they used them. There were sounds their dialects had that his didn't—r's trilling where there were none, words running together, sounds completely dropping, and not in the way he did with cognates. Rodzjiek had the occasional lisp like Elspeth, given their fangs. But most noticeably, the measured tone he'd heard all his life was entirely absent.

"I think you're right," he whispered to Elspeth as they wove around a man bartering with a woman over the price of eggs.

"Right about what?"

They stepped into the square, passing through the flow of people skirting around carts and stalls and a great fountain in the center.

He didn't answer her. He almost didn't want to.

Her elbow bumped into his side, jostling him nearly into a passing man with an armful of maps. "Sorry," he said, then immediately began to question if his articulation was too noticeable even in that single word.

"Aleksander?" His friend nearly sang his name, which would have sent blush to his cheeks were his head not reeling. "Right about what?" she repeated.

A tug stopped them both. Her eyes bored into his, so intensely he had to look away. In his attempt to escape, he found Inaya's Apothecary once more.

The answer he gave came out so quiet, he wasn't entirely able to hear it himself.

"I don't belong here."

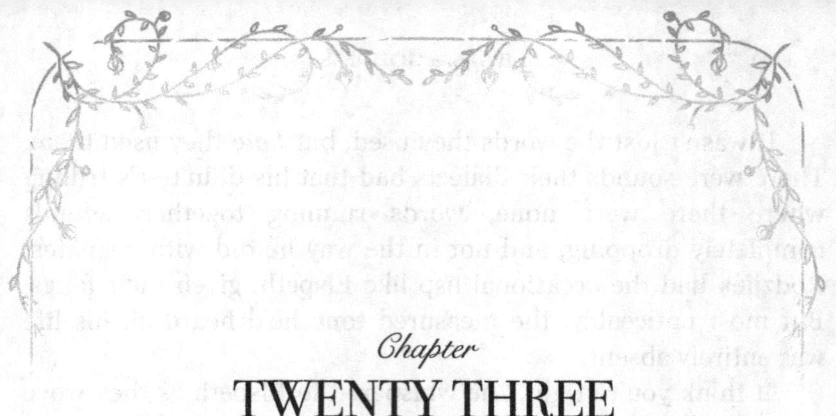

TWENTY THREE

After a moment, where the noise around him began to die and turn to a garbled mess, Elspeth shoved into him with a hearty laugh. "None of us do, Aleksander, that's what growing up in demesnes do to a person. Now come on, I'm hungry. That was a long walk—we should find something to eat, don't you think?"

"El, look at me." His chest tightened. "Do I look like a person who belongs here?"

Her eyebrows scrunched together, nearly making one long caterpillar across her forehead. "Who looks like a person who belongs anywhere? It's a large town remarkably close to a manor—there are all kinds of people here. You're fine."

But he wasn't fine. She was completely missing the point. He had passed among the people in the city at the feet of his castle home all his life, and had somehow, foolishly, thought he was one of them. Or at least, that he could be...if he tried hard enough.

Being here made that idea feel immeasurably stupid.

Swallowing his words, he stuffed his hands in the pockets of his fur coat and followed Elspeth's winding path through the square. He didn't speak further on the topic—he wished he didn't think more about it, but it couldn't be helped. As they walked along the main road, he scanned the scenery, the people. There were few parallels to be found to the polished streets of Brewith, even down to the smells. And yet he felt as though he should belong. As though it were wrong for him to feel so out of place.

Try as he might, he couldn't dredge up memories of his first five years, and that house with his parents and their blurry faces. Varek was right, on the balcony. Aleksander should have grown up in a town like this.

Someone bumped his shoulder, and as his wide eye met the indifferent stare of this stranger, something like relief flooded him.

Maybe Elspeth was right. Here they were, just two strange kids wandering the streets of a gorgeous, though small, city. One he'd never truly visited, unless one were to count the time he'd split off and cried in front of a random girl who bought a statuette of his friend. He certainly didn't, and by the way Elspeth grabbed his arm and pulled him across the square to buy small jelly treats coated in powdered sugar, he assumed she didn't either.

He stayed silent as she spoke to the vendor, nodding at the flavor choices as the old Ölmesuz woman listed them. A withered hand wrapped up the ones they selected in parchment and passed them across. From within her vest, Elspeth withdrew a single gold piece and laid it on the counter.

The woman's eyes grew wide. "Oh, dear, that is too much."

Elspeth shook her head. "Keep it. It wasn't mine anyway." She dissuaded the woman's concern with a wink. "Don't worry, I was given it to spend as I please." Only then did the dark bronze of the vendor's face gather like curtains on the side of a wide, genuine smile.

She winked back. "Alright then. You two have a lovely day."

Aleksander ignored the warmth now burning within his chest and smiled at his friend, only speaking once they were out of her earshot. "Did you snag that from me?"

"Oh, no." The parchment rustling partially silenced the low roll of Elspeth's laugh. "It was given to me by Lord Asghar this morning. I said we might be stopping in to town and he told me to use it wisely. Want one?"

Pinched between two of her fingers was a cube of the confection. Powdered sugar dropped off in small puffs each time she took a step.

"Why not." As it hit his tongue, the sweetness washed over him, followed quickly by the strong floral note of rose.

Aleksander did not notice he stopped walking until he looked up to see Elspeth in front of him by a few paces, grinning wildly, the open parcel still held carefully in her cupped hands.

"This is amazing."

"I know."

"I need more of this."

"I have more." She giggled, bouncing towards him foot-to-foot. Before Aleksander could open his mouth to respond or ask for another or say anything in general, her fingers interlaced with his. With one strong tug, he stumbled down the street behind her, laughing.

Even as his boots refused to gain a solid footing on the dusty cobblestones, his heart soared.

They wandered through the town, picking out shops to visit when they were less busy, pointing at vendors wares that twinkled in the sunlight, and giggling at the vulgar shapes of some of the statues for fertility. There were two necklaces Elspeth spotted on a stall, and one dress in the window of a very busy shop. She'd pressed her fingers gingerly to the glass, oohing over the olive silk, the embroidery, the beading.

Aleksander nearly offered to buy it for her, until they both looked down and saw it priced at a hundred and thirteen gold coins.

Eyes wide, Elspeth spun on her heel. "I'm going to have to forget I ever saw that dress," she muttered, looping her arm through Aleksander's once more and dragging him down the street.

"Oh!" she exclaimed, pointing at the corner shop that had all sorts of hats in the windows. "The hat shop! Asghar said there was a tavern down the street from that. He said the food was good but they also have a live band!"

For a moment, Aleksander debated if a tavern was safe. He'd heard stories from Janek of the seedy men that frequented places like that. Thieves and drunks, soldiers with no merit—never mind that Janek had a favorite tavern in Brewith. He'd still told Aleksander they weren't safe places, especially for women.

But Elspeth's grip tightened on his hand, and her mention of a live band settled in his mind.

They could dance.

◊ ✳ ◊

THE TAVERN WASN'T busy, not by a long shot. Just past midday, most of the others in there had books, journals, or other projects alongside their plates, and hardly any were sipping from the tankards Aleksander knew were usually reserved for hard drink.

A Rodzjiek woman sat at the bar, a book open in one hand and a fork with a scoop of potato in the other. She didn't glance up from the page as Elspeth slid onto a stool a few down from her, though the Ölmesuz behind the bar immediately appeared before them. As his opalescent eyes met Aleksander's, he slung a dishrag over his shoulder.

"What brings you two in here so early in the day?" His voice rumbled in a similar way to Varek's, though not as weary. There was a clarity to it that seemed long worn from the mercenary's own.

"We're looking for a meal," Elspeth said, her gaze wandering the interior.

Aleksander tried his best not to look around. It was nice, from the corners of his eye. Not the dim den of sin Janek had made taverns out to be. The ceiling seemed to have small patterns painted along the rafters, and the lamps hanging from them were incredibly reminiscent of the ones he'd seen littered throughout Chione's library. Still, he saw the way the man's eyebrow raised at Elspeth's clear awe, and opted to do his best to not appear as new to this place as she clearly was.

"Well," he said with a great breath, "we have them! Lunch is finished for now, though we do have an after-lunch snack board available, and dinner will be ready to be served in just a few hours."

"How many hours is a few more hours?"Aleksander asked.

The woman seated beside them took a bite and glanced up from her novel, catching Aleksander's eyes and nodding before stifling a grin as her gaze landed on Elspeth. "We've finally convinced them to make *zure*."

"Probably two hours, at the longest," the man said. "But you're welcome to wait here—band is on their way for the evening, they'll start playing soon."

"What's *zure*?" Elspeth whispered, leaning further towards the other woman.

Dark eyes, like fertile soil, narrowed ever so slightly, confusion drawing lines around them. "You're Rodzjiek, yes?"

Elspeth grinned, showing off her fangs. "Yes."

"And you've never had *zure*?"

"No, I was raised mainly with Zekharyans."

The woman's eyes softened. With a deep breath that visibly shifted the blouse beneath her embroidered vest, she sat taller, marked the page in her book by folding down the corner, and slid it into the satchel hanging off the back of the chair. "Ishyahu, I'll have dinner with these two. Add their soup to my tab when the time comes."

He nodded. "Of course." His duties of gathering plates and wiping tables soon removed him from behind the bar, and it was just Aleksander and Elspeth, hands still entwined, a few seats away from this woman with her long, wavy, black hair and deep eyes. She scooped one of her two braids over her shoulders and brushed a few flyways out of her face before acknowledging them again.

"Come, sit closer," she said. When neither of them moved, she flashed a bright, fanged grin not unlike Elspeth's. "I'm not going to bite, scoot. I just want to talk."

Elspeth's hand slid free from Aleksander's. The stool grated against the wooden floors as she pulled it out and climbed onto the red cushion.

Something felt strange to Aleksander. This woman was nice —there was nothing she'd done or said to make this situation seem dangerous. But this was a city, a city he hadn't been to, a city where no one knew him. And they were in a tavern. Aoife, once again, was not on his hip, and memories of how he wished he'd had her last time replayed in his mind. He and Elspeth were just existing, entirely on their own.

But Elspeth clearly wanted to speak to her. So, as much as this woman's demeanor and general existence felt off to him, he climbed onto the stool beside her and leaned with both arms on the counter.

The woman shoved a large bite of potatoes and beef into her mouth, washing it down quickly with a sparkling glass of what appeared to be a cider of some sort, and turned in her seat to fully face the pair.

Her face was round, with a strong chin and large, downturned eyes ringed with thick lashes. Lips painted a fading red parted in a smile.

Aleksander would have been foolish to not acknowledge that, as beautiful as this woman was, there was a strange element of ferocity to her. He found himself both drawn in to her gaze as much as he wanted to cower beneath it.

"I'm Marzena."

"I'm Elspeth," his friend said quickly, "this is my friend... Edwin."

Marzena snorted. "Oh, that's a Zekharyan name, alright."

"Is that a problem?" Aleksander asked. Within his chest, his heart was pounding a frantic beat. Still, it was not enough to force him up and out of the tavern.

"No, no," Marzena took a slow sip of her cider. "Not unless you're one of those Zekharyans who think we're more monster than man."

His brows furrowed. "No. I mean, I'm no stranger to what

people say, but I've been hearing there are more and more people welcoming non-Zekharyans into their courts. There are Ölmesuz in the royal court now, you know. I've even heard of some Rodzjiekim being held in high esteem by the royal family."

The healer he frequently sent people to appeared in his mind for a flash, with her soft moss-green eyes and brown hair the shade of old cedar.

Marzena's eyes rolled beneath her lashes. "Sure, we're given positions as healers and soldiers within courts, but that's not the same as being accepted as equals. There are no Rodzjiek lords or ladies, but look who controls our fief: Lord Femi Asghar. A man whose history lies across the sea."

"They're not even from here, and still, *we're* closer to animals," Elspeth muttered. Her eyes shot up to the man behind the counter. "Sorry."

"Don't worry about it, you're right, this isn't our land the way it is yours. And I wouldn't say animals," Ishyahu's eyes adopted a far off, dreamy veil to them, "more like...spirits. Like something from a folktale, easily twisted good or bad depending on the stance of who is telling the story."

Aleksander's friend nodded. "Like the Dzera."

The name sent a jolt of discomfort down his spine. Even in the center of town, for a moment, he felt It watching him.

"It's the teeth, we get it," Marzena said, running her tongue over the sharp points in her mouth. "Humans have flat teeth, Ölmesuz have flat teeth but silly ears—no offense, Ishyahu."

Their eyes shifted to where he was in the tavern, a stack of plates in one hand. His ears bounced with a laugh. "None taken, Marzena."

She shrugged, running a worn, calloused hand over the mouth of her glass. "We've got the fangs, the eyes, the *magic* that reminds them we're born from the Untamed and all that lies beyond. Same way the Mekartlim have the wings as a reminder that they're from the mountains and the skies. That we're always something they'll not fully understand, nor fully control."

"They tried to get me to file my teeth down when I was little,"

Elspeth said with a chuckle. For the first time since she'd first told that story, however, there was no humor in her laugh. No sparkle in her eyes. When she'd tell Aleksander, she glazed past it, like it was nothing more than stating what the weather was like, or what color the walls of her childhood bedroom were. Her thumb nail fitted over her left fang, and as she flicked it, Aleksander's heart sank.

He'd not noticed it before, but that one was flatted more than the other.

Marzena nodded. "They tried that with a lot of us. I see they got you a little."

Elspeth shrugged. "Yeah, but I bit them, so they stopped."

Pain churned in Aleksander's gut. "You've mentioned that before. Have they stopped?" he said. His voice seemed soft, weak —unimportant. "I mean...I know there were rules around what you all could or couldn't do for jobs in Zekhar, until a decade or so ago, but..."

"They've stopped. Mostly." The woman nodded towards Elspeth. "I'm guessing your friend here was one of the unlucky ones, born in an outer village that turned a blind eye to such cruel practices."

Elspeth shook her head. "It was in the Keep. My commander didn't like us."

"They're just teeth," Aleksander's voice shook. "Normal teeth, like I have, but...just that little bit different. Special. None of you would be Rodzjiek without them."

Marzena's thick brows lifted. "Well, we're always Rodzjiek, with or without fangs. If you have fire in your bones and trees in your chest you're one of us. It's not about appearances. But some Zekharyans hope to make us a little more *tame* if we don't have them."

After a moment, her eyes flitted from his to the girl between them. When they landed on Elspeth's face, those dark depths welled with care. She extended a hand and gently placed it over the one still marked, ever so faintly, with burns.

"You may have a name from them, but you're Rodzjiek.

Right?"

Elspeth nodded, a wavering grin forming. "Right."

The older woman patted her hand and drained her drink. In the thin shafts of light coming through the windows, the flickering of the lanterns above them, Aleksander had initially thought Marzena was older than both of them by a good decade or so. The lines around her eyes and mouth were too deep for her to be in her twenties, but too fine for her to be much older than thirty. Yet, as she stared at her cup, her thumb absently flitting along the etched detail near the base, Aleksander couldn't help but parallel her to Varek.

Don't Rodzjiek also have extended lives?

"I've got a few errands to run," she said, scooping up and chewing at the last of her meal. "But meet me back here for dinner in two hours. I'll pay for your *zure*, I wasn't lying." Her skirts ruffled as she slid off the stool and hit the floor, standing just a hair taller than him. A hand, calloused as well as wrinkled, patted Elspeth's cheek. "You're going to love it."

The pair watched as she left, and once the door swung closed behind her, Elspeth turned to face Aleksander.

Deep within him, that pained ache started twisting his guts again. There was so much going on in her eyes.

"I love her," she laughed, "we're coming back here for dinner."

But it was a strained sound. There was a tightness around her eyes, her mouth. Her eyebrows were pulled together slightly too far. It made the whole of her expression desperate, even if she didn't intend to appear so.

"Are you okay?" Aleksander slipped a hand onto her wrist. She instinctively flipped her hand over and wove her fingers with his.

"Yeah." But she hopped down off the stool and tugged Aleksander with her. "Let's go wander a little more! I think I've finally decided which necklace to buy with all the coin Asghar gave me."

Aleksander let her drag him from the tavern, from the

warmth radiating from the wood interior and out into the chilled autumn afternoon. It was enough for him to have the unease churning in his stomach. It was enough for the voice at the back of his mind to start bringing up what Chione said in the library, about how maybe the others in Zekhar were scared of the Zekharyans. Were scared of Aleksander in particular.

But now, with the unease in Elspeth's stride, the forced glow in her eyes, trying, *straining* to refocus on something different...

It was more than what Chione was saying.

More he'd have to figure out. More that... somehow...did not feel like blasphemy. Even though the voice in his head said it was.

Stepping into the cool sunshine, hand in hand with his friend, a wave of peace flooded him, despite the war still raging in his chest and his mind.

Elspeth's eyes caught his, and she smiled.

The Presence, somehow, smiled too.

Chapter

TWENTY FOUR

B Y THE TIME THE CLOCK in the square was ringing four, Asghar's coin purse was a lot lighter and Elspeth's appearance was a lot shinier. Her eyes glittered, the confusion and discomfort from earlier finally having gone. Dangling from her ears were two red beads, polished to a shine, and around her neck was a string of red and gold to match.

The decision had been clear, she'd told him striding up to the stand. The man across from them greeted them as they returned, his beard scraggly but eyes bright as he pulled out the box once more.

"Like rowan berries," he'd remarked as Elspeth lifted an earring, peering into the dusty mirror hanging just a bit too high. "For protection."

"Protection from what?" Aleksander asked.

"Everything," Elspeth had responded, slipping the earrings in. "But mostly monsters. How much?"

"For you?" The old Rodzjiek scrubbed at his dark beard. "Twenty silver."

Elspeth raised an eyebrow. "And what if it was him paying?"

"Thirty."

Elspeth's head threw back with a laugh, eyes shut and fangs flashing. "How about fifteen and I get the necklace to match?"

"Twenty, and you get the necklace to match," he'd countered, a matching smile peeking from his untrimmed mustache.

Walking away, Aleksander's mind swam. The man had increased the price just by looking at him. Once they had gotten out of earshot, Aleksander had brought it up only for her to laugh at how dramatic he was being, but the fact remained.

How much have I been overcharged? Has this always been going on, even in Brewith?

No matter how serious he tried to sound when bringing up those fears to Elspeth, she still would buckle over with a laugh, tell him he was being silly, and drag him further down the road. She bounced along the path back to the tavern, and as they approached, Aleksander actually found himself excited to see Marzena again.

As strange as the woman was, his apprehension towards her, he decided, was purely born of his own anxiety around new things. Being raised in the castle his whole life, everything was some sort of a routine. From his prayers in the morning, to his training, to his daily goings on—even down to how he got himself dressed and what he said while brushing out his hair.

He ran a hand through it now, ruffled by the cold wind as it was. It curled around his ears and brushed his eyebrows. The ends got stuck in the collar of his doublet. It had gotten longer— almost to the point it was in that dream he'd had months ago.

His stomach twinged.

He still felt uncomfortable whenever he remembered that nightmare.

Especially now—knowing that Varek did indeed, at some level, have plans to turn against the crown. He told himself it would never matter the man's reasoning, or on what level he commits his treason. And yet, some small voice in the back of Aleksander's mind kept telling him he was overreacting.

Aleksander clenched his jaw.

What was Varek's reasoning?

A tug on his hand slowed his steps, dragging him back to the present. He heard Elspeth's teeth clack together in a grimace.

"Oh, looks busy," Elspeth muttered, slowing her steps as they approached the tavern once more.

In contrast to when they'd been there earlier, the windows to the street were thrown wide open. The panes, filled with abstract stained glass, scattered not only the fading sunlight across the square, but the beginnings of flickers from the street lamps.

Aleksander glanced towards the lighter part of the sky, where, past buildings and trees, he could see the lower range of the Pozhontecs. Beyond that hovered the sun, just beginning to dip behind the smaller mountains.

He'd never understood why the peaks in the north were so jagged, so tall, and these were much smaller. He supposed it had to do with the curve of their earth or the way the land had been formed, but he had never been good at remembering things like that from school. Besides, those kinds of topics were left for the scholars, not the soldiers.

"Should we just... go in?" Elspeth stared at the door, propped open.

The sound from the band echoed out with the chatter from the patrons.

Aleksander shrugged. "I suppose. I don't expect them to invite us in, so if we want to go, then we will have to walk in."

Elspeth elbowed him with a snort.

He smiled at the gesture and nudged her back.

The fading sun gilded her hair and skin with a pink glow, bringing out the chilled blush in her cheeks and nose. A puff of breath blew from her lips and she looked up at him.

"Alright. Let's go then."

Squeezing her hand, Aleksander took the lead.

He wasn't sure why she was so nervous, but he didn't stop to ask. Now wasn't the time, and she didn't need to be pressured into explaining the workings of her mind.

He felt her strong hand resist momentarily before falling forward into timed steps, the pair eventually entering the tavern nearly side by side.

"Hey, you two!" a voice called.

Aleksander's eyes darted around the scene before him. Patrons sat at each table, more than one at a time now. The booths in the corners and along the walls were nearly packed, some were so full a townsperson or two sat on the arm rests of the benches or the tables themselves. Women sat in men's laps, drinks were passed around—this was what he'd expected. This was what Janek had warned him of.

Straight across from the door, tables had been cleared in favor of a band. The music was not familiar to Aleksander—it was not the jaunty, smooth tones of the tunes he heard at court. It was so much more lively. Violins and accordions and flutes melded together in what he expected to be a horrible display of "art," but instead was something that sent goosebumps down his arms. An Ölmesuz woman sang with short, lilting, peaking tones at the front of the stage. Behind her, a Rodzjiek man with a thick beard and a black brimmed cap keyed along on an accordion. The band was comprised of mainly those two peoples, save for the single Zekharyan in the back with her smooth black hair pulled up into a bun. She sat with a bodhran and a wide smile, nodding at Aleksander once his eyes lit on her.

He smiled, and nodded back.

"Don't ignore us!" The voice shouted again over the chaos, and Aleksander finally found the speaker by the bar, a glass of cider in hand once again.

Marzena waved them over.

"Come meet my friends!"

Elspeth squeezed his hand and dragged him through the crowd, even as that slight tug of nervousness began in his chest.

Marzena grinned wildly as they approached, her lipstick a bright red, contrasting her tan skin and the pale, ivory fangs peeking out from them. "Come take your seats! Hope you don't mind it's not just me anymore," she said, glancing over her shoulder. "Everyone, this is Elspeth and Edwin! They're having supper with us tonight."

Aleksander craned his neck to take in the selection of people behind her.

"Good to meet you," one of the men says, nodding at Aleksander. His eyes were a pale, bright blue—paler than any Zekharyan's he'd ever seen. Almost white. With a smile, his fangs came into view.

Rodzjiek, Aleksander thought, *okay.*

"I'm Cezary." He reached a hand around Marzena, and Aleksander felt nearly out of control has his own hand floated up to meet his. The man let out a laugh. "What, are we too startling of characters for you? Must be used to the palace, eh?"

Aleksander's blood froze. "What?" he squeaked.

Marzana threw her head back and elbowed Cezary, flapping her hand dismissively. "Come on, you think they'd let one of us into the palace?" She snorted as she sipped her drink. "No, but he has a point. Neither of you talk very village. Where are you from?"

"Duke Elmere's Keep, to the northeast," Elspeth answered, sliding between Aleksander and Cezary to shake his hand as well. "That's where I was raised."

Aleksander was thankful for the redirection and the explanation. His racing pulse calmed enough, and he took a deep breath, a nervous smile flitting onto his face. A single nod tied him to Elspeth's statement. He'd been to the Keep recently enough that he could fabricate a convincing enough story. "Thank you for letting us dine with you all," he managed.

"Of course," the man's eyes sparkled, and his laugh was soft despite how loud he was. With a slap on his thigh, he turned, gesturing to the others. "Lets get names out of the way—that's Piotr, Lena, Eliana, and—"

Any semblance of reassurance he'd gathered faded. Blood pounded, fresh and hot and terrified, in his ears. "Inaya," he said the name at the same as Cezary, and the man's face snapped around to him once more, decorated with a bright grin.

"You've met! Wonderful."

But Aleksander's eyes did not leave those of the old woman farthest down the counter from him. Beneath the wrinkles and drooping lids, her gaze did not leave him either.

Goddess, please do not let her say it. Keep her mouth shut, push the words from her mind—perhaps she is old and senile enough to have forgotten me. Forgotten us.

Aleksander nodded. It was tense. He could swear he heard his neck creak as his head slowly bobbed.

"Yes," came the weathered voice. "I remember him, he helped one of the mages at the manor buy supplies from my shop." A smile curved her wrinkled lips moments before it was covered by a mug. "Did your lady find success with the components I sold her?"

He blinked. Did she? He had to answer, it would seem far to strange to ignore the question, especially since she acknowledged that they did, indeed, know each other.

"Not yet," he answered, trying his best to draw in some of the slurred, joined speech patterns from Elspeth, "but I think she's getting close."

Her grin widened, head dipping in a slow, earnest nod. "Good. I'm glad to hear it."

"Ooh, working for a mage, are you?" Cezary's eyebrows bounced. "What's that like? Is she spooky and terrifying? I've heard Zekharyan mages are no more than witches."

"Oh, shut it Cezary, you know they say the same things about us."

Images of Carissa flashed through his mind—her towering over him when they were children, the corner-of-the-eye glares he was shot across many a feast table, even the way she leaned over Duke Halkin's desk and whispered poisonous words into his ear to convince him to let them bring Iscah...

The corner of his mouth twitched, hardly able to contain a smirk. "She certainly can be. Spooky and terrifying that is, I don't know if I'd consider her a witch."

"She's a fair mistress, though," Elspeth said, waving down the barkeep. "What do you all recommend here?"

The trio of Rodzjiekim and two attending Ölmesuz exchanged looks.

"How old are you?" Lena leaned back, her black eyes

scanning Elspeth.

"Sixteen," she responded. "I was born on the full moon of the month of Holy Fire, I think it was technically the fifteenth day."

Aleksander blinked at her. Her birthday was during their journey around Zekhar. The tail end of it, either right after or right before their battle with Lord Terrell, but... how had she not told him? Told anyone?

"She can have a *little* something," Marzena said, waving her hand in that way Aleksander had quickly become accustomed to. "She may not have the heart for it like most of us do, but that doesn't mean she can't partake. Besides," the bartender caught Marzena's gaze, and she nodded once, indicating for more drinks. Then, she fixed a smile back at the pair of them. "They'll need the energy if they wish to keep up with us tonight."

Something twisted in Aleksander's gut. This wasn't right, they shouldn't be partaking in the beverages this establishment offered. They weren't married—only married people drank wine. For the most part. At least, that's what he'd been told.

Still, Ishyahu set down an ornate crystal glass with a shimmering near-amber liquid in it for Elspeth, alongside a steaming bowl of *zure*.

Everyone watched intently as Elspeth stirred the mix a few times, bringing up chunks of meat and vegetables and the occasional cut of a boiled egg. Aleksander's own fist clutched his spoon, poised above the bowl placed before him. He wasn't about to eat before her. Not when this was *her* people's food.

"It's more of a spring soup," Lena said around the others, wringing her hands. "But they didn't make it this spring, so we finally convinced them to make it now."

"I brought most of the ingredients," Piotr said. It was the first time he'd spoken since Aleksander and Elspeth had sat down. His voice was melodic and smooth, yet held a gravelly ending to his sentences. His cheeks rounded with pride. "It was tough, since season's almost done for them. But I made sure it's all good."

Flashing a momentary smile, Elspeth's eyes darted down to

her spoon, raising a chunk of meat and whatever the broth was towards her lips.

She took a bite.

Marzena's face split into a grin as she chewed. "It's good, isn't it?"

After a moment, her shoulders shook and a strange choking sound came from her throat.

"Elspeth?" Aleksander's hands flew to her back, her shoulders—her spoon clattered into the bowl. His panic did not abate when she lifted her head, her eyes watering.

Then she swallowed, pressing the back of her hand to her nose. "I think my mom made me this," she whispered. Her voice cracked with each word. "I...she...she must have. I ate it sitting before the hearth, in... She... That was before she..."

Instinctively, Aleksander lifted his hand and swiped a tear before it trailed too far down her cheek.

Before she gave Elspeth up.

She sniffed, eyes wide as she stared at the bowl.

Aleksander wiped another tear. His friend smiled. "Try it." Her voice cracked. "It's really good."

Over her shoulder, every member of the group beamed.

IT WAS GOOD. A SORT of sour, savory flavor that washed over his tongue and sat in the corners of his mouth. Even after his bowl was empty, the back of this throat and jaw twinged, asking for more.

Marzena, Piotr, Cezary, and Lena took turns conversing with him and Elspeth—though, truth be told, mainly with her. Aleksander didn't mind one bit. The less he spoke, the less likely it was that he would be found out to be high born.

And with what they'd been sharing about their feelings towards Zekharyans, he figured just being one already made them wary enough.

After a lull where Elspeth finished her drink and the others began to stand and stretch, either to take their leave home or whatever else they had planned for the evening, the band struck up another tune.

The man on the accordion was playing as though his life depended on it, the other musicians doing their best to keep up.

Cezary whistled with the beat for a split second before looping his arm through Lena's and dragging her into the center of the floor.

Aleksander couldn't help the grin that spread across his face as he watched the pair of them jump and twirl and spin around each other. Their dancing was much less contained than that which he'd grown up around. Lena threw her head back, long hair not unlike the pale-brown of old wood trailing behind her in the single, long braid she wore. Cezary's eyes were nearly entirely hidden by his cheeks from how great his smile was.

The boy found himself tapping his foot along the support of the stool.

He should grab Elspeth, the way Cezary grabbed Lena, and drag her onto the floor. He didn't know the dance, and he was certain he would stumble his way through it, but as others joined in, the notion dawned on him that this song did not have a planned dance. Everyone moved in their own way, only the rhythm of their movements determined by the music. Some spun nearly without stopping, until they whirled to a nearby table for balance giggling all the while. Others kept up a more methodical style. And still others shifted from moment to moment, entirely driven by the feeling of the song.

It thrummed in his blood. The joy of the tune was infectious, he had to—

"I don't know, I suppose I figured they would get over this and I wouldn't deal with it in my lifetime," Elspeth's voice rose over the music, catching Aleksander from his thoughts and the music. Before he could turn to look at her, she dropped her voice again. "Sorry, it's just... With all that's going on, I'm worried."

"And that's understandable, *złotka*, but trust me. We've made it through this before and we will again. We're strong, you and I. All of us are. And we're even stronger together. You've always got friends, and a home—whether that's here in Hadiqin or deep in the Untamed. Or even past the Pozhontecs, where our people still hold power."

The music left Aleksander's body altogether. His fingers stilled on his thigh, the pattern they'd been tapping in time with his boots dying immediately.

"Thank you, Marzena." Elspeth's voice was even lower now. "I appreciate it."

She doesn't want me to hear, he noted. Not only was she

quiet, but his friend had begun to lean quite far from him, her chin resting in a hand propped on the bar.

"I...I'm not lying when I say I'm proud of it, it's just..."

"It doesn't feel safe," Marzena finished for her.

His friend nodded. "Yeah. That." A cup scraped against the wood of the counter. "It's something I've heard Rodzjiekim strive to perfect, and it comes so easy," she confided. "It scares me. I... what if I lose control?"

At this, Aleksander looked over.

Marzena's brows drew close. Her gaze flicked to his for a moment, before returning to Elspeth's, whose back was still solidly turned to Aleksander. "Most of us in the cities struggle to keep a candle lit these days. Add on to that the fact that some people still think you're going to kill them just because you have fangs and...it's hard, I know." Her hands reached for Elspeth's, taking them gently. "But you have a gift. Keep up your studies. Talk to that librarian more, she sounds like good folk. And if you ever want another taste of home, or anything, you come find me, okay? And if not me, then others of us."

The few wavy strands that had fallen free from Elspeth's braid bounced in the candlelight as she nodded. "I will. Thank you."

Marzena's lips stretched across her face in a broad grin, deepening every line of age and experience she'd gathered. She must have been at least forty, Aleksander finally assumed. One hand patted Elspeth's cheek before waving down Ishyahu and ordering another drink.

"Worrying for your friend?"

The quiet voice rumbling at Aleksander's shoulder caused him to jump, which in turn caused Inaya to snort out a laugh.

"Please, it's just me."

Aleksander's eyes grew wide. "Sh, you shouldn't—"

"Oh, hush," a withered hand flicked away his admonition. The old apothecary leaned further on the counter, scooping a newly refilled glass of red wine towards her. "If I wanted to out you, I would have already," with a smirk, she added on in a whisper, "your holiness."

He pressed his lips together tightly. The chilled Presence clamped its hands down on his shoulders, the small, beginning ripples of anxiety fluttering through him.

"You didn't answer my question though, are you worried for her?"

"Why should I be?"

The old Ölmesuz laughed. "Oh, that's your question to answer. I've heard from a bird or two that you're looking in to things your sister would not appreciate."

Aleksander's brows pushed together so tightly, the skin of his forehead felt as though it was near to bursting under the pressure. Despite the stretching, burning sensation along his nose and forehead, he kept the expression and shook his head. "What are you talking about?"

Her wrinkled lips pressed together. "Nothing, I suppose. Nothing I need to say out loud." Two glistening, citrine eyes slid to him. "I just hope you're as smart as everyone says you are."

Draining her glass, she stood, patting the table. "Ishyahu, thank you for a lovely meal and drink as always."

The Ölmesuz man bowed, grin wide. "Always a pleasure, *h'met'r* Inaya."

She pushed her long hair over her shoulder and adjusted the robes cascading over the top of her gown that appeared to be woven from starlight itself. The woman cast one final glance to Aleksander, eyes winking in a partial smile. "You have a good night, *Edwin*."

Despite her use of his fake name, his skin still crawled. Deep within him, his heart began to pound. She knew too much. Someone had told her what was going on with him—

Someone was watching him.

His head began to swim again, and he was grateful he'd refused Marzena's offer of a drink. Along with fear and frustration, anger began to curl in the pit of his stomach.

Suddenly, he couldn't stop himself from scanning the crowd. Spies could be anywhere. For Varek or the Scourge themself, he didn't know, but...

Herself, Aleksander corrected himself. *If she is indeed still a "she" in this lifetime.*

As his gaze drifted, he found a shock of dark auburn spinning in the center of the dance floor. It was enough to shake him out of his trance, if for a moment.

Elspeth spun with Piotr—he was older than her by a good decade or so, and they both laughed as she stumbled through steps she'd never been trained for.

Warmth bloomed in his chest. It had been too long since he'd seen her face that open, that bright. In fact, maybe he never had. There were glimpses of the Elspeth before him in his memory, but never truly this vibrant. He smiled.

"She's a natural," Marzena mused quietly.

Aleksander nodded, even as Elspeth tripped over Piotr's feet for the fiftieth time.

"I hope she stays safe wherever you lot are."

Again, Aleksander's brows furrowed. "What do you mean?"

Marzena finished her drink, pushing the tankard as far from her as she could. "I mean, it's not always safe for girls like her during times like these. The... What's the crown calling them in all their bulletins? The groups of Scourge-sympathizers popping up around the country?"

He swallowed hard. "Blights."

"Right," she said, "the Blights."

The pair's eyes turned towards Elspeth, still twirling, cheeks red and eyes closed.

"You wouldn't understand, purely because you're Zekharyan," the woman's voice was low and dark, but not cruel, as she spoke. "But for us, times of unrest are always worrisome. Anyone looking or acting even a little off is cause for concern. And now we have these people so full of hate to deal with alongside the..." Those dark pools turned to him. "I just... Promise me, Edwin, that you'll keep her safe. Not just from the Blights, though they'll want her if they find her. She's young and talented, moldable. Keep her from them. And from..." something flickered in her eyes. A remnant of that fire he'd come to search for in Elspeth. "From others."

His heart beat hard. He didn't want to say it, didn't want to finish the sentence for her...yet—"You mean the crown."

Marzena's eyes widened, thick lashes blinking rapidly. "Yes. I do."

Gazing back out at Elspeth, his mind swirled. Whether he believed it was rational or not, Chione had voiced the same concern. As stupid as it was, as blasphemous as it felt in his very soul, this was El they were talking about. His El.

He nodded. "I promise."

The tension leaving Marzena was nearly tangible as she deflated in the corner of his vision.

"Thank you."

Elspeth's eyes caught his, and he smiled.

She was brilliant. Bright. Beautiful. For a moment, he wondered if this could have been her life had she not joined the service of the Elmeres at such a young age.

Before he knew what he was doing, his feet hit the floor.

The song ended and Piotr guided Elspeth, gasping and giggling, to the counter. Ishyahu pushed a small glass of water towards her, which she eagerly gulped down. A few drops dribbled down her chin, making her lips glisten as she bared her fangs in a wild grin.

The Presence danced within him, and his own pulse hastened its pace. Energy built in his chest. He wanted to scream, sing, cry, laugh, hug her and squish her face in his hands and—

He blinked rapidly. That rush of feral joy was nearly enough to wash out all the panic which had been building prior.

Another song started up, and Elspeth's eyes sparked, nearly catching her lashes aflame.

Aleksander caught her hand, spinning her back towards him before she could make another escape onto the dance floor. "Can I dance with you?"

In an expression he thought nearly impossible, her smile

split from ear to ear. With a tug, they were out on the floor, her hand firmly on his bicep, his on her waist, the other two intertwined with no intention of ever letting go.

"Just follow my lead!" she shouted over the music.

Aleksander stumbled, his gaze fixed on their feet. He was smiling, he realized, despite all the mistakes.

The warmth of her hand met his jaw, tilting his head up.

His heart skipped when his eyes locked onto hers, so bright and full of a kind of life he'd never seen in them before.

"Just watch me, don't look down," she said.

He nodded, hesitant smile splitting into a full grin.

How foolish he had been to ever look away.

Chapter

TWENTY SIX

"I DON'T KNOW WHAT YOU'RE thinking," Elspeth whispered, pressing her back to his door. "But I'm thinking two things right now."

Her eyelids began to flutter down over her eyes, but she blinked herself back to life, just in time for Aleksander to reach around her and turn the knob to open the door. She stumbled back. A crack echoed as she accidentally threw the door into a side table.

"I'm thinking," he started towards his wardrobe, "that we change, splash our faces with fresh water, and go to sleep."

Her hands clasped behind her back. "Oh, no, you're not thinking what I'm thinking at all."

"Then enlighten me." Aleksander began to undo the clasps on his doublet, cringing away from the awful feeling of the wool, now damp with the cold autumn mist they'd walked the last twenty minutes back to Aarua in.

Boots sounded behind him, followed by the *frush* of blankets. "I think we stay up, look at the stars, talk."

"Why?"

"Because I want to. Because you're fun to talk to."

He scoffed. A single glance confirmed that she had indeed sprawled herself on his bed once more. "We talked all day today."

"Not all day!" She sat up, brows furrowing. "Are you...bored of me?"

At that simple statement, at the genuine hurt simmering behind the humor, pain shot through his chest. He spun to face her. "No, never. Don't say things like that."

A smile crept into her cheeks. "So can we talk more?"

"About what?"

"I don't know!" Her hands flapped at her sides, patting the quilt. Exasperation bent her shoulders inward. "Things! People can just talk about *things*, Aleksander, it's what friends do."

He studied her for a long moment. The pull of sleep had already started to undo bits of hair from her braid, drag down her eyelashes in erratic flutters. That bend to her shoulders and spine got worse until she was sitting like an old woman without her cane to support her.

"Go get changed, stop laying on my bed in wet clothes." With three strides he gathered her hands in his and pulled her to her feet. "Then come back and we can talk."

Still held within his own, her fingers curled into excited claws. "Open the window, it's so nice out!"

In a breath of whirling fabric and swaying hair, she was sliding out the door.

"It's raining, El!" A sigh heaved from his chest, his call falling on deaf ears. Slow steps scuffed their way back to his wardrobe where he finished taking off his disguise and slipping into his normal nightclothes—soft linen pants and a matching shirt.

For a moment, he wondered why he didn't protest. His entire body ached in a way it never did from his usual forms of dancing, his belly was full of soup, and as exhaustion curled its heavy fingers into his joints, all he wanted to do was collapse on his nice, plush bed and let the darkness of sleep claim him.

Yet he found himself undoing the latch on the window and pushing it open just enough for a damp breath of cold air to swirl in.

"Okay," came the low word from his doorway. "I'm changed,

happy now?"

Aleksander said nothing. Just leaned on the windowsill, letting the rain dapple the face he'd just dried off. Moments passed and a figure took up residence beside him. She leaned forward in a similar way, eyes closed. Casting one glance her way resulted in him staring. At the way her lashes fluttered when the rain hit her eyes. The way her nostrils flared with each deep breath. The way her hair shimmered as it fell over her shoulders.

The way her lips parted ever so slightly, curving at the corners.

For a moment, he saw himself cupping her jaw the way Janek held Carissa's, gently bringing his face to hers—

"The world just smells so good tonight," she whispered.

His cheeks burned, and his gaze shot out into the darkness. There was that warmth again, that energy that collected in his chest and made his heart race much too fast.

The smell, she'd mentioned how it smelled.

In an attempt to steady his breathing, he slowly inhaled.

It was sweet, the night rain. Autumn decay mixed with the earthy freshness of the water, and even as goosebumps began to raise on his arms, he found he couldn't move from his spot.

Clearing his throat, he shifted. "Wh—what do you want to talk about?"

She shrugged. "We don't have to talk. We can just stand here together."

He scoffed, hands shaking lightly even as the burn in his face abated and his racing thoughts calmed. Elspeth was right, though. They could just stand together, and everything would be completely fine.

He took another deep breath. And another. And then, he closed his eyes too.

How long they stood there, he didn't know. But eventually, a weight began to press on his left arm, and eventually, hands looped around his wrist and up under his arm to steady the body bearing that weight.

"Today was a good day," she whispered.

"It was."

The rain began to shift from a light mist to a consistent drizzle. The dark evening coupled with the rain was enough to make anything beyond the glow reflecting off the windows deeper than pitch.

Straightening up, Elspeth backed away. "What are you doing?"

"Closing the window, the rain is getting worse."

She didn't have to speak for Aleksander to know she was pouting. Clumsy fingers pulled the window back in and latched it. "I want to go to bed," he muttered.

A long minute passed and he turned to his friend, waiting patiently for a response. She pursed her lips and offered another shrug. "What?"

"I want to go to bed, that means it's time for you to leave."

Any exhaustion she was holding dissipated for a moment, replaced with dramatized shock. Her hand slapped against her chest like she'd been hit with an arrow. "I can't believe you're telling me to get out."

He chuckled, but pushed himself off the sill. "I am."

Her head flopped back with a sigh, eyes wide, but then that tired smile crept back in. "Thank you for coming with me today. If I haven't said that already."

"I mean," the pair shuffled towards the door. "It was mostly my idea, if you remember."

"Still, I appreciate it." She stopped before the door. "Are you sure we can't talk more?"

"I think we're both much too tired for that." His shoulders rose with a heavy, slow breath. Every muscle in his body felt as though it was vibrating, as if the simple act of keeping him on his feet was more than enough to wear them to failure.

"Dancing was fun," Elspeth continued.

He raised an eyebrow—a gesture she met with a simple, dazzling smile.

She's not going to let me go so easy.

Heaving another sigh, Aleksander stepped aside. "Elspeth,

would you like to come in and talk a little longer?"

Her eyes blazed. "Oh that's such a nice offer! I'd love to." Smooth, flowing steps took her around Aleksander and directly to his bed, where she once again sprawled out, taking half of it for herself. "I think your bed is nicer than mine."

"They're all the same."

"Mm, I'm not so sure."

With a laugh, Aleksander flopped down on the other half. The moment his body hit the plush quilt and sank further, cradled by the mattress and all the down within, sleep began to pull at him. Any movement he wished to make, from yawning to stretching to simply breathing, was slow and laborious. Tension leeched away from his muscles. For the first time in a long time, his brain fell quiet. "You realize we're not talking again," he asked.

A squeak was all he got in response as his friend stretched indulgently over the cushions. "Dancing," she finally said. "Dancing was fun."

"You said that."

"But it was."

He exhaled sharply, the only thing close to a laugh he could muster. "It was."

"Save a dance for me at the solstice. I never know what to do with all those courtiers."

"Of course." His head rolled to the side, catching her profile in the dim candlelight. "Court is an...interesting place. For newcomers, of course, but... I don't know. I don't think I'll ever be used to such grand parties."

Silence fell again, punctuated by the occasional patter of rain pushed by a gust of wind and the rhythmic breathing of the girl beside him. His eyes fluttered shut, and even that began to fade away.

"Aleksander," she whispered. "Can I ask you something?"

"Of course."

"We're friends, right?"

At this, Aleksander did laugh. "What would we be

otherwise?"

"I'm just checking."

Something in her tone hit home in Aleksander's chest. His eyes opened, heart shifting from that calm, steady, contented beat to a frantic erratic pace driven by fear. "El," he rolled onto his side. "What's wrong? You don't actually think we *aren't* friends, do you?"

"No," she rolled too, propping herself up on her elbow. "No, I just...wanted to make sure. With everything going on, I..." Her face fell. "I talked to Chione, you know."

He nodded.

"And aside from giving me advice in regards to my fire, she told me...well, that girls like me get killed by boys like you. Zekharyans, I mean. Especially..."

"People who worship Tulathne," he finished.

She nodded.

"She...told me about that stuff too," Aleksander confided. "But I promise it's nothing more than craziness. I'd never do that. It won't happen to you."

"See, that's what she said you'd say."

However tired he was did not beat out the panic building in his chest. "Do you not believe me?"

Elspeth snarled, pushing herself up to sit. "I don't know! I don't know, okay, because I've heard stories of this all my life from other low-born, especially Ölmesuz and a the few Rodzjiekim I had with me. And I want to believe you because I—" her eyes met his. She froze. "Because I like you and I want to trust my friend. But I'm scared."

Aleksander pushed himself to match her. "Elspeth. You can trust me. I'm not scared of you, and you're not... I know this is about people mistaking you and others like you for the Scourge, but I *know* you're not and I'll make sure they know it too."

"Do you think I'm dangerous?"

"What? No."

"Tell me the truth, Aleksander, am I dangerous?"

He did not look away from her eyes. From the serious brows

pressing down on them. From the bars he was watching close between them. Her shoulders and clavicle bounced with erratic, frantic breaths.

Yes, he wanted to say. *You are, but that's not a bad thing. You're not dangerous to me.* "No."

"Don't *lie* to me." Her lip curled back, fangs flashing. Light caught on the tears gathering along her lash line.

Nothing he could fabricate to smooth down that snarl, no carefully woven half-truth to comfort her. He grabbed her forearms and leaned in—without hesitation, her hands flipped up and curled around his. "The truth is you are," he said.

Bright fear bloomed in her eyes.

He shook his head. "But I don't care. You'd never hurt me and I know that, and I'd never hurt you. We swore ourselves to each other, don't you remember that? I don't break my oaths. Is your fire terrifying? Yes, but I'm more worried about you." For the first time since the incident, his eyes roved the fading scars on her hands. "It hurts you more than it does me."

Slowly, her chest began to rise and fall in deep, even breaths. "You don't think I'm cursed?"

"No." There, sure and steady, was no lie. Nothing needing a coat of sugar, nothing to hide from her. He matched her slow, measured breath and leaned in. The words left his mouth quiet and earnest. "Not at all."

Her lashes fluttered with a blink, and she nodded. "Okay."

He mirrored her. "Okay."

Shoulders slumping with a heavy sigh, Elspeth leaned forward, forehead resting on his collarbone. Flyway hairs tickled along his jawline, her breath warming the front of his shirt. "I just...I've been talking to Chione and Varek and even Asghar, and they all think I'm okay, but the things they say about what has happened in the past, I just..."

Aleksander cut her off with an embrace, welcoming her further into whatever comfort he could provide. "I know. They've told me too."

All he had been told and all he had overheard swirled in his mind, mixing with the faded scent of smoke and rosemary wafting from Elspeth. The truth about the Scourge, the riots and the hatred of the crown. Spies and treason and every horrible thing he didn't let himself think about, but knew deep down were connected. Even as she rested in his arms, breathing a slow pace that meant she was safe and she knew it, his chest constricted at the contents of his thoughts. They were lies, his mind screamed back at him, pushing down whatever came up that caused his heart to twinge. They were threats to him, his family, his country —Chione was wrong, Varek was a traitor.

And yet, two strong hands closed around the back of his shirt, and pulled. The pressure dropped his shoulders, and both he and Elspeth sucked in a great breath.

"I'm scared," she whispered. "I know I'm...safer, working with you all. But I'm scared."

His arms tightened around her. "I know."

No, he was wrong. Not Chione. Varek was a traitor and who knew if anyone else in the manor was a spy—but neither of them were lying about this. He didn't know why that statement was indisputable. It came down to the simple fact that when he weighed his frantic attempts to label what they say as blasphemy against the actual things they said, he felt more like a blasphemer.

And with his friend trembling in his arms...

His stomach sank, and his eyes darted towards the edge of his mattress.

He needed to read it.

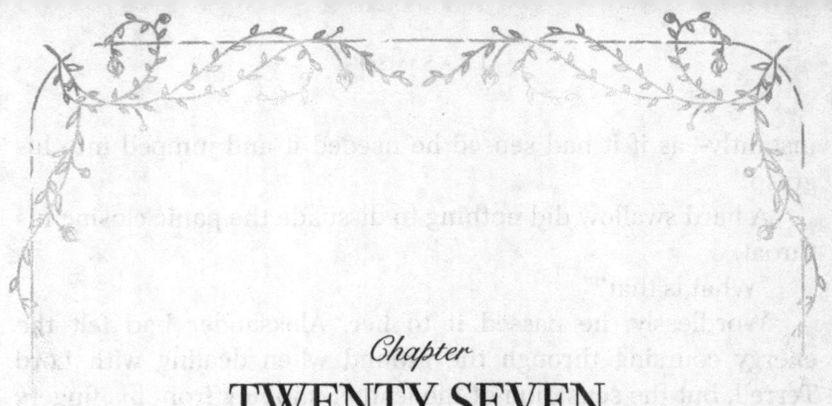

TWENTY SEVEN

ALEKSANDER HARDLY FELT THE FABRIC of Elspeth's night dress shifting beneath his hand—she slid from his chest, catching herself on the mattress. His pulse thundered in his own ears, legs slowly shifting towards the side of the bed. He hoped she couldn't see the way his hands trembled.

"What's wrong?"

Elspeth's voice hardly broke through the cacophony in his skull.

The cold from the floor radiated up, his feet hovering over the wood slats.

What was he *doing*?

A distant feeling of warmth and pressure began to rub between his shoulder blades. "Are you feeling okay? Do I need to call for a healer?"

There was no doubt he looked pale. The churn in his stomach was not one to leave the rest of him unaffected, but it was one he could easily dismiss. He'd done it in classes, at funerals, when the village girls in Brewith would press their faces to glass store windows in embarrassing attempts to catch his attention.

In one smooth gesture, Aleksander's hand disappeared beneath the mattress and reappeared with the small volume in his grasp. The spine of the book fit between his fingers perfectly, instantly—as if it had sensed he needed it and jumped into his grasp.

A hard swallow did nothing to dissuade the panic closing his throat.

"What is that?"

Wordlessly, he passed it to her. Aleksander had felt the energy coursing through the ground when dealing with Lord Terrell, but the sensation of the leather slipping from his fingers was a painful jolt unrivaled by even the strongest lightning storms.

When he finally got the courage to look at Elspeth, her face was downturned, unreadable, lost to the tiny pages and their words. Her fingers brushed over the paper, tracing gilded swirls and painted vines. "I remember this, Chione showed it to me." She looked up. "Why do you have it?"

"Chione let me borrow it." He spoke with a steadier voice than he'd expected. "There's so much... I mean, it's just..."

Elspeth's lips flattened, and she kept flipping through the pages.

Blasphemy. He'd meant to say blasphemy. For some reason, the word refused to leave his lips. He couldn't even get it into the back of his throat where it could make a dull croaking sound. It raged in his mind, but never broke past the gates.

"She showed me something about the Sword and the Scourge," he said. "It's what you were talking about—how...how she was a woman and so we all hate women now, or..." If only that pounding in his head would *shut up*. "Or something."

"She was a woman, and because she was naturally skilled in magic now any non-Zekharyan girl who has a similar gift gets killed," her eyes flared when they met his. "Believe me, I've become very familiar."

Her finger traced the words on a page, illuminated with vines and flowers and pale blue fire tipped with gold. "I can't read well —wasn't a strong skill they nurtured in the Keep—but it's talking about how Alesathne was the first Zekharyan to land on the continent. Back when it was just Mekartlim and us Rodzjiekim who lived here."

The bed creaked, Aleksander's only indication that he was scooting closer, straining his neck to read over her shoulder. Once he could clearly make out the name, he recoiled.

Never mind that, for the first time, That Name truly felt like another person, entirely disconnected from him.

"I can't read much at a time," he stuttered. "It's just...it's just *wrong*."

"According to Chione, it's factual. She said these were translated from Old Zekharyan. Look, they even have it on the opposite page."

Only his eyes moved to look.

"And it's all of Aithne's prophecies, not just the ones about you. There are poems about the Scourge, about the Temple... there's even a story of the Scourge desecrating it."

Aleksander straightened. Now, that was a familiar story. It was part of the reason why the Scourge was so hated. Alesathne had brought men to these shores with the intent of setting up a town and a temple to his Mother. One person, someone close to Alesathne, secretly hated him and the goddess so much that they —or, she, he supposed—desecrated it and killed Alesathne's wife, Liadain, as retribution. Tulathne cursed them, creating the Scourge, and Alesathne swore revenge.

"—how she was so heartbroken and upturned a brazier out of anger," Elspeth muttered.

He blinked, drawn out of his daze colored by years of study with the priestesses in that very temple. "What?"

"She upturned a brazier and smashed a bottle of wine on the statue's feet," she said, pointing. "Here."

His eyes scanned the words, deciphering as best he could from the flourishes and accents any word he might be familiar with. And she was right.

> *Rife with anger and pain in pair,*
> *She turned up a brazier*
> *And beckoned the air*

> *To come fill this place,*
> *Make the fire grow,*
> *For the wine she had spilt*
> *Was done just so—*

He pushed it away. "I don't need to read that, I know the story." It had been burned into him in every class he'd ever taken from the priestesses. From Lenore. The Scourge was hateful, and while they never used "she" to refer to their enemy, while that was a new element of this poem, he remembered the way the lines lilted and hopped along, painting the twisting, dark face he'd seen in his nightmares.

His friend blinked at him. "Are you sure?"

"I'm sure."

Lips pressing flat, Elspeth flipped through until she found another page. "Read this one."

After a moment, she handed it back to him, the pages open to a beautifully illuminated poem. Around the corners of it were flowers—dahlias, snapdragons, and marigolds. And around them were gorgeous geometric and nearly woven designs, accented with four and eight pointed stars.

"This is what she gave me. Chione. Back when I..." A sharp inhale cut her off. "She thought it might help."

Aleksander took the book from her. He'd wanted to read it. He'd wanted to learn more. But as his fingers brushed the leather, they shook. "But it didn't."

Her lips tightened against one another. "No."

With a deep breath, Aleksander let his eyes wander from his friend's face to the words confined within the glowing gold border.

The Ballad of The Scourge of Tulathne

His stomach twisted, a pang of disgust souring his tongue.
But he read on.

With courage to do
What others wished not,
The sorrowful rose
From her downcast spot

And brushed off the ashes
She had been forced to pile
'Cause a Mother's words struck pain,
And left her reviled.

There was nothing more
This woman could do
But rise from the floor,
And start anew.

Yes it's true.
At her a curse has been spat,
One that, through time,
Will always come back.

But this is not unavoidable,
Or fate,
No.
Not that.

Though the world may damn her,
From a few windows, her banners fly.
She was undeserving, we all were.
Both you in the future, and I.

So peer into her eyes,
When they're again born anew,
And remember her love
For everyone.
Especially for you.

He blew out a deep breath. "I should throw this into the sea."

Elspeth said nothing.

Aleksander's gaze drifted up. Her eyes drooped, tired by the words and the time of night. "Chione gave you this thinking it would help?"

Again, his friend did not answer. Her eyes were shadowed, dark as charcoal, dancing beneath fluttering lashes back and forth between the different elements on the page.

Again, he studied the page. He did not read it—he couldn't read it again. "Of course it didn't help," he muttered.

How dare the seeress say such things. How dare she record something about the Scourge having supporters, and doing so in a positive light—he knew the supporters existed, that's why he joined his sister in the south. To figure out how to uncover them, kill them, stop this war before it became more than spies, the occasional attack, and threats painted on walls.

Opening his mouth, a question forming, he looked to Elspeth once more.

But her eyes were already on him, empty, faded. She'd opened up to him about her fears, about how she worried she was dangerous, and had assumedly done the same with Chione. And she had given her this...blasphemy. Not at all the comforting embrace of Tulathne she deserved but one step away from pointing the finger at her and saying she was no better than the Scourge.

His lips closed tightly.

None of this made sense. Not the way he'd hoped it would. Not in a way that gave him any answers.

He wouldn't question her anymore. He didn't need to. The book, the prophecies, the talks he'd had with Chione... Aleksander needed to do more than just sit and think and talk about all the same confusing things, over and over, like a farmer expecting his dead ox to magically rise and plow the field on its own. He needed to do something. Whether it was blasphemy contained on these pages or not. He needed to stop sitting around.

The book closed with a snap. Elspeth jumped, eyes wide and searching until Aleksander extended his hand, rising from the bed. "Come on El."

She blinked at him, a small spark of light flickering in her eyes.

He needed to preserve that spark.

"Let's get you to bed."

TWENTY EIGHT

H E THOUGHT OVER EVERY WORD of that poem for the rest of the night. Face turned towards his ceiling, drifting in and out of sleep. At one point, Aleksander nearly swore he saw the carved stone above him twisting into words, faces, anything that brought to mind the dreams he hadn't had in a long time, or the so-called "accurate" translations of the prophecies.

That was what bugged him the most. He'd spent years—nearly a full decade—studying most of the other poems in that book. Different translations, but still, he'd recited and analyzed them day after day. Carissa too. And Janek. And any other children of nobles that lived near enough to the Great Temple to take their lessons there. The words he was familiar with had been woven into songs, into plays, small books and toys for children. They defined not only him, but the whole of Zekhar.

But mostly him.

These were not any of those. That ballad wasn't even mentioned. They even messed up the prophecy, the most important one.

Everything around him dissolved, his mind centering on one thing:

What was the original prophecy about Alesathne's return?

"When his time on earth has come to an end/ Trust through

all things that he shall..." the prophecy trailed off, his whispers dissolving into nothing.

Sitting up, he snatched the book from his mattress once more and stalked to the window. The moon was nearly full, bathing everything in a pale light. If he squinted...

He flipped through until he found what he was looking for. The Prophecy of Alesathne, made by Seeress Aithne in the year 251.

That number had never struck him before. It was old. Back when Toprazi was new. Very new. It seemed a far cry from the year 1398 that the country would be welcoming in at the turn of the winter solstice.

Beside that number, however was a small notation he'd never noticed before.

251 *S.C.*

He'd have to ask Chione about that later.

The words on the page were entirely unfamiliar, not even seeming to be Zekharyan—until he glanced at the opposite page and noticed the words he knew.

Interesting that it had both the old Zekharyan, copied straight from Aithne, and the translated newer edition of the language. He would have taken more appreciation in it had he not been entirely unfamiliar with the old speech.

"*Though* when his time comes," he recited to himself, nodding along with the familiar words, "put flesh to the earth/ And trust that in all things/ He shall return." It didn't rhyme. The prophecies he was familiar with rhymed, though he didn't doubt that it was simply a side-affect of doing a more direct translation. "It will not be as it once was."

The bridge of his nose scrunched involuntarily.

He didn't remember that line.

Skimming through the rest of it, his brow furrowed deeper. The part about his parents remaining human through all following incarnations was still there. And when he got to the part about the Cursebringer, the Scourge herself, that verse was still there—"this accursed shall too be revived/ Shall too remain fit for the reaper."

But after that...

But time will blur fact.
We must not forget.

What did that mean?

A frigid breeze blew through his window and Aleksander startled, snapping the book closed and nearly fumbling it through the crack between the open panes.

He stuck it back in its hiding place, and part of him wished he hadn't sent Elspeth to bed.

And Varek.

She'd said she'd been talking to Varek. But on the balcony, Varek had mentioned using Elspeth as a ploy to bring Aleksander to their side. Hadn't he?

The words were so jumbled now by time, and further by lack of sleep, that he couldn't think straight.

There had to be some way to gain clarity. He would try snooping again, he decided as he tucked himself back into his bed, before Varek returned. If he looked around and was simply caught again by Lord Asghar, a servant, or one of his own companions, it would be much easier to explain himself.

If Varek caught him...

He had a hunch the man would figure things out immediately, and either kill him on the spot or bring him into an awful cycle of blackmail and threats to keep him quiet.

The image of him, clad in black leather, a towering, nearly writhing shadow on the balcony that day was enough to send a shiver down Aleksander's spine.

He curled deeper into the blankets, pulling them around himself as if the layers of down and cotton and linen and silk would protect him.

Even as he felt that distinct tug of the Presence, attempting to lead him in to dreams he knew would be full of monsters and sorrow and despair, he buried himself deeper and deeper. His breath was hot, trapped in the blankets. But he did not care.

At last, the Presence relaxed too. Closing his eyes, he saw that shape—that writhing, swirling mass of ash and darkness, and the two blazing eyes peeking at him from within. But this time, he did not shy away or run. None of that fear flooded him as it once did. Instead, he sighed, and peered back at the monster.

"I want to sleep," he muttered. "Leave me alone tonight, please."

With a slow nod, and what appeared as an almost pitying smile, the Scourge did.

Chapter

TWENTY NINE

A RAVEN CAME FROM BREVINDUN!"

Across the table, Carissa's head snapped towards the entry to the dining room. As the weather got colder, the tenth month inching ever closer to the eleventh, it had become less and less enjoyable to have breakfast outside. Thankfully, this morning, they had shifted it indoors to a smaller banquet hall, decorated almost entirely in columns and gauzy, draping fabrics. Candelabras flickered in the corners, scattering extra light into the room when the grey day peeking through the windows was decidedly so scare with sun.

Held in Elspeth's hand, high above her head, was a curled letter. She waved it back and forth, frantic. With the movement, Aleksander couldn't make out the seal on the bottom. But he didn't have to.

She strode towards his sister without so much as a glance in his direction. Her hair was braided neatly, showing off the stern, concerned look etched into her strong features. "It's Demir."

A pang of fear shot through his chest. That could mean any number of things. It could mean Demir sent it, and it's an update on the castle and his and Janek's duties there. It could mean Demir sent it and it's an update on nothing important, though that wouldn't make sense.

But "it's Demir" brought one thought to the forefront of his mind: the man was injured or in danger. Had his broken wing caused complications? Did he get hurt again? If he did, how?

He still hadn't written him a letter. Maybe he would have known if he'd reached out sooner.

Carissa's plate crashed against the table, a hard boiled egg bouncing off and rolling on to the floor. The letter crumped within her grasp. For a moment, Aleksander feared she'd tear it in her haste. "Have you read it?" Her pale eyes were wide.

Elspeth nodded. "Only part, that's why I brought it to you."

Both women looked at Aleksander momentarily. Then, Carissa's head dipped to read the message.

Elspeth's eyes stayed on his.

He hadn't seen her this morning, not until now. The heaviness that wore on him seemed nonexistent on her. She wasn't pale, her eyelids didn't droop, and her clothes weren't wrinkled as his were. Though, after an extended moment of eye contact, her brows did scrunch together slightly, the creases around her eyes smoothing. That small shift was enough to change her expression from concern to sympathy.

Snatching a muffin nearby, lemon with poppy seeds, he held it across the table.

Are you okay? he silently asked.

A smile softened her face, for only a moment. *Yes, thank you,* she seemed to answer. She plucked the muffin from his outstretched hand and began to nibble away at the puffed top, watching Carissa scan the letter.

Her movements, which started out stilted but still relaxed, had become rigid. Fingers hooked into the soft paper like claws, the veins on her neck stood out with strain.

Aleksander set his plate down. "Carissa, what's wrong?"

Teeth sinking into her lower lip, a breath huffed out from her nose. "Demir writes to inform us of an attack on Farnich."

Air refused to enter his lungs. *So close to the castle.*

"There was a group claiming allegiance to the Scourge, mostly Zekharyan." She spoke slowly, rereading and paraphrasing. "They set fires in the eastern part of the town, coming from the fields and woods, and moved through towards the Kallendrine's estate. They were calling the royal family and all who side with them a stain upon the continent. They were..." her voice caught, and she looked up to Aleksander. "They were calling you *anerois*."

Aleksander's blood turned to ice. He'd read it in classes as a child, knowing that people still used it. But alongside the facts came the priestess's warnings that echoed in his mind. And hearing it spoken made them grow to a scream.

Old Zekharyan was a strong language. A powerful language. One that, if you gave the right words the right energy, the right belief, could topple kingdoms.

And they'd called him...

"What does that mean?" Elspeth's features were contorted in a mix of confusion and fear. The tension in the room was thick, painful—no wonder she could feel it too.

Aleksander swallowed hard. His heart battered against his ribs, making his voice shake. "It's Old Zekharyan. For 'unholy.'"

"Not *just* unholy." Carissa's hands began to shake. "It's practically a curse. It's usually tied to the Scourge and to call our Sword of Ages that is just—"

"What else does it say," Aleksander asked, desperate to leave that word in the past for but a moment.

His sister returned to the page, eyes flickering as she scanned Demir's words. "Kallendrine's men were able to push them back well enough. Out of the twelve only four were taken to the dungeon in Brevindun. They'll likely be interrogated and executed within the month."

"Was anyone hurt?" Elspeth's fingers twisted the soft paper that had, minutes ago, held the muffin. Crumbs stuck to her fingers and rained on to her boots, but she paid it no mind.

"Twenty"—Carissa blew out a breath—"twenty five are dead within the town."

A shuddering breath slowly lifted Elspeth's shoulders.

"One of them was a soldier Demir had joined with. Houses

were destroyed, shops are burned to ash. My father is giving them aid and resources to rebuild."

"Homunculi?" The word left Aleksander's lips quietly. Fearfully.

To his relief, his sister shook her head. "No. No, it seems there are no new sorcerers yet." After a long moment, she folded the letter, passing it back to Elspeth. "Thank you. Have they kept the raven?"

She nodded. "The girl told me she did, just in case you wanted to reply."

Carissa sucked her teeth, picking her plate up from the table. "I do." The porcelain was already piled high with smoked fish, baked goods, and the last of the autumn berries—after a moment, she began piling more. "I'll be in my study in the mage's wing today. There's... a lot I need to work on. I won't take visitors."

For a moment, a pang of guilt entered Aleksander's gut. He'd never considered visiting his sister while she worked. Most of the time, he was just as busy with his own duties. Should he have made more of an effort to visit her?

"There's this response," she muttered to herself, "that stupid spell Theresas wants me to develop, meanwhile I can't even *do* magic without hurting myself right now so I need to..." she raised her head. "Would Old Zekharyan work?"

Aleksander sipped his juice. "For what?"

"Bypassing the toll."

Elspeth's head snapped up from the plate she had begun assembling, eyes wide enough to make them fall out of her skull. They landed only on Aleksander.

"I...uh, I don't know," he stammered. Beneath their shared gaze, his body began to buzz with anxiety. "I mean, there's always been a toll, right? Even for old mages who spoke the Old language."

Elspeth's chest rose and fell in short, quick breaths.

Carissa took one, deep, long inhale. "I suppose. But there have been some who managed around it." She picked up a cup of cranberry juice and nodded to the both of them. "Everything else alright with you two? This letter seems to have spoiled our morning, I'm sorry for that."

For a moment, Aleksander considered answering truthfully. About Elspeth's trouble with her fire, about Chione and the book he'd been hiding under his mattress. The thought passed by about turning in Varek, giving Carissa a win when she clearly was drowning in issues that did not have single solutions. It had been so long since he'd sat on a rug or against a tree, spouting off all that was wrong in the world to his sister for the sole purpose of having someone share that burden. But he popped a hard boiled egg in his mouth to keep silent.

These were burdens he couldn't share. Not yet.

"We're doing fine, Carissa," Elspeth murmured, placing a gentle hand on the princess's arm. "Don't worry about us. Everything is just as it should be."

A quick, genuine smile turned her lips. "Good. I'm glad something is."

With that, his sister stormed out of the room, a trail of crumbs following after her as she held her plate with one hand and munched on a cinnamon muffin with the other.

"I don't know if she read all of it," Elspeth mused, peeling the flesh from an orange slice. "He wanted to talk to Varek—I figured she would have mentioned that seeing as the old man isn't here."

Aleksander furrowed his brows, still doing his best to chew up the egg he partially feared he'd choke on. "Why did he want Varek?"

She shrugged. "He didn't say, just that there were things he wanted his opinion on." The corners of her mouth turned down in a frown, her lips pushing out and the points of her fangs forming two bumps beneath her lower lip. "He better come back soon. I'm getting sick of running over the same drills without him, not knowing whether we're even doing it right."

As she spoke, her tone shifted from the frustration and anxiety it had been laced with while Carissa was here. Now, it drifted softer—annoyed, but with an undertone of warmth.

She missed him.

Aleksander let himself miss the Ölmesuz too. Just for a moment, while the memories of him being strangely kind during the ball celebrating their return circled his head. Then, as the images of him on the terrace with Asghar replaced them, he swallowed hard.

"Um, El?" He didn't want to ruin whatever bond they'd formed. Not completely. It would cause more harm than good if she suddenly began avoiding him and said it was Aleksander's doing. No, if that happened, they would all be in a great deal of trouble. He just wanted to warn her. Make sure she kept her eyes open.

Elspeth looked up from pouring a glass of cranberry juice. "Yes?"

The words stuck in Aleksander's throat. What could he say? "I would...not get to close to Varek. If you can help it."

Her brows furrowed. "What? Why?"

"Just..." his heart thundered in his chest. This was his secret to keep, not Elspeth's. It was his burden. "He can be harsh. Irrational. I don't want you to think everything is fine and friendly and then have him tear you down."

Those thick brows nearly touched now. Her lip lifted in a confused snarl. "What are you talking about? You think I don't know the man? Of course he's mean, but he's our teacher, Aleksander. He wants to keep us safe, even if he doesn't go about it in a nice way. Him yelling at me for a sloppy form isn't going to damage that, so long as I deserve it."

The room was electric. At least, it was to Aleksander. Elspeth radiated pure confusion and frustration, but within Aleksander sparked full bolts of fear.

His eyes fell on the pitcher of cucumber water and he poured himself a glass, shaking his hair free. It was so long it half-covered his eyes, now. "I know. Sorry. I'm just on edge with all of this."

"Is this about last night?"

The glass pitcher hit the table with a thunk, nearly slipping from Aleksander's hand. "No," he said.

Though he wasn't entirely sure that was the truth.

"Good," her voice dropped. "I figured we were fine but you're acting so weird this morning I..." she shook her head. "Is there anything else going on? Did you have a nightmare?"

"No." He took a sip. The water was slightly bitter, but in a fresh way. "I haven't had nightmares since coming here. Thankfully."

He missed the ice they served in the palace. There was a cellar deep within the mountain the castle sat at the foot of, full of fresh water. They'd grow and store their own ice blocks there. Even in the middle of summer, if there was a grand meal, each goblet would be nearly crusted over with a layer of frost.

Looking up from it, he saw her brows drawn down, serious and concerned.

"Sorry El, I'm fine." He smiled. "I promise. After going to sleep so late last night, everything we talked about, and now this I'm...I'm a little out of it. But I'm alright."

A moment passed, and she nodded. "Okay. I believe you. Sorry if any of it was my fault."

"No, no," he rushed to dissuade her of that concept, his plate hitting the table as he reached over the eggs to grab her forearm. "No, don't ever blame yourself, that wasn't your fault. It's my fault I couldn't quiet my mind enough to sleep. Not yours."

Her hand left her plate, and after and awkward battle for a grip, she clasped his fingers in hers. "Next time, if I'm there too late, tell me to get out."

His cheeks burned momentarily. "See, I did, more than once, and you still didn't go."

"And don't forget, I'm here for you as much as you're here for me. You need me, just ask. To listen, to distract, whatever you require of me, I will give." She offered a smile and a squeeze of his fingers.

He returned the smile and the gesture. "I know. Thank you."

Except he couldn't. Not everything. They'd vowed themselves to one another's service, that was true. They'd grown beyond their initial roles outlined by their vows, Sword and Soldier, and into friends, that was also true. But it was not easy to be that, not now. All this—his issues with that book, the knowledge of Varek's treason, and so forth—were things the Sword should tell his Soldier. They were *not* things he should burden his friend with.

"Of course," she whispered, patting his arm before lifting her glass of juice in a salute. Steady backwards steps took her towards the door. "I'll see you soon for training, right?"

"Right."

She spun on the heel of her boot and trotted off.

Aleksander watched her go.

He wasn't hungry anymore.

Chapter
THIRTY

$\mathcal{D}$UE TO THE COLD, THE fountain near the ring had been shut off that morning. No one told Aleksander, and it seemed Elspeth didn't care. By the end of their first hour in the frosty air, Aleksander's nose and lips were frozen while the rest of him baked inside his armor.

Whether as retaliation for his criticism of Varek earlier, or simply because he wasn't there, Elspeth had taken up their mentor's attitude. She wasn't as mean as Varek. It was there in her eyes, that slight pang of guilt at each insult she shouted at him.

Through his numb lips, he offered the same, until they were tripping over their own feet every match, swinging lazily and shouting back and forth nonsense meant to distract the other.

There was no malice in their taunts. Aleksander hardly registered them after the first match, and aside from an occasional laugh or louder taunt in response, Elspeth didn't acknowledge them either. But it was enough to push them forward, until the sun went down and they finally trailed inside, sore and stiff and hobbling. Elspeth leaned on the wall as she got inside and called for the nearest servant, ordering dinner be taken to their rooms and baths prepared for each of them.

Any attempts to dissuade his friend from making requests on

his behalf were met with a pointed stare.

"We're exhausted, in more ways than one," she huffed, removing her sabatons. "Take a bath, eat some food, and relax for once."

Her voice echoed an hour later as he sank beneath the warm waters, full from the roast goat and spiced rice he'd been brought. Lavender and vanilla mixed with the steam spiraling up in the candlelight. Slowly, the stress wound deep in his muscles began to unravel.

Ice seemed to be flowing through his pores, that bone-deep chill from the training ring finally leeching out of him.

With each exhale, his shoulders relaxed, his fingers uncurled, and his mind began to wander to places that did not send him into a panic.

He thought of the fields outside Brevindun first. How green they were. Then how he used to play there with Janek and Carissa. Then how he wished Elspeth got to see them in the height of summer, and how he'd make sure they all got to have a picnic next year—his thoughts began to veer off into the topic of "if" there would be a next year, and he brushed them aside.

Watching the shadows shift on the ceiling was a much less fear-inducing alternative.

Aleksander lifted his fingers, twirling them the way he'd seen Elspeth twirl hers, commanding the smoke from their campfire to weave between them, to dance.

As he expected, nothing happened. The steam spiraled and floated with his movements, but not in that magical way he'd envisioned. To test it further, with a smirk twisting his lips, he snapped his fingers towards the nearest candle. Nothing happened, save for a slight waver of the flame when the wind caused by his movement finally reached it.

If only Elspeth wasn't terrified of something so incredible.

He sank back further, eyes drifting shut.

Just rest for once.

◇ ✳ ◇

THE LIBRARY'S LANTERNS were, on the whole, unlit. The stacks were cast in deep, eerie shadow, and for a moment Aleksander wondered if he should have come here at all. Still he wove through the maze-like shelves, until finally finding the gold, red, and blue glow of those glass lanterns that were lit further in. Footsteps and rustling paper echoed from the same direction. He'd come here to talk to Chione. There were still things he needed answers to, though some part of him said he already knew those answers.

What were those questions again?

He followed the sound of that other person, recounting the thoughts that plagued him. If he had recorded past lives, were there any for the Scourge? Was there any news on Varek? Why did she give a blasphemous poem to his friend, and above else, was there any written record of the horrors she claimed had befell those young women? He'd tried so hard to relax in the bath, but he'd kept thinking about Elspeth and their discussion, and that vile tome he'd been harboring.

But, he had fallen asleep, hadn't he? Everything was a blur after training. Dinner, the bath, then...

Aleksander stopped.

The stacks were *not* laid out like this. Chione wouldn't stand for such winding rows.

Bookshelves began to swirl in on one another, the path shifting before his eyes. Aleksander stumbled back, watching as the light, the shuffling, the...the *humming*, was closer than ever before.

There hadn't been humming before.

His heart began to pound. This was a dream, he knew it was. Of course he had told Elspeth his dreams and nightmares had finally stopped, only for him to be thrust back into another disconcerting vision.

It was naïveté alone that had convinced him they would never happen again.

His footsteps echoed strangely as he walked.

The light did not get any closer, but still he continued on.

Titles stamped onto the spines in gold foil caught his eye—*Róisín's Barter, Jadzia and the Aerie, When Osier Swallowed the Sun*. He didn't recognize any of the names, nor any of the stories. Róisín was a northern Zekharyan name, that much was certain. Osier sounded Ölmesuz. He paused in his path, lifting a finger to brush the name Jadzia. A warmth blew through him, and with it the smells of mountain sage in the summer, fresh air, the crispness of high altitudes.

His throat tightened.

He hadn't smelled it that closely since he'd been a child. The grounds around the castle and the capital were too manicured, and besides, the sage normally grew higher, at the edge of the trees, once forests and ferns gave way to outcroppings of rock.

A great clattering startled him, and the scent, the warmth, the comfort he'd been given momentarily, disappeared.

On the floor, about fifteen feet away, rested an open book. Pages down, crumpled on the polished, waxed wood floors, the only thing that gave him any indication of what the book contained was the entirely unembellished cover.

For the first time, Aleksander realized the Presence was not there. It had become so constant, so normal to sense its shifts and reactions, that once the only fear he felt in his body was his own, everything felt off. He felt lighter, like the presence had offered a true, physical weight—but also hollow, as if something was missing.

How he wished it could give him guidance in this moment.

Hesitant steps guided him to the book, and he lifted it.

Smoothing out the pages, the little firelight that bounced down the aisles caught on thin gold script.

I'm waiting.

Goosebumps flared up on his arms, down his back, his legs. Flipping from page to page, he found nothing but the same script, the same message.

I'm waiting.

I'm waiting.

I'm waiting.

The snap of the book closing echoed, and the humming grew louder. It was a strange, lilting tune, holding long notes before fluttering between a few and shifting to a minor. It was haunting and filled this strange other-library with a tangible smoke, smelling of incense.

He didn't throw the book aside, though every nerve in his body was telling him to. For some reason, his fingers curled into claws around the thick spine. He tucked the book against his chest.

They're waiting.

Swallowing his fear, he walked on. The floor switched as he did—wood planks took on the fluidity of fabric, shifting beneath his feet before solidifying again into their straight, knotted boards and changing his path.

Now the voice was behind him.

Now to his right.

Now his left.

His boots echoed louder, louder.

His steps came faster, faster.

Frustration began to wind his jaw. If they wanted to talk to him so badly, why couldn't he just *get there* already?

The shelves shifted one final time and he stopped.

There, just a handful of paces away, at the end of this strange, living hallway, hung a collection of lamps from the ceiling. Their flickering glow cast patterns, colors, and shadows onto all around them—the shelves, the books, the pages flipping underneath the gentle guidance of thin, pale fingers.

Aleksander's breath caught in his throat.

Even with her back turned, her eyes downcast, and the lights turning her silver-white hair to a mosaic, he saw the broad stretch of her shoulders, the long, white lashes fluttering just above her cheeks. That downturned nose dotted with freckles.

"Finally," she said, still not lifting her gaze from the book in her hands. "I was wondering if you'd ever find your way through that maze."

The book snapped shut and she lifted her head, turning to face him.

Three strides ahead of him, glowing like a goddess in her draping traditional gown, with pink in her cheeks and a glow in her eyes, Iscah smiled.

Chapter

THIRTY ONE

LEKSANDER'S KNEES CRACKED AGAINST THE hardwood. The vision before him blurred, becoming a watercolor of silver and rainbows. Tears streamed down his cheeks.

Any word he attempted to voice failed.

Iscah took measured steps towards him, holding out a hand. "Stand up, Aleksander."

He shook his head. The breaths that came from his throat were ragged, hoarse. "Iscah, I—"

She closed her eyes, letting her hand fall back to her side. "Yes, yes, you're sorry, I know, I've heard you. Stand up."

Frustration swirled in his chest, along with all the guilt he'd ever felt for her death and all the joy at seeing her again, even in this strange dreamworld. His teeth ground together, emitting a sharp squeak. "What?"

His dead friend raised an eyebrow, but she didn't speak.

His jaw hurt. "You *know* this has been eating at me and you won't let me make amends? Iscah, do you *want* me to suffer more?"

That lavender gaze softened. After a moment, her robes rustled as she knelt before him. A hand touched his cheek, and tears sprang anew—she was *warm*. Warm, like living flesh. She was alive, somehow. Maybe this wasn't the dream, maybe life was the nightmare he escaped from.

A barked sob escaped his lips, and he fell forward, crashing his head into her shoulder and throwing his arms around her. She wobbled, unsteady in her crouched position, but after catching them Aleksander felt two strong arms wrap around him. Her cheek pressed against the side of his head. It was almost too much, being this near to her after so long. Actually, he'd never been this close to Iscah. All those days together on the road and he'd never hugged her, never thanked her, never said anything to indicate just how much he appreciated her and all she did, all she gave up for them.

"I'm sorry," he whispered.

She sighed. "I know."

"And..." Aleksander sniffled, his voice catching on the tears. "I did an awful job leading you. I never told you how much I appreciated your Creations, how much I appreciated you and your kindness and the way you protected my sister and Elspeth in the fight and Demir and I—"

His breathing became too fast, too ragged. Aleksander lifted his head from her shoulder, gasping for air. Two warm, soft hands closed on his cheeks, thumbs swiping his eyes.

He pressed a hand against his chest, hard, desperately trying to stop the panic, the grief, from consuming him.

"Hey, listen to me. Aleksander. Aleksander, *listen to me*," Iscah repeated. Her voice was smooth, soft. It still had that bounce it had in life, but it was more measured, silkier, almost in the way Varek's was. Rapid blinks cleared his vision enough to focus on her face.

She inhaled slowly, raising her chin, her eyes on his.

As she exhaled, Aleksander followed along.

In.

Out.

His ears burned.

After a moment, she looked down. "I won't lie and say I don't blame you for it. That won't do anyone any good."

The words hit Aleksander like a punch in the gut. His whole

body shook, threatening to vomit, cry, scream—to lose all sense of control over the amount of guilt he was trying to hard to control. Panic flooded anew, and he struggled to breathe.

"But I'm not mad at you." Her hand left his cheek momentarily to swipe a lock of hair from his eyes.

In this moment, he remembered how close she and Carissa were. It made sense—the way she stared at him, the way she wiped his tears...his sister had done it a fair share when they were children.

She continued, "You did not ask for any of this, just as I didn't ask for it either. You were named the Sword because your mother went into labor on a night with a specific constellation in a specific place in the sky. I joined because I saw a way to help my people, *maybe*, no matter how much I dislike the crown. And your sister..." her voice caught, "your sister brought me in because I could fight and would be useful in more ways than one."

Aleksander nodded, slowly letting her words sink in.

"I don't care if you were involved in my death. You're a kid."

He furrowed his brow, momentarily incensed. "I'm not a kid," he said.

"You're fifteen."

"I'm fifteen and a *half* years old, that's not a kid, I'm practically an adult."

Her fingers pressed in to the sides of his head sharply. "You. Are. A. Child." Anger flared in her features, but it was not directed at him. "I'm not saying that to insult you. I'm saying that because it's fact. And the role you've taken on is not one fit for a child, but it's a role you're in nonetheless."

The weight he'd thought he'd shrugged off returned with full force, threatening to pull him through the floor. It was a dream, after all. He could slip through those floor boards if his subconscious wanted him to.

Iscah shook her head, sliding her hands to his shoulders. "That's not what I wanted to talk about, though."

The weight pressing atop him darkened his vision. He

blinked to clear it, trying desperately to focus on her face and those strange amethyst eyes that no longer needed to blink. "What? Isn't this a dream? The things that happen in dreams, they're never real."

The woman scoffed, rising to her feet. "You Zekharyans, you love magic and all the forces in the world that you lack understanding of, you make every attempt to harness it in a way that does not come naturally to you and actively hurts you, yet you refuse to learn about the magic that each living being on Toprazi is blessed with." She selected a lock of hair to slowly detangle as her gaze wandered the shelf before her. "Dreams are work of the subconscious, yes, that is true. Scholars and Crafters alike will tell you that. But that does not mean they cannot be influenced by other things around us. Situations, people," she waved to herself, throwing a grin back at Aleksander, "spirits. *Especially* spirits, in my opinion."

"So..." his heart raced. Aleksander pushed himself to his feet, wringing his hands together in absence of the book he'd carried moments ago, now lost to the folds of the dream. "So you are real? I'm not entirely making you up."

Iscah plucked a book off the shelf and cast a sidelong glance. "Well, you're making me up to an extent. But I am here. I am always here." She flipped through the pages absently. Thick eyelashes brushed her brows when she glanced up at him. "I must say, I had no idea you were so troubled when I met you. You seemed strangely mature for your age." A light laugh rang through the dark library. "I supposed it was because you were royal, but that should have tipped me off. You're not royal though, are you?"

Aleksander blinked.

The darkness around him whispered *no*.

She cocked her head to the side. "Tell me, Pride of Tulathne...who are you?"

A shiver ran down his spine. Everything he'd ever been told, everything he'd ever believed raced through his mind as possible answers. The Sword of Ages. The Champion of Tulathne. The

Blessed One. Alesathne Reborn.

Then, it all faded away, leaving one name. A name he'd only spoken once.

Aleksander Fylan. Who even *was* the boy who carried that name? The one born in the foothills, to a mother and a father with a vegetable garden?

Aleksander licked his lips, and answered honestly. "I don't know."

His friend smiled. "And why *don't* you know?"

She sat down, instantly cradled by a plush chair not unlike the one Chione had sat him in.

Checking behind himself, Aleksander found an identical chair waiting for him, different only through the blanket draped over an armrest. He sat, tucking his feet in like a child.

"I...I know who I am," he mumbled, staring at the flickering colors on the floor. "I know my name, I know what I like and what I dislike, I know what matters, I know *who* matters...to me." His eyes flicked up to catch Iscah's momentarily.

She suppressed a smile. "And yet?"

Aleksander blew out a long breath, dropping his gaze again. "And yet, I don't know if I am who they say I am."

"Why not? Don't you believe in Tulathne? In the prophecies?"

"See, that's just the thing, I...used to. I did. At one point. With my whole being. I... I loved Her and being Her son and every word of the prophecies, of our poems and scriptures, it was true to me, it was *real* and I felt it. But now..." Aleksander caught Iscah's eyes again, this time holding them. "What do you know about the Scourge Scare?"

A hard swallow worked down her throat. "You and I both know what I know about that."

He frowned. "Tell me then, if we both know."

Iscah's mouth pressed thin. Deep creases formed between her eyes, nostrils flared with heavy breaths. "It's not *easy* for me to talk about, Aleksander."

As if echoing from different spaces, different times, a faint cacophony of screams echoed through the library.

Aleksander's hair stood on end, his head snapping this way and that to catch the source of the screams, weaving through the air as though carried by a looping butterfly. Women, girls, *babies*, crying—*screaming*—for help. It cut him to his core.

His eyes stung, his throat grew tight.

He heard people trying to help them. Parents, siblings, friends stepping between them and what he could only assume were the mobs after their heads.

He wanted to throw up.

"She's just a girl!"

"She has done nothing to you!"

"Get your hands off my daughter! Mona!"

"You cannot take her from me!"

"I will gut every last one of you—let my baby go!"

Glancing across to Iscah, his blood ran cold.

Her eyes glowed with a vibrant purple fire, jaw locked in rage, tears shimmering in rivers down her cheeks, her neck, into the neckline of her dress.

He swallowed hard. "Make it stop."

"I *can't*, Aleksander." Her words were tight. The hands that once rested gently on the arms of the chair curled, her nails tearing into the fine upholstery. "None of us ever could. You wanted understanding, you're getting it."

The screams rose to a pitch, accompanied by the snaps of flames, the ring of blades and axes and knives, the breaking of glass, the spat curses on innocents in the name of Tulathne.

My goddess would not condone something like this.

"Tulathne wouldn't let this happen," he gasped. The tears continued to flow as the screams grew.

"It's not up to Her, Aleksander, the gods don't meddle in our lives the way they once did. This is the fault of the people and the people alone. For centuries. Ask any Ölmesuz older than I what they've seen. Ask any girl *younger* than I what her biggest fear is."

And just like that, the screams stopped.

His ears rang. His hands twitched with latent tremors from too much adrenaline.

The glow in Iscah's eyes faded until it was just the lamplight reflecting off them like a cut jewel, sparkling in that entrancing, disconcerting way all Ölmesuz eyes sparkled. She blinked, her chest heaving. Then, one hand unhooked itself from the chair, and she wiped her cheeks.

Aleksander swallowed hard. Dream or not...those sounds were too visceral to be entirely made up. And if Iscah was right about dreams being able to combine reality with your subconscious in deeper ways than most Zekharyans understood, then...

"What else," he asked. "Surely that wasn't all you wanted to tell me."

"No, it wasn't, but that was more than I expected."

Suddenly, she looked mortal. Bags appeared beneath her eyes, her hair wasn't that perfect, melted waterfall of pale silver she'd brushed her fingers through minutes ago. The tears left tracks on her cheeks, shimmering with forgotten starlight.

He shook his head. "If you don't have the energy to talk, then —"

"No," she interrupted with a raised hand. "No, I...I don't know when I'll be able to do this again. So I would like to get it all out before you wake up." The woman wiped her cheeks and rubbed her eyes, leaning forward with her elbows on her knees. Her gaze locked on him. "Listen closely. You are whoever you need to be. It's your job to decide who that is, not theirs."

Aleksander nodded. "Okay."

"I'm not done."

"Sorry."

Another hard swallow, and she continued, "I felt had no choice to join your party. And while it got me killed, that does not mean I regret it—not now, not ever. I met you, Carissa, Demir, Elspeth. Even Varek. I fought for the sake of my people. My sisters. Even though it was a short time. And I'm grateful for it. And I'm sorry for the weight put on you, I wish I could take it away. Still, I have to ask you to do your best. You know things now. Don't keep them to yourself."

Again, Aleksander nodded. "Can I ask a question?"

"Of course."

"Varek..." he hesitated. He'd been fighting himself on this for weeks, ever since he'd overheard that conversation on the balcony. But this was a dream, and there was no way anyone outside of this would hear him insinuate Varek's treason. "I overheard Varek talking to Lord Asghar. It sounded like..."

"Treason, I know. That was even a word he used." She smiled. "Again, Aleksander, I was there. I'm always there."

He clenched his jaw. There was a chance this wouldn't work. There was a chance that this *was* all just a dream, and he was making all this up, and all these answers to his questions were just things he wanted to hear. Things that would take away his guilt and grief bit by bit. Still, he licked his lips and spoke. "What do you know that I don't know?"

Iscah's eyebrows raised, her gaze drifting off into the distance for a moment. "Quite a lot, actually." Her vision refocused on him, and she sat back in her chair. "I won't give you answers, you won't truly learn that way. But know that—just like the prophecies and the Scourge—there is more going on than you know. And sometimes, those who you think are your enemy are meant to be your greatest ally."

For the first time in weeks, Aleksander felt a drop of peace swirl within his soul. He hadn't realized truly how much this chaos with Varek had been disturbing him, but hearing from a mostly-reliable source that his fears were directed towards the wrong man, he breathed easier. Even if he didn't fully believe it.

"Thank you."

She nodded. "I'll let you wander the library, if you'd like. But before I go" —she reached across the gap between the chairs, the floor warping so their knees pressed together, and took his hands in hers— "Tell Varek thank you, from me. And tell Demir I loved him. I'm sorry I never got to say it."

"Of course."

Tears welled in the woman's eyes. "Tell Elspeth I'm proud of her. Tell her she's strong, and powerful, and should never, *ever* be ashamed of that. And...tell Carissa I loved her, too. I wish we could have been friends longer. And tell her I'm so happy for her, she'll know what it's about."

Aleksander nodded.

Iscah sniffed. "And Aleksander?"

"Yes?"

A wavering smile crept onto her face. "You're strong enough to be who you are. Whatever that means to you. You're kind and caring, and yes, you're ignorant in the ways of most of us commoners, but you try. Keep trying. And never let your heart grow callouses."

Aleksander blinked his tears away.

When had they started to fall again?

The warmth where her hands pressed to his cheeks dissipated, and he sat alone on the floor, a single lantern overhead.

Chapter

THIRTY TWO

WATER SPLASHED OUT OF THE tub as he shot up. The start of her name clawed its way up his throat, but as the room around him came into focus, all that came out was a strangled "Ih..."

The candles had mostly burnt out. It was dark, and a chill had begun to creep into the bath, leeching through the metal from the stone surrounding him.

Shivering, he stood and drew a plush, quilted robe around him.

You'd think Ölmesuz would make a heat-retaining tub, with all their Crafters.

At the notion of Crafters, those bright eyes flashed in his vision once more. They froze him to the spot.

She had asked things of him. She had hugged him and held him and spoken to him more than she ever had in life, and yet she still had seemed fully herself. Maybe he should go talk to Chione, or even Asghar himself about the Ölmesuz belief regarding dreams.

Pulling on pants, he swallowed hard.

Or maybe he should just trust her.

Aleksander's mind reeled as he dressed. It was strange, spending all that time those few months ago actively pushing away anything that happened in his dreams, only to turn around and be told he needed to hold to them. Remember them. Act on them.

He needed to pass on her messages to the others. And...he needed to find out, once and for all, what Varek was doing.

Without a second thought, he threw open the doors to his wardrobe. It was late. Everyone would be asleep. With Varek gone, there was no one to catch him snooping. The guards here mainly stuck to Lord Asghar's chambers and the grounds, adorned in light, ceremonial armor as if they didn't have any fear sudden attacks, or their lord's life being threatened.

If he wore dark clothes, if he stuck to the shadows...

The door creaked open, and his heart jumped into his throat. Every terrified breath was tight, shallow. He pulled the door closed. When that near-silent *click* echoed through the hall, he took a step back and stared at it.

Varek would call him an idiot for doing this. He'd say he was being stupid and careless, proving that the royal family shouldn't be trusted.

But as Iscah said, Aleksander wasn't royal.

Aleksander swallowed hard and clenched his hands into fists, only to stretch out his fingers with a long exhale. He could do this. He had to. It wasn't just because of what he heard on the terrace—this was his only way to make sure his family was safe. To make sure his country was safe.

To know if Iscah was real in that dream, or not.

Silent steps, padded by soft leather slippers, tiptoed down the stairs. Only a handful of lanterns were lit, as usual. Outside, clouds gathered and a crisp breeze wound its way through the mosaic halls, sending a shiver through the boy. He did not turn around to get his cloak.

Everything was different in the dark. He'd been wandering these halls for a month at this point, technically a few weeks more, and had become so familiar with each curve, each painting, each mosaic pattern and how it shifted on the floor beneath his feet. Yet, just like the last time he'd wandered into this wing of the manor at night, everything warped. It was like a dream—like the building itself was doing everything in its power to keep him from knowing exactly where he was going. Doorways looked all the same, the dark gauze of night obscuring the carvings and symbols that usually denoted what lay beyond the ornately carved oak.

Footsteps echoed down the hall, and he darted into an archway, pressing flat against the wall before sinking to a crouch. That was something he'd learned as a child, playing hide and seek with Carissa and Janek. The taller someone was, the less likely that they would look down for any intruders. Usually, they'd look in the range from their chest up to up above their heads. The more he snuck around beneath benches, the less likely it was they'd find him.

His breathing was remarkably calm. As the footsteps grew louder, closer, scuffing tiredly along the stones, Aleksander pressed his lips together and drew deep breath after deep breath. He was allowed to wander the manor freely. He was not a prisoner. And there was no one here who would dare threaten him even if he shouldn't be in this wing.

The steps passed by, and in the dim, strange mix of moonlight and distant lantern light, he caught the familiar bowed form of Mage Theresas. Her stick stretched out before her, loosely flitting back and forth, ensuring a clear path in the dark.

It took everything in Aleksander not to step out from his hiding space and offer help to the woman. Though as the mage shuffled on, it was obvious she did not need help.

He stood slowly, waiting until she was far enough down the hall that she would not pick up on the shuffling of his shoes traveling in the opposite direction. Then he turned and continued on his trek.

It came up faster than he'd thought—the door before him loomed tall, just as it had those few days ago. Closed. Beside it, nearly unreadable, was the sign confirming that this was, indeed, Asghar's private office.

A steady hand lightly pressed on the handle. The brass was cool beneath his hand, so much so he nearly jerked his hand back as though he'd pressed it flat into a fresh snowbank. But he grasped the knob tighter. He started to turn it, and was met with awful resistance.

Embarrassment flooded his gut. For all the planning he'd put into this, though admittedly it was not much beyond wearing a dark robe and pants and going where he knew the guards wouldn't be, it had never once occurred to Aleksander that the door would be locked.

And why would it be? It was never locked in the daytime, and it certainly wasn't locked the other time he'd broken in.

His hands flew to his pockets of his robe, searching for anything that would serve even remotely well enough to loosen the lock. All he found was a folded slip of parchment paper—the scrawl on it was smudged, so he had no known use for it.

I can work with this.

Aleksander folded it in half once more to create a thicker slip and creasing the edge between two fingernails, exactly the way Janek had shown him years ago, moments before the doors swung open to reveal Clauden hunched in the light of a single candle, helping himself to a tray of pastries before the boys could do so themselves.

It was hard to see what was happening in this light. There was no moon, and there are no lanterns lit at the end of the hallway. Nevertheless he crouched, squinting at the dull glint coming off the door handle, and felt his way for the tiny space where the door fit into the frame. Once he came upon a small indent, he slipped the paper in, slowly lifting it until it hit the pin of the lock.

The pin was curved so as to better fit into the door without causing much fuss to the individual interacting with it. However, that meant that if he turned the handle this way at the same time he moved the folded paper this way...

The lock clicked, and the door swung open.

A swell of triumphant pride raced through his chest, turning his cheeks in a smile. For a moment, Aleksander reveled in the feeling. It was that same rush he'd felt the first time he'd broken in. But stronger.

Pushing down the guilt that attempted to ebb in after the sensation, he let the door close behind him.

Thankfully, it seemed the clouds had parted just enough that he might be able to make out general shapes in the room. Beyond the large window loomed a deep, threatening evening. The clouds shimmered as they thinned. Rays of silvery moonlight found their way through the panes of glass.

One deep breath, and draw after drawer was ripped open, his eyes and hands flying through their contents. He had seen no guards on his journey here. Asghar was asleep in his bed a floor and a wing away. The walls were stone.

Blood pumped furiously, excitedly through his veins.

The ledger was found easily, like it was waiting for him to return. The leather was smooth beneath his fingertips, waxed and sealed to keep the rich brown of the tanned hide.

Lifting it revealed a stack of parchment, curled oddly here and there, bound with a short length of twine.

Every muscle locked up, the gears in his mind turning as he peered at the papers glowing in the moonlight.

That was not there before.

He blinked, tearing himself away from the letters and bringing the ledger to the window. The full moon was like a candle, no matter how hard the clouds tried to snuff it. Still, the writing was so small, and written with loops and curls he wasn't used to seeing past. A quiet curse slipped past his lips, and he threw the ledger onto the desk.

The panes of glass creaked as he leaned back against the doors that were locked to the tiny balcony. The ledger had been his best bet, and the first time he'd looked at it, he couldn't read through the smudges. Now, he couldn't read the anything.

Teeth nearly squeaking against one another, he locked his jaw and pushed himself forward.

His heart had begun to still with each measured, frustrated

breath, but as he gathered the stack of letters, it pounded anew.

As he struggled to untie the twine, the paper suddenly seemed much too loud in such a space. It bounced off the walls. In Aleksander's ears, it was near to the sharpness of a scream. Finally, just as his stomach had begun to twist with nausea and his mind repeated that he'd never get them free or at least crease them so much that Asghar would know someone was here, the string fell to the side.

The first three were dated over the last few days.

Ravens. They were curled, folded—they'd had to have come by raven.

None of the scrawl on the first one was decipherable. The loops were all in the wrong places, marked with dashes and dots in a style he had never seen before.

He placed it on the table, beside the pile.

The next one was the same, all wrong.

On the next letter, his eye caught a triangle, or at least part of a triangle, with a swoop on one side.

A "V."

He knew who wrote their V's like that.

Swallowing hard, he turned the paper around. His hands shook. How dare they shake now?

Femi,

Sorry I had to leave so abruptly. There were issues I had to attend to.

I'll be in Belharrow, should you need to send a raven.

I don't know if this is the work of the Blights. In fact, I fear it's no more than Zekharyan zealotry gone wrong.

Should you hear anything of the Scourge, write immediately. Even if it's another false alarm.

Expect another letter.

Varek

Blinking rapidly, Aleksander went to the first letter he'd discarded, turning it around. This, he was correct in discarding. No matter how he turned it the writing was unreadable, not in any language he'd ever seen. But the next in the stack...

Femi,

Sing a hymn to the Kutsalyot for me.

This is driving me insane, old friend. I regret every word of that oath I made all those centuries ago. I don't care if its serving me well now, I should have died and gone with her. ~~If I had known what~~

Our time is nearing. I feel it in my bones. I have sent ravens, and have been receiving responses.

Ogaden's face is all I see in Carissa. The drive, the thought that they're the only ones who know best. Theres his bloodlust there too, whether she knows it or not. I'd tried to tell myself it wasn't there, ever since she was a child. But she's starving for it.

I'll be back soon.

Varek

Iscah was wrong. She was deeply, utterly wrong. There was nothing more going on than he'd thought—Varek explicitly spoke against the crown. Against *Carissa*. He called her by name, saying she was bloodthirsty.

His hands began to shake. All images became muddled in the dim lighting, and he suddenly worried if he crumpled the paper too much as he folded it and put it back, tying the twine too loosely but who *really* cared at this point?

Nausea swirled in his gut, his heart racing and turning his whole body cold. For the first time, he realized just how much he truly wished this were not happening. He had needed to be wrong. That's why he finally came here. It wasn't to find proof, no matter what he told himself. He had needed proof that he was *wrong.*

And he hadn't found it.

"Goddess, oh Tulathne." The admonitions came out broken, breathy. "What do I do?" he whispered. The words were tight, strangled. He leaned forward, bracing himself against the desk his chest heaving.

Then, Aleksander's breathing stopped altogether.

Something was wrong. Goosebumps ran down his arms, his hair standing on the back of his neck. Just as he lifted his head, a flash caught the light and settled beneath his chin.

Even in the dark, Aleksander knew what a dagger looked like.

"I have to admit," came the low rumble, just over his head, "your awareness has gotten better, your holiness."

THIRTY THREE

ALL HIS YEARS OF TRAINING, all his days of fighting with the very man now threatening him, washed clean from his mind. Panic, anger, hurt, and fear swirled within every part of him. A tempest of betrayal, shackling every part of his mind and body to the exact spot he stood.

"I'd really hate to make a mess of the good Lord's office, kid. So tell me—why should I spare you?"

The blade was cold. It pressed against his throat, not so much to cut but just to further remind him the position he was in.

Mind racing, fear reigning, he swallowed. What could he say? Varek knew exactly what he'd just read, and it wasn't a leap to assume he'd run and tell Carissa. She would then report it to her father, and there would be all out war, not against the Blights, but against their own people, traitors they may be. Interrogations and executions would be carried out in the court, and soon—

"Nothing to defend yourself?"

Every sense in Aleksander's body bent toward the man's voice. To the erratic breaths now huffing over his shoulder. To the waver when he said "nothing."

To Varek's fear.

Aleksander raised his chin, one sentence cutting clear through his own panic.

"Iscah says thank you, Varek," he croaked.

Behind him, the breathing stopped.

The knife slid away for a split second, wavering in an unsteady hand in the moonlight, and Aleksander used the moment he was gifted to fit his hand between his shoulder and Varek's forearm, shoving hard enough to send the assassin stumbling back while Aleksander launched himself over the desk and towards the door.

Things clattered to the floor in his wake—a pen, an inkwell, a statue, a pile of books. He threw himself forward, scrambling over the rug as it bunched beneath his feet, hands stretching for the door.

Those hands met leather, and Aleksander jerked back. The tip of the blade now rested just beneath his chin. Varek stood before him, towering, terrifying. More expressive than ever, his brows sat low over his eyes, entirely obscuring them in darkness. It looked as though he had two black pits where those polished spheres of tiger's eye usually rested. His lip curled back in a snarl.

Aleksander stuttered backwards, tripping over the rug and all he'd toppled onto it. A shock burst up his tailbone, then his spine hit—his head landed on the ledger, mere inches from the hardwood desk.

Varek crouched over him, dagger still brandished.

"What did you say?"

Aleksander didn't answer. Part of him hated that he relayed Iscah's message in the first place—she was wrong, he was a traitor. There was proof of that. Her message could very well have been made up by his own mind in a desperate attempt to make him believe—

Varek's knee crushed Aleksander's chest. The air rushed out of him, and when he tried his best to take in more, he found the man's knee still there—not forcing any more air out, but not letting him take a full breath.

"Varek." The name left his lips a plea. An earnest, terrified plea.

The man's eyes flickered, head cocking to the side. "*Aleksander.*"

He coughed, his hands working their way up from their twisted places by his sides, and started trying to push Varek's leg off him.

Metal glinted. The dagger angled right above his right wrist— his sword arm. "Answer me, kid."

Desperation dripped from his words.

It was a challenge, part of him thought. Like in training. He had to match his trainer until one of them backed down.

But the sharp steel point pressed against his skin, right where the bones of his forearm separated.

Varek won't kill me.

He blinked up at the dark specter over him.

If he was going to, I'd be dead already.

Air gone, the words left his dry lips in a crackling whisper. "Iscah said 'thank you.'"

The pressure abated from his chest at once and he flew up, gasping for air. His vision swam, and some light returned to the room as he regained his faculties.

A venomous glare twisted his features, eyes flying to meet Varek's—but Varek wasn't looking at him. There was an emptiness in his eyes that told Aleksander he wasn't even looking at the blade cradled loosely between his open palms. His shoulders hunched, his hair fell in his face. He looked...mortal.

It felt wrong.

After a moment, he straightened with the assistance of a deep inhale. "What did you see?"

Aleksander's jaw flexed. "Your letters to Lord Asghar. And I heard you, on the balcony. Weeks ago."

"No." The old man grunted, shifting out of his strange crouch to cross his feet in front of him. He leaned back against the bookshelf. "What did you see with her?"

It took everything for Aleksander not to scoff. "What makes

you think I was serious about that?"

"What did you see, Aleksander?" His gaze hardened, though not with true malice.

The boy opened his mouth, ready to explain, only to close it again. The screams still hurt, like they were trapped inside his head. Whenever his thoughts strayed towards that dream...

"Just her," he said. "She was waiting for me in the library."

"How did she look?"

At this, Aleksander's eyes burned. "Divine."

Varek's mouth pressed thin, his chin jutting out. A conscious attempt to stop tears from forming. "Did she say anything else?"

Aleksander nodded. "She had messages for everyone. And she said not everything was as it seemed...but I think she was wrong about that."

Varek turned away with a sharp laugh, shaking his head. "What was our Kutsal wrong about?"

"You."

The statement left his lips so suddenly, Varek's head snapped to face him. Shock painted his face. Then, his countenance shifted, eyes darkening and the lines of his aged features becoming more prominent. "How?"

"She said you weren't a traitor. That there were things I didn't understand. But I saw the letters. You are."

Aleksander's accusation hung in the darkness, waiting for either man to acknowledge it and drag the discussion further. His eyes shot down to the dagger still resting in the old man's palm. It was unnerving, the way he held it so surely and so carelessly all at once.

Varek nodded. "Okay. What else?"

No words came. No thoughts dared form. There was no logical response to that, not one that Aleksander could come up with so quickly. He'd accused the man of being a traitor, and the man *agreed*. More than that, he asked what *else* Aleksander had to accuse him.

"Y-you are planning a coup. I think. You have allies around Zekhar, probably spies too, and you definitely have some in the court."

The old man shrugged. "That's the short of it, I suppose. Yes."

Rage, only a breath away from the kind that drove Aleksander to slice through Terrell's windpipe, flooded his body.

How. Dare. He.

Varek had been training him for months. He'd been in service of the crown since the crown *existed*. And now, he's accepting all these accusations of treason. Willingly. Easily. And he's sitting there with his toes tapping the air, his head leaned back against a bookshelf, like none of this is a big deal.

Aleksander's hands shook. "That's my *family*, Varek. You know that, right?"

"And that's why I didn't tell you, your holiness." With a deep sigh, he pushed himself to his feet. "Aside from the chance of you running and telling your sister, I knew if I tried to explain it without you knowing more, you'd see it as a betrayal."

"Because it *is*." Aleksander shot to his feet, stepping in Varek's path towards the door.

He raised his eyebrow. "Tell me, your holiness, are there people in Zekhar who don't believe in Tulathne?"

"Of course."

"And do you think people should be murdered because a prophecy from a religion they don't follow says so?"

Deep within his mind, between the crackling of flames on a pyre, a girl screamed.

"Of course not. And the prophecies don't say they should be murdered. I've read them front to back, I've memorized them since I was a child. Nowhere does it say you should kill someone you think is the Scourge. Her judgement is left to be carried out by the Sword."

At his words, something deep in Varek's features thawed, and for a moment, Aleksander saw a man. A normal man. Not an assassin, nor a mercenary bound to his family's name. A man. From a normal town, who worked a normal job. Maybe he had someone he loved. Maybe he was a father. A friend. A son. That version of Varek faded, but stayed just beneath the surface of the mask Aleksander now realized was just that. He nodded. "Wise words from such a young man. But not everyone agrees with you."

Aleksander did nothing to stop Varek from walking around him towards the door. His eyes fell from where Varek's face was to the desk, still painted in watery moonlight, still strewn with papers and missing most of the decor Aleksander had thrown to the floor.

"Prove Iscah was right," he said.

A pause. "What?"

"Prove to me that Iscah was real. In my dream." Aleksander turned towards the door and the man about to walk through it. "Prove there's more going on. Prove you're not a traitor."

Nothing passed over his features. No matter how hard Aleksander looked, how deeply he dug into the smallest of shifts in Varek's eyes, there was nothing he could point to as proof the man would agree.

"But I am."

Aleskander clenched his jaw. "No. She said you weren't. She said there was something going on that you were a part of, and that I needed to know what it was. So tell me."

At this, the man smiled. "No, see, you asked me to prove it. You didn't ask me to tell you."

"I'm asking you now."

"And I'm saying no." He shrugged. "You want me to prove whose side I'm on, kid? I'll prove it. But I'll still be a traitor. My question is..." he bent down and stared, unblinking, into Aleksander's eyes. "...are you?"

The question threw him back a step. He wasn't. Not yet. But if Iscah was right... "I'm not sure."

Varek straightened slowly. "I guess we'll both have to prove ourselves then, won't we?" That smirk faded. "To calm your nerves, I'm not with the Blights. They're vile, and I've had to clean up their messes more than I'd like. They hurt the people I want to protect."

"And those people are?"

"You know."

Deep in Aleksander's gut, he knew Varek was right. On a broader scale, everyone in Zekhar. On a smaller scale... "The girls that are going to be targeted."

The man nodded. "Correct. One of them is going to be blamed for all this, singled out as the one you're meant to kill. And when she is..." Varek's voice caught, a rare display of emotion that he quickly shoved down. "When she is, I'm going to stand between you and her, and hope to the Mother and all the Kutsalyot that you're the smart, kind boy I've seen you become. If it turns out you aren't?"

With a flourish, he sheathed his dagger.

"Are you threatening me?" Aleksander wished his voice hadn't wavered.

"If you end up making a stupid choice, yes. But I've got... faith. In you. For some Saint-forsaken reason." Varek ran a hand through his hair, sighing so deep it nearly sounded painful. "Reincarnation or not, she doesn't deserve to be killed in every life. And you don't deserve to be a killer."

Aleksander scoffed. "A little late for that."

"Yeah," the man breathed, "but it doesn't mean it's right."

From its place on the carpet where Aleksander had kicked it to in his haste to escape, the overturned desk clock's steady *tick, tick, tick* floated through the room as the two stood in silence.

Aleksander was not at ease. Far from it. His mind reeled, his heart still threatened to break into a race...and yet, his soul was quiet. The Presence was not flaring, nor writhing the way it did when something was wrong. There was something in the old man's words that situated in his body the same way the Presence did. Not invasive, not threatening, just there. As constant and true as his heartbeat.

He was a traitor. And traitors couldn't be trusted.

But maybe this traitor had a point.

And maybe, somehow, whatever drove him to be a traitor was worth it.

Aleksander extended his hand. "To proving ourselves, then."

There he was again, for a flash. The man before the bloodshed. Whoever that kinder, open, earnest version of Varek was.

A large, leather-clad hand took his.

"To proving ourselves." He flashed a grin before he turned towards the door. "Now go get some sleep. Come sunrise I'll have no clue you were up so late, and I'll be expecting you in the ring, ready to go."

The door opened, and Varek was soon swallowed into the pitch black of the hallway.

After a moment, he reappeared from the void, his brows knit in earnest inquiry. "She really thanked me?"

Aleksander nodded. "It was the first thing she asked met to pass on. 'Tell Varek thank you, from me.' I don't know what she means by it, but..."

"It's alright." A strange mix of grief and peace flashed over his face. "I know what she means." Eyes, softer than Aleksander had ever seen in the old man's face, found his. "'Night, kid."

"Goodnight, Varek."

Chapter

THIRTY FOUR

FROST DUSTED OVER THE LARGE window's glass panes, obscuring the world beyond so heavily Aleksander wasn't sure he remembered it accurately. He tugged his blanket tighter, rubbing his face on the soft linens to wipe away any remnants of exhaustion and sleep. It felt like a morning from his childhood, when the snows would pile up so high around and on top of Castle Brevindun that the stones themselves threatened to grow ice. There was a certain crispness to the air that always served to simultaneously wake him up and call for nothing more than a hot cup of apple cider and a seat before a roaring fire.

No matter how tempting that childish desire was, he rose and stretched, dressing in warm clothes and finding a place at his borrowed desk to comb his hair and splash rose water onto his face. He only paused twice to draw figures in the frost, smiling at the way it curled up into tiny spirals as he scraped it free from the glass.

The moment he opened his door, the temperature shifted. It was cold in the hallway. Not so much that he needed his fur cloak, but enough that he considered turning around to get it just in case he needed it later.

Unfamiliar sounds echoed up the stairway and through the halls. Scraping and smacking and occasional heavy clunks grew louder as he descended, eventually stumbling on a group of servants shoveling snow out of the terrace doors.

Snow.

Aleksander's pace slowed involuntarily until he was stopped, staring at the drifts of snow sticking to the tiles and how the white blanket extended beyond.

It wasn't a thick layer, the snow. But it was enough to obscure most of the shapes of the stairs, the bushes, the trees. Each branch was coated in it, fuzzy and thick and already beginning to bow under the weight.

He couldn't help it—he smiled.

Kneeling down beside the workers, Aleksander stuck his hand into the snow and watched as his body heat melted the shape of his hand, compressing it perfectly along the curves of his palm. His hand stung when he pulled it back, but that did nothing to dim his joy.

Snow meant it was almost the end of the year, which meant it was almost the solstice, which meant he'd get to see Genoise again.

Aleksander jolted to his feet, blinking away that thought.

No. He wouldn't see Genoise this time.

It had been a long time since he'd last thought of her. Months since he last saw her. He didn't need her pretend friendship, not anymore. There was no honesty to what they'd had, and he half hated himself for thinking about her.

He shook the snow off his hand and blew on the pink skin to warm it.

Perhaps Genoise would be at the solstice party in the court. In fact, he would be shocked if he didn't see her. But this was the year he'd spend time with Demir and Janek and Carissa.

This was the year he'd get to dance with Elspeth.

He'd make sure of it.

"My lord Champion!"

Aleksander spun towards the echoing voice to find Lord Asghar himself, draped in heavy layers and furs, waving him over.

"Good morning Lord Asghar," Aleksander offered a slight bow upon approach, his heart racing.

He'd cleaned up the lord's study the best he could, but there was still the chance that he'd missed something in the dark. An ink spill, a decoration that rolled under a chair and escaped his notice.

There was also the chance Varek told Asghar what happened.

But the lord simply smiled at him. It was a short smile, tight and curt, but it was otherwise genuine. "Varek returned last night, just before the snows came. And this morning, her highness wishes for us all to gather for a meal so that she might discuss some developments with us."

Those few words were all that were needed to turn the growing anxiety in his stomach to full fear. "What developments? Is everyone alright, has anything happened?"

"Oh, no, nothing dramatic," Lord Asghar said, turning to guide Aleksander to the breakfast room. "Her highness has been in contact with the palace and a Commander there—Polat?"

Aleksander's pace hastened, matching Asghar's and even challenging the lord to speed up his own steps. "Demir, yes he's a friend of mine. I knew he'd sent a raven yesterday—was there another?"

"There have been quite a few. He sent a handful in succession it seems, and Varek sent one off to him this morning as well. We're still waiting for a response."

The doors usually open to the terrace began to shut, closing out the early winter chill best they could.

"I didn't expect it to snow yet," Aleksander muttered, really to no one.

"It's almost the month of Darkest Nights," Asghar responded, "I just can't believe I have missed the start of the snows so utterly."

Any of the excitement Aleksander had felt when watching the servants shovel out the first snow faded. As they walked down the hall, he kept finding his gaze flit between the path ahead of them and the lord beside him.

Asghar's face was stern, his usually relaxed features tightened over his skull. Deep bags stretched beneath his eyes. His eyebrows drew tight. Even his mouth, constantly held in a glimmer of a smile, had flattened into a firm line.

Every step was measured.

Aleksander's heart raced.

"Nothing dramatic" sure seemed to be something dramatic.

"Do we know what this is about?"

Asghar shook his head. "Not yet. That is why we have been called to a meeting."

Down the hall, voices grew louder and louder. Varek's was above them all, still indecipherable in the ricocheting cacophony echoing through the tile and columns.

Even getting to the doorway, no single word was shouted out above the others.

Large carved doors had been thrown and propped open, and a group crowded around the long table stretched through the middle. Only drinks had been served—warm, steaming beverages scenting the air with sugar and rich, roasted spices. Varek sat across from Chione, his brows knit together as they ranted away together in a mix of Zekharyan and Ölmesuz, hands flailing and gesturing emphatically.

Aleksander had never seen the two so emotional. Not in the sense that there was water in their eyes or cracks in their words, but that their faces were shifting with every word. Eyebrows bounced, lips pursed and frowned and blew puffs of frustrated air. Hands flipped and waved away the statements of the other. Their voices alone traveled in dramatic ups-and-downs, punctuated by guttural consonants and rolled R's. Never in all the months he'd known the old man did he hear him utter more than the passing word or the lilted funeral song for Iscah.

Somehow, a simple sentence about goddess-knows what held that same, melodic quality.

Even as Varek scoffed and waved his hand dismissively.

Elspeth sat back in her chair, brows knit and lips taught against her teeth. Lashes fluttered against her eyebrows with each glance between the two.

And there, at the front of the table, hands braced against the flat expanse of polished and oiled wood, was Carissa. She wore her hair down, the wild curls cascading over a single shoulder. A cup rested between her hands, steam curling up towards her downturned face. The golden fur collar of her winter robe mixed with her hair, creating the image of a wild lioness when her head raised and those pale, firm eyes met his.

"Good!" She stood tall and brushed her hands against each other before folding together her fingers and letting them rest before her. "Sit down."

"Carissa," Aleksander strode past the table, all the chairs, and the bickering Ölmesuz. "What is going on?"

His hand brushed her arm, and she released the lock on her fingers for a moment, squeezing his fingers once. "Go sit down. I'll explain."

Everything that could have happened raced through his mind—a Blight attack, a homunculi attack...a coup. His fingers shook within the grasp of his sister's. "Is Demir okay? Janek?"

"Listen to the Princess," Theresas said, feeling her way towards the table from the doorway. "Take a seat, dear Champion."

Asghar gestured to the seat beside Elspeth and across from the lord himself.

Aleksander's eyes shifted between everyone. Varek and Chione had fallen silent. The old man crossed his arms once more, leaning back in his chair and recreating the image of himself he projected when Aleksander had first met him. The librarian took the mug before her in both hands, lifting it to her face but not taking a sip. Tendrils of steam curled around her nose. She rolled the ceramic across her lips, eyes downcast towards the empty table.

Theresas slipped into a chair beside Asghar, and Elspeth finally lifted her eyes.

Nothing but fear crackled there.

Aleksander sat down.

Carissa cleared her throat, fingers splaying across the table once more. "We have received recurrent updates from Commander Polat, who works alongside my husband, Sir Unwin, in the war council headed by my father. As we all know, Blights have been popping up all around the country. The most recent attacks have been closer to the capital and to Hadiqin." She swallowed hard, brushing a curl from her eyes. "We initially assumed they were trying to antagonize us. The smaller attacks, the vandalism, testing the limits we are willing to go through for small disruptions. My father and Sir Unwin have been diligent in dispatching armed forces to each site of disruption, but that seems to have done nothing to discourage them. In a recent attack, one outside of Brewith in a small trading settlement to the north, we have discovered what their priorities have shifted to."

The princess's voice dropped, her eyes falling to a letter on top of the stack to her right. Thin fingers hesitantly snatched it up. She scanned the letter for a moment before reading it. "Demir writes, 'we've noticed in recent attacks that they've been leaving messages for the Scourge. And...'" a deep breath broke her speech, "'they have been claiming that they've found her.'"

Chapter

THIRTY FIVE

EFORE ALEKSANDER COULD PROCESS, HIS sister continued. "Through rumors, letters, or outright shouting in the streets, we've heard of various young women being claimed as the Scourge. If retaliation was not swift enough and Zekharyan civilians did not kill them first, their bodies have been found mutilated, with a note stating that they were no more than false gods.'" Swallowing hard, she dropped the letter, muttering the final sentence. "'We assume, in these instances, they were killed by the Blights.'"

A heavy weight fell over the room. Aleksander's tongue failed, refusing to allow him to even *think* of words to say. Part of him was thrilled that they hadn't found the Scourge yet. That he didn't have a face to put with the title, a name that he knew he would have to wipe from history.

And yet...

Those screams in his memory echoed afresh. This time it wasn't just the Zekharyans or the Blights they had to worry about —it was everyone. With the tensions ramping up across the country, it didn't matter who you served, what people you belonged to. Anyone could turn against you.

You could turn against anyone.

For a moment, he swore he saw Iscah's eyes flicker in the

back of his mind, the remnant of her sorrow and anger flooding through him. After, came that breath from the Presence.

It was tinged with enough sorrow to churn his gut.

A quick glance to Elspeth, and his blood ran cold. His friend's face was pale, eyes wide and unblinking.

There was no fire there.

Carissa folded the letter. Her voice wavered. "Thank goodness, they've only killed three so far. Our people got to one, and she was killed before being brought to court."

"Thank goodness?" Varek spat. "Thank *goodness*?"

"Only *three*," Carissa's voice was firm. "Would you rather they kill more?"

"I would rather you didn't *thank* anything for the wrongful deaths of innocent young women."

Aleksander leaned forward. Varek's eyes blazed, refusing to leave the princess's careful, practiced face, carrying as much fire as Ölmesuz eyes could. He'd seen it before, and after last night... "So what do we do?" The boy asked.

Varek's eyes shifted to him, and ever so slightly, that fire fell.

If you end up making a stupid choice, he'd said. Varek would only threaten Aleksander if he ended up making a stupid choice.

Aleksander hoped this was the right one.

Carissa folded her hands. "What do you mean?"

"You wouldn't bring us here just to tell us this and then send us on our way. You have a plan. You always have a plan. So what is it?"

If his sister were anything, erasing her smarts, her visions, her kindness, and her royal status, she was cunning. And she always had a plan.

Aleksander leaned forward. "What's your plan?" he repeated.

She pressed her lips together, chin raising. "I wanted to keep our presence here quiet, but after what's happened during my trip to town, it seems futile." She let that sit for a moment. Thankfully, the room remained quiet. All eyes stayed on the princess. "Lord Asghar."

The man straightened at her attention.

"The last body that was found, that I was told of, was in Belhaven."

Bellhaven.

Aleksander stopped his head from snapping towards Varek. Thankfully, a slow drew his attention towards the lord seated with them.

"For those of you at the table unfamiliar with the south," he said, careful and slow, "that is half a day's ride from Hadiqin along the shore to the east. They have no lord to protect them."

"Their town is unincorporated," Carissa continued. "But it's likely the Blights' search will take them to the nearest fief, which is Hadiqin. Mobilizing Asghar's forces would be too obvious, and likely deter them—I don't want to do that." A dark, focused intensity fell over her face. Any waver, any casual tone within her voice fled. "There are two things we will be focusing on. The first is figuring out what girls will be...chosen as the Scourge, or at least hopefuls for the role, and collecting them to the nearest manor house. I would say ideally to Brevindun, but that can be dealt with at a later date." Her eyes shifted to Varek. "I don't care how many spies you have to use, I don't care how many horses are burned out from the journey. The moment you hear anything, those girls are swept up to us."

Varek's jaw twinged beneath his beard...but he nodded.

"The second...is the Blights themselves. They're a threat to my people. They're a threat to us." Something cold swam through her eyes. "I want these men found and slaughtered like the pigs they are."

Her words struck a chill through him. The Presence shrugged awake from its place of rest along Aleksander's spine and blew a wind through him so frantic and fearful his heart began to pound.

The blurry, dark words from one of the only readable letters in Asghar's office floated along that wind.

Ogaden's face is all I see in Carissa.

His bloodlust is there too.

With great effort, Aleksander looked over at the Ölmesuz. He was good at concealing himself and his thoughts. There were perhaps a handful of moments where Aleksander had witnessed emotion enter his features unwillingly.

This, with shallow breaths barely moving his doublet, the tight hold to his lips, the wide grief in his eyes...this was certainly one of them.

"Varek," Carissa said. "You have served my family for centuries as both a mercenary and an assassin. I..." the princess swallowed hard. "I trust you to oversee these operations from here, partnering with my husband, father, and Commander Polat to cover the country, from the sea to the mountains."

He did not respond.

"You have your contacts still, don't you? If I remember correctly my father used your skills only a handful of years ago. Surely you did not let all those within your employ go."

"No, my lady," Varek grumbled. "I did not."

Her brows rose. "Good. Then I'll need you to contact Sir Unwin and arrange a network for the girls. As for the Blights, he will arrange surveillance for the east, Demir is covering the west, and your group must operate here in the south. The first they hear, see—even smell of a Blight forming, they report it to you, and you report it to me. Then, we will form a plan to corner and dispatch them from there."

Varek rolled the neckline of his doublet between his fingers. "You want all of them dead?"

Her jaw clenched. "No. We need at least one alive. I believe I'm nearly around the block I've hit with the Flow. Once I am, I have found old writings on how to control the Flow within a person." Her features hardened beyond anything Aleksander had ever seen her express before. "I'll wring it out of them myself."

Aleksander glanced across the table to find Elspeth's terrified gaze locked on him.

"Something you disapprove of, Lady D'orde?"

Elspeth blinked, her gaze redirecting to the table and all the cups of tea on it. "No, your highness."

A long breath blew from his sisters lips. She sagged at the

head of the table, bags darkening beneath her eyes. "I know it's not ideal. I know this worries you. But I will do anything, *anything* to help my people. To keep my brother safe." Her head cocked to the side, akin to an animal's. "I only ask that you prioritize those same goals. This country belongs to all of us, you know."

Silence stretched through the hall. Chione looked up, meeting Varek's eyes. There was some conversation that flitted between them, silent.

Without a single word, Varek reached forward and poured a fresh cup of tea and slid it to Aleksander.

A silent peace offering.

A silent alliance.

Aleksander took it and drank.

"Alright," Varek said, some sort of looseness entering his form and leaning towards Carissa. "How many ravens do you have to spare? I've some messages to deliver."

Chapter

THIRTY SIX

WHEN IT SNOWED AT CASTLE Brevindun, his studies were often shifted more towards the cerebral. Aleksander spent his days huddled in warm, quilted outfits lined with furs, reading over prophecies or the history of the continent and the royal family. Once a week, he'd don his armor and enter into a smaller indoor arena normally kept warm, for soldiers and guards to train daily. It was heated by large fire places on either end. Tall windows allowed for a fresh breeze to pierce the indoor ring every now and then, drying off some of the sweat that would build up on his brow. And after, the boy would go out to the garden in his underclothes, stick his face in the snow, and continue on with his day.

As the chill of his armor bit into the back of his neck, his elbows, and his waist, Aleksander realized how much he'd taken that heated room for granted.

His warm up stretches and swings were stiff in the cold. The forms he ran through were choppy. Elspeth joined him after a few minutes, stretching along the wall and complaining all the while about the cold before giving one big huff and drawing her sword.

The rhythm of their cuts and the clanking of their armor was somehow soothing to him. Snow crunched beneath sabatons, breaths followed swishes. Once they'd done enough to be properly warmed up, Aleksander had dropped to his knees and taken a bite out of a clean patch of snow. It froze his tongue. He didn't mind.

Beside him, leaning against the wall of the ring and heaving slow breaths, Elspeth practically steamed.

"Is that your fire? Doing that?" He stood, eyeing the swirls coming up from the cracks in her armor. "Or do you just naturally sweat a lot?"

She raised an eyebrow. "Which do you think?"

It felt like a trap. The mischief dancing in her eyes pitted a knot in his stomach. "Your fire?"

With a smile, she shook her head. "No, I just sweat a lot." The face guard on her helmet slammed down with a flick of her head, and she strode out in front of him, leaving boot prints in the snow.

He paused a moment, then called out, "What do you think of Carissa's plan?"

His friend stopped. Though she did not turn to him, there was no mistaking the deep discomfort that entered her body. "What do *you* think?"

"I think it's..." his tongue fell dry. It was under-planned. It was fueled by fear. "Interesting."

At this, Elspeth turned. "How?"

He shrugged. "Killing people on rumors seems like it could cause issues. It's not what we normally do—especially not Carissa. Even traitors get trials." The smell of Terrell's cottage flooded his nose. The Presence huffed. "Well, usually."

After a moment, Elspeth pushed her guard up. Thick eyebrows peaked over a stern, scared face. "Why does she want the girls gathered?"

Her voice was small. It made his chest hurt.

That, Aleksander did not have an answer for. Carissa didn't give one. He swallowed. "I'd like to say it's to protect them, but..."

Elspeth's lips pressed thin. The look in her eyes was enough to tell Aleksander he did not need to finish that sentence. She knew exactly what he was worried about.

"Glad to see you both made it," Varek's voice rumbled over the arena.

The clank of Elspeth's face guard dropping echoed through the crisp air. Both turned to watch the Ölmesuz stride in, entirely devoid of his leathers or any plate armor. Instead, a large fur cloak rested around his shoulders, and beneath it came flashes of the purple quilting he was so fond of for his doublets.

Elspeth moved into position, but he raised a hand.

"I need to talk to you both before we get into our drills today."

Aleksander's eyes flashed towards his friend. Within the visor, he saw two glowing eyes flash to him as well.

"Come on," Varek rolled his neck. "Don't look at each other like that. What could I say that earns that look?"

Plate rattled as Elspeth shrugged. "I don't know. Something that makes us feel like we're failures."

Varek's lips pressed thin in response. "You're not failures. And I'm making *sure* you're not failures. But that's why I need to talk to you." He waved his fingers. "Sheath your swords, come here."

They followed suit, walking the ten paces it took to get within regular speaking distance of the man. Elspeth removed her helmet, resting it against her hip. Waves of hair that had crept free of her crown braid stuck to her cheeks. They were a bright, rich pink, dappled with beads of sweat. Her brows tucked tight over her eyes, heavy and stern and focused.

Varek cleared his throat, and Aleksander's eyes snapped towards him.

Embarrassment warmed his cheeks. The boy swallowed hard, bracing for the inevitable scolding—but Varek simply slid his eyes over to Elspeth, and began. "You were both in the meeting, so I won't bore you with a repeating of the facts. I'll only say this." His chest expanded with a deep breath. Varek took a moment before speaking. "This is not about the Sword and the

Scourge."

Aleksander's brows furrowed.

"What we are doing, what *you* two are doing, is about the people. It's about their futures. Forget the Sword, forget the Scourge, even if that title belongs to you. What matters here and now are the people of Zekhar. *All* the people." His brows dropped, stern and steady over his eyes. "Their lives are on the line in this conflict, and it is up to you two to be a part of ending it. So when you train today, remember that you are *not* going to be fighting each other. You will be fighting people who do not deserve to be called 'people.' You will be fighting against people who do not care about the men, women, and children who cannot defend themselves. You will be fighting against monsters who see anything they disagree with as a stepping stone to their own success and the realization of their own agendas. You will be asked to leave your morals at home..." his eyes slipped over to Aleksander, holding a steady gaze. "And you must respond no, and hold on to what gives you a soul with every ounce of strength you possess."

Aleksander swallowed hard.

The man continued, "It's not easy, and Mother knows if I was given the choice, I would *not*, in a thousand millennia, have placed you in the roles you now inhabit. But we do what we can with what we've been given. So as this gets more and more serious, as it gets more and more *real*..." he shook his head. "Don't forget there is a real enemy out there, bent on destruction. And don't forget who it is you *really* serve."

Without prompting, the clearest image appeared in his mind. No sound came with it, there was no screaming or begging like he'd expected. Instead he saw a group of women—newborns all the way to those the same age as Iscah and Carissa—standing together. Rodzjiek, Ölmesuz, a few Zekharyan, and one Mekartlim with wings a shimmering white-gold.

At the front of them was Iscah, Elspeth by her side.

The image made the Presence dance within his spine. It raced up and down, sending jolts of panic and joy and fear all at once through his body. All at once, it felt strange and wrong to be so moved by such an image. He knew what it meant. He knew that, to some extent, it was Iscah's doing. And he knew that, though he wasn't quite ready to say it out loud, he would not make the stupid decision Varek feared he might.

So he nodded. One firm, steady nod. "I don't think I'll ever forget."

Something flashed within the man's eyes. Aleksander could swear he saw a shimmer along his lower lash line before he blinked, stepping back from the pair. "Alright then. Drills, let's see it."

"But we just finished our drills," Elspeth said.

"Was I here?"

She shook her head with a sigh, putting her helmet back on. "No, sir."

At this, Varek let a smile slip. "Then I'll say it again. Drills."

Just as Aleksander turned to stand beside Elspeth and unsheathe Aoife, the door to the manor burst open.

"Aleksander!"

Panic flooded his chest. The cry was so urgent, so frantic, he thought for a moment that the castle had been attacked, that Demir and Janek and Clauden and Lenore were all gone. Aoife dropped from his fingers, an icy scrape of metal on compacted snow echoing through the ring. As he turned, all he saw was a wild mane of curls the color of wheat throwing themselves over his shoulder.

"I did it!" Carissa squealed.

Aleksander's heart pounded. His sister's arms embraced him, rocking side to side, her laughter ringing out into the still winter day.

"What?" he said, slowly lifting his arms to her in the intention to return her hug, but she pulled back. Fine fingers gripped his pauldrons, a smile the likes of which he'd never seen on her face nearly blinding him.

"I did it!" she repeated. "I figured it out! Aleksander, I can do magic again." With another laugh, she threw herself around him again. Her weight caused him to stumble, and as he caught himself and held on to her, his eyes slid to Elspeth.

Even within her helmet, she did not hide her disapproval well. Her brows fitted low over her eyes, crackling with embers. A subtle shake of her head was all she gave before swinging her sword and striding towards one of the dummies near the wall. With a single stroke, she split its head in two. Snow shuddered off its false shoulders, plopping onto the rest that had accumulated beneath it.

Just as Aleksander looked at Varek, he realized he'd been nearly silent. "That's great," he finally said.

Carissa separated from him again, holding out her hands to reveal a flower. "Watch."

Aleksander did. He watched as she held a pale blue blossom in one palm, and a smooth cut of obsidian in the other. He watched as she whispered something, not anything in a language Aleksander knew, and he watched as the flower wilted as an image appeared on the surface of the stone, as if carved.

Janek, drinking an ale with Demir.

Aleksander watched even as his stomach soured and his heart pounded.

Even as the Presence grabbed him and shook, seeming almost on the verge of screaming.

The flower turned to nothing more than crumbled brown bits and fluttered away on the wind. With it, the image left Carissa's scrying stone.

Her eyes blazed as they found his face again—but that blaze fell instantly. Puzzlement twisted her features. "I thought you'd be more excited, Aleksander."

"Oh, I am," he blinked rapidly and ran a gloved hand over his sweat-matted hair. "I am, I just...the way you'd screamed, I thought someone was dead so..." a nervous laugh leapt from his throat. "Forgive me for not being more enthusiastic. That's... that's very...good, Carissa."

"Oh," she sighed, grasping his hand. "I am sorry, I just got so excited. I didn't even think about..." Her other hand covered her mouth for a moment. When it dropped, she smiled again, but this time at Varek. "I'm going to take my brother for a moment. There are a few things I need to discuss with him after this change."

The man's expression was nearly unreadable. "Fine. Though I do have work to do regarding the spy network you just had me set up and I've limited time for training, so do make it quick, your highness."

If Carissa heard the vitriol with which he'd delivered her title, she didn't show it. Her grip around Aleksander's hand became tighter, and she dragged him from the ring without so much as a backward glance.

Halfway to the door, however, Aleksander twisted his head over his shoulder.

Varek was muttering to Elspeth, both of them watching as he left.

He couldn't do anything to quell the guilt that began to bubble in his stomach.

Chapter

THIRTY SEVEN

T HERE WEREN'T AS MANY CANDLES burning in the chapel today. A distinct lack of heat swirled with the usual incense and smoke, making a shiver ripple over his skin. Strange how a single flame can really affect something much larger than itself.

Aleksander had taken off his armor, but only his armor. He kept the gambeson and pants he wore beneath his plate. Hair still stuck to his forehead, around his ears, against the nape of his neck. Varek had asked them to make it quick, and that was his intention.

Training took his mind off things.

Today, he *needed* to take his mind off things.

Carissa stood at the sound of his approach, spinning to face him from where she had been seated. The princess had chosen a pew directly between Tulathne's statue and Iscah's. If Aleksander were more of a superstitious boy, he would have held on to the notion that perhaps this meant she was trying to find a middle ground. But he wasn't, so it passed by just as quickly as it occurred to him.

Her pale green eyes flicked towards the statue of their friend. "I have to admit," she started, "I talked to her."

Aleksander swallowed hard. "You...what?"

"I know," she smiled, a blush creeping into her cheeks. "It's not right to pray to anyone else, but…I had to. I don't know if she even heard me, I just…" That smile faded, and she turned once more. The light from Iscah's candles danced along the loose curls framing her face. "I miss her."

His fingers fiddled with the cuffs of his gambeson. "I'm sure she misses you too."

She huffed a sad laugh. "She's dead, Aleksander. Dead people don't feel."

Teeth sunk into the inside of his bottom lip. Those words just felt…wrong. They were true, to an extent. Those who weren't here anymore can't feel the way living individuals do. Yet…

"You don't know that," he said. Slow steps took him to the end of her pew. "Maybe she's been waiting for you to come talk to her."

"Well, I did. And she didn't say anything back, so…" There was a bitterness to her words. But when she faced Aleksander, there was nothing but joy in her eyes. "Sit down. I want to talk with you."

He did as she asked, smoothing his hands over the bunching fabric on his torso. "Varek wants me to make this quick."

"Varek can't make *me* do anything," she hissed, then immediately closed her eyes. A slow inhale whistled through her nose, followed by a soft puff of air from rounded lips. "Sorry. I'm just…I've had it with him thinking he can tell me what to do just because he's older and knew my however-many-great's grandfather." She pulled him into a soft, focused gaze. "Besides, what I have to say is important."

"Okay," he said. His voice was soft. There had been many times over the years where Carissa had pulled him aside—away from a dinner, a party, a meeting, class—and stared with that same, quiet intensity. What followed was always earnest. Whether it was a critique against him or a critique against herself that she asked forgiveness for, Aleksander knew this look was one that implied she meant every word she spoke to the very center of herself.

"I am sorry," she began, "that I've been so caught up in my work."

Aleksander shook his head. "You don't need to apologize. So have I. We're both busy."

"Yes, but we're *family*. And family is supposed to make time for each other." The pew rocked as she leaned back. "I could have made more of an effort to show up to meals over the last month or so. Could have watched a training session or two. Gone to town with you more."

"I wouldn't have been there," Aleksander said. The words left his lips without thought, and the meaning of what he said fell upon his shoulders only when Carissa's eyes widened. "Not like that," he covered, "not that I wouldn't have wanted to. I love you, you know that."

She smiled and patted his hand. "I know."

"It's only…" the last month swirled about his mind in a tempest of flashes. "There's been so much on my mind. So much I've been working on. Even if you made time…I'm not so sure I'd have been able to. Besides, you were able to figure out everything with your magic much faster this way."

"That is true," she agreed, stretching her arms above her head and leaning back over the pew. A few cracks sounded from her spine before she relaxed back into a regular seated position. "I am glad for that." A light took to her features. "Oh, you have no idea how hard it was. I don't know how Terrell did it with his lack of education, I mean…it took me months." At this, she laughed and shrugged. "I suppose it could have taken him years. Anyway. It's so fascinating, the way it works."

As she launched into her explanation, about how everything in the world is gifted with the Flow and all she had to do was shift how she approached it, nausea grew in Aleksander's gut.

He hated how he felt. Carissa had been so overwhelmed with this, so stressed after the occurrences from the last time she used her magic so constantly. He'd seen how it had worn on her. That specter she'd become over a handful of days had been a sight he'd never wished to encounter, nor a condition he'd ever wished upon her. He had no right to feel so...angry with her. No, not angry. Just frustrated. She had finally found a way around something that was giving her immense fear and truly damaging her, but was it really worth it?

Especially as she discussed how easy it was to transfer the toll to a plant, a candle, a mouse—a flower, like the one she used in her demonstration.

How *easy* it was to inflict the suffering that should be hers on something undeserving.

"Carissa," he started, weighing his words carefully. "I understand that you want to find a way to use magic that's more...sustainable. But do you really think doing it like *this* is the right way?"

A single, thin eyebrow raised.

Aleksander cleared his throat. "I mean, the Flow works with everyone differently for a reason, right? We're not supposed to be...moving it from us. Isn't that what the priestesses always said? Deal with the Flow directly? Mediators only cause issues. And..." His mind stuttered on his next words, but he managed to get them out. "I'd be irresponsible if I didn't bring up El's concern. That this was the same thing Terrell did, only he shifted his magic through—"

"I am *not* Lord Terrell," she snarled.

The Presence awoke, shivering in the back of his mind. He could feel it reaching for his consciousness, trying to tell him this was not a safe situation anymore.

He pushed it away. But the rapid pace his heart beat continued on, unchanged by any amount of convincing he tried.

"You all keep saying that. I shouldn't be doing this because of that *traitor*. I am not a traitor, I am not doing this to tear down my country and damn my family, I am doing this to *help* us." Tears glistened in her eyes, rimmed red with frustration. "Stop comparing me to him, I *hate* him."

"Okay," Aleksander wrapped an arm around her shoulders, pulling the princess close. Her head dipped, hitting his chest. "Okay," he repeated. "I'm sorry. You're right, you're not Terrell.

It's just...it's unnatural what he did, and El is worried. I'm worried. But I'm sorry, you're right. You deserve our trust."

Silent sobs bobbed her shoulders. Her face pressed into the front of his gambeson, and he prayed he hadn't sweat enough that he'd end up suffocating her with odor. Thankfully, she showed no sign of minding, even if he did stink.

His chin dropped to the top of her head. "I do trust you, Carissa."

She nodded. "I know you do. And I know you're worried." Sitting up, she swiped at the tears pooling beneath her eyes with the sleeve of her gown. "And I understand why. I'm not saying you're crazy for having those fears. I'm just saying that I have had them too, so often through this process, and I've finally worked past them. I don't need you to bring them up again. Or anyone else."

"I won't," he said. "Promise."

She sniffed. It echoed off the vaulted ceiling. In the silence that stretched between them, the princess allowed her eyes to wander the room.

Aleksander's, however, never left her face.

He'd promised he wouldn't bring it up again.

That didn't mean he approved of what she was doing. And it certainly didn't erase his concern.

Another heavy sigh cleared the air, and she turned back to him. "I had a vision. I've had a few, actually."

Aleksander nodded. "I'm not surprised. You'd been going without them for a while, it's only fair you've had more as you started exercising with the Flow more."

"Yes." Her ring glistened as she untangled it from a thread in her skirts. Once it came free, she wound her hands in it, crumpling the velvet and lace. "The first one was what made me realize I needed to change my interaction with the Flow. I couldn't keep doing it as a mage, not anymore. I'd put too many lives at risk if I did that. And the second one, well..." she looked up at the altar before them. Aleksander couldn't tell if she was looking at a statue or a candle, but it didn't matter. "The second one showed me I'm on the right track."

He leaned forward. "Do you remember it?"

She nodded.

"Are you willing to share it with me?"

Again, she nodded, shifting in her seat. "Of course. Um..." her eyes fluttered shut, brow scrunching in thought. "It was quite fascinating, actually. I started in the palace this time. I was on the second level, and as I walked out, I saw rows and rows of pikes lining the road down to Brevindun. Heads sat on each one. Marked with a symbol—I can't remember it, not now. It wasn't one I've seen before. But for once, the city was silent. Everything was peaceful. No one was yelling, no one was dying, there were no homunculi—in fact, their bodies were burning in a pyre down by the Great Temple. I was made queen, and my reign was one of peace. I had children, Aleksander," she opened her eyes at this and turned to him. A smile curled her lips. "By doing this, I will bring an age of peace. Such a deep peace that I will have to be long dead and buried by the time someone dares to even try and break it."

That peace she spoke of flooded her face. Her eyes relaxed, her smile was languid. She felt it. Aleksander could see that it was a very tangible feeling in the moment. But all that writhed within him was disgust.

What Carissa spoke of as peace sounded to him like a massacre. In his own mind, the silence was caused by an empty city. Rot clung to the air in her vision—hadn't she smelled it? But he hadn't been there, hadn't stood beside her on the balcony overlooking the pikes and the city and whatever her reign would bring about. There was peace in her features, yes. But her tone was tinged with a darkness that send the Presence into a panic.

He blinked at his sister.

She had changed over the month they'd spent apart.

"Our people will be safe, Aleksander."

Or perhaps he had.

Whose heads were on those pikes in her vision? He couldn't help but envision Varek's, Chione's, Asghar...even Fazhia and

Lady Kallendrine. Were those dead truly the enemy? Were they truly followers of the Scourge?

Or just people who didn't agree with Carissa?

He sniffed and licked his lips. "I hope that's true."

How dare he assume such horrible things.

"It will be." Her smile grew. "Aleksander, I've never felt such peace and stillness from a vision before. Tulathne is letting us know we are on the right path. That *I* am on the right path."

He nodded slowly. "She could also be warning you," he said softly. Carissa's brows furrowed in confusion. The promise he'd made moments earlier came back to him, and he shook his head, waving the thought from the air with a lazy hand. "Sorry, forget what I said just..."

Out of the corner of his eye, he swore Iscah moved. Focusing on her painted face, however, he was sure he'd imagined it.

"I just don't want you getting your hopes up. Remember, none of this is certain."

Carissa's fingers laced with his, offering a reassuring squeeze. "I know that. But I have proof this one is."

Nausea swelled in Aleksander's throat. Fear wrapped itself around his lungs as he asked, "Really?"

Even as she nodded, he prayed it wasn't true. There was no way she knew what was going to happen. There was nothing in their lives at the moment that could prove the tragedy she'd witnessed—the tragedy she planned to orchestrate—would happen.

"Yes, Aleksander." Her curls bounced along her cheeks, brushing the side of a wide smile. With their fingers still intertwined, she pressed his hand to her abdomen. For the first time, he noticed how strangely her dress sat about her midsection. How she'd kept it loose for the last two months and now even the laces weren't enough to accommodate for the extra space needed.

Aleksander stopped breathing.

"You're..."

Tears welled in her eyes. "I get to be a mother."

Chapter

THIRTY EIGHT

E SHOULD HUG HER. He should hug her and pick her up and scream and laugh and congratulate her. Janek and Carissa had been married for years with no children on the horizon, despite how much they both desperately wanted to be parents.

When they'd only been engaged, he'd sat in on many conversations where they'd plan out their family. Six children, no, eight. No, Carissa wouldn't want to go through labor that many times, so three. Three is a good number. Besides, as royalty they didn't need to worry about infant or mother mortality as much, they had better midwives and healers than the rest of the country. If anything happened to the baby or Carissa, there was little-to-no fear that it wouldn't be taken care of. And once they'd been married, he'd sat with Janek as the man expressed his fear of never being able to be a father. He loved his wife and wouldn't leave her for anything, she was more important than that desire. Their love didn't take away the sorrow of it all, though.

Growing up with Janek...he was a natural at it. There were times when Aleksander saw him more as a father than a big brother or even a friend, and imagining him without a flock of children following him felt strange.

And Carissa. They were siblings, yes, but more often in his

memory she occupied a space that Lenore should have occupied. She was kind and stern and loving. She *deserved* to have her family.

He'd always wanted to be an uncle.

So he threw his arms around her, mouth agape, eyes unblinking. She returned the hug fervently, with all the excitement of a new mother not yet aware of all the struggles she would be undertaking.

"I'm so happy for you, Carissa," he said. The words were flat, but he meant them. He really did. Regardless of the conversation they'd just had, regardless of the fact that she essentially admitted that this child was the proof she needed to enact a massacre, he was truly happy.

She laughed into his shoulder. It was such a bright, carefree sound.

It stung his ears.

Pulling back, he actually smiled. It wasn't forced; the joy on his sister's face was enough to break through the grim veil that had been draped over him. Even just a little. "Does Janek know?"

"No," she said quickly, "not yet. I'm planning on telling him once we get back. I wanted to wait to ensure this one stuck, and it has." She was practically bouncing in her seat. "I just feel like everything is lining up now. My breakthrough with the Flow, this child, my visions coming less frequently but still being overwhelmingly clear..." she sighed, dipping her head back and staring at the ceiling. "The next few months are going to be tough. But we have so many different omens for good, Aleksander. And with this new method—Aleksander, I can do magic and I will be fine. The baby will be fine."

"That's good," he said. "Good that the baby will be okay."

He was glad she couldn't see him. He was so, so glad she couldn't see the way his brows pinched together, the way his nostrils flared. He was glad she couldn't see the way he fought against the disgust, the anger, the confusion.

Her head tipped forward and he tossed his hair out of his eyes, refocusing on the statue of Tulathne just a few meters past the princess.

The white marble glowed with the candles beneath it, but for the first time, Aleksander did not regard the statue as being alone. When he'd first entered the chapel, all those weeks ago, he'd seen it as mildly disrespectful and sad, his goddess being so out of the main area, so tucked away. There had been a mix of indignation and frustration; he could recognize the feelings now. As much as he'd not cared to kneel there and pray every day, that had still been *his* goddess. *His* mother

Now, She felt like a strange, looming figure. Distant. Cold. Content to watch, but not caring enough to step in as the world around him crumbled—as the lives of his people were so clearly placed in jeopardy.

This was why he was the Sword of Ages, the priestesses had said. Whenever he'd make a comment like that—"Why doesn't She just do it Herself"—they would always admonish him with the reminder that Tulathne was a goddess. It was *his* duty to mediate and enact Her will upon the earth.

Aleksander swallowed the bile rising in his throat.

All his life, he'd become content with that notion. That he was the one acting on Her behalf.

Not anymore.

He hoped those eyes, hidden within Her stone veil, turned to him. He hoped She saw the look he gave Her.

We will talk, he said. She was a goddess. She could listen if She wanted to. *And I will get my answers.*

Carissa heaved a sigh, the simple, delicate sound rocketing Aleksander back to the present. Back to the cold still leeching from his bones, back to the sweat that had dried on the nape of his neck, back to the soft hand that squeezed his.

She smiled. "Well, I suppose you need to return to training. I think I'll take a stroll around the grounds."

He furrowed his brow. "It's snowed, Carissa. There won't be any paths for you to walk—none of the plants will have leaves, it won't be worth it."

She waved him off, pushing herself to stand. "It's fresh air and a way for me to stretch my legs. That's all I need."

She bowed her head, hand cupping his cheek. Her full face, glowing with renewed hope, was cast in flickering shadows as she offered him a final smile. A burst of purple sparked within her eyes. "Our people will be alright, Aleksander. Our family, Janek, my children—we'll be alright. I'm certain of it."

Her lips met the top of his head, the way she used to kiss him when he'd woken from a nightmare, or performed admirably against Janek in training, or any other occasion where the pride she felt for being his family radiated clearly from her wide eyes and wide grin. Only now, it was subtle. There was more here she was proud of.

As much as he watched the back of her dress swish out the doors—the same dress she'd worn for the last two winters, the same cloak, the same tangle of hair—something had shifted in his chest when her lips left his crown.

He hadn't asked it. It hadn't come to mind quickly enough. She'd left before he'd formed a thought, well before he formed a word.

The back of his gambeson stuck against the pew, squeaking strangely as he shifted to face Iscah.

"Was I there?" he asked the statue. Aleksander's voice was small, light—it faded as quickly as a breath.

She said nothing, of course.

Dread sunk in his stomach.

The cords in his throat felt thin and reedy, as if voicing his wonderment was enough to snap them, so he needed to be extra careful when he spoke next.

Shifting forward, Aleksander rested his forearms on the back of the pew in front of him.

It wasn't a question. He knew it wasn't. Every time Carissa told Aleksander a vision, she never failed to include everyone she saw, whether she knew them or not. When she'd first had the vision about his troupe, she'd called them "spirits," and identified them based on their energy, what they brought to the table—their steadfastness, their free spirits, their drive.

She had listed Janek, her children, and herself.

And the severed heads on spikes, lining the main road to the castle.

"She didn't see me, Iscah," he breathed.

The realization sank deep into his chest. It was a heavy weight, sinking deeper and deeper as the Presence awoke, frantic and spiraling and curling through is mind, his spine, his back. Aleksander was numb. There was no fear—no emotion at all—when he voiced it plainly.

"I wasn't in her vision."

◇ ✳ ◇

THE DOORS TO the library were open. Aleksander did not need to shove them aside, though his arms ached for a use, ached for some sort of release to the pressure building in his chest and shoulders.

He'd sat in the chapel for a long moment, staring back and forth between the statues—Tulathne, Iscah, and the five other Kutsalyot scattered around whose names he didn't know, and wasn't sure he ever would.

When that got to be too much, when that tension started in his hands and his neck, writhing through the tubes and vents in his heart until it hurt, he stood and paced back and forth.

He knew he had to go back to training. He knew that was what Varek was expecting. And he didn't want to make the man frustrated with his already-busy schedule, nor deprive Elspeth of any practice that could better prepare her for the massacre he now was certain would soon crest the horizon.

And yet, though every part of him wanted to go back to the training ring and let loose on Varek, Elspeth, and every dummy Asghar stocked for his men, Aleksander had found himself veering off towards the library, just a little ways down from the chapel.

The librarian, he'd decided, would know more than anyone here. After all, it was the tome she had given him that made him react this way in the first place.

Books sat piled on Chione's desk at the front. Along it all was a scroll, opened and pinned with four weights. A pen sat on it. Its nib still dripped ink onto a blank portion of the parchment.

She herself was nowhere to be seen.

"Chione?" he called. Her name did not echo the way he'd hoped. In his dream, the library was vast, empty, and everything echoed.

He'd forgotten the real thing was silent, devouring every bit of sound anyone attempted to introduce into its various pages and scrolls.

Aleksander started to walk. His boots hit the slatted wood in quick, heavy stomps. Every shelf he passed, he'd throw a glance down the rest of the aisle.

Empty.

Empty.

Empty.

His glances grew frantic, his steps faster. He'd never run in a library. In fact, as a child he was punished for it.

But now his hand caught on the corners of the heavy wood shelves, swinging himself into aisle after aisle, keeping that speed and momentum and desperation as it grew.

He turned a corner, opening his mouth to call out once more for Chione, only to have the gentle crackle of flames in the hearth he'd sat at not too long ago pull his attention. His tongue froze in his mouth as he wove through the stacks, eventually coming upon the fireplace and the seats around it.

The window nearby had a soft flurry of snow caressing the glass in a gentle greeting. Snowflakes stuck and melted there.

He stopped, and from her seat in the chair, Chione looked up.

"Aleksander?" She put aside her cup of tea, moving to stand.

Across from her, seated in an identical chair, wrapped in blankets and cradling her own cup of tea, Theresas lifted her head, her pale eyes drifting aimlessly past him—though he could tell the older woman knew exactly where he was.

Decorum called on him to greet the pair, ask to sit, and only then express the turmoil writhing around within him.

But his voice cracked, the fear that had been thundering within his mind finding sound in a single sentence: "Tell me Carissa won't kill Elspeth."

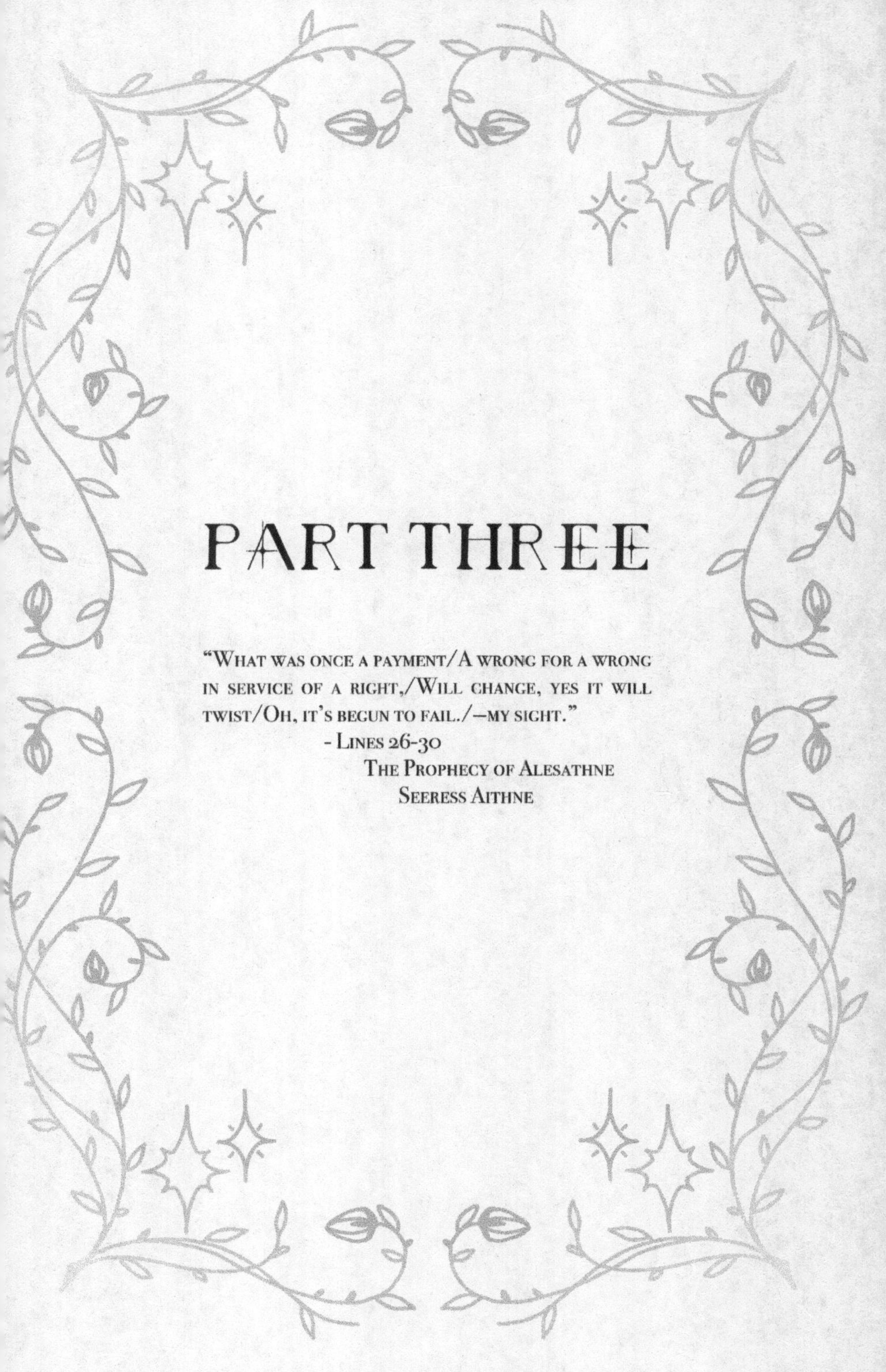

PART THREE

"WHAT WAS ONCE A PAYMENT/A WRONG FOR A WRONG
IN SERVICE OF A RIGHT,/WILL CHANGE, YES IT WILL
TWIST/OH, IT'S BEGUN TO FAIL./—MY SIGHT."
- LINES 26-30
THE PROPHECY OF ALESATHNE
SEERESS AITHNE

THIRTY NINE

I T WASN'T WHAT HE HAD intended to say. It wasn't even what he should have said. His mind emptied of every other imaginable question, every notion and topic he'd been consumed with on the walk here. All he saw, as tangible before him as the flicking flames of the fire, were spikes topped with the heads of everyone he loved. There were so many other people in danger, so many other girls than just those he knew personally. But his mind narrowed, and the only eyes staring back at him were *hers*.

His chest rose fast with his breaths, both frantic from the dread he felt, and desperate to intake oxygen after that flurry of action he'd taken to get here.

Chione blinked at him. She froze in her chair, leaning forward as if to stand—one hand poised on the arm rest, the other on her knee. Swaths of shimmering steel-toned hair slipped past her shoulder. It reflected the light of the hearth, glowing as though it would melt like the metal it resembled. "What?" Her response was quiet, breathy.

Shocked.

Aleksander swallowed and shifted his weight. "Carissa just confided in me that she had a vision. Of a peaceful, silent Zekhar. One without war or malice or hate. She saw pikes lining the road to the castle, topped with the heads of the people who caused the unrest. I think she interpreted them as the heads of Blights, but I..." his mouth ran dry. Aleksander stuck his lips between his teeth and wet them before continuing. "I'm not sure. The way she spoke, Chione, I'm...I've learned things. I've seen things. And —"

Chione stood abruptly, rushing towards him and enveloping him in a hug. He froze at the sudden contact, at the crushing pressure she exerted on him. As his face pressed into her shoulder, he became aware of the dampness scattered on his cheeks.

She said nothing as she pulled back; soft, ink-stained thumbs wiped below his eyes. Pillows appeared out of nowhere and were arranged on the ground for her to sit.

He took the chair she'd been in moments earlier.

Once they'd all settled, Theresas fixed her empty stare on him.

"So she told you," the woman's crackling voice harmonized with the fire.

Aleksander nodded, then caught himself and said, "Yes. All of it."

"I half wondered if she'd keep it to herself." The mage leaned back. One hand drifted to her right temple, picking out a tight ringlet streaked with grey and twirling it through her fingers. Thick eyelashes fluttered as she thought. "What did you take away from it?"

Aleksander swallowed. "That she's going to enact a massacre."

Beside him on the floor, Chione stiffened.

Theresas lifted an eyebrow. "A massacre? Or a war?"

The question hung in the air. For the first time in his life, Aleksander found that a difficult distinction to make.

Throughout his time in school, in the temple, pouring over history books and the records of battles and ambushes and invasions and anything else Clauden deigned important enough to teach him as the Sword, it had been easy to differentiate between the two. A war had two opposing sides. A clear winner. Massacres were carried out by one force, and though they were sometimes considered to be the winners, it was never a fair fight. The "win" was never genuine.

Perhaps this time it was both.

There was a war coming. That was certain. Not only was there growing unrest with the Blights, but there was growing unrest in the people themselves, separate from the struggles with the Scourge—or perhaps parallel to it. But Carissa's vision still stuck out in Aleksander's mind as a definite tragedy. A definite massacre.

Though his sister hadn't said it, he *knew* not all of the dead she saw were the Scourge's forces. There's no way they could have been.

Though his sister hadn't said it, he knew the reason Brewith was so peaceful was because almost no one remained within her walls.

"It's a massacre," he finally said. "There may be a war with it, but I know what she told me. I know what she saw, even if she doesn't."

Theresas pursed her lips, nodding slowly.

"I mean, look at what she's doing with the Flow. What's your opinion on that, Theresas?" His lips wavered, failing to stop himself from speaking further. "You of all people should know humans aren't meant to wield the Flow in such a way. It's…it's dangerous not only for us but…she's actively harming other things, other creatures, for the purpose of not harming herself. In the meeting this morning she posited taking members of the Blights and using the Flow to get truth out of them. It sounds…" He swallowed hard. "It sounds like torture, and…I can't help but worry that she'll sometimes grab the wrong people. And what's going on with the girls she wants gathered? She gave us no reason, no purpose—Theresas, how do we know she isn't going to do the *same* to them, forcing confessions until she can find the Scourge herself?"

The fire crackled in his pause.

"Does that not concern you?"

"Of course it does," the old mage said. "But she is our princess and if she refuses to listen to my reason, then she refuses and must face the consequence." For all the sorrow in her features, her lip twisted momentarily into a smile. "Besides, the Flow will take from an unruly wielder. It always does. Just not the way one might think."

"Why did you ask about Elspeth?" Chione finally spoke. She looked up at him, her eyes sparkling in the light. They were clear, tired. First the briefing this morning, where she'd been arguing with Varek, and now this. "Is there something I need to know? Is she alright?"

Aleksander quickly shook his head. "No, she's fine, she's... there's nothing going on yet." He swallowed hard, allowing his gaze to drift towards the flickering within the hearth. "She just... She told me about the poem you gave her, but then she...she asked me if it was gonna happen to her, what's happened to all those other girls. If *I* was going to kill her." His stomach ran cold with a rush of adrenaline, his heart racing with disgust and fear as he let the thought linger for too long. "I told her no, and that's true. I don't care what happens—she could be the Scourge herself for all I care, I'd never raise a hand against her."

"But Carissa is not you," Chione said, filling in the gap for him.

Aleksander nodded slowly. His tongue was fat and numb as he spoke. "Carissa is not me. And what she's doing has me worried." He took a deep breath in an attempt to calm the tremors passing through to his fingers, savoring the warmth fluttering against his hands, his legs. He hated what his words implied. That Carissa would be capable of killing. That Carissa would be capable of killing a *friend*.

It was a shock to hear her so violently wish for the deaths of the Blights, but he'd understood. They were evil, purely, and they'd proven that. To some extent, he'd agreed, and he would take them out if any were found within his purview.

But her vision had made him worried.

Perhaps she did have the nerve required to slaughter innocents. Even those she knew.

After a moment, Theresas cleared her throat.

Her hair was arranged into long, thin braids, with gentle curls fluttering out here and there. A slight hand dragged down the side of her head, gathering a section and pulling it over her shoulder. Small metal clasps rang against one another, against the rings on her fingers. Her chest rose and fell with a steady breath.

"She's a skilled mage, your sister," she began, "if often too...I hesitate to say greedy, but that's the only word that comes to mind." She tilted her head. Considering something. "I understand where she's coming from, why she feels its her only option. Even if she is wrong. Even if it's going to hurt her more in the long run."

The three of them sat in silence. He'd come to get answers and in search of that comfort Chione managed to provide. So far, his mind had gone blank in his rush to find her.

That number, beside the prophecy he'd stumbled upon in that tiny book, came to mind again. "What is S.C?"

Chione blinked. "Sorry, what?"

"After a year." His hand went to his side, where his heavier doublets often had a pocket as though he had concealed the book within his gambeson and not kept it beneath his mattress. Biting the inside of his lip again, he folded his hands. "In the book you lent me, there was a year that had S.C. after it."

The woman's eyes softened. "It's in old Zekharyan. *Synaté Calvantia.*"

"It's used to denote time after the gods made themselves known to us. Tulathne, named usually as Calvantia, was the first." The old mage spoke with such passivity, Aleksander almost didn't grasp all she'd said.

She smiled at the confusion and shock he was sure sat clearly on his face. "Yes, there's more than just Her. And yes, the name you've called Her is not Hers. Well," she bobbed her head to the side, "it is and it isn't. Names are funny that way. The others, they didn't get that change. Just faded, except for those across the sea, from what I know." She waved her hand. "But that's not for now. That's for later, when you have less pressing matters."

His head swam. All his life, he'd been taught that Tulathne was...well, Tulathne. The Lady of Balances. Of life and death, giving and taking. The *only* Lady, the only goddess, at least for Zekharyans. Ölmesuz had the Mother and all their Kutsalyot, the Rodzjiekim their Bozkei and spirits, but—

"You've made him confused now, my love," Chione chided. "This is why you stick to magic and I share about history and politics."

Theresas laughed, a bright crackling sound tinged with exhaustion and humor from years gone by. "As if those three subjects are never entwined. How many times have we counseled each other over the years?"

Chione sniffed back a laugh, dropping her gaze from the warm features of the mage seated beside her. When her eyes once more rose to Aleksander, the light that had danced there momentarily was gone. "My young champion," she breathed, "what will you do?"

Aleksander could have laughed. What a question. There were so many things he could do about so many problems. And yet... "I..."

He wasn't sure.

Everything was changing. Not just on the levels of the towns and the Blights, but in the courts as well. Within the royal family. Carissa was not herself, just as he was no longer himself. They'd both shifted and grown. The face Aleksander saw in the mirror was one he would always recognize, but it somehow felt more and more distant each time he looked. And Carissa...

Her eyes were the same, that pale green hue like lichen streaming from old pines, but the light within them was different.

The Eyes of Time, it seemed, had come to stay within the body belonging to his sister. The girl he'd grown up with wouldn't have seen a vision of a silent city and severed heads lining the main street as an omen of peace. The girl he'd grown up with—the sister he'd grown up with—would have fallen to her knees and sobbed at the destruction, the lives lost. And maybe she had. Maybe she'd come out of the vision and crumpled, overwhelmed, trying to find a way to balance the grief and the sorrow with the promise of a family and a peaceful city. But he *hadn't* seen that.

Maybe he was making excuses for a woman who no longer deserved them.

"I think..." he spoke again slowly. Both gave him space to parse his words. "I think I will go back to training, and then I will go write a letter to Demir." Blowing out a breath, Aleksander stood. "Thank you," he muttered softly to the women.

"Of course." Theresas said. She picked at her nails, holding them up as though she could see them. "If you have more questions, we'd love to hear them."

"Not now. I mean, I know I have more, it's just..." Nervous hands tugged at the long hem of his gambeson. "you got me to think a lot, and right now I think the best course of action for myself is to go and...make sure the people who need protection are getting it."

"Of course." Chione looped her fingers thorough his, hanging by his side. She smiled when he looked down at her. That usual tinge of sadness to it was more potent, but alongside it ran pure contentment. "I'm sorry we couldn't give you more guidance."

The corners of Aleksander's mouth twitched with a smile. He couldn't bring himself to offer a full one. There was too much going on in his mind to use the energy he'd need for a full smile. But it was enough.

She gripped his hand and tugged. As he helped her to her feet, Aleksander felt like he should say more. Like there was so much he needed to say. Were Theresas not there, he may have considered sitting back down and telling Chione all about his dream. What Iscah told him, what she showed him.

Instead he nodded, turned, and disappeared into the shelves once more.

For the first time in a long time, he was oddly at peace. He was not comfortable by any means, yet his heart had slowed to a relaxed pace; there was no tension in his hands, no rage locking his jaw. A great darkness pressed in around him, and those simple, worrying facts floated through his mind—Carissa's vision, the coming war and inevitable massacre, the danger Elspeth could be in, Varek's spies and continuous treason, the new possibility of Tulathne *not* being Tulathne—but they were not overwhelming. They were simply there.

With a deep breath, they even settled.

Things were going wrong and, unlike his sister, he was never one to formulate a good, complex plan. But he could react. If anything came up, he could swing his sword in time to block or counter. That's what he'd been trained to do—not to plan, but to fight.

As long as the threats made themselves known, he wouldn't have an issue dealing with them.

Aleksander did not pause as he strode out the doors, nor as he continued down the hall back to the training arena. Not a single servant or noble wandered the halls—or if they had, he'd not taken notice of them. His boots alone echoed off the stone and tile around him. By the time he reached the arena, it was empty.

A scuffling cut through the muddled ambient noise of wind and barren trees, and Varek stepped into the doorway, blocking Aleksander's entrance into the training ring.

The Ölmesuz regarded him with an inquisitive eye. "Everything alright, kid?"

Aleksander nodded, slowing to a stop before him. "It will be."

A single eyebrow rose. "Anything you need to talk about?"

"No." Aleksander strode past him to the bench where he'd laid his plate armor, immediately busying himself with strapping it on. Every movement was sure, controlled. Each tug of a leather strap, each shift of metal—everything was more calculated than Aleksander had ever been. There was no hesitancy in his grip. No trembling in his fingers.

Not anymore.

He was too angry for that now.

"Elspeth's done. We worked on her training without you. You can take the rest of the day if you want, I've other duties."

Aleksander shook his head. "I'm training."

Varek watched him as he armored up, in the corner of Aleksander's eye, not saying a word. Not moving from his place in the doorway. Arms folded, chin dropped so he stared at the boy through his bushy eyebrows and strands of loose hair.

"How did the talk with your sister go?"

"Good," he lied. Aleksander lifted his left arm, fastening the lower strap for his pauldron. "She found a way around the Flow's toll for mages. She's pregnant. She's had a vision she's sure promises peace." After slipping on his sword belt, he met the man's eyes.

"Does it promise peace?"

For a man who was not religious or superstitious, there seemed to be a genuine, desperate hope swirling within that complex gaze. The usual slight squint he held was gone, allowing the lower part of his eyes to droop and make their usual almond shape more exaggerated, more rounded. Desperation was painted in every inch of his features.

Aleksander blinked once and drew Aoife, swinging her a few times to reacquaint himself with her weight. Once she fell still again, he met Varek's unrelenting stare.

"No." The word was quiet.

Beneath his mustache, Varek pressed his lips into a firm pout. "Alright." There was disappointment in the word, but not as much as Aleksander expected. The man pointed at him as he retreated into the hall. "Make sure you watch your left—you've been leaving it undefended lately."

Chapter

FORTY

ALEKSANDER NO LONGER FELT THE tension in his shoulders. When he raised a brush to smooth his hair, there was a struggle, as though his arms did not want to be put to work like this, but it was short lived. Candles illuminated the stone walls of his room.

Outside, more snow had begun to fall.

The bin given by Asghar sat open on his desk—he'd used the paper and ink to write a simple, short message to Demir and sent it off on a raven before they were retired to their roosts for the night. In the letter he'd laid out all he was worried of. Writing it was cathartic, and when that bird took off into the darkening sky, it felt as though a weight left and went with it.

But now, his mind swam with more thoughts than he'd had before.

He wondered if the spies had already been sent out, and if they were in all black, like he'd seen Varek wear that one night. Those leathers were silent, he didn't doubt the usefulness of them. But on a night like this, it seemed their dark tones would only serve to hinder their mission.

Disgust still lurched in his stomach at the notion. There was more at stake now, he knew that. There always had been, he supposed—there was always the promise of a war, the decimation of his country, its towns, its people. But it seemed so much nearer. As he was cleaning Aoife, sat by a window that radiated a sharp chill, he'd decided to put aside any of the things he was unsure of, like Varek's still-unclear stance or the spies he controlled. He sent them on behalf of Carissa, that much was true.

But they were his.

That was how the old man referred to them. He had to gather *his* spies. Had to prepare *his* spies.

Not Asghar's. Not the crown's. *Varek's.*

That was not of his concern. Not right now. Especially with what he learned and the deal he'd made with the man, there was a chance Varek would be one of the only people here that he could trust.

Right now, he had to prepare for a war. He had to find a way to stop his sister from murdering innocents, just like he needed to find a way to stop the Blights.

Just like he needed to find a way to keep Elspeth—and all the other girls like her—safe.

How many, he wondered, were across the country in this very moment, with shaking hands, capable of tremendous magic?

How many were already being found?

He put his brush down. Dark gold waves fell over his forehead, shining almost like Ölmesuz hair.

It made him sick, thinking about how he needed to find a way to stop Carissa as much as he needed to stop the Blights. They were not the same. They never would be.

His eyes seemed to glow in the flickering candlelight, warped by the mirror in a strange mimic of the dream he'd had months ago, where he became Alesathne.

But they both pose a threat to the people. And that is why I need to step in.

He didn't trust his sister to meet those girls with kindness. She was collecting them to test their identity herself. He knew that, even if she never said it.

With a puff of breath, the candle on his desk extinguished. Aleksander changed into clean underclothes and pulled down the blankets on his bed.

For the first time in more days than he could easily count, he backed away and placed a pillow before the windowsill, dropping to his knees.

There was no oratory in his room here, not even a place for a statue of Tulathne, but he would make do.

Clasping his hands together, he inhaled deeply and let his eyes drift shut.

The new name he'd learned passed through his mind, dying on his tongue before it could be voiced. *Calvantia.* It meant nothing to him, and the way it whirled like a breath through his mind was strange.

"Tulathne," he started, "Lady of Balances, I kneel before you tonight asking for guidance." The prayer felt stiff coming out. Forced. As if he'd forgotten how to pray properly. "I apologize, first and foremost, that I have allowed such a great stretch of time to pass between my speaking with you. To you." He swallowed. Ran his tongue over his teeth. "There has been a lot of new things I've been learning. A lot I've been thinking about. And honestly, it's all left me with questions. I think I know the answers but...I wanted to come to you first." His knees began to squish into the pillow below him, dispersing the down strangely. "My sister Carissa has had a vision. She says it promises peace, but when she told me about it I can only think of disaster. There are things people have done in your name that I cannot bring myself to accept. Innocents have been slaughtered, and now Carissa aims to do the same." He bobbed his head, considering. "Well, I *fear* she aims to do the same. I don't think she knows exactly what she's doing."

Silence stretched after his words, and agitation flared in his throat.

It was not the Presence, not the frustration he usually felt from it when he prayed. No, this was his own emotion.

It felt wrong, he realized. This prayer. He did not need to ask for guidance—he already had it. Aleksander did not have all the answers, and most of what he had learned still felt strange and wrong beneath his skin, but he knew somehow that what he had learned was true.

A prayer to a misnamed, silent goddess was not going to change things. And he would not hear anything telling him what he didn't already know.

He unclasped his hands and pushed himself up. There was no need for this. If his realizations were guided by the goddess, fine—if they weren't, fine. At least he'd learned.

The pillow sailed through the air, guided by a deft, agitated flick of his wrist, and flopped against the headboard before rolling down the slope of his other pillows and onto the half-pulled-back comforter.

Prayer was not what he needed this night.

Aleksander considered climbing into bed and closing his eyes. As much as his body sagged at the thought, his mind still whirred at that slow, steady pace. Nothing agitated him, it just... didn't let him rest.

So he grabbed a heavy robe, shoved his feet in to a pair of fur-lined slippers that had been waiting by his wardrobe after he'd returned from training earlier that day, and shoved open the door.

His hand slid against the wall as he walked down the hall, the steps, through a maze of corridors. There was no goal in his mind, no destination. Only wandering. The more his feet wandered, so did his mind.

With each step, a new way to deal with his issues came to the forefront.

He could get information from Varek, or perhaps the spies directly, and take action against the Blights before anyone else. Carissa wanted them mostly dead and a little captured, that much was true.

Aleksander wanted to know *exactly* what they wanted. And then to kill them.

If he managed to get Carissa alone—perhaps for a cup of tea

or hot milk, like he used to do when they were kids—he could open a discussion about the vision she'd had.

Elspeth would stay by his side, he'd make sure of it. At the next meeting, he'd declare her his right hand. Then no one could touch her. She would be his equal. Slighting her would be like slighting him. Like slighting the goddess Herself.

Voices sounded up ahead, and he stuttered to a stop. His mind fell silent. Every inch of him strained to focus on the warped conversation.

"You're a brilliant man, Ilya."

Varek.

"Thank you for bringing this to me."

"Of course," the man said. He'd never seen him, but just from the way he spoke, Aleksander already envisioned the fangs poking into his lower lip. "I'm just sorry I wasn't able to get the others out. Couldn't find them in time."

"You did what you had to, that's fine. They'll find me when they're ready, when it's safe to."

A pause. Aleksander inched closer.

"Did you find her family?" Varek said. His voice was low, mournful.

Peeking around the corner, Aleksander watched the Rodzjiek shake his head. "No. There were very few identifying marks. I didn't know her—she was Ölmesuz, and from her dress, she seemed to be more on the outskirts of town. We left her for the local authorities, and I've heard there's a funeral tonight, so..."

Varek's head hung low. A quiet curse spat from his lips, and then he raised his head, eyes searching the ceiling. "Mother carry her soul," he muttered.

Ilya shifted from foot to foot, obviously nervous.

"Are you looking to leave?"

He shook his head. "Not unless you say I can, sir."

The old man rolled his neck. "We'll keep this quiet. Not everything needs to get back to the princess right away. Besides, I want to gather more. See if any of our men can get into that barn, gather information on whoever their contacts are. If they have any."

Barn. Aleksander latched onto that word.

That barn.

That. Barn.

A specific barn. A specific barn they now knew of. A pit of rot where a Blight had begun to grow.

His fingers began to tingle, itching for action. For his sword.

"One of the boys was already there, he got involved quick. Saw them dumping the body, was able to convince them he wanted in."

Varek's brows shot up. "*Min-fe-hira*, that quickly?"

Ilya shrugged. "They're desperate for new members. For anyone that could give them more of a foothold. They're crazy, Varek. Sure they've been a pain to track down so far, but they're not geniuses."

Aleksander swallowed sharply. *Tell me where*, he thought, staring directly at Ilya as though he could telepathically convince the man to give up the exact location. *Tell me where to find them.*

"I'll keep checking for notes from him, but this is all I've got so far." A folded slip of parchment passed between the men. Varek unfolded it, skimmed it, nodded, and placed it in the breast pocket of his doublet. Ilya continued, "We've set up this drop at the ruins of a house halfway between the barn and Hadiqin. That's where I found this."

Varek nodded. "Do we know whose land they're on?"

There was a pause. Ilya's dark eyes flickered back and forth between the empty darkness of the hallway and suddenly seemed to refuse to fix on Varek.

"The family died years ago," he said. "Their only kid was lost in a tragic accident, the rest fell into grief. Some left the area or took their own lives. People in the town say their land is cursed. That's why we stay away from it." He shrugged. "That's why the Blight moved in so easily. It's not hard for biesy to move in where ghosts already dwell."

The taller man shifted, his boots making little to no sound on the tile floor. With a heavy sigh, he nodded. "Thank you, Ilya. Keep up the good work."

The Rodzjiek momentarily flattened his lips in acknowledgement. They both stood there for a moment. Not looking at one another, both of their gazes fixed on the ground, shoulders sagging—Aleksander wanted to ask where this house was. He wanted details, information, things he could act on. But he stayed crouched. Kept his breathing shallow, light.

Finally, Ilya nodded. "Before I go, can I ask you something, sir?"

With a grunt, Varek straightened. "I suppose."

"I know where I stand," he started. The words came out slow, careful. He bobbed his head as he thought, lips moving silently, until he finally spoke again. "I just...do you trust the kid? Some of the boys, they say he came into town and pretended to be a commoner. He...he *knows* we don't like him. And I know you've got some messed up deal regarding him and the princess but—"

"He's a kid, Ilya." Varek responded quickly, cutting off whatever the spy was going to say next. His frame stiffened. "He's fifteen years old. You and I both know that's a spit of time. He's been taught certain things his whole life and is just now learning they may be wrong. I'm giving him the opportunity to make his own choices. If he makes bad ones, don't worry—I'll take care of it."

The other man stared at him for a long moment, his gaze piercing through the pale brows he'd pushed over his eyes. Finally he nodded, taking a step back. "Alright. If you think it's smart."

"Doesn't matter what I think is smart, boy. Matters what's right. He has an opportunity to fix the wrongs of all before him. And I'm *letting* him." Those words hung in the air.

He's letting *me.*

He's letting me fix things.

For some reason, that word stuck out. There was no expectation, there was no demand, no duty—it was an option.

When it came to fixing things and doing what he was

supposed to, there had been no question about it. There was a demand for it. But here, it was an option. If he chose wrong, it would end bad, yes, but *still.*

Aleksander puffed out a breath. Varek's ear twitched, but he didn't turn around.

"Goodnight, Ilya. We'll talk more later."

The spy nodded and turned first. His boots were loud, heavy —the kind you'd wear to work on a farm or in the forests, not the ones you'd use sneaking around a castle. Once that noise finally retreated, Varek sniffed once and cleared his throat.

"Well? Are you just staying in the shadows again, your holiness?" He spun, eyes training on the corner Aleksander was peeking around. "Or do you want to talk?"

Chapter

FORTY ONE

ALEKSANDER STEPPED FORWARD FROM HIS poor hiding place, and pulled his quilted robe tight around himself. "We can talk," he said.

He didn't want to talk. He wanted to leave, to find this barn Ilya spoke of, to get whatever sort of upper hand he could on the vile individuals murdering the people he'd trained his whole life to protect.

He'd been taught to react, to fight. And now, he *needed* to.

But Varek took three slow steps towards him and tilted his head back. "How much did you hear?"

"Only that they found where the Blight is hiding."

Varek chewed on his lower lip. "Anything else?"

Aleksander shifted his weight. "And the girl," he said softly. "There's another girl dead."

In the winter, when snow blanketed the palace, it always dulled the sounds of the world. Though in Brevindun, there was always enough action happening somewhere that being alone and quiet did not make it feel like you were standing within a void. At Asghar's manor, with all asleep and the windows and doors closed tightly against the buffeting wind and flakes, it was like a tomb. Aleksander could not so much as hear his own breath echo off the walls. Silence and darkness pressed in around him, choking him. He cleared his throat, desperate to break its hold—Varek obliged to speak.

"What are your thoughts on that?"

"It's despicable," he spat. "That's nothing I'd ever turn my back to."

Thoughtful nods shifted Varek's hair around his face. "I'm glad to hear it."

Aleksander lifted a finger to scratch at an itch on his neck. The sound of his nail scraping on his skin echoed through empty ears.

"You know, your holiness," Varek trailed off.

Aleksander lifted his eyes to his, finding those darkened shards of tiger's eye fixed on him, unblinking. They did not glow in the dark of night the way Rodzjiek eyes did—the way Elspeth's did. But they were no less unnerving.

A sigh heaved from Varek's lips, and he continued, "I do not *expect* evil of you. If you're worried about that."

"I'm not," Aleksander said, but he was. It wasn't that Varek expected awful actions wrought by his hands. It was the simple fact that Varek was preparing for them anyway. He shifted his weight. "Where is the barn?"

"Now, why do you want to know?"

The boy shrugged. "I'm assuming I'll go there eventually."

Varek did not blink as he studied him. Aleksander quickly averted his gaze from the prying, dissecting eye roaming his face, his clothes, the way his arms clasped around his midsection as though he were a child who had broken a lamp or strolled into his parents' room in the wee hours of the night to let them know he'd been sick on the floor.

Under the old Ölmesuz's eye, he indeed felt more childlike than he preferred. Too young. Too inexperienced. Too stupid in the ways of war and politics.

He shook his head. A slipper scuffed the floor. "I can just go to bed, I'm sorry. You'll tell us all this tomorrow anyway."

"I won't," Varek muttered. "Not all of it."

Aleksander squinted at him. "What?"

A grin split across the man's face. It wasn't broad and boasting. Not the usual smile he wore. No, this one was much more subdued, almost...regretful. "Perhaps you were quick to forget our meeting in Asghar's office, but I still have a need to keep information from her highness. She'll know we have a lead, and she'll learn about the most recent murder in detail. I want her to see what the continued belief in this nonsense is bringing upon her people."

A knife twisted within Aleksander's heart, one he'd forgotten was there. "You still think this is all nonsense?"

Varek nodded.

"Even with the Blights, the murders—the homunculi?"

"Is all this happening because the prophecy said it would, or are they carrying this out because the prophecy said they would?"

Aleksander's nose scrunched. "What?"

Varek held his gaze a moment longer, then he shook his head, directing his attention elsewhere in the darkened corridor. "It's to the east," he said finally, "The barn. Go to town, cut behind the milliner, and keep walking until you jump over broken down fences. There's a crumbling well near the house, don't go near it, it's liable to drag you in. The barn is just past the edge of the forest." He shrugged. "It wasn't a forest when I'd last been there. They had goats and cows. And they made good cheese."

He rolled his neck once more, a light crack echoing through the vacuous space, and turned to walk down the hall.

"You're just...telling me?" Aleksander said. His heart raced within his chest. There was no way Varek was going to give him that information out of nowhere. Was he suspicious? Did Varek know what he planned to do?

Was this his way of giving Aleksander his approval?

Varek paused at the boy's words and glanced over his shoulder. "I figured I'd tell you now, so you didn't spend hours trudging aimlessly through the snow just to get get hypothermia by morning." He continued on his path, the dark, towering form of him melting once more into the evening hallway. "Dress warm, kid."

Even after he was gone, Aleksander stood there. This was not like Varek. He wouldn't just give Aleksander everything he needed to pursue these men alone, it was stupid. It was reckless. But Aleksander felt that same rage growing within his chest that he'd felt when they found Terrell. That same pull for justice. For blood. Before he could fully realize what it was he was doing, Aleksander darted down the hall, up the stairs, and back to his room. His breaths came heavy and fast as he climbed the steps.

The door to his bedroom swung open, and he didn't bother to close it. Instead he went straight for the wardrobe, throwing the doors wide and letting his robe drop onto the floor. He pulled on a fur-lined doublet—half of the garments in his wardrobe had been replaced overnight, it seemed. Everything was warmer, thicker, newer—the fur had been brushed, the leathers conditioned. The boots he pulled on were stiff, not yet worn in. They were wax-sealed, to keep out the water and keep in his body heat.

He strapped on his sword belt.

Looking in the mirror, he certainly did not feel ready.

His hair hung down loosely around his face in tousled waves. Suddenly he felt that his cheeks were too soft, his eyes too gentle. Maybe it was the clothes he was wearing, so indicative of a nobleman and not at all of someone about to creep through the snow in the dead of night just to kill some men trying to hurt his people.

Maybe he should just wait for Carissa. This was her plan, after all. Find them, rally them up, kill them and interrogate one.

But she was going to control him. Terrell could manipulate the dead well enough—horribly enough—but what would Carissa do with the living?

No. It was better this way.

He snagged a scarf that hung on the back of one door and looped it around his face, pulling it over his nose the way he and Varek did all those months ago.

There. That helped, a little.

He closed the doors carefully and snuffed every light. Slipping into the hallway, he was silent.

"Aleksander?"

Every muscle in his body froze. He turned slowly, only to see Elspeth a few feet away. Her hair fell limply from her braid, and even in the lack of light, he could still see the way her eyelids drooped and darkened with exhaustion.

"Elspeth."

She furrowed her brows at him. "What are you doing?"

His heart hammered in his chest. What was he to say? The truth? He couldn't lie to her. This was Elspeth—they didn't lie to each other. "I've...got something to deal with. In town."

She folded her arms. "Yeah?"

"Yes," he said, "I won't be gone long. I just...I couldn't sleep, and then Varek told me—"

"Varek? What did he say?"

Aleksander licked his lips beneath the scarf. He was grateful she couldn't see his multiple attempts at speaking, the way his mouth opened and closed and pursed and grimaced. "He said there was another murder. In Hadiqin. That an Ölmesuz girl was falsely identified and the Blight massacred her before our people could get to her. I want to see if there's anything I can dig up."

Color drained from her face. Her lips hung open, trembling fingers hovering a hairs breadth from her chin. "What?"

He swallowed hard. "Yeah."

Those dark eyes, still somehow smoldering with embers, drifted to the floor, then the wall, then the ceiling. Finally, they landed back on him. "Give me a moment, I'll come with you."

"No." The words came too quickly, too harshly. In a few steps he stood before her, hand hovering above her arm.

For some reason, he couldn't bring himself to touch her right now.

"I...it'll be better and faster if I go alone. Varek knows where I'm headed, if anything happens, you go with him."

At this, her eyes widened. "If something happens?

Aleksander, what—"

"No, never mind, nothing is going to happen," he stuttered. At this, he took her hand in his. It was strange, the separation his glove caused. Nothing more than a thin strip of leather and fur, but all he felt was the ghost of her hand pressing in his. "I'm just saying, if anything does, because of what's going on in general, Varek knows where I am and everything will be fine."

Her fingers tightened their grip on his. "Are you okay?"

A long moment passed. His throat constricted, his chest burned. *No.* "Why do you ask?"

"You don't..." her eyes roamed his face. "You seem different. Unsettled. You've been more and more unsettled lately, Aleksander. It...worries me."

Grief flooded through him, and for a moment any trace of his growing lust for vengeance was washed away. The muscles in his face relaxed. His eyes ached at the release of tension, and he blinked them rapidly, taking Elspeth's hands together in both of his own. "No, El, I...I'm okay, trust me. I'm fine."

But she didn't. He could see it in the way her brows pressed closer together, as if they wished to close that gap above her nose for good. Sparks flickered in her eyes. Her full lips pressed thin and firm.

"I'm okay, El, really. I just...I'm mad and I feel a little helpless right now. So I'm going to do something about it."

She shook her head almost imperceptibly. "You don't need to be helpful right now, Aleksander, we don't have any orders. It's okay to be mad, I'm mad too. Furious, actually. But...we *can't* help right now. We don't have enough information, and we haven't gotten any marching orders to act on the little information we do have."

He chewed his bottom lip. "I just...I need this to end." Tears began to burn in his throat. He didn't expect it, the sudden rush of grief and emotion. Aleksander cleared his throat, pushing it away. "It's my job. I am the Sword of Ages, it's my *duty* to keep my people safe. So I'm going to do that."

After another moment, she squeezed his hands. "I can't stop

you?"

He shook his head.

Her eyes searched his face, tired and weary and glowing with concern. "Okay then. Come back before sunrise. I'll leave my door unlocked, I better be woken up by you and not the clock on my desk."

Heart still clawing its way into his throat, sending shivers of panic down his spine, he nodded. "I will. Trust me, I won't be out long."

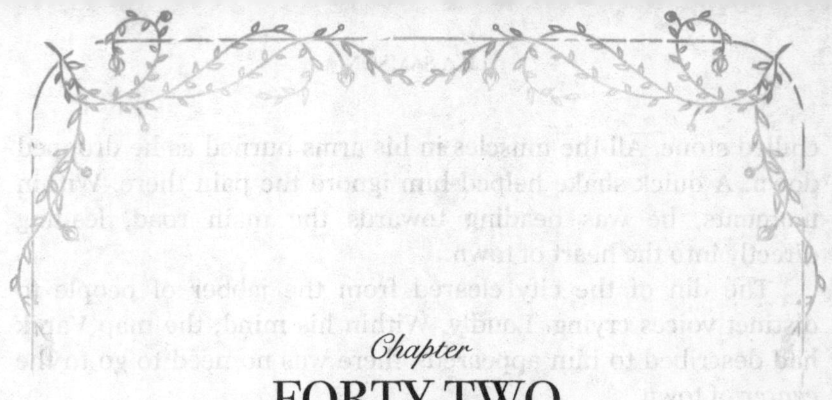

Chapter

FORTY TWO

HE EARLY-WINTER SLUSH THAT everyone else called snow melted quickly around his legs. The layers he had donned were certainly not thick enough, and there was no wax over the top of them. With each step, the damp, quilted fabric stuck to his skin.

At least his boots were warm.

A single, gloved hand stayed wrapped around Aoife the whole time. Secured beneath his cloak, Aleksander was not worried about losing her or damaging her in the snow. He just couldn't let her go. Each time his hand left the slender grip and detailed pommel, his pulse shot up as though there was a geyser in his chest—so he kept hold.

How long he had been walking, he didn't know. After leaving Elspeth and the castle, he'd started the long trek down the path to Hadiqin. The city was alive this evening. Each step he took led him nearer to the glistening buildings, the flickering lights along the streets. Constant noise rose up from them.

Aleksander held his scarf up around his nose and mouth, desperate to keep it in place lest one of the guards along the wall see him as he climbed over and recognize that he was not someone who was supposed to be leaving at this hour of night.

He slid over the top of the wall, sword clacking against the chilled stone. All the muscles in his arms burned as he dropped down. A quick shake helped him ignore the pain there. Within moments, he was heading towards the main road, leading directly into the heart of town.

The din of the city cleared from the jabber of people to distinct voices crying. Loudly. Within his mind, the map Varek had described to him appeared—there was no need to go to the *center* of town.

But that *wailing*.

The pitches cut to his core, speeding his pulse and twisting his stomach.

Diverging from his planned path, Aleksander made his way further in to town. Around him, the lights got brighter. Nearly every window had a candle or three in them, tall flames flickering and working together with the street lights to paint all the town, laden with snow, in a golden glow.

Even as he walked, he continuously corrected his eyes to the frosted stones before him. His mouth gaped when he caught sight of a processional. Moments later he snapped it shut and looked down again, reminding himself it wasn't nice to stare, open-mouthed, at strangers. They each carried lamps, old oil lamps similar to the ones Chione had scattered on stands and tables around the library. Mostly Ölmesuz, their unbound hair dancing like spider silk in the cold wind. Leading the way was a holy woman, bearing an oil jar, her face solemn and her usually glittering attire instead traded for a single, thin garment of pale blue. It fluttered in the breeze, and Aleksander watched as goosebumps pricked up along her exposed arms. Following her, mourners mouths moved slowly with whispered prayers, or not at all. Directly behind the priestess, however, stood one woman.

Tears streaked her face, eyes red and puffy and squeezed shut as she stumbled along, arm linked with another holy woman.

Her hair was short. Just cut below her ears. The ends were jagged, the resulting mess looking more kin to tangled steel wool than the silver that seemed to be her usual tone. Every step from her was met with a heavy sob.

Aleksander's throat began to close.

He didn't stop himself as he followed the procession. People on the sidewalks stopped, bowed their heads, or began whispering their own prayers.

From the whispers, he gathered the keening woman was the dead girl's mother.

In the center of the square, beneath the fountain where a statue of Iscah sat, lamps and candles adorned her feet and the rest of the fountain beyond. Tall Ölmesuz towered above him, blocking his view as he got closer.

A whispered "pardon" here, an "excuse me" there, and he was able to move through the crowd of mourners to watch as the mother bent before the statue.

Everyone fell silent.

There was no body. Seeing as they'd come from the edge of town, Aleksander assumed they'd already buried her.

Still, it was as silent as if she were among them, hands folded the way Iscah's had been, surrounded by flowers and all the things she loved.

Then, the mother lifted her head to the sky. Tears streamed as she wailed, gently falling snow dotting her dark face, her hair, her dark orange gown. Her feet were bare and even with the rich complexion a deeper bronze than even Lord Asghar, he could see the red and pink from where the walk in the snow had frozen her skin.

The sound shocked Aleksander to his core, his blood pumping furiously, terror working into his chest.

As her cries faded, someone to his left began singing.

Each word uttered was still foreign. He hadn't heard the funeral song in months, but he bit his lip to stop it from quivering nonetheless.

After the first line, more singers joined in. Guttural consonants and rolling syllables, lilted in a deep, earnest grief, rang through the town.

Aleksander pressed a hand to his nose, stifling a sob, as the song faded out.

He should go. This was a private affair.

Yes, it was in the middle of the town, and many people gathered around him in all manner of clothing, from all manner of peoples, but—

"I am in agony."

He halted; the cracked, exhausted voice of the mother at the fountain created the only sound in the square.

"I have never felt such pain," she managed through stilted gasps.

"We hear you. We see you," the crowd responded.

Silence fell again.

Snow whispered through the air.

"I do not...I do not know how to hold this pain."

Aleksander choked on his tears.

Around him, the response echoed, "We wish you did not have to."

"I have lost my daughter. I do not know how to go on." Her words were stronger now. In her agony, the grit of anger creeped in to the edges of her voice. "I fear I will forget her laugh. Her eyes. The smell of her hair and the music she would hum."

"We will not let her disappear from this world."

Behind him, a stifled sob echoed his own.

The mother swayed on her knees, dropping forward with a heavy breath. When she rose again, her eyelashes fluttered shut on glistening cheeks. A wind ruffled her hair, and she took her time to breathe it in.

"I feel so alone."

That single sentence echoed, but not for more than a moment.

Aleksander opened his mouth in tandem with the mourners around him.

"You are not alone."

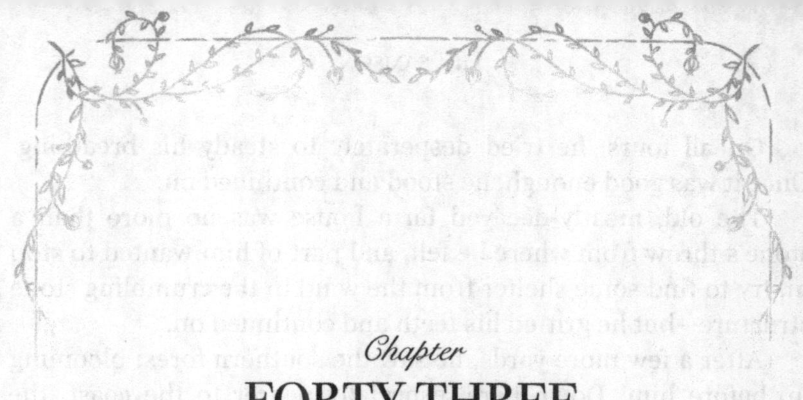

Chapter

FORTY THREE

IS BREATH, STILL STALE WITH tears, made his scarf hot and wet against his lips. Once did he draw down the woven wool to take a breath of fresh evening air, and only that once did he regret it. The inside of his nose still stung.

He'd left quietly. He did not know the mother, the daughter, or really anyone present at the funeral, and though his tears were real, he couldn't shake the feeling that he did not deserve to shed them.

Then a gust blew through, swirling up the dry snow, catching on his eyes, his cheeks, that small gap between the scarf and his doublet collar he hadn't managed to tuck in properly.

With a shudder, he ensured his cloak was clasped and swiped any remaining tear tracks from staining his cheeks.

The night darkened as he got further and further from the town. The crying and singing faded into silence. Whispers passed by on the wind, each tiny sound making his heart beat faster, the hairs on his neck stand straight up. Fear circled through his chest.

He found the first fence Varek had told him about. It was worn, broken down and half rotting. Swishing his cloak out of the way, he climbed over it. The weak wood snapped beneath him and he tumbled into the snow, pain kicking up the left side of his body.

On all fours, he tried desperately to steady his breathing. Once it was good enough, he stood and continued on.

The old, mostly-decayed farm house was no more than a stone's throw from where he fell, and part of him wanted to stop in, try to find some shelter from the wind in the crumbling stone structure—but he gritted his teeth and continued on.

After a few more yards, he saw the southern forest blooming up before him. Down here, especially nearer to the coast, the trees were shorter, thinner. As he approached, those waves of panic brought on by the nearness or even the thought of the Untamed were absent.

That didn't make them any less foreboding, though.

Branches shuddered in the wind, shaking off clumps of snow only to whip around and threaten to snatch the hood off Aleksander's head.

He'd begun to count his steps. Two hundred since the house, and he hopped another fence. This one was sturdier, it only creaked when he put his weight on it.

For some reason, he'd expected this barn to be easy to find. Maybe it was his anger, telling him this was a quick job, an easy thing to do. Maybe it was simply the fact that the last time he did something like this, he'd followed Varek's commands. Everything seemed quicker when you had someone telling you what to do—there was no room to make your own decisions. The time that passed in silence was time spent waiting for the next instructions.

Now, he had to decide whether to go over this log or around it.

He went around, and when he did, his heart stopped.

It was shrouded in snow, one side of it nearly caked in it due to the wind. But he could still make out the large black doors, the flicker of light behind the drawn curtains, the tarps and patchwork covers on the roof to keep out the snow.

Aleksander was an idiot.

He was. He was so completely stupid.

His breaths came faster, sending small curls of fog before his eyes. The edge of his scarf began to crust over with ice.

Yes, he had years of training. Yes, he was a skilled swordsman. But he suddenly realized he had no clue who these people were. Or how many they were.

Or if they had homunculi.

Not that taking down his scarf to sniff the air would help. The freezing night air wiped away any scent and replaced it with the cold, fresh bite of winter.

Something shifted to his right, and he dropped down behind the log. It was dark, the rotten bark and innards of the tree holding on to the remaining heat of autumn decay. Snow had just started to stick to it. From a distance, his dappled cloak shouldn't look much different.

From the woods came a dark figure, roughly the shape of a man, if he were wearing layers upon layers of winter clothes. He seemed only about Aleksander's height, maybe slightly taller. He moved slowly, raggedly. Aleksander blinked to clear his vision, and it was then that he noticed the shape the man was dragging behind him in the snow.

Aleksander swallowed the bile rising in his throat.

A corpse.

Of course.

The man dumped it into a pile beside the barn and dusted off his hands before going inside. In the quick flash of light and warmth, Aleksander counted 2 more people inside. Not many. Certainly not the ten or more he'd expected.

This he could do. Just a few men. No problem.

Aleksander glanced side to side. The rest of the forest was dead still. It seemed as though even the wind paused its blowing, the snowflakes settling around him in a silent, simultaneous end.

He swallowed hard.

Closer and closer, he managed to cast a glance to the corpse that had been brought. It was old—their clothes were decaying, a skull half-skinned with clumps of long, broken hair rolled to the side, barely connected to its neck.

So they're desecrating graves. Again.

Aleksander heaved a sigh.

At least they're not creating the corpses for themselves.

Creeping towards the door, he unsheathed Aoife. The quiet ring of her blade leaving the scabbard was more than enough to send a jolt of fear into his heart.

It wasn't long until the rest of him started shaking.

Aleksander pressed his eyes shut tightly and took slow, deep breaths.

No. He was the Sword of Ages, he was Alesathne.

He was not made to falter.

He was not made to break.

He clenched his jaw, willing the spiral of thoughts to dissipate entirely from his mind. Who cared who he was? In this moment, Aleksander decided, it did not matter. He was not the Sword, he was not Alesathne—he was himself, and that was enough.

Voices escalated inside, laughter and jeers muffled by the thick, rotting walls of the barn and whatever things they'd cobbled onto the dilapidated boards.

He nearly choked on his heart, the beating strong and violent against his vocal chords. With one deep breath, he prepared himself.

The door flew open with a single kick, sending the three men backwards. One, directly to his left, hanging up the cloak Aleksander had seen him wear, toppled entirely onto his backside.

"Hey!"

Across the room, a man stood abruptly, jostling a half-drunk bottle of ale onto the floor. It bounced and rolled before hitting an old plow and cracking the top off it.

Aleksander leveled his sword at him. "Do not take one *step* closer."

The man's eyebrows raised slowly, in tandem with his hands. "Oh. What have we here?"

To Aleksander's right, the man who had been hanging up his cloak regained his footing. "Kid, I think you've got the wrong barn." He took a single step forward.

With a deft flick of his wrist, Aoife's blade sliced a cut along the man's chest. He stumbled back, crying out, and on the other side of the room the third man stood, brandishing a weapon.

"You don't get to just come in here and hurt my men, kid." His voice was low and commanding. He stood taller than the others too, and when he stepped into the light, Aleksander's gut sank.

The man from the town. Who had stopped the teens from harassing Carissa.

Get answers. That's the first goal. "Tell me why you target girls who have nothing to do with this." His voice was loud, if unsteady. Aleksander's grip adjusted on the sword. Sweat and tremors made her loose in his hand.

Recognition flashed in the man's eyes, and that same smile he'd seen on the street stretched across his face, cracking with a hatred that hadn't been there before. Or at least, had been suppressed before. "Oh, your *holiness*," he practically sang. "I hadn't expected to see you again so soon! To what do I owe the... pleasure?"

The ring of a blade preceded the man's movement, but he didn't lunge or strike.

Just let the long, cracked blade glint in the lantern light.

The sight made Aleksander's stomach twinge. He could handle it. He'd been in fights before. But if that cut him, he'd likely suffer an infection worse than any wound it could inflict.

"You don't get to walk around *my* country and kill *my* people." His own voice dropped, low and certain. Like before, in that muddy field surrounded by homunculi and facing a traitor, Aleksander was washed with calm.

Aiofe's handle was no longer slick and loose in his hand. He gripped it firmly. His arm ached.

The Presence swirled, warm and sure, in his chest.

For once, he was truly grateful for it.

The tall man laughed. "Oh, yeah? And why is that? It's my country too, you know." His eyes narrowed, scanning

Aleksander's form. "Isn't it my duty to protect people from the *real* threat?"

Aleksander didn't answer. He didn't know how to answer. What this man saw as the real threat were his family, the crown, Tulathne. But wasn't he himself coming to that same conclusion?

A grin spread further across the man's face, greasy, sweaty blond hair drooping into his eyes. "Come on, kid, you've been so confident up until now. Cat got your tongue?"

No. Carissa was in the wrong, of course, but in this moment —on the whole—the real threat was the men around him.

Whatever threat the crown posed, it was slimier than these before him, like fishing a leech from a jar. These men...these he could grab easily. These he could crush.

"Kieran." The man who had dropped the bottle stood from his new position, pressing in to the wound on the third man's stomach. "The sword."

Aleksander's grip on Aoife tightened.

Kieran's grin widened, dark eyes now stuck on the arming sword within Aleksander's grasp. "You boys are just now picking up on it, huh?"

Before he fully knew what was happening, the man to his right lunged, hands stained with his friend's blood. Aleksander wheeled back, striking a solid cut across the man's forearm. With a shriek he stumbled backwards, and when his eyes met Aleksander's again, they were full of rage.

A flash of metal from the left. Aleksander flung Aoife to block Kieran's blow. The collision rang down his arms.

His heart fluttered against his ribs, deep in his mind a voice screamed that he was stronger than he'd expected—but Aleksander steadied his footing and dodged, hitting the heavy blade aside a second time and landing a strong strike on the man's shoulder.

A fury bloomed in Kieran's eyes.

Beneath his scarf, Aleksander smiled. Breaths already huffed between bared teeth.

Movement behind him tried to take his attention, and for a

moment it was split between the man before him, and the two behind him.

Kieran caught it and twitched.

Aleksander reacted, throwing himself backwards against the door. His feet slid beneath him easily, and he would have uttered thanks to Varek for all the agility drills if he'd had the time.

A laugh burst from Kieran just as the first man, still bleeding, lunged with a set of iron shears.

His heart leapt into his throat, and he sliced up, knocking the shears out of the way.

A string of curses flew from the man's lips, and through his fingers wrapped around the new wound, bits of white bone splintered among the steadily flowing river of blood.

Aleksander's stomach lurched, his vision wavering for but a moment.

He swallowed it down.

Now is not *the time*.

Pain blossomed, sudden and deep, against Aleksander's side. He twisted his head, but the hood blocked his view.

His heart raced faster, movements becoming imprecise. The cloak, which had flowed so effortlessly behind him, tangled with his arms. It wrapped around Aoife's hilt.

Every breath became rapid, terrified.

A hand shot out from where he couldn't see, grabbed his cloak, and tugged.

The dirt and dust covering the floor spun him without effort.

His hands flailed, trying to get free of Aoife, trying to see.

A sharp snap sounded, and Aleksander screamed.

It felt like fire racing up his left arm—his fingers, his forearm, his elbow burned with the sudden pain. Instinct made him move his fingers.

They did not respond.

Tears blurred his vision, his body buzzing in response to the attack. A poorly aimed strike with Aoife hit nothing but air, and his vision swirled.

Something impacted him from behind. All the air rushed

from his lungs—in an attempt to breathe in, Aleksander inhaled the scarf. The fabric choked him. Aoife clattered to the ground and his knees hit alongside her. Frantic hands clawed at the wool, and one his mouth was free, a shaking, unsure hand dove for his sword.

A shadow clouded his vision.

Blood red streaks seared across his vision in a fresh wave of blinding pain.

He barely registered the impact of his face on the disgusting, splintered barn floor before his eyes closed.

Chapter

FORTY FOUR

Everything was cloudy. Nothing made sense, not the voices he heard, not the pain that had been sewn into his very bones.

He was so cold.

Aleksander licked his lips, and all he felt was frost.

I can't die here.

His fingers twitched, searching for Aoife—they only scraped along wood and stone.

Darkness swam in the corners of his vision. He pressed his eyes shut, forcing it away, but that only drew it closer.

No, no.

The boy turned his head and pain streaked down his spine.

I can't die here.

Those shadows closed in.

Chapter

FORTY FIVE

HIS EYES CRACKED OPEN, BUT THEY didn't stay that way. Some unknown force was tugging them down, fighting against Aleksander's attempts to open them, focus on something, *anything*. Someone was talking. He couldn't see who it was. There was a growl to their voice—it sent a shiver down his spine.

Don't move, he told himself.

Somehow, he managed to ignore his own words of warning and lifted his head. The back of his head throbbed. His jaw felt loose, like it might just fall off from the pain, and his eyes couldn't focus on any of the figures moving around in the dim lamplight.

There were more now, that was certain. One crouched by the door, peering through a crack.

Aleksander was only able to make out the strip of early light contrasting the gold of the lamps.

How long have I been here?

He shifted a leg, boots scraping at an angle he didn't expect along the floor.

With a gasp that sent explosions through his vision, he looked down—his legs weren't broken, thank Tulathne. Just tied.

"He's awake." The muddied words wormed their way into his

ears.

"Get him food. Water."

"Kieran, you can't just—"

"I *said*, get the kid food and water."

Aleksander might as well have been underwater, or tossed into a well. Every word spoken in the barn echoed in a disconcerting way within his ears.

He half expected everything around him to fold in on itself. Maybe this was all a dream after all.

"You know we have to keep him alive. For now."

A rough hand grabbed his chin, forcing his mouth open.

He winced, but drank quickly once the ice cold water started dripping over his lips and down his chin. Never mind he couldn't breathe, never mind each gulp sent pain screaming across his skull.

By the time the cup was taken away, he could feel his pulse within his own skull. Like his brain had been a dry sponge that just got entirely soaked.

It was enough for him to keep his eyes open and watch the spoon reach for him. The carved wooden spoon moved slowly, cradling a soup of pale broth and strings of egg. He could smell the green onions in it.

The soup was warm. Not hot, but warm enough.

His head rolled to the side and soup dribbled down his chin. The loss of the meal was enough to coax a short whine from his throat before it started to close with tears.

This cannot be happening, I—

"Careful, kid."

Aleksander blinked at the voice, lifting his gaze enough to catch the pale stare of a Rodzjiek man.

A Rodzjiek man Aleksander knew.

Cezary lifted his eyebrows momentarily, as if to tell Aleksander not to respond. Not to do or say anything that would indicate they know each other.

Aleksander wasn't even sure he would be able to speak if he tried. He opened his mouth again, leaning forward, a silent plea to try eating again. A gentle hand cupped the back of his head, just below the spot he'd gotten hit.

It felt hot, and pounded with the desperate pulse of a body trying to repair itself.

Cezary assisted in guiding his head to the spoon for a few more bites. "That's all I can give you, kid," he whispered. "I hope you understand."

Aleksander's head rolled back against the wall and he winced. *It's okay,* he wanted to say. But all that came out was a whine. He resigned to close his eyes.

Tulathne, Mother...anyone. Tell Varek I'm stuck. Tell someone where I am. Don't let me die here.

Tears burned in his eyes. One dropped on his cheek, and Cezary quickly brushed it away.

"I'm going to change his bandage," the man said over his shoulder. Then, quietly to Aleksander, "I'm sorry. This is really going to hurt."

Before Aleksander could even open his eyes to see what the man meant, lightning shot up his arm. A strangled scream escaped his throat, but soon, everything faded back to darkness.

FORTY SIX

BLOOD THRUMMED IN HIS EARS. Faint and slow.

Elspeth.

His head swelled so big, it rolled on his shoulders.

Varek.

Someone.

Fresh air and clean linens and warm earth swirled around him. Only for a moment.

Mom.

Chapter

FORTY SEVEN

EAT.

All he felt was heat. It pressed in on each side of his face, unforgiving yet gentle all at once. Then, it shifted. It moved under his eye, through his hair, along his jaw.

"Aleksander," the voice floated to him.

Opening his eyes was a struggle, but he recognized it. It was that same voice in his dreams, reaching for him, calling to him. Part of him did not want to take in what he knew would be that same, dark, swirling form. The glowing eyes, the reaching claws. There had to be another way—this couldn't be death.

Not yet.

It took every ounce of strength he could muster to shift his head away from the being's touch.

"Aleksander, please, look at me. Open your eyes, *please*."

Wait. No, he *did* know that voice. He knew that voice like he knew his own name, like he knew the way Aoife fit into his hand. It crawled into his chest as intimately and sure as the way she'd smile at him, fangs peeking from her lips.

His eyes cracked open, and staring back at him, red, watery, and desperate, were two wide eyes, flickering with embers.

Glowing like planets.

Warmth rushed through him, turning his stomach, swelling

within his heart. His throat closed instantly and his vision began to warp with tears. "El."

"Oh, gods," she gasped, her eyes roving his, taking in every portion of his face, every wrinkle, every bump, every bit of dried blood and dirt he now felt caked in. A tear dripped down her cheek and he gently raised a hand to wipe it.

He didn't get farther than her waist before pain caused him to stop. Hooking his thumb in her sword belt, he let his muscles hang limp there.

She shook her head, fixing him with a stare. "You're an idiot, you know that?"

"Is Varek here?" His voice didn't sound like his. It was raspy, cracking. For all intents and purposes, he sounded as though he should be dead.

"No."

Any trace of hope that had blossomed within his chest faltered.

"It's okay," she said quickly, taking his face once more in her hands. "It's okay, he knows I'm here, he's going to meet us halfway, he went to get some of Asghar's soldiers and a healer." The warmth of her touch left his face, working to unbind the ropes around his feet and elbows. "I couldn't wait—Varek told me where you were, I had to get you."

"He should be here, he could—"

"They're coming back, Elspeth."

Aleksander's head twisted to find Cezary by the door.

He glanced back at them. "Get him up, you have to go."

"*We* have to go," she spat back, "You're not staying here with them, Cezary."

He rolled his eyes, baring his fangs in a frustrated grimace. "I'll do what I need to do. If that means staying and being the guy who got beat up in an attempt to stop you from taking him, then that's the roll I'll play."

The rope around his legs was finally pushed free, and in a single swipe of her blade, Elspeth cut the one holding his arm to the wall.

Everything swirled around Aleksander as he stood. His body felt heavy, as though it had been filled with water sloshing against the inside of his skin, throwing him off balance. His head tipped and Elspeth gasped, rushing forward to catch him.

"Can you walk?" she asked. Her voice shook.

Aleksander tried and failed to shake his head. "I don't know."

Her hand pressed against his chest and she studied his face. "Stay here, I'll bring the horse closer."

"No time." Cezary's call was laced with panic. Aleksander turned to look at the man. He was met with a look of pure, unbridled fear. Loose strands of his hair fell in his eyes with every shake of his head. "They're coming through the trees, I can see them—Elspeth, go."

"No, come here," she said. Her hands left Aleksander's body and he stumbled back, bracing himself against the wall. His left hand hit—

A scream he'd never expected to hear from himself tore from his throat. His entire left hand—entire left *arm*—was shooting with the most torturous pain he'd ever felt. Exposed nerves screamed in agony, and through tear-blurred eyes, he looked down.

His stomach churned, throat burning with bile.

He hardly had a hand at all. It was bloated and wet, with streaks of red and black spiraling beneath his skin. The skin itself had a strange green hue to it and was much lighter than his usual coloring. A few inches up from his wrist was wrapped, but through the blood and the bandage, he could see the outline of a bone.

"My...my..." he stuttered, his breathing growing faster, his stomach churning.

"Aleksander, no, don't look!" Elspeth tilted his face up, eyes wide. Terrified. "We're going to get you to a healer. Cezary has been doing what he can, you'll be fine."

"I'll say it once more!" Cezary shouted, drawing his sword.

Aleksander's stomach flipped.

"Back up and leave him, or you'll be the next girl butchered in this village!" His face was stern, but his chest moved with frantic breaths. He tossed a quick glance to the door.

Elspeth nodded, drawing her own sword.

She isn't in armor—none of us are. This will be useless if both of us end up injured or dead.

He caught her free wrist in his good hand. "El, let's run."

The look she gave him said they both knew he wouldn't be able to.

Cezary stepped aside, and four other men burst in. Two he'd known before. Kieran and the one whose forearm he'd sliced. The other two were strange, and as Aleksander met the eyes of the shorter man, they widened.

"You weren't joking," he said softly. "You really got him."

He smoothed his riding doublet, thick for the winter, and his signet ring flashed in the lamplight. If Aleksander could only have taken a few steps closer...

"And who are *you*, girl?" Kieran snarled, taking a step forward. "Cezary, why didn't you kill her yet?"

"I was getting to it, she just got in," Cezary lied.

Aleksander prayed Kieran wouldn't notice the way Cezary's chest heaved with fake exertion—and very real panic.

The large man's dark eyes shifted between Elspeth and Aleksander, a somewhat amused grin growing on his face. "You didn't answer me, girl. Who are you?"

Elspeth swallowed hard. "I'm just a girl trying to get this wretch to a healer so our Lady of a Thousand Deaths can have a fair fight."

At this, Aleksander's entire body ran cold. He'd never heard that term, "Lady of a Thousand Deaths," but it *had* to be referring to the Scourge. Death of a Thousand Ages, yes. But not specifically "Lady." The way the men reacted, though, showed it *was* a proper term for her.

Kieran's eyebrow raised. "My, so you're on her side as well?" A slimy gaze slithered over her form. "With that regalia, you look like one of Asghar's pets. If not the Sword's himself. Come to think of it, weren't you standing with the princess when those two boys were harassing her?"

She tossed her chin towards the man Aleksander couldn't identify. "Is that one not from the court?"

The shorter man huffed.

The name still refused to come to him, but Aleksander was certain now. He *was* a lesser lord. To the...south east, if he remembered right.

"And yet, that doesn't incline me to give him up." Kieran sniffed, wiping some snot from his mustache on the back of his sleeve. "So tell me, miss..."

Elspeth just set her jaw and held his gaze.

"*Miss*." Kieran smiled. "Why should I listen to you and not kill you? We've already got a lot of false Scourges, what's one more to add to the pile?"

Aleksander watched her mouth drop open ever so slightly, eyelashes fluttering with panicked blinks.

"You don't want to do that." Her voice wasn't strong or commanding, but there was a severity in it that sent a shiver down Aleksander's spine.

"And why is that?"

She swallowed hard. "Who ever said I'd be another false Scourge?"

Now Aleksander was certain he was about to faint. Not only was Elspeth here alone, but she was trying to get him out by claiming that she was the Scourge.

Sure, she had enough skill with fire to scare them, but they'd see through it soon enough.

Kieran's eyes widened. Then he threw his head back and laughed. "You're a bold one, I'll give you that."

"It's not bold to tell the truth," she said, doubling down. With her wrist still firm in Aleksander's grasp, he could feel her starting to shake. "And I'd hate to kill you just to prove a point."

The short nobleman sniffed, taking a step forward. "I've seen you in court, *girl*. You're part of the Princess and the Sword's entourage."

A snarl slipped across Elspeth's face. Only Aleksander saw

how her lip wavered. "And? You're there too. Doesn't mean I'm lying. I think you'd agree if I said that the court was the best place to tear down a country from. Like a parasite, eating a doe alive from the inside out."

"She *is* lying," he said, turning to face Kieran. "Kill her and be done with it, that's what I would do."

Nobody moved. Aleksander's heart raced, ready to break through his chest and kill him right then and there if it needed to. He could barely see, barely stand with the way his head swam from the rush of adrenaline.

Kieran studied them.

Beside him, Cezary's sword began to falter in his grasp.

Elspeth sucked her teeth. "Well? Are you going to take my word or will I have to prove it to you?"

A deep breath swelled through the room, and when Kieran exhaled, he shrugged. "Cezary, kill her."

"No," Aleksander croaked, leaning his head against the wall. He couldn't stand much longer. Even if she did manage to survive all of them, if he wasn't able to walk, they were still stuck. "Please."

Cezary swallowed hard. His eyes flashed from the man beside him to the two children in front of him, and the ice within them melted. It nearly spilled over his lower lashes. Desperation fluttered across his face when he looked at Elspeth, and Aleksander could practically hear him begging her to fight back.

She readied her sword.

Setting his jaw, Cezary readied his and lunged.

Aleksander let go of his friend's hand, allowing her full range of motion, and staggered along the wall in an attempt to distance himself from the fight.

Elspeth parried Cezary's blow, sliding to the side and landing a punch square on his jaw.

The Rodzjiek staggered to the side. When he looked back up, there was no malice in his eyes. "Kill me if you have to," he whispered, launching himself at her again.

Aleksander could barely keep up with the flurry of blows. He kept his injured arm to his chest, staring out at the ensuing fight with terror setting every nerve in his body alight.

She was doing well. The way Elspeth shifted her feet was the Ölmesuz way, and though she did not have their innate skill for speed, it did certainly improve her fighting. She parried a blow, staggering back and immediately raising a foot to Cezary's chest. The man nearly went flying from the kick.

He hit the wall and slumped, groaning in earnest.

Her shoulders heaved with anxious breaths, glancing back and forth between Cezary, still on the floor, and Kieran. He watched intently with his arms crossed.

The look in his eyes made Aleksander's stomach clench.

"That proves nothing." He slid his sword out of its sheath. That same metallic whisper Aleksander heard moments before—

A deep rumble began to echo through the space. Not a rumble, not really—a gust. Almost like wind. It set off alarms in Aleksander's brain, throwing him deeper into a panic.

The men looked between each other, Cezary watched Elspeth with fear.

Even Kieran's tough facade dropped momentarily as the static noise became louder, louder—deafening almost.

Elspeth raised her hand, her first finger extended.

It did not shake now.

Shadows crawled from the corners of the decaying building around them, snaking through the lamps set on barrels, hung on walls, snuffing them out one by one. Within moments, everything fell silent. The barn was shrouded in darkness— Aleksander couldn't see Elspeth, couldn't even see his hand when he raised it before his face.

He was nearly blinded when Elspeth burst into flames.

Chapter

FORTY EIGHT

ALEKSANDER'S HEART JUMPED INTO HIS throat at the sight. It was horrifying as much as it was entrancing. Nothing was burning. At least, not yet. Whatever practice she had been doing with her fire seemed to really help her control. There was a shell of sorts around her clothes, lighting the shape of her on fire but not her actual body. It crawled along her, dripping down the sword still within her grip, coating the blade in flames while dissipating from her body.

Casting a glance over her shoulder, Aleksander's soul felt as though it was trying to tear free from his body.

He could see the fire dancing through her veins.

The smoke and the shadows she had summoned from the barn wrapped her in swirls of darkness, curling through the loose hair that flew out behind her. Sparks danced through it all, sparking and twisting in a stunning display.

But her eyes were alight. No longer could he see those sparkling irises—not when the flames that licked from those sockets blazed so brightly.

At once, Kieran's three henchmen launched at her.

Elspeth turned and parried one attack, twirling her empty left hand to gather smoke. It twined together and appeared nearly solid within her grasp. Loops of writhing shadows and particulate ready to be commanded coiled together. She kicked the next man, allowing him to stagger back.

Flicking her hand out, she loosed her fingers from their grip on the coil. The long, braided smoke lashed out, snapping against the face of the other man Aleksander recognized from earlier, still trying to figure out the best grip for his dagger.

The dagger fell to the floor and he toppled back, screaming. Aleksander watched as he scrambled against the wall pressing his left eye. Blood poured through the cracks in his fingers.

The whip snapped around again as she parried a hit from the nobleman. His rapier warped under the heat and pressure of Elspeth's blade, and as the whip found its home around the wrist of the second unknown man, she got in close enough to land a cut against the nobleman's neck.

He fell instantly.

Elspeth turned, pulling the whip and guiding the man's hand. His grip loosened and the sword clattered to the ground.

Aleksander's stomach churned violently as flames crept up the still-coiled smoke, into the hand and beneath the skin of the hand it held. He screamed as it licked along his bones, bubbled his skin, burned him from the inside out. Elspeth did not let go, even as the veins in his face began to glow brighter.

"Enough!" Kieran's shout echoed through the space. Aleksander felt his voice vibrate within his ribcage and start a ringing within his ears.

The man slumped to the ground, smoke creeping from his mouth, nose, and ears.

Cezary had rushed along the back wall of the barn and now stood beside Aleksander, his face pale as a ghost, eyes wide and unblinking.

Even though he did not want to, Aleksander looked at Elspeth.

She'd distanced herself somewhat during the fight. Whether it was an intentional attempt to keep him safer or just something that happened in the heat of the moment, he didn't know. But he was grateful.

Her shoulders heaved with great breaths, and even as Kieran slowly approached with his hands up, she kept the smoke and fire swirling around her, covering her. She had no need for metal armor, he realized—she had her magic the whole time.

The flames licking from her eyes flared as he approached.

"You've made your point, my Lady." His voice still held its gruff, intimidating quality—but it nearly broke as he spoke. Slowly, he dropped onto one knee, then the other, and sank back. His hands rested on his knees as he looked up at her. His eyelashes fluttered, thickening in the soot that wafted off of her. "You didn't have to kill my men."

"You didn't believe me," she spat. "They were going to kill him if I hadn't done anything." She pointed at Aleksander, all but one finger still curled around the whip.

He flinched.

"*You* were going to kill him!" A snarl contorted the shadows of her face, and from the dark mask she'd given herself, her teeth shone brilliant and violent.

Kieran shook his head. "I was saving him for you, my Lady. Hoping we'd find you before he was well enough to escape and find his way back to those royal heathens."

She shook her head. Finally, the air in the room relaxed. Her shoulders drooped ever so slightly—then she caught herself and straightened again.

As the fire went out on her sword, small sprites darted off the metal and zoomed around the room, finding homes once more in the lamps she'd turned out.

"I would have preferred if you had simply let him kill you," she hissed. "At least then he would have gone home and been more fit for me."

Kieran's head dropped. "I am sorry my Lady."

"You should be."

Aleksander had never heard Elspeth speak in such a way. Every word, every *breath* was laced with more vitriol and malice than he'd ever thought her capable of possessing. He couldn't tell if she was looking at him, but he hoped she wasn't. He didn't want her to see the fear he knew was written all over his face.

He didn't want her to see that there was hatred there, too.

She bent down on one knee, reaching toward Kieran's face as the smoke dissipated from her grasp. Her nails curled into his jaw like talons.

Pain streaked across his face momentarily, but it cleared as she leaned closer.

"I am taking the Sword. None of you will follow us, and you will *not* make a move until the time has come."

He nodded. As much as he could with her gripping his chin. "When will I know the time has come?"

Aleksander was startled to hear actual anxiety wavering his voice.

"You'll know." Elspeth held him there for another moment, flames licking back and forth in mimic of eyes searching a face. She didn't smile. With a violent shove, she pushed Kieran's face away. He wobbled to the side and caught himself.

"Of course, my Lady." Trembling hands steadied him as Kieran bent forward, pressing his forehead to the cold wooden boards of the barn's floor. "I'll be waiting."

Elspeth said nothing as she turned and walked towards Aleksander and Cezary. The sword slipped back in its sheath and her arm looped around Aleksander's waist, supporting him as he walked.

And he had no choice but to accept the help. Cezary went along with it, holding Aleksander's right arm and giving him assistance on that side, but Aleksander couldn't ignore the terror in his eyes.

He hoped he'd hidden his own enough.

Cold wind hit their faces. Behind them, the door to the barn closed, and all the smoke that had been concealing Elspeth's face drifted away. The flames settled in her eyes, and when Aleksander turned to her, she refused to look at him as she unbuttoned her doublet and sank into the snow with a groan.

"I...I'll get the horse." Cezary dropped Aleksander's arm and took off through the snowdrifts as fast as he could.

Chapter

FORTY NINE

*E*LSPETH, FACE DOWNTURNED, NO LONGER burning within her own skin, kept walking with Aleksander.

His mind swam. Not just from the pain, not just from what he'd witnessed, but from what it meant. This was Elspeth. *Elspeth.* The girl he'd danced with in the tavern, the girl he trusted more than anyone.

"Was that an act, or real?" The accusation was painful to think about, but when the words left his tongue, he felt his own heart crack.

Her jaw tightened and they paused at a tree so Aleksander could catch his breath.

"Elspeth," he snapped.

"Real." At this, her eyes lifted. They were rimmed with red. Tears tracked down her cheeks, dry and soot-stained in the stark daylight.

He wanted to scream at her. Everything he'd learned about the Scourge came rushing back in a matter of seconds—forget what Varek and Chione had said about young girls being condemned wrongfully, this was *the* young girl. This was *the* Scourge. The person who, generation after generation, would attempt to destroy his way of life. His people.

Him.

And yet, at the same time, his throat closed. Tears burned his eyes. "How long have you known?"

It wasn't a question, it was a demand.

By the way Elspeth's eyebrows twisted and her lips pursed, she heard what he *really* meant. It wasn't about her knowing. Not fully.

Aleksander leveled a glare at her. Every ounce of strength he had left

How long have you been lying to me?

"People have been whispering about it since I was a girl." Her voice was small. "Saying that's why my mom left me. But...I didn't know for sure until we came here. Lots of girls hear that, you know." Tears flooded her eyes anew, carving new tracks down her cheeks. "I promise you Aleksander, I do not want to be her."

Her voice broke on his name.

He couldn't look at her.

"You have to believe me," she stepped forward, and while Aleksander needed the tree for support, he shifted away.

The feeling of her grief was like a bolt of lightning. His gaze fixed off at one of their footprints, he saw her pull her outstretched hands back to her chest. One fluttered up to cover her mouth.

"I..." he started, but stopped. What could he say?

More frustration and anger than he'd ever felt swirled within his chest. It ate at him, making his hands buzz and his muscles run tight. She deserved to be yelled at, she deserved to know how much this hurt. How *wrong* this was.

But she was his friend. And he couldn't forget that.

So on top of all that anger was a thick, writhing layer of sorrow.

He shook his head, ignoring the stars it brought to his vision, and looked up at her.

She stood in the middle of two trees—the one he'd been leaning on and the one across from it. Snow from the branches settled upon her hair, and if it weren't for the spectacle he'd witnessed moments earlier, he'd have no clue she had just become a monster from his nightmares.

"I've been raised to hate you." It wasn't what he'd expected to say. The words were measured. Their arrows aimed. "You know that, right?"

Her eyelashes fluttered. "I know."

"I'm supposed to kill you."

"I know."

"In every lifetime, Elspeth, I kill you."

"I *know*."

"And you lied to me. You knew this and you lied to me."

Her chin quivered. "I tried to tell you."

"When?"

She shook her head, wiping her tears away with a dirty hand. "So many times."

"Who else knows?"

At this, her eyes widened. "What?"

"Are Cezary and I the only ones who know?"

After a moment she shook her head. "Varek and Chione know, too. Asghar has his suspicions, but I don't think he's fully put it together yet."

Varek. Of course.

That was why he was so set on telling Aleksander to protect Elspeth. *That's* why he was defending all the young girls getting accused, because he knew one of the young girls getting accused was in their midst.

Even if this accusation was correct.

Snow fell around them now in a quiet mist.

Aleksander shuddered and glanced into the forest for any sign of Cezary.

"Do you hate me now?"

The words caught Aleksander, but not as much as her tone. Never in their months of knowing one another, in their late nights and early mornings, in all their moments of vulnerability where Elspeth would laugh off things that turned Aleksander's stomach, had he never heard her so...hopeless.

Turning back to the Scourge once more, the Elspeth he'd known looked like she was dying.

Her eyelids hung over her eyes, jaw slack. Circles had appeared beneath her eyes. Her nose was red from crying, and that water didn't mix well with the cold woods they stood in.

Her lips twitched before she spoke. "I'd understand if you did."

Damn it.

Aleksander looked away, chewing on his lower lip. He couldn't. He knew he couldn't. "No," he said, meeting her gaze again. "But that doesn't mean you haven't hurt me. And it doesn't erase how angry I am right now."

She nodded frantically. "I'll take it."

Repetitive footfall sounded from up ahead. Snow crunched, buried twigs snapped. Through the trees, Aleksander could make out the shape of Cezary, walking with Elspeth's war horse. Without asking, Aleksander limped back towards Elspeth and let her hold him up again.

Their steps fell in sync, crunching through the snow.

"Are you going to tell them?"

Now *that* was a question. If Aleksander was any sort of man, especially if he were the man he was supposed to be in opposition to Elspeth, he would.

"No. Not unless I need to."

Beneath his weight, she sagged. A sigh floated out and turned to mist as it passed by his face. "Thank you, Aleksander."

She shouldn't be thanking him. Keeping her identity a secret was a horrible choice.

Cezary helped hoist him onto the horse with minimal yelps of pain. Elspeth swung up behind him, arms encircling him just to grab the reins of the huge animal. Just as she was about to click to it, usher it forward, he turned around.

"Cezary!"

The man stopped his walk away and turned.

Aleksander swallowed hard. "You don't tell anyone about this. You don't tell anyone about her. Or Varek will kill you."

The muscles along Cezary's jaw flared, but it was clear he knew as much as Aleksander did that Varek was his biggest threat should Elspeth's secret get out. He offered a curt nod. "Be well, Aleksander," he muttered. To Elspeth he said nothing.

She nodded to him regardless. Her thanks was clear on her face, but as she turned back to direct the horse, Aleksander caught a glimmer of grief pass over it.

The horse's speed picked up. Snow flew around them as she cantered on, and despite the severe pain in his arm, the way his cloak bunched around him was cozy. He rested his head back against Elspeth's shoulder, and allowed his eyes to close.

Somehow, despite the jostling he endured in the saddle, he managed to drift off to the smell of smoke and rosemary.

Chapter

FIFTY

ALEKSANDER WAS THANKFUL FOR THE amount of Crafters, mages, and healers in residence at Asghar's estate. Once they'd run into Varek and the men he'd brought with him, Elspeth and Varek had rushed Aleksander back to the manor. The soldiers continued on with a single order from Varek: kill everyone still breathing in that barn.

He'd told him about Cezary, and Varek had smoothed back his sweaty, blood-soaked hair, promising that his spies weren't idiots. If he had any knowledge of the men racing towards that barn, he'd have left the moment Elspeth turned away.

The Ölmesuz had practically carried him up the steps of the manor, screaming for healers, mages, anyone who could help.

A few minutes later, and he was laid out in a room in the mage's wing. People he'd never met were fluttering around him. He drank bitter tinctures. They snipped at his already-rotting flesh. He asked how long he'd been gone.

Just a day.

It felt longer.

He wasn't sure if he believed them when they said that.

He couldn't look when they set his bone. One of the healers, a Rodzjiek woman who reminded him of the healer they'd found in Farnich, talked to him as the others shifted it. Then, she gave him a pillow to bite down on.

The grind and crunch reverberated up his arm and he screamed. Feathers stuck in his mouth when they took the pillow away.

It wasn't technically broken. It had been shattered. There were sections that weren't there anymore, in that thin bone of his forearm, but it didn't matter, the healers said. The missing shards were so small his body would find a way overtime to close them up.

But he wouldn't be without pain.

It was lucky, they said, that it was his left arm and not his right.

He likely wouldn't have the kind of mobility he used to in his hand anymore. Kieran's strike had injured the tendons too much.

Overtime, he'd grown quiet. When he'd first arrived, everything was a flurry of activity. From Varek's shouting for help, and then all those who answered trying to talk to everyone at once in an attempt to figure out what happened and what needed to happen in response. Even as they sat him on the bench and turned his head away from his arm, administering whatever medicines and tests they needed to, they kept talking. He kept talking, too. Laughter rang through the room, down the hall.

Theresas joked with him while she wove a blanketed wall around his mind with the aid of mint and licorice root and a small shard of amethyst. Others entertained him with party tricks, like conjuring lights and using whisper spells to move their voices around the room.

Crafters came in, mildly confused about him, but kind nonetheless. They offered Creations to hold his bones in place, to reduce swelling, to check the state of the impact on the back of his head.

Then the pain shifted. No longer was it a strange, aching numbness that spiked through his bone when he put pressure on it or moved it in another way. Once they'd set the bone and closed up the skin as best they could, it began to throb. They slathered an ointment on the part of his skin that had already begun to suffer from the infection, they put a different ointment in the wound to stave off further ailment. It burned. They wrapped it in gauze and linen.

It was easily the worst long-term pain Aleksander had felt. Wounds were short. You had the initial pain at injury, and then occasionally as it healed.

This was certainly worse than anything he'd endured before.

Aleksander stopped laughing. Stopped talking at all.

"There," the head healer said, washing her hands off in a basin. "That's all we can do for now." She was a kind woman, one he hadn't met before. Rodzjiek, like most of them were. Her eyes were somehow a brighter gold than Varek's. "I know it'll hurt, but you'll be up and moving in no time, I'm sure of it."

He did his best to respond to her offer of a smile. "Thank you, Vlasta."

Drying her hands off on her skirt, she reached for him. "Let me help you up, my lord." She was careful with how she took his injured arm, grabbing just above the elbow before shifting him enough to grab the other.

Simply the act of moving his body—and thus his arm—through space was enough to make it feel as though his hand was going to fall off.

"Does it hurt awfully?" she asked, studying his shift in expression.

He shrugged. "It feels like it almost got cut off, if that helps."

Vlasta pursed her lips. "I'll come up with a pain remedy for you. Don't worry."

The pair walked in near silence down the hall. Servants passed by slowly, each of their movements suddenly measured much more than they needed to be. If one was to accidentally meet Aleksander's eyes, he often received a worried look and a nod that he took to mean "glad you're alright."

Nothing was more appealing to Aleksander than getting to his room and curling up in bed for a good, long rest. A true rest.

They followed the paths of tile and murals that he'd become

so familiar with. Eventually, the door to his room swung open.

It was just as he'd left it, save for the single figure seated by his desk, chin in her hand, eyebrows furrowed intently at the frosted window. When the door opened slightly too far and squeaked, the princess's head whipped around. Relief flooded her face.

"Aleksander!" She nearly began to cry, her voice cracking and eyes welling with tears as she flew from the seat she'd taken towards him, arms outstretched. The embrace she took him in was careful, but it was not gentle. "Oh, thank the goddess, I was so worried."

He dropped his head into her shoulder. "I'm alright, Carissa."

Pulling back, her brows drew low over her eyes. "What were you *thinking*? Did you *want* to get killed?"

And there it was. The side of Carissa that only ever came out when he had done something entirely inexcusable.

She had often taken the role of the mother as they grew up, but it was these moments when she truly proved to be Lenore's daughter.

"I'm sorry," he sighed. The room was already starting to spin, and Vlasta was still trying to get him past the door to his bed.

"Sorry is not good enough! Aleksander what possessed you to sneak out in the middle of the night and go seek out the very people who want you dead? The people who side with our enemy —who want our whole country to fall?"

He winced at that. "I'm...Carissa, can I lay down, please?"

She flapped her hands at her sides. "I just...yes you can lay down but...*Aleksander*."

"I know, Carissa, I know." The bed sagged beneath him as he sat. A welcoming shift from that barn floor and the bench he'd been on for the past few hours.

Carissa stared at him with damp eyes and crossed arms, watching as he carefully shifted his injured hand around the blankets. "So what happened?"

A deep sigh blew from his lips. "A lot."

With a few steps, she joined him on the bed and leaned down, taking off the boots he'd somehow entirely neglected to take off. "I just...tell me what happened, Aleksander."

Tucked safely in bed, with his sister arranging his pillows and blankets and sticking her head out in the hall to call for a tea service, he shared everything. From the anger he felt at not being able to act, to the stupid decision to act once he ran into Varek during a walk around the manor. He told her all about the fact that Varek seemed to know he wasn't going to give up and told him about the barn and the Blight anyway, which made Carissa's brows furrow even further.

"It's not his fault," Aleksander snapped, "I'm the one who should have just pocketed what he told me and moved on."

"I'll still wring his neck for it," came the immediate response.

He did not tell her about Ilya and Varek's discussion, but he did mention that Cezary was there, and instrumental in getting him out.

There was no way he could look at her as he described the disastrous attempt he'd made on attacking them. How he'd broken in, only managed to land a few hits, and then got his arm wounded and his head bashed.

He tried to ignore how his face heated when he recounted the joy he'd felt waking up to Elspeth's presence.

"How did Elspeth fare?" his sister said. "She was terrified when you were nowhere to be found."

Aleksander's stomach turned. As mad as he was at the girl, he couldn't shove aside the sorrow he felt at making her worry so.

"She said she'd found you leaving your room in winter clothes and when she asked where you were going, you said you'd be back by morning." The princess brushed aside a curl with a huff. "And then you weren't."

"She was fine. Better than fine, actually." A lie. He knew it. Plain as he knew Elspeth's stance on her identity, on their destined dynamic, he knew she was not fine. No girl who was content with such a destiny would have cried before him like that. "She fought well. Varek's training is really paying off."

"Good."

"She took on three men at once, Carissa." Aleksander couldn't help the swell of pride in his chest as he said it. "She took on three at once, killed two, partially blinded another and got the fourth to surrender."

Carissa's eyebrows rose.

Too far, too much I should have kept quiet.

He swallowed hard, shifting as though his head or arm was hurting him. Out of habit, he placed his left hand flat on the mattress to push himself up. A strangled shriek broke from his throat and Carissa lunged forward, helping him adjust.

"That's impressive," she mused. Her eyes roved the bandage on his arm. Something shifted. Aleksander wasn't sure exactly what it was, but when her eyes met his, the smile she gave was strained. "Get some rest. We'll be traveling back home tonight."

"What?"

She stood, brushing her skirts smooth. "I've completed my training. With the Blights getting worse and now you and Elspeth having unearthed the local group and killing some of its members, Lord Asghar's men can handle it from here. We're going home." Her hands folded before her. "We have work to do in the castle. My husband is expecting us."

Aleksander nodded slowly. It all made sense. And he wanted to go home.

Yet something pulled him to stay here.

"Are we all going?"

"Yes," his sister nodded on her approach to the door. "Varek will be following shortly behind, you and Elspeth will ride back with me. Bunc has been staying around the manor anyway, he should be readying the horses as I speak."

The door creaked as she pulled it shut, but her grasp lingered on the polished wood.

"Rest for a while." The command was soft, gentle. Those pale green eyes held within them deep pools of care. No matter that Aleksander could see wheels already beginning to turn in the princess's head. "I'll come get you once we're ready to leave. You can even sleep in the carriage, I'll make sure it's comfortable for you."

The latch clicked behind her, leaving Aleksander alone in his room.

He tried to shimmy down into his pillows, pulling the blanket up around him best he could with one hand.

This bed was one of the most comfortable beds he'd ever had the pleasure of resting in.

And yet, as he tried to close his eyes, nothing felt right.

For once, he knew it wasn't the fault of the book beneath his mattress.

Chapter

FIFTY ONE

THE FAMILIAR GRAND FIREPLACE CRACKLED before him as he lounged in one of the smaller sitting rooms at Castle Brevindun. It scattered brilliant refractions of light though the crystal glass he held. Aleksander studied the pungent brown liquid as it swirled, leaving droplets and streaking down the sides of the glass the same way he'd seen imported wines from the west form rivulets along the inside of Janek and Carissa's cups. Vlasta had gotten the tincture to Bunc just as they were about to pull away. It was thick and dark, and to be diluted in water—or even fruit juice if they had access to it.

They were royals, she'd said. Of course they'd have fruit juice in the winter, how silly of her.

He took another sip. Aleksander had already drank half of this first glass, and while it made his nose screw up and his lips pucker, he had to admit, the pain in his wrist was finally beginning to fade.

Footfall sounded behind him. For the first time in his life, he didn't turn to see who it was. On one hand, yes, his head hurt if he moved too much. But on the other hand, he'd spent a solid hour before this fireplace, letting others unpack his things, and he'd finally gotten over the guilt of not being able to help.

He'd risked his life multiple times in the last year. He could let someone take his attention if they needed it, instead of offering it to them should they want it or not.

A familiar ruffle echoed through the space.

"How's that arm doing?"

Aleksander turned and wished he had more energy and strength to launch himself at the Mekartlim smiling at him.

To compensate, his face nearly split in half with a grin. "It's awful."

Demir laughed. Oh, how *good* it was to hear that laugh. Aleksander hadn't realized how much he'd missed the man's company until he smiled so wide his eyes closed, shoulders and wings bouncing in amusement. "And yet you've got a glow the likes of which I've never seen on you."

Aleksander rolled his eyes. "That's just because I get to see you again."

Demir's laughter quieted, but an earnest smile stayed softly affixed to his features. He lifted a wing over the back of the chair beside Aleksander and spread them as best he could. "Mind if I sit?"

"If you can."

It took some maneuvering, but eventually, the man was able to lean forward, elbows on his knees, and stare into the fire alongside Aleksander. "Varek told what happened."

The boy's gaze turned back to the swirling drink. "He did?"

"Mmhm."

The crackling of the fire filled the space between them.

"I'm not mad, if that's what you're thinking. I'm not here to lecture you," Demir said softly.

"No," Aleksander shook his head. "No, that's not it." And it wasn't. He knew Demir wouldn't be mad at him. If anything, he expected the soldier to understand. He figured Demir would have done the same thing had their roles been reversed.

"Then what is it?" He shifted forward, the movement causing Aleksander to match his gaze. Those clear eyes seemed almost predatory, the way they searched his face. The corner of his mouth twitched up in a smile. "I know there's something wrong.

I've seen enough of yours and your sister's moods to know when either of you are hiding something."

The first thing that came to mind for Aleksander was the fact he had been grappling with since the moment he and Elspeth left that barn. But he couldn't tell Demir.

He knew the man wasn't on the side of Tulathne, not fully. But he knew he was loyal enough to Carissa and Janek that, even if he sided with Varek, he would likely tell them. And that would only end horribly.

So he shrugged and rolled his neck from side to side. A series of cracks sounded, and for the first time in a few days, the tightness in Aleksander's skull lessened. "Well, you got my letter, didn't you?"

At this, Demir snorted. "Yes, I did. Sorry I couldn't send one back in time but it seems you move faster than me."

A laugh choked its way out of Aleksander's throat. "Yes well… it's been…"

"I know," the man said. "I did read the letter."

"And I've been…" Again, Aleksander was at a loss. How could he tell Demir what he'd discovered in the last few days? It was more than likely the man already knew about the Scourge scare— he had been the one updating them on the young women being murdered.

It still felt so strange, those words leaving Aleksander's mouth that, just a month ago, he had seen as a form of treason. "I've been thinking about the Scourge scare a lot," he said softly. "And that's ultimately why I'd gone to the barn alone I…I needed to do something. Me. As Aleksander." His eyes met Demir's. "I've been raised to help people. If I'd continued to turn a blind eye, I'd be a disgrace not just to my title, but as a person."

The man smiled. It was soft, mostly visible in the crinkles around his eyes and the way his mouth curved slightly, twitching his facial hair up. "I'm glad to hear that, Aleksander." His voice dripped with warmth. With pride.

Aleksander took a sip of his drink to quell the sudden tightness in his throat.

"Not many in your position would have done that, I think."

The strange, almost-minty liquid slid down his throat. "You're probably right." He turned to take in the man beside him. Demir had not changed much in the time he'd been gone. His winter clothes were different—the shirt he wore was a similar style to his usual, with a special pattern of ties so that he could easily take it on and off with his wings, but like Aleksander's doublet, the strips of fabric were lined with fur. His left wing was still held tight against his back, but it drooped more than it had.

"How's the wing?"

A heavy, deep sigh caused the fire to flicker. "It's a wing," he said simply. "I still have it."

Aleksander's face bunched up. "That's all?"

"I can't fly." His tone was flat. "It's still too tight and by the feel of the tendons..." He sat up straighter, momentarily flexing the wing out. The instant he pressed too far, his wing began to twitch. It only stretched to half of its usual span. Demir winced, his features contorting not in pain, but in effort and frustration. With a gasp, he folded it back against himself.

Aleksander's heart seized. He had known there was a strong likelihood Demir would never fly again, but somehow, he'd convinced himself if he hadn't told Demir, it wouldn't come true. He'd thought it to be a cruel trick, the healer suggesting that. Nothing bad ever truly happened to anyone he knew about. No one had lost limbs. No one had gotten so ill they died, or lost the ability to taste for the rest of their life.

In all his fifteen years, whenever anyone got hurt, they healed completely.

"I'm sorry," he said.

It wasn't enough, he knew that. But it was all he had.

Demir didn't respond.

"You should be up there," he continued softly. "You were made for the air."

"All Mekartlim are," the man sighed. "But I knew, going in to this, that there was a chance I would die. All things considered, I'd take being crippled over being dead."

As the fire continued on, they both sat there in silence. No other topics of discussion came to mind, even though Aleksander was desperate to say *something*. Anything, really, to shift the mood that had suddenly become incredibly oppressive and sad.

He couldn't help but compare Demir's crippled wing with his injured arm. It was different, he knew that. Demir had lost the ability to engage in something innate to his people. Aleksander lost the ability to make a full fist with his left hand.

Still, it weighed on him.

A log snapped in the fireplace, and Aleksander spoke. "Iscah wanted me to tell you she loved you."

The words were out before he could even preface them, or stop himself from saying them all together. A message from her, however kind and hopeful, was not something that would lighten the mood.

Demir blinked at him. "What?"

Aleksander downed the last of his pain medication and set the glass on the painted table beside him. "Iscah told me to tell you that she loved you."

The man stared at him for a long moment.

"I had a dream," Aleksander started to clarify, "she was in it, and...she gave me messages for everyone. Yours was that she loved y—"

"I heard you." Demir's voice broke. His thick lashes blinked rapidly in a futile attempt to clear the tears forming. "When was this?"

"A week ago. I think."

His lips pressed together firmly. One, steady nod was all he gave in reply. "How did she look? Was she whole?"

Aleksander knew what that meant. Did she have her wound? Was she still suffering, even in death?

Or was she safe?

"She was beautiful," he whispered.

A strangled sob clawed its way up Demir's throat. He looked down, his soft curls and the braids adorning them forming a curtain from the rest of the world. After a moment he raised his head and swiped the tears from his cheeks. "Thank you, Aleksander."

He nodded fervently. "Of course."

Demir dropped his wings to the sides, his head tilting as much as it could to rest on the back of the chair. His chest rose and fell with a deep steady breath.

On it came a soft, muttered prayer—bits and pieces gathered together in thanks to the Orzei and the Mother for protecting Iscah.

Aleksander wished he had more of that awful drink to busy himself with.

Finally, Demir dropped his chin, focusing again on the fire. "I needed to hear that. Maybe now my dreams will finally rest."

"Dreams?" Aleksander's heart stumbled at the word. It conjured up his own memories from the realm of sleep—memories he now saw as much too real.

"I'd been having nightmares," his friend said, brushing off the worry in Aleksander's tone. "Nothing much, just different forms of that night. I don't know what the Ölmesuz believe, their religion is much different from ours. Much more complicated. But I hoped they got restored in the afterlife. Mekartlim do," he shrugged, "but there are also stories of specters looking as disfigured as they did when they died. So...I didn't know. It was eating me alive. Thinking she'd be in pain for the rest of time."

"Oh," Aleksander leaned forward. "No, she's entirely safe. Entirely herself."

"Good."

"Aleksander!" The voice boomed through the halls. It was muffled enough as to obscure the full identity of the speaker, but the urgency in it set both Demir and Aleksander to their feet instantly.

"Aleksander!" The call came again, clearer.

"Varek?" he shouted back, already starting for the doors of the sitting room. "Varek, I'm in here!"

The Ölmesuz's towering form slipped around the door frame. His eyes were wide, his shoulders heaving.

Aleksander's blood ran cold. "What is it?"

He almost didn't want to ask.

Part of him feared he already knew.

"It's Elspeth," Varek heaved. "They've arrested her."

Aleksander's whole body began to vibrate. Nothing felt real, not the clothes on his frame, not the breath in his lungs. Every inch of his body flew into panic, and yet he couldn't move.

"No," he said, "no, they can't."

Varek's eyes closed tightly. He sucked in a deep breath, shifting his weight. When his eyes opened, the only emotion Aleksander saw there was pure terror. "Aleksander. She *knows*."

Chapter

FIFTY TWO

"CARISSA!" His SISTER'S NAME TORE from his throat, rattling and desperate. Forget the pain in his arm, forget the pain in his head—he pushed on, running as much as he could down the hall with Varek and Demir close behind.

His chest grew tight, but he clenched his lips shut and sucked in a large breath through his nose. It didn't stop the burn, but it did still its progression.

With a new lungful, Aleksander screamed again, "Carissa!"

Varek's hand closed around Aleksander's arm, tearing him into the office he nearly ran past.

There she sat, behind a fine mahogany table, laden with spell ingredients and tomes rich with magical and religious texts. Half of them Aleksander recognized—they'd read varying selections from them in school. The others were entirely new.

Her eyes lifted, dripping with regret. "Aleksander…"

"No," he snapped. "No, Carissa why are you doing this? Where *is she*?"

A hard swallow traveled down her throat. Fine fingers splayed out across her desk, and she pushed herself to her feet. "Aleksander, please, breathe. I told Varek to let me break the news," her smooth gentle tone twisted into a snarl as she regarded the Ölmesuz with her usual venom. "I knew this would be a shock to you but, Aleksander—"

"She..." His chest heaved. Tears burned in his throat, his pulse pounded in his ears.

This was not happening. They hadn't taken her. They wouldn't do that to Elspeth, besides he'd not told anyone, and Varek would have known if any of his spies spread the news—if Cezary spread the news.

He shook his head. "Carissa, she..."

"Shhh," she slid around the table, skirts swishing behind her.

Within a breath, she encircled him in a tight hug. Her head dipped to his shoulder. The curls that were beginning to fall loose from her bun tickled his nose as his stilted, fractured breaths pulled the coils in and out at uneven intervals.

"I'm sorry, Aleksander," she cooed. "I...I wish it wasn't the truth, but she didn't deny it."

He pushed his sister back as best he could with one hand. "What. Happened?"

She blinked at him slowly, then glanced at the two men behind him. "Would you both wait in the hall?"

Aleksander heard Demir begin to step back.

Varek stayed exactly where he was.

After a moment, Carissa fixed him with a burning glare. "Let me rephrase that—go wait in the hall. Now."

A sharp huff expelled from Varek, but his boots soon joined Demir's as they clicked across the polished stone. The door latched behind them, and Aleksander found himself being dragged forward, his sister's fingers woven between his.

Get off me, that voice in the back of his mind snarled.

She had no right to touch him. How *dare* she think he would even allow it, after what she just did?

But that numbness had returned, and with it, the inability to command his hands.

So he let her drag him to the table, and help him into the seat across from hers.

"I know this is a lot, Aleksander." Her tone was honey. As warm as the sun and as sweet as it spread over toast.

It only served to make him angrier.

"I had been wondering for a while. She's skilled with fire, but I have heard of every Rodzjiek wielder with a prowess near hers, and it was strange that it seemed to be something even she didn't know she could do."

When did this start? Had the friendship he'd watched them share, their closeness...had it all been a lie?

"I know Elspeth was your friend, but—"

"She *is* my friend," he bit. Every word hurt to speak. "She is, Carissa."

A wave of condescension rolled off of her as she tilted her chin down and looked at him through her eyebrows. The realization nearly knocked the wind from his lungs: she truly did not care.

"She's your friend too," he breathed. "Are you forgetting *everything* she's done for you?"

Carissa scoffed. "What has she done for me? Are you talking about the time she let me stay in a vision that was clearly hurting me? Or what about when she didn't tell us to leave a cave full of bodies that had been ravaged by homunculi? She's been manipulating all of us, Aleksander, she's just like Terrell."

"She is nothing like him!" A screech echoed through the room as the chair jumped back. His hand splayed against the table propping him up. Pain shot between the tendons, his fingers splaying wider than they normally could.

Rage flared across his collarbone, and not even a gentle swirling chill from the Presence did anything to abate the inferno growing within him.

"You forget everything she's done for you." The words hissed between his teeth as steam from a closed pot.

Carissa's lips laid flat against each other. "And you allow everything she has done for you to cloud your judgement."

"She is a good person."

"She—" hands slammed the table, propelling Carissa to her feet "—is a monster."

Never had he gone up against the Eyes of Time. At multiple

points in his life, Aleksander had watched as his sister shifted into this other person, with a sickly sweet poison on her tongue and violence writhing right behind her pale green eyes. Lords had bent to it, priestesses had bent to it—as a child, he fully expected Tulathne Herself to bend to it, had Carissa ever been given reason and chance to confront the goddess.

But now, with hot breath and a chest full of anger at things he'd never even considered before, Aleksander knew all those people were weak.

It wasn't that Carissa wasn't strong. She was.

The simple fact was that no one had gone against her with the same conviction she threw at them.

Options flashed through his mind. There was physical violence, but the rage of a thousand men couldn't push him to lay a hand on his sister.

So he flared his nostrils and snarled. The chair tipped slightly when he dropped back into it.

Perhaps he was weak too.

The tension running through her hands relaxed and Carissa stood straight.

Aleksander couldn't look at her. "What are you going to do to her?"

In the corner of his vision, Carissa's gaze fell to her desk. She began to stack papers with lazy, absent movements. "It's not what *I'm* going to do to her," she said, "it's what you're going to do."

His eyes closed. It was all he could do to keep from crying. "And what, exactly, am I going to do?"

The rustle of papers and a swift *plop* sounded through the room. Once Carissa's shifting subsided, all he could hear was the faint whisper of snow blowing up from the windowsill behind her.

"She has two options," she said slowly. "Death by waiting, or death by sword."

He did not open his eyes.

"Death by waiting is simple," she said, "she'll just rot in that cell. I had one of Asghar's Crafters put something together before we left, in case my hunch was right. She won't be able to use her fire to escape, and since she has no need for food…"

An all-too-vivid picture flooded his mind. She sat hunched against the wall of a cell, slowly wasting away. Her cheeks grew sallow, her hair thinned. Everything that was bright and warm about her faded away in his minds eye, until she was nothing but a corpse with rotting teeth.

Nausea churned in his gut. He opened his eyes.

Carissa smiled. The way it reached her eyes made it clear she was trying to show kindness.

To Aleksander, it felt more like the grin of a homunculi before it lunged.

"Death by sword is even simpler." Her head cocked to the side. "You kill her, and this is all over. I may even let you bury her."

A heavy, dark cloud settled around Aleksander's shoulders. It pressed down and in, threatening to suffocate him. Running his tongue over his teeth, he grimaced. "So either way, she dies."

At this, Carissa's smile did fade. "You know she has to."

Aleksander's hand cradled his head. His empty gaze roamed the woven rug visible in the space between his feet.

"I know you think I'm happy about this."

"No," he sat up. "I don't. But I don't think you're *nearly* as mad about this as I am."

For the first time, tears welled in her eyes. "I'm furious, Aleksander. You think I'm excited that Elspeth is the one destined to destroy us? The one who poses a real, dangerous threat to *you*? No, I'd be insane to be happy about that. But I have so much more to think about than one single girl." Her hand drifted to her stomach.

She didn't have to speak about it for him to remember the vision she'd had.

"There is a whole country out there that I must protect. There is a family *here* that I have been praying for the last few years that I must protect. And if that means I have to lose someone I briefly considered a friend in the process, so be it."

The heat and anger coursing through Aleksander dissipated with her words. No matter how much he wanted to, he couldn't blame her. They'd been raised in the same classes, prayed the same prayers, learned the same stories. Elspeth was the Scourge. She admitted that to him, she held that truth within herself. And if he still had the same mindset as Carissa, maybe he too would be okay with putting his best friend to rest. If he had the same mindset as Carissa, she wouldn't be his best friend anymore.

But he didn't. So while he couldn't blame his sister for her decisions, he did hate her.

A hard swallow worked its way down his throat.

Hate was a strong word.

When he met her gaze once more, however...it was the right one.

"When do I need to decide?"

Carissa shrugged. "You can decide whenever. She'll starve in the meantime."

The cavalier way she said that locked in a vice around his stomach.

She'll starve in the meantime. As if it was that simple. As if she wasn't condemning a so-far innocent girl to death. She hadn't killed anyone that Carissa wouldn't have already wanted dead. She hadn't rallied these forces.

Elspeth hadn't even been fully aware of her identity until a few months ago.

With disgust boiling in his stomach, Aleksander stood. "Can I at least go see her?"

He didn't need to hear a response. It was visible in the way Carissa's brows came to a point, her gaze dripping with sick, poisonous pity. She shook her head ever so slightly.

"Fine. Can I go to my room?"

"Of course," Carissa cooed. She rose slowly, hands outstretched.

Aleksander stepped back, and did not let the hurt that flashed across her face affect him.

"You take all the time you need, brother. I'll be here for you. We'll all be here for you." An earnest smile flashed over her lips momentarily. "Talk to Tulathne about it."

He said nothing on his departure. Fists clenched at his sides, pain riveting up his left arm, even as his fingers refused to fully close.

The last thing he wanted to do was talk to the goddess responsible for this mess.

Chapter

FIFTY THREE

THE CONTINUOUS SCUFFING OF HIS boots threatened to wear a strip along the rug beneath his bed. Not that anything done to stone or woven wool should matter—the floor can be buffed and replaced, a new rug could be woven. There was nothing he could do to help Elspeth if she died before he made a choice.

So he paced.

In the corner, the old tapestry of Tulathne stared down at him. He hadn't looked at it since re-entering, and he didn't look at it now. His eyes traced the path before him, marking out where his feet should fall between the grouted stone, what woven flower he needed to cover, what tassel his toe should avoid. And all the while, his mind reeled.

Aleksander's shoulders were tight, his breathing shallow. Anger and fear wove in tandem up and down his spine.

How infuriating it was that Carissa had made such a rash decision like that.

Why did his toe keep catching on the rug?

It came as a shock to everyone but could they not see that Elspeth's past and current behavior warranted respect?

He meant to step slightly forward, why couldn't he step just a little further?

She was a good person. In all their time together, she had proven that.

Stop stumbling. Step *further*.

How *dare* Carissa?

The fingers on his left hand refused to make a full fist. *Gods* how he wanted to make a fist.

If he were truly the Sword of Ages, taller and stronger and older, he would walk down to the dungeon, find her cell, and demand her freed. And they would listen to him. They'd have to.

How come they didn't listen to him now?

Goddess above, why couldn't he close his hand?

Tension streaked up his neck. In a burst of movement, Aleksander grabbed the screen blocking off the oratory and hurled it across the room. A yell tore from his throat as it caught air and wobbled in its descent, crashing against the trunk beside his vanity. The fine fabric, woven intricately with stars and flowers, tore at the corners.

Had the wood shattered even a little, he may have felt better. But it didn't, and Aleksander still seethed.

His mattress sank beneath his weight. Held by only his hands, his head felt unbearably heavy. More than a normal head should ever weight, as if the knowledge he'd acquired and the grief he'd endured in the last few days was a tangible, measurable thing.

There was no way he could fight. Not with his injuries. His hand wouldn't be much use gripping a sword, and while Aoife could certainly be wielded with one hand, he didn't feel comfortable without having the backup strength of both hands. Besides, any rush of adrenaline past what he was already enduring would certainly spike the pain already building behind his eyes and send him into an episode of flashing lights and immense dizziness.

What was he thinking, anyway? Fighting off armed palace guards? Alone and injured?

It was idiocy.

Were he to attempt it, he'd be hauled back to his room and

locked up at best. At worst, he'd be named a traitor to the crown and either exiled or killed.

No, fighting for her freedom was out of the question.

Maybe he could just visit her.

Visit her and get a better grasp of the situation. Sneak her an iron file, perhaps. He'd read books about people getting imprisoned and breaking out by using a farrier's file to cut the bars.

But that would take time. And with no food, no water, she'd be weak or dead within days. Humans didn't last long without water, and though Rodzjiek were heartier folk, he assumed it was mostly the same.

His thumbs pressed into the space above his eyes. A deep breath blew from his pursed lips.

The door creaked slowly as it opened behind him. Another deep breath heaved out of Aleksander, and the door closed.

"Not taking it well, I assume?"

He scoffed. "What, should I be?" Sitting straight and turning, Aleksander took in Varek's visage. His breath hitched at the image before him.

Normally the man held his shoulders broad, proud. Almost threatening, if you looked at him from the right angles. And his eyes were stern. But the Varek before him...

"No," he said softly. "I'm certainly not."

The man before Aleksander radiated utter defeat. His frame drooped, arms crossed loosely before his torso. That normally sharp tiger's eye gaze was dampened, lazily roaming the room, taking in the tapestry, the broken screen, Aleksander himself. Each breath looked like it hurt.

Aleksander scooted to the side.

Varek sat without a word.

A heavy, slow breath raised his shoulders. "I would go down there and destroy that jail if I could."

"You say that as if I don't want to do the same thing," Aleksander muttered, dropping his head back into his hand.

Silence passed between them, dark and teeming with anxious

energy.

After a moment, Aleksander lifted his head. "When did she tell you?"

"She didn't have to tell me, kid."

Aleksander rolled his eyes. "Fine. How long have you known?"

The man beside him sucked his teeth before answering, "I've had my suspicions since that fight in the Untamed. Against Terrell."

Since Terrell. What Aleksander expected to hit him full force now echoed as no more than a drop in the cave of his mind. It didn't surprise him. Not that Varek knew, and not that he figured it out that early. The man was smart—he let his gruff exterior push that notion away, dummied down his own portrayal to simply "fighter." But if there was anything Aleksander had learned since the Summer Solstice, it was that nothing and nobody were ever exactly as they seemed.

The man now seated with him, dressed in fine Zekharyan courtly wear, commanded more spies than Aleksander truly knew. He trained both him and Elspeth in the Ölmesuz style of fighting. He had guided Carissa in manners of magic.

If anyone should have been untrustworthy, it should have been Varek.

And yet, here he was.

Aleksander nodded. "Alright. And you didn't think to tell me?"

Varek snorted. "Do you think there would have been a good time?"

"All things considered," the boy rolled his neck, "no."

"Hm. See, there you go, then."

He had a point. Aleksander hated to admit it, but Varek was right to keep it from him then. Just as they were right to try to keep it from Carissa, Clauden, Lenore, and the rest of the court.

But Elspeth had let Kieran go. Had let that other man go too.

"She kept two alive," he sighed, falling back on his bed. As a child, awaking from a nightmare, he would scan the canopy above for any imperfections in the dye or the weave. It was a source of grounding, a source of comfort.

It all just looked red to him now.

Varek shot him a quizzical look. "Hm?"

"The Blight members," he clarified. "She kept two alive. If they were gone by the time your men got there... It was only a matter of time."

"Doesn't mean it was a good time."

Aleksander nearly laughed. "No. It doesn't." As quickly as that strange curl of humor disappeared from his lips, the sorrow he'd managed to keep at bay rolled in and took hold of his chest with a clawed grip.

He swallowed hard, pushing down the hot tears that threatened to spring up yet again.

"What do we do?"

The question was small, quiet. Aleksander wasn't even sure Varek heard it—he could hardly decipher the whisper himself. But Varek sighed and leaned against one of the bedposts. "See, that's the thing, kid. I'm not sure."

"You're the spy, though." Aleksander pushed himself upright. "You're the one who has been trying to stage a coup. You...you have to have *some* idea, don't you?"

At this, the old man laughed. It was a bitter sound. "My biggest plan was keeping her from getting discovered in the first place. At least while under Carissa's control. We could try breaking her out, but..." The man trailed off, shrugging.

Aleksander's teeth pressed together, grinding terribly. Varek's ears twitched but he didn't do anything to stop the boy.

"Then we get her out," he finally said.

He expected opposition from his teacher. Questions about how, or how feasible did Aleksander *truly* think that was? Instead, when he looked up, he was met with a steady gaze.

Varek's jaw tensed. Gone was the despair that had etched deeper the lines already in his face. In his eyes flowed determination.

Aleksander blinked sharply.

And pride.

The man did not blink, did not dare break his gaze. "Tell me what to do."

FIFTY FOUR

THE DUNGEONS HAD NEVER BEEN a place Aleksander enjoyed visiting. Many times growing up, Janek had dared hm to sneak in and find a skull, a dead rat, or something else to bring back and prove his bravery. But even with torches lighting every inch, and the King or a priestess to guide him and issue history lessons, his tiny heart would hammer so hard he usually forgot what they'd said the moment they left the dank tunnels.

The archway to the cells, however? That was forever imprinted on his mind.

Servants didn't offer a second glance to him or Varek as they walked. Aleksander's heart pounded in his throat, his hands clenched at his sides were shaking, but somehow his anxiety was all outward. His breaths were steady. His mind was clear.

The calm he felt did nothing to quell his desperation and rage. He still was prepared to tear the castle apart brick by brick until he got to her, if that's what it took.

"My boy." Clauden's breathy greeting sounded as mournful as Aleksander felt.

He came to a stop and met the king's sorrowful gaze.

He did not want to.

"I...I am so sorry it ended up being this way." The old royal's bushy brows arched over his eyes, half covering them in that eternally sad way of his. Only now, the emotion seemed intentional. Genuine. A smile flickered beneath his beard. "Over the last few months I had engaged in many intriguing conversations with that young lady. Truly a shame."

Aleksander clenched his teeth so hard he feared his jaw would snap. "Truly," he managed.

The king's eyes flicked up to Varek, where he offered the Ölmesuz a sorrowful nod. "I'll let you two on your way. No doubt you've much to figure out, with..." Clauden swallowed sharply. "With her death, and all."

But he didn't move. Eventually the king raised a hesitant hand and patted Aleksander's shoulder. "Should you need anything, my boy..."

There was no fighting the smile that passed for a mere moment. "Of course," he whispered.

Clauden pressed his lips together and nodded sharply. With one final pat, he left.

As they walked on, Aleksander had to hand it to him: Clauden had much more empathy than his daughter.

After turning down a hall, Varek caught Aleksander's arm. "Do you know where you're going?"

Cold metal pressed into the boy's hand. Aleksander gripped the gift tightly and shoved it deep within the pocket of his fur-lined pants. "Trust me," he whispered. "I couldn't forget that archway even if I tried."

"Good." Varek lifted his head to acknowledge a passing courtier before once again turning his dark gaze to the boy beside him. "Once you're in, go down to the second level. It's going to be cold and it's going to stink—breathe shallow. Once you get her out, tell her to run to the back and take a left. There will be a door. Go through it, go up the stairs, and then take a right. Three panels down there is a servant's door on the left side. Go until she hits the back kitchen, then out that door." His eyes flashed around the hall. A large hand closed tightly on Aleksander's shoulder, drawing him in to the tall man's space. Varek's breath burned against his ear. "I'll be there with a horse. She has to do this alone."

Aleksander nodded, adjusting the ring of keys that now felt very bulky and obvious in his tight, quilted pants. Heart racing, he glanced up at Varek one last time. "You talk like you've had experience breaking out of our dungeon."

The man only flashed a smile before turning and disappearing down a connecting hallway.

Aleksander's pulse was loud in his ears. Were he standing by a rushing waterfall, it would have had the same effect—muffling his thoughts, numbing his senses. His heartbeat traveled down his fingers, his spine.

With a deep breath, he straightened up and walked on.

Soon, the archway appeared before him.

That familiar arch, with a single, heavy door and two torches on either side. The handle was cold in his hands and scraped against the rest of the metal in the mechanism as he turned it. A creak sounded from the hinges and his stomach turned.

A quick glance secured that he was, indeed, alone. Strange, considering the person imprisoned below. But he was not one to question a blessing.

The door closed behind him with a heavy clunk, and darkness consumed him. A faint glow illuminated the bottom of the stairs. With careful steps and a hand dragging along the damp wall to steady his descent, Aleksander entered the first level of the dungeon.

Every time he had set foot on this floor throughout his childhood, it had been empty. Now, chains rattled as he came to the bottom of the steps.

"Who is that we've got?" A tired voice echoed from one of the cells.

Aleksander paid no mind and ducked his head, sticking to the shadows. His eyes darted to the side once, catching the crumpled, filthy image of a man in rags.

He curled back a lip and spit before turning in to the cold wall, muttering to himself.

The next staircase was illuminated by yet another torch at the other end of the level.

Taking a deep breath, Aleksander ran.

No one was here. The guards were gone, likely assuming that no one in their right mind would attempt to get her out. Half the torches were gone or extinguished.

Carissa didn't just want to starve Elspeth.

She wanted her to die cold and alone.

She wanted Elspeth to suffer.

With a deep breath and a sharp *gulp,* he laid a hand on the stone of the next staircase and descended into darkness.

The second level was much lower than the first. Janek had told him the First King had built it along with the outbuildings in the back, well before the castle itself was completed. It housed war criminals and rebels, often those who wielded the Flow either as a mage or simply by the nature of being Rodzjiek. There were even rumors they'd kept a few Ölmesuz down there.

Aleksander had eventually decided that was an exaggeration. If they'd imprisoned Ölmesuz, there would still be Ölmesuz. And as far as he knew, there weren't.

At last, his boots hit the bottom floor, and his head swam with the overwhelming darkness and stench.

Unlike the first floor of the dungeon, the second was nearly a maze. The staircase he'd taken was placed smack in the middle of the main corridor, and out to each side stretched a long hall that ended in a T shape. How many more branched after that, he didn't know.

He didn't *want* to know.

But she had to be close.

Doing his best to still his breathing and focus past the pounding in his ears, Aleksander's eyes widened to take in the dimly lit space. "Elspeth?" he whispered.

Even that small breath of her name bounced off the walls. The metal and stone warped it, so by the time his own word got back to him, it sounded hissed and garbled.

"Elspeth?" he tried again, a little louder.

Somewhere in the dungeon, someone shifted.

He didn't dare move. It could be anyone, but if it was her, he couldn't lose the sound of her boots scraping on the dirty stone to his own noise.

"Aleksander?"

Her voice was quiet, shaken, but there.

His head whipped from side to side, trying to pinpoint where she'd spoken from. That dull ache from the bump on the back of his head began again, but he couldn't care less. Not when his veins were full of adrenaline and his heart was ready to burst out of his chest. "Yes," he answered, "it's me. El, where are you?"

"Here."

To the left. He turned, and in the dim firelight, he saw two sets of strong, long fingers curl around the iron bars. "Over here," she said again.

He nearly tripped over his feet as he began to move. It was difficult to balance his need for speed and efficiency with the simultaneous need to be quiet, but he did it. "Elspeth," he breathed, grabbing the bars just above her hands.

Bloodshot eyes met his.

"I'm here."

FIFTY FIVE

THUNDEROUS ROLL OF SORROW rang through him, threatening to drown out anything and everything else. For only having been in here less than a day, she looked awful. A bruise had begun to form below her left eye. Her lips had been picked raw by her teeth, her eyes red and puffy, still glistening with tears. Around her throat was a thin gold chain, locked here and there with inscribed runes. It was tight. Even in the dark, he could see the way it nearly cut into her skin.

He reached through the bars, a gentle thumb wiping away what dampness was left on her cheek.

"Thank the gods," she breathed.

For a moment, he wanted to smile. Here she was, before him, still alive. But it was not the time or the place. "Here," he whispered, retracting his hand from her cheek. The keys were warm now in his pocket, and he was careful to use two hands to muffle the jingling of metal on metal.

Her eyes widened. "Aleksander—"

"You need to run, El," he panted. The key shook in his hand, struggling to find purchase in the locking mechanism; panic was already setting in. Any drop of water, any distant sound of rats scurrying, and Aleksander's hands shook worse.

Elspeth leaned through the bars, her nose and cheek

pressing through one of the gaps. "Aleksander, no, where am I going to go?"

A heavy *click* sounded and he pocketed the keys, drawing her hands into his as the door swung open and away. They were cold. So, so cold. He rubbed his thumb over her knuckles, raising them to his lips and blowing warmth on to them.

Thank whatever god gave Vlasta her intelligence. With that tincture, he could open his fingers just enough to dance them over the back of her hand.

Aleksander shook his head. "I don't know. But you can't stay here. It's not safe, El, Carissa..." Eyes pressed shut for a moment in a desperate attempt to steel himself. "Carissa wants you dead and in a gruesome way, and I can't... I'm *not* letting that happen. Is there some way we can get that off of you?"

His eyes stayed on her neck, and when she swallowed, the chain bulged.

"I don't know, I've been trying but, Aleksander, I—"

Dropping her hands, he dug in his pockets for anything. When he came up empty, he shifted behind her.

It seemed to have been soldered on to her.

"Are you okay? What is this doing to you?"

"I don't know." Elspeth shook her head. "It's like it drew a veil between me and the Flow."

His fingers were too thick, too numb to fit between the chain and her neck. There were no clasps. It was gold, and gold was weak...

"Let me try something." The words barely left his mouth before he placed his cheek on her neck, fitting the chain between his molars and crunching.

Metal and something hot and sweet splashed over his tongue, but when he let go, one of the amulets had broken. With a great sigh, Elspeth ripped the chain from her neck and threw it to the ground.

"No!" Aleksander skittered after it, scooping up the damaged gold. "You keep it with you. We can't leave anything here that would insinuate you had someone helping you. Now, listen." He tucked the chain back in her hands, even as she winced, and continued. "Varek's waiting out back with your horse and provisions for you, he gave me instructions on how to get you out of here."

"I'll be found," her voice cracked, "they know who I am now. They want me, Aleksander. And if I'm alone... they'll find me, I'm sure of it." Those tears began afresh, spilling down her cheeks. Her hands shook in his. "Aleksander, I can't do this. I... This shouldn't be *happening,* I don't know what to do."

"Yes, you can. You can do this. I've seen you in the heat of battle. I mean, everything I saw you do in that barn—El, I... You were amazing."

She blinked at him. "I was?"

He nodded, ignoring the heat that rushed into his cheeks under her stare. "You were. Listen to me, okay?" Raising their joined hands between their faces, he stared at her over her knuckles. "You are an amazing warrior. You are fierce, and mean, and strong, and I—"

"See, that's just it," she shook her head and pulled her hands free. Her voice lowered and that gaze dimmed more than he'd ever seen it.

His blood froze. Even the Presence didn't move. To Aleksander, it felt as if it, too, wanted to see what she meant by that. What she'd say next.

"I am fierce, and mean," each word was slow and deliberate. "And *strong*. And I see things I shouldn't. And when I become... *her*...it's like nothing I've ever felt before. There's so much of... everything. I *feel* everything ten times more. Anger, hate...love." She swallowed hard and finally met his eyes. "I'm so angry, Aleksander. Have been my whole life and I hold it in, I know I can't be...that. But when I'm her it comes so easy." Her eyes fluttered closed and for a moment, a terrifying kind of peace passed over her face. "There's no guilt. No fear of how I'm seen. I feel like I'm doing something good, even when..." her eyes opened, the peace falling. "Even when I know it's not. *She* is who they want, Aleksander. And I cannot be her because when I am it is so hard to *stop*. Not that I can't, but because I don't want to. And if they get me to give in to her?" Her chin quivered, voice cracking. "Who I am, *this* me, right here...she may never come back out."

Aleksander's eyelashes fluttered. He cleared his throat, fighting back tears of panic. Of fear. "Now, I know that's not true."

He didn't.

"You're going to be fine, El."

"I won't," she said. "I know I won't be fine, and I'm scared."

Their hands trembled in unison, desperate and terrified.

"You'd be even *less* fine if you stay."

"I can't do this, Aleksander," she whispered.

"Elspeth." For a moment his voice steadied. A tear dropped from his clouded eyes. "If you stay here, they are going to make me kill you."

She breathed in sharply, tucking her lips between her teeth.

He knew that's what would happen. It was between him killing her, quickly, as painlessly as he could, or letting her starve. That must have been why Carissa had given him that option. Because it wasn't *truly* an option.

If he cared for her at all, he'd give her a quick death.

Her fingers slid smoothly from Aleksander's and before he could grasp for them again, she flung herself around him. She was cold to the touch, but warm where they met. Her breath mingled with the chill of the dungeon, tickling his ear, her cheek warm against his. Fingers dug into his back and neck, desperate to keep them together.

For a moment, all the pain that had been ricocheting around his body for the last few days didn't matter.

She smelled awful—of dried blood and smoke and mildew and sweat. How he wished he could smell the rosemary oil she used just one last time.

Her grip tightened. He was the same height as her now, but he'd become broader over the last few months as well. The arms encircling him were tipped in claws that nearly cut into his doublet in desperation.

Deep within Aleksander's chest, something began to break.

"I'll go," she said finally.

"Good," he muttered.

Pulling back, she wiped a shaking hand down each of his cheeks. "Aleksander, promise me something."

He nodded. *Anything.* "Anything."

"If we meet again—"

"*When* we meet again."

"When we meet again, it will likely be on opposite sides of a battlefield. And...I won't be *me*. I'll be her." Each word cracked as she spoke. "I do not hold any anger towards you. I need you to know that. I never will, I never could. But if I'm too...consumed by it..." Her teeth clenched, hands and eyes roving his chest, adjusting the straps on his doublet, smoothing fabric.

Distracting herself.

"I'm going to need you to...to..."

He shook his head. "No, no I can't do that."

"You need to promise me that if I try to kill you, you don't let that happen."

"No."

"Aleksander, *please*."

Somewhere, the creak of a door echoed. Aleksander's breath stopped, and in the silence he could swear their heartbeats were echoing in tandem.

A gentle hand guided his cheek down, tearing his gaze from the ceiling and fixing it on her. "I need you to promise me that. If I'm not me, then I don't want to be anything."

His throat burned. "I promise."

"Good." Her bottom lip quivered as her eyes searched his face. "I'm going to miss you."

This couldn't be happening—he knew he was going to let her go, that she was going to run, but...

No, this wasn't actually a goodbye.

It couldn't be, he didn't plan for that. There was more he wanted to say, more he wanted to do—

They were supposed to dance together at the solstice.

He couldn't bring himself to tell her he'd miss her, too.

After a moment, Elspeth's eyes flickered around his face and widened. She looped a hand around the back of his neck, pulling his face to hers, and kissed him.

Aleksander's heart shattered.

Her lips were cold, her breath sour from crying, but even as she tried to pull away to leave, he looped his injured arm around her back, grimacing through the pain because at least it meant that she was still here. He kissed her again, desperate to hold her and live, for a moment, in a world where they were entirely honest with one another about everything. Where they had some mangled, cobbled form of happiness. But she pried her lips from his and leaned back.

"If you want me to go, then I need to go now."

No more sounds had come from above. No one knew he was here. No one knew he'd set her free. Except Varek. And he wouldn't tell anyone.

But maybe someone figured it out, and maybe they were running out of time.

Aleksander's whole being ached as he dropped his arms to his sides.

He nodded. "Go. Down the hall, take a left. There's a door. Go through it, up the stairs take a right. Three panels down on the left wall there's a servant's passage. Follow it to the back kitchen and go out that door. It's hardly used this time of year. Varek's waiting there with your horse."

"Thank you," she breathed. Her boots scraped dirt against stone as she slid away from her open cell, fingers flexing in anticipation. Not once did her eyes leave his.

Then, she turned and ran.

Aleksander couldn't move, even though he knew he needed to get out as quickly as possible. Everything hurt. Not just his injuries, but his very skin. Being alive hurt.

He stood there and waited, his panting breaths mixed with the fading of her footsteps. A door latch echoed as it opened, then as it closed, and the only sound that remained was his frantic heart.

Chapter

FIFTY SIX

ESPITE THE ABSENCE OF CANDLELIGHT, the soft blue glow emanating from the snow beyond his window, and the familiar embrace of his bed, Aleksander could not sleep. Since the dungeons his heart had not slowed its pace.

He had returned the keys with no issues. None of the guards noticed. They were not commanded to bring Elspeth food, just check occasionally on rounds, and that other person down there had been left to rot as well.

The castle was not yet on high alert. That gave him some semblance of comfort—at least they didn't realize she was gone yet. At least she had a chance to get further.

Nervous fingers fidgeted with the quilt tugged over him.

Were he in better shape, he would go train.

A bolt of hot pain shot up his arm and down his fingers. Aleksander's face contorted, but once the jolt passed, it fell once more into perfect apathy.

He sat up. It could not be *that* late, there was still the faint glow of a torch beneath his door.

Still, there was no way he could sleep this evening.

Casting a glance once more, the flickering of the firelight that reflected off the polished stone began to shift and fade.

A heavy sigh propelled him back onto his bed. The impact of

his head on his pillow caused his head to hurt again, but he only squinted past the dancing stars in the corner of his vision for a moment.

Footsteps echoed outside.

When he turned his head again, the torch was wholly gone.

The boy swung his feet down onto the thick rug and waddled over to his wardrobe, wrapped in a blanket. The embers in the small hearth had begun to fade hours ago. Winter's damp, chilled breath had already begun to leak through the stone.

He knew he needed to sleep. But all he could do was turn over and over in his mind where Elspeth was. What she was doing. If the Blights had caught her, and if they did, what she could have done to them.

She was their patroness, in a way. The one they'd been waiting for. But she was still a young woman, and they were all violent.

His stomach churned as he dropped the blanket to the floor.

There was no need to think about what they might do to her. That thought held nothing but fear that he could not control.

Right now, control was the biggest thing he needed to regain.

Slipping his feet into boots, he was sure to choose ones with a soft sole. They were nearer to slippers—meant for perusing the colder parts of the palace and going onto the parapets that did not get dirtied easily. They merely had rain and snow battering at them, and the occasional trod of a guard's boot. During times of peace, they usually stayed to their towers, stationed in the corners of the castle.

In fact, all his life, Aleksander had never seen more than one guard at a time patrolling the parapets.

No doubt it would be different now—they thought the Scourge was wasting away in the cellars below them, but those who followed her were still out there.

Regardless, Aleksander offered a silent plea that he would get lucky and be on the walls alone tonight.

He tugged that same heavy cloak around his shoulders that he'd been given at Asghar's and let the door swing shut behind him, not worrying about the noise it might send shattering down the hallway.

With the fur hood up and around his face, each step quickened. His heart began to race.

Gods, he felt ill.

Unreasonable panic flooded his body, threatening to swallow him whole.

Where is the door to the roof?

His thoughts muddled together, the maps he'd made of Brevindun and Aarua Manor warped together and he found himself lost in the very palace he'd grown up in.

Maybe they hit my head harder than I thought.

Spots began to cloud his vision. Numbness worked its way into his hands, his feet. His boots scuffed along the stone floor.

Where was it?

This had never happened before. This wasn't him, he could navigate this castle with his eyes closed.

His heart began to race even more. For the third time that year, Aleksander thought he was going to die. Right there in the hallway, stumbling around in his winter clothes, vision zoning in and out. His pulse would be too fast, his heart would get to tired, and he'd drop.

Beneath him, his legs turned to jelly.

The click of a door closing caught his attention.

Where was it?

Silence radiated through the hall.

Focus, Aleksander, where was it?

The door clicked again, and he started walking. Hand pressed to his collarbone, he forced himself to take deep breaths, widen his eyes, take in the scene around him.

There—at the far end of the hall, a door swung on heavy hinges. The whistle of a breeze passed through it.

Of course. When he was a child he'd hid from Janek on the parapets just past that door.

He wasn't losing his mind.

He just needed to breathe.

Pulling his cloak around him, another gust pushed the door open wider. A few snowflakes twirled in ahead of him.

Aleksander caught the door and inched out onto the wall.

The swirling sky around him was black, painted with swaths of grey where the low clouds had become heavy with snow. Even within their casings, the few torches were struggling to stay alight in the heavy winds.

"Close the door, kid."

Aleksander almost couldn't make out the voice. A quick glance to his left, and his gaze landed on Varek. The old man nodded towards the door.

"Latch it better than I did."

The boy threw his weight against it, pulling until his head nearly touched the merlons. The dull click of a latch echoed into the night.

On his feet again, Aleksander pressed his back to the stone outside of the castle. Through the wind and fur whipping in his face, he was able to focus on Varek, standing little more than an arm's length away. A small paper was held between his first three fingers, rolled into a tube. Without so much as looking at Aleksander, the man adjusted his other hand—on which sat a large raven—and began to stuff the note into the casing strapped to the creature's leg.

"What's that?" Aleksander asked.

Varek shot him a side-glance before turning his attention back to the raven. "Just a letter."

Aleksander opened his mouth to ask the next logical question —"a letter to who?"—but the massive creature twisted its head, locking one pale, beady eye on him. A heavy swallow worked down his throat.

It was a messenger raven, one Varek had set up for communication, that much was obvious. Still, the way it moved was unnerving. Especially up close.

Somehow it had never occurred to him that these birds were, in fact, large.

The casing snapped shut, and Varek held out his hand. The

raven balanced for a moment, wings out, flapping slowly as they were buffeted by a strong gale. Once the wind died it launched itself into the sky, disappearing into the dark of night.

"Is that why you chose ravens?" Most noblemen preferred hawks for messaging. Aleksander had never quite understood why Varek had gone a different route, but in this moment, he was glad for it.

"Not entirely," the man puffed. "It's only an advantage that they blend into the night."

"Then why?"

"They're smart. Much smarter than most birds, and some people. I'd wager good money on Deina there being able to outsmart even your sister." At the notion of such a silly competition, Varek's mouth twitched with a smile. "Besides, they're important. We believe they're the eyes of the Kutsalyot. I'd rather have the saints watching over us and our secrets than anyone else."

"I thought you weren't a religious man."

The old man shrugged, settling back against the wall. "I'm not. But the saints aren't just religion, they're history. They're family." He fell silent, nuzzling his face down into the ruff of fur he'd created from his cloak's hood. His eyes, however, still peered out over the land.

An age seemed to pass. Aleksander's face grew numb from the wind, the cold. It even began to leech through the layer's he'd donned, a light breeze somehow finding a fissure in his clothing and sneaking through to brush across his chest or arm.

"I know why I'm awake," Varek said, breaking the silence. "What about you?"

"You first."

The Ölmesuz snorted and adjusted his cloak tighter. "I'm the one who asked the question, kid."

Aleksander's eyes felt on the verge of freezing. Each blink made his lashes stick together. "I can't stop thinking about what's going to happen when they don't find her." His voice was quiet.

Varek didn't say a word.

The silence made his skin itch, his mind run. "They wouldn't know it's us, right? They wouldn't be able to figure that out. And..."

"I covered our tracks, we have alibis, she had a fast horse." His words were steady, and when he turned to Aleksander, more warmth than he'd ever seen from the man flooded from his eyes. "We're going to be okay. And so will she."

Aleksander swallowed. He couldn't look at Varek anymore. "You can't be sure of that."

"I can," the words rumbled from the man's chest. "Because I'm the one that made it happen." His voice caught, and he swallowed hard. Varek shifted forward, leaning over the flat top of the parapet wall. Loose strands of hair caught on the wind, covering his face almost completely from Aleksander's view.

Beyond him, shrouded in a fine blend of fog and powder snow that just began to fall, were the glittering lamps of Brewith's streets.

"I'm not... I don't talk about this. Not usually. But..." The low tone he spoke in was already beginning to break.

Aleksander debated stopping him. He didn't need to get into whatever this was. For a moment, Aleksander actually missed the gruff old mercenary who called him "your holiness" and trained him so hard he landed his strikes purely because he'd begun to imagine Varek's face on the targets. It was easier having trust for him as equally as annoyance.

Empathy...that was new. It felt strange, uncomfortable beneath his skin.

Regardless, he didn't stop him.

"I'm old, kid." A wind picked up and blew some strands of his hair around his face, fluttering at his cheekbones and catching in his beard. "I'm real old. Been around a while, and that means I've seen a good bit of history." Varek quickly brushed at his cheek, nearly snarling at the small drop of wetness on his hand, as if his own body was betraying him by shedding tears. Still, he continued. "There was a girl, centuries ago. Smart. Young.

Skilled in magic—frankly, she's the one who taught me everything I know, everything I've passed on to Carissa. Though that's not saying much. And because she was skilled and strong..." he trailed off.

"They thought she was going to be a bad person," Aleksander said. He meant they thought she was the Scourge.

He couldn't say the name. It felt different to him now.

Varek nodded. "And I didn't get to see all the wonderful things she'd do with her life. Didn't get to see her choose a job, find someone to love, become a Crafter like she dreamed. Did you know that for Ölmesuz, because we live so long and births are rare, each person is considered to be a soul the world could no longer move on without?"

A long silence stretched between them.

"Her name was Mona."

That name rang through Aleksander.

He felt unbelievably hollow.

"Why is it," Varek said, voice softer than the mist around them, "that when people are looking for an evil the world, and they see a young girl who is *different*, who is smart and strong and proud of who she is, they're so quick to point the finger?"

Silence buzzed between them. Even the wind died, not knowing the answer.

Aleksander moved forward, leaning on the parapet beside the old man. All the titles, all the masks Varek had donned over the years stripped away—assassin, mercenary, commander, spy, none of them mattered.

None of them were reflected any longer in the worn face before him, creased deep with wrinkles not just of age but of unending worry and unfathomable grief.

Weary, red-rimmed, banded-gold eyes met Aleksander's. "I've seen this play out before. I saw how the praise affected other young men, drove them to make dumb decisions in the name of a goddess they'd been taught had their best interests at heart. And I saw firsthand what the hatred of the Scourge does to people. What that *fear* does. And then, ten years ago after serving out in neighboring countries and across Zekhar, I was called back into the palace to meet *you*."

Blood ran cold in Aleksander's veins.

"I saw a boy from a poor family, pampered and praised and being told that *this* was his duty—to eventually kill for his goddess. And all I saw was my little girl, asking me why she got called a demon, when she had done *nothing* to deserve that title." He swallowed hard, his words turning sharp and clipped. "The six year old I met had a good heart, and I was praying to anything that would listen for you to still have it all these years later. I still am."

Varek's gaze drifted out over the dark countryside beyond Brevindun, beyond the lights of Brewith.

"Do you think my daughter deserved that title?"

Aleksander shook his head sharply. "No."

"Do you think *Elspeth* deserves that same title?"

A sick rot situated in Aleksander's gut as every single thought he'd been repressing, ignoring, and actively avoiding crashed in on him at once. And there was that cold, right at the base of his skull, crawling down his neck. Words swirled in his mind; all the things he could say, all the stances he could take, all the things he'd been taught. But it all settled, and there at the center was an image he'd not thought of for months: two emerald eyes in an old woman's face, and a wrinkled mouth mourning him and the job he was given with three simple words.

I'm so sorry.

He understood now that her mourning wasn't just for him. It was for what he didn't know. For what he was going to be made to do. For the girl she knew Aleksander would inevitably be made to kill.

Aleksander turned to look out over the parapet. His lungs struggled to get a breath but there was no desperation in it—it was almost as though they simply wished to stop breathing.

"No," he said. His already shattered heart broke more with each beat. "No, she doesn't." Wind tore past Aleksander's ears, his chest swelling with the fresh, crisp breeze. "Varek?"

"Hm?"

"That man. Who killed...a lot of Zekharyans. In a town to the east. Did you know him?"

A long pause. "Yes."

The boy's throat tightened more. "Did *he* deserve what you did to him?"

"Yes," came the cracked reply. "But that doesn't mean I don't see his face when I close my eyes."

Through the heavy shroud of night, alarm bells began to ring throughout every guard tower in the castle. The clanging hit Aleksander to his core, his leather soled boots sliding across the slick stone wall until he pressed his back against the parapet, staring up at the nearest tower and the bell within it.

Varek merely stood tall, set his jaw, and huffed. "Sounds like they checked the dungeon."

CHANGEBRINGER

BY LILA SAMSON

EVERYTHING GRATED ON THE YOUNG man's mind. It was as though the evergreen crown that had been placed on his head by his sister just hours before had sprouted thorns, digging deeper into his scalp with each chord from a violin, each laugh, each echo of his name or title from across the room.

The solstice was lovely. Of course it was. The days leading up to it had been as usual, with the queen in a flurry of activity, Mrs. Buckneel on her heels, barking out more orders in the hopes of easing her Lady's burden. Arrangements had been ordered, approved, and set in place. Servants caught their breath when they thought no one could see them, red faced with blank stares. Food had been prepared for days, making the whole palace smell of pastries and pies and rich, succulent venison stews. Gowns were ordered. Fabrics were draped over his shoulders. Praise was cawed and in the temple, special hymns to Tulathne were practiced.

Normally, he would have leaned into it. Mulled ciders and decadent chocolate drinks would have been brought to his room each morning, with a warm pastry so full of dried berries it was almost entirely blue or red. He would hobble about in his thick dressing gown, trying on new suits with Carissa's advice guiding him towards the perfect outfit. He would have sung the hymns with pride. His offerings to the goddess would have been the most meaningful.

During the party, he wouldn't say no as often to the ladies who requested a dance with him.

With a quick scan of the room, Aleksander found his old friend on the arm of a young lord. The son of a man from the north. From the Islands. Aleksander could never remember his name, nor his father's. Her dark eyes flashed in his direction, and with the gaze was a split-second of longing. Then, it cleared, and plastered back on her face was that smile she used to save for him.

A slight twinge of disgust, frustration, and sadness poked at his abdomen, but it left as soon as it came, and that dark, dreary cloud descended on him again.

It didn't matter anymore. He'd long accepted his distance from her. The loss of that friendship and whatever else he had been considering pursuing.

What he did struggle with was the loss of a parter for these events. Half the time, he'd be floundering about, following Carissa or Janek, and when he had enough he'd sneak off to find Genoise or she would find him.

It was clear that was no longer an option.

The music swelled around him and he darted off the dance floor, towards a side table laden with food and drink. For the first time, as he watched a servant prepare a mixed drink, topped with berries and a sprig of rosemary, he considered asking for one.

But as the servant's bright eyes turned to him, cheeks painted with rouge to mimic the flush of cold, dappled with fine glitter, he offered a half smile and took a single chocolate orange.

He chewed as he turned away, and once again, disgust settled in his stomach.

None of the opulence was exciting this year.

Aleksander gritted his teeth, tugging on the sleeve that constricted his left arm. This room was too warm, with the roaring fires and all the people.

In the month following his injury, surface healing came quickly. The rest...

The young man flexed his fingers. A sharp, tugging strain ran from the tips of each of them all the way to his elbow. It took everything in him to not scratch at the tendons beneath his skin. No matter how stuck and itchy they felt.

He still could not fully open or close it without discomfort.

The gloves were a small blessing—they hid the way his skin had regrown around his wrist and fingers, looking as though he'd suffered a burn or had his arm cobbled back together with stitches, not unlike a training dummy's burlap body.

Weaving through the crowd, his eyes landed on the two men

in the corner, laughing and joking and taking in the picture of holiday joy. As he approached, the taller one straightened, his smile faltering slightly. "Aleksander," Demir said. A fist pressed against his heart. "Blessings." The Mekartlim offered a short bow. His left wing twitched with the movement.

"Demir." Aleksander allowed a smile across his face—for his friend's sake.

"How are you enjoying the party?" Janek asked. His dark eyes scanned Aleksander's form, meeting his gaze with barely-hidden concern.

The Sword of Ages shrugged, stiff hand resting half-open on the hilt of his sword. "I've not run off yet, have I?"

Janek's brows furrowed, surveying the boy before him.

He should have felt bad. Aleksander had come back distant, searching out Demir or Varek before the man he'd grown up with. The man who was practically his brother.

His chest tightened. He cleared his throat. "Sorry," he said, making a visible effort to release the tension he could already feel snaking through his shoulders and down along his spine. Aleksander smiled. "I'm just...overwhelmed. As I think we all are. There's so much going on and we're...throwing a party."

At this, his old friend nodded. "It is overwhelming. I can't imagine how much more for you than us, though." Janek's lips pressed together. "I'm...here, if you want to talk about anything, Aleksander."

He'd said that a lot over the past month. Whispered over the dinner table, murmured earnestly by crackling fires.

But what *could* Aleksander say? What could he tell Janek that the man did not already know? And, above all, what good would telling him what happened do, truly? He couldn't say anything about Varek's spies, about the fact that Aleksander now firmly believed that the crown and most followers of Tulathne as a whole were manipulating the prophecies—and, by extension, him—so that he might fall in line for them and enact violence against unarmed, innocent women.

Most of all, Aleksander could not open up about the fact that his best friend, a girl from across the country with eyes that glowed like planets and fire around her heart, was the Scourge. And he couldn't even hate her for it.

He simply missed her.

Deeply.

Aleksander bobbed his head, muttering his thanks and keeping his eyes trained on the scuffling of his boots beneath him.

His throat tightened.

"My Lord Champion," a voice beckoned from behind him.

His heart seized with recognition, only to drop with grief a moment later. The voice belonged to someone he'd been missing, that much was true; he just had no desire to see the owner. Not right now.

Turning slowly, he took in the form of Genoise, free from the arm of that lord's son. She stood before him draped in a rich blue dress. It was velvet. Within the long, flowing sleeves were several layers of white chiffon, trimmed in silver so that when she moved, it caught the light and glittered like fresh-fallen snow. Bright red berries had been woven into her half-up hair, along with cascades of diamonds and sapphires.

Something felt...familiar about the image.

It only made the pit in his stomach deeper.

Her cheeks were pink, rounded with a shy smile that grew wider as he met her glittering eyes.

Aleksander raised his chin. "Yes?"

With a hard swallow, she glanced between him and the two men behind him. "Might I have a word?"

"Don't you have someone to spend your evening with?" The words came out more bitter than he would have liked, he could admit that.

The lady shrugged it off. "I do, but he has duties of his own to attend to while here in your castle. I'd still like a moment to talk to my friend."

She was earnest. He could see it by the way she dipped her head. Gone was that loud, excited girl he'd grown up with. Now she was a woman—tall and demure and fully aware of her place in the court.

How awful.

He nodded. "This way."

Her cold, thin hand snaked through his elbow, pressing right above the bandages still trying to hold his bone in place that it might heal. Pain shot up his arm. He offered no reaction and instead continued to lead them through the throng of people flowing on and off the dance floor as the music changed from a slower tune to a jaunty rendition of a seasonal hymn. Past the courtiers, the dais with an empty throne, and out the back door, there was a thin servant's hallway. It led to the garden and the kitchen, depending on which side you took at the fork, but Aleksander stopped and removed her hand. "What did you need to speak about, my Lady?"

Those cold hands, now released of his elbow and her skirt, wrung together. They were dry, the soft scraping sound akin to parchment rubbing against itself echoed through the passage.

"I wanted to see if you were alright," Genoise said softly.

"Just that? You could have asked that outside."

The woman lifted her chin, eyes wide, voice raised, "No, Aleksander, I needed—"

He raised a brow and she paused.

"My Lord Champion," she corrected. "I needed to ask it in earnest. And...I ask for an earnest answer. Are you alright?"

A gentle hand extended, resting lightly on his uninjured forearm.

No. Of course he wasn't.

"No," he said. The word was soft, quiet. Raw.

She nodded slowly. A single step closer. "I'm sorry."

He didn't say anything.

The silence that stretched between them felt muffled, strange. Through the stone walls and the thick hidden doors, the thrumming of the base and the muddled chatter of courtiers enjoying the longest night of the year still came through.

He'd never admit it to her, but it felt like he was drowning.

"I know she was your friend. And...I'm sorry I couldn't be there for you. I am sorry I had to break it off the way I did. You're a wonderful person, and a wonderful friend. You didn't deserve that. From me or her. I'm not much, and I don't know if anything I could do or say would fix what happened or even fix your outlook on it, but..." Her fingers slid down, wrapping through his. "Know that I am here for you, if you need me."

Aleksander did not meet her gaze, though he felt it on him. It burned through his bangs, the wavy golden locks that had grown long enough to brush his shoulders and curl around his cheeks, shaggy and rough-cut as they were. He watched as her thumb methodically brushed over the back of his hand, offering comfort. Offering physicality.

He slipped his hand from hers.

"There is nothing you can do now." He meant it. "You've chosen to distance yourself, and I think you were right to do so. This isn't about you, and it shouldn't be." At this, he finally looked up.

She had stepped closer, so close he jolted back in surprise when he could make out the fluttering eyelashes mere inches from his in the pale blue dark.

Blush creeped up her cheeks. Genoise took a step back.

"You were a good friend, and if you can be honest with him, I'm sure you'll be a good wife. A good Lady of your manor. And I hope when the time comes you can think about what's really going on and choose the right side."

At this, her face paled. "You...Aleksander what are you saying?"

People had been talking to her. That was one thing he'd never forgotten from his stay at Lord Asghar's. Whether she accepted it or not, she knew bits of the truth.

"You know exactly what I'm saying." Hand on his sword, the other pressed in a fist against his heart, Aleksander bowed deeply. "Thank you for your time, your care, and your friendship, Lady Elmere." When he straightened, he swore there were tears glistening in her eyes. "I wish you a long, happy life."

The tip of Aoife's scabbard scraped against the wall as he turned, but it didn't matter. There was so much more going on that mattered more, how could he be so concerned about the wellbeing of a sword that he could get fixed, a leather scabbard he could have buffed out?

When the door creaked open the noise of the hall slammed against him. That crown of evergreen tightened around his head, poking deeper, probing for his brain through the plates in his skull.

Through the din, one cry echoed.

"Aleksander!"

Acknowledgements

This book took much longer to come out than I had ever initially intended, but here it finally is! Let this be a lesson (for myself and any other eager authors):   let your story take its time. If I had rushed to meet my initial May publishing date, nothing would have turned out remotely as good as it did here.

I'm once again in the space of having to thank people. Not having, sorry—*getting* to thank people. There are a number of individuals whose contributions and guidance and support made this book what it is.

First, I'm thanking Cameron. My chief beta reader, in this book and the last. This chapter of Aleksander's story would not be complete, would not be as it is, without your ever-pertinent critiques and comments.

Thank you to Emily, for your constant assistance and encouragement with things as I got stuck and discouraged.

Thank you to my husband for staying beside me and getting excited once I told him the book was finally, at long last, done.

Thank you to my parents, my author friends, and everyone else who encouraged me to take my time amidst all the work this book entailed and the big life changes that were happening behind the scenes. This story wouldn't be out if it weren't for you.

And as always, thank *you*, dear reader. I'm glad you've chosen to join up with Aleksander and his friends again, and continue the journey. As bittersweet as it will be, I can't wait to take our final steps with them all in the final book in this trilogy.

Lila Samson is a Minnesota born-and-raised author and artist. Reading since she could make up words and exploring since her hands could grip tree branches, there's always a story working its way through her mind. With a Bachelors in Theatre, a fascination with culture, and a never ending love of the otherworldly, her works primarily span Fantasy and Sci-Fi, though that's bound to change at some point.

She resides in the forests of Minnesota with her husband and their two cats, Winston and Wesley. You can find her on TOME at @lilasamsonauthor and on Instagram at @shelvedbylila.